LADY OF LIGHT, LADY OF DARKNESS

She Would Be Queen . . . but She Refused to Be a Sorceress

The Master of the Junipers looked into the innocent face of the future Queen and spoke softly.

"The mind rules all. Were it not for our belief, this world of forms would not exist at all. You *must* know this if you are to wield the Jewels."

"I won't . . . I must not wield them. . . ." she replied, thinking with a shiver of her guarded secret, the terrifying intimations of inner power that had tormented her as a child. "Such things should not be meddled with. You cannot understand – there are dark things in me that would be too powerful. . . ."

"No!" The Master's eyes were bright. "Don't you understand? The power that you fear is not darkness, but light. . . . ."

About the Author

Diana L. Paxson is a science fiction and fantasy writer living in Berkeley, California. She studied medieval English and French for her Masters Degree at the University of California, and this knowledge has been used as the basis of many of her short stories and novels. She has written a number of fantasies, including THE PARADISE TREE and WHITE MARE, RED STALLION. Her most recent novel is THE WHITE RAVEN, also published by New English Library.

Diana L. Paxson is married with two sons. She spends her spare time playing the harp and writing poetry.

Lady of Light, Lady of Darkness

Diana L. Paxson

NEW ENGLISH LIBRARY
Hodder and Stoughton

First published in the United
States of America in
1982 by Pocket Books

First published in Great Britain
in 1990 by New English Library
paperbacks

An NEL paperback original
British Library C.I.P.

British Library Cataloguing in
Publication Data
Paxson, Diana L.
  Lady of light, lady of darkness.
I. Title
  813',54 [F]

ISBN O-450-50938-9

Printed and bound in Great Britain
for Hodder and Stoughton
paperbacks, a division of Hodder
and Stoughton Ltd., Mill Road,
Dunton Green, Sevenoaks, Kent
TN13 2YA (Editorial Office:
47 Bedford Square, London
WC18 3DP) by R Clay Ltd,
Bungay, Suffolk.

To my husband . . .
Jon DeCles

LADY OF
LIGHT

Contents

Prologue

From the interaction of light and darkness, of spirit and matter, the world was made.

In the beginning, a spark whirled in the void. It slowed, cooled, became a sphere where the sovereign elements of earth, water, air, and fire combined and recombined in an endless dance. Continents grew, rivers carved paths to the sea, soil was formed, and living things appeared.

Each thing that came into existence followed the pattern of its kind, yet each was unique. Everything possessed awareness – a continuum of consciousness from the smallest particle to the Mind that had created all. Then the lesser minds, which were both cause and effect of the aggregate individuals, became aware of themselves and of each other and walked upon the infant world. They were the Guardians of their kinds. And above them all there was in every region a Guardian of the land itself, whose spirit determined its character, just as the Guardians were the patterns for the kindreds they ruled.

Species were born and disappeared. A new creature walked the earth who imprisoned consciousness in words, and whose name, in whatever language it made, was Man. For millennia men remembered their beginnings, revering the Guardians and living upon the earth without marring it. But at length the people began to change and desired to bend the earth to their own wills. Sooner or later in every place the new races pushed those who held to the old ways

1

to the very edges of the habitable lands, and the Guardians withdrew from the knowledge of men.

Yet a time came when the land itself rose against men: earth trembled, and fires were fanned by the winds until the waters stilled them, and every plant and animal was at war with Man. Then the remnant of humanity cried out to the Creator for fear that men would perish utterly.

And the Maker of All Things commanded those Guardians who were the souls of each land to appear. For each region a new Law was made, appropriate to its nature, but however the countries of men were henceforth to differ, in all of them it was decreed that humans should no longer be masters, but only the tenants of the land.

On a fair coast washed by a sunset sea, the survivors made a Covenant with the Guardian, and wishing to forget the past, they called Her, and their country, Westria. Those who remembered the old skills and the old rituals that would help them to live at peace with the land were made their teachers, and they began to build a world that was at once very old and very new.

Two centuries after the Cataclysm human wars threatened the Covenant of Westria. In those days a priestess made four Jewels of Power, one for each sovereign element, and her son wielded them to heal the land. In the years that followed there was always an heir of that line to bear the Jewels and to rule Westria.

In the sixth century of the Covenant the Estates of Westria petitioned the King to marry, for he had no child. And so the King and his companions set out to find a Lady for Westria – a woman who might be equally the mistress of the King's heart, and the Mistress of the Jewels.

1

Stormfire

Light slashed across the darkness, illuminating in bas-relief the snow-powdered mountains and the outworks of the Hold, the glimmer of Faris' face in the window she had just pushed open, and the livid scar that twisted up the inner side of her left arm. She took a deep breath of damp wind, blinking as the radiance faded and night swept back over the world. Thunder crashed and rolled around the fortress and Faris jumped, though she had been waiting for it to come.

"May the Lords of the Elements have mercy on the King, for surely they are at war tonight." Faris heard her friend Rosemary speak behind her, the customary calmness of her voice belying her words.

"Perhaps he has taken shelter somewhere," said Faris' brother, Farin. A few fragile harp notes echoed his words as he picked up the melody he had been playing when the thunder came. Reflected in the windowpanes she glimpsed a stretch of frescoed wall, Rosemary's owl on his perch, the gleam of the fire.

A gust of wind lifted Faris' dark hair away from her face. She heard the trees sighing in the walled orchard below as they stretched their arms to the storm, and a few petals, whirled up by the wind, clung to her hand. She wondered if any blossoms would be left for the Festival of the Lady of Flowers.

"Jehan promised my father he would be here in time for the ceremony tomorrow," said Rosemary.

"It would be a pity if he missed it – every girl in the Corona is hoping that the Lady will help her to attract the King," Farin replied.

"Not me – Faris is more beautiful, let her be Queen!"

"Hush, Rosemary! Don't encourage her to think such things. She will only be hurt." Farin's voice came too clearly as the wind eased. "Our family gained honor enough when our sister Berisa married your brother, who will be Lord Commander of the Corona one day."

Rosemary sighed. "You all protect Faris too much. No man worth marrying would care about her arm."

Automatically Faris tugged her sleeve down. Her eyes blurred and her disfigured arm throbbed as if the lightning had seared her flesh and not the sky. *My father cares . . . Berisa was right, I should have stayed at home!*

The wind was rising once more. Faris blinked as lightning flashed again and again above the white peak of the Father of Mountains, glowing through the boiling clouds. As if to escape Farin's words, she thrust the window fully open and leaned out into the rain, gasping as energy pulled her fine hair into a cloud about her head and tingled over her skin. The charged air dizzied her. *I must not do this,* she thought, but already her spirit was surging to meet the storm.

Thunder billowed around her, but it was a deep, unhuman laughter that Faris heard. She saw the sky people, bombarding each other with handfuls of cloud, spinning themselves out in lines of light that shattered as the lightning struck, then taking shape again. The elementals were playing, an abstract sport of force and pattern that she almost understood. Her spirit danced in the vortex of the storm, and she stretched out her hands to its power.

. The heavens gathered themselves around her, then were torn asunder as if the fabric of the world had been rent to reveal the glory it veiled. Faris cried out and fell back as earth and heaven quaked to the thunderbolt.

"Faris! What are you doing? Do you want to get a fever again?" The ancient glass of the window rattled as Farin slammed it shut.

"Your hair is soaked – let me get you to the fire." Hardly aware of her own body, Faris felt Rosemary's strong arms half carry her toward the hearth. Her eyes followed the swing of the other girl's golden braids as Rosemary bent to poke up the fire and then pulled a shawl out from under the sleeping sheepdog and drew it around Faris' thin shoulders.

Now she could feel water trickling down her neck and the ache in her fingers as the circulation began to return. *A moment ago my hands had the strength of the storm,* she thought, ignoring her brother's scolding. *What a weak thing this body is. My father was right to forbid . . .* She closed her eyes against the memory of his words. Her mother had had the power to call the winds and talk to the trees, and her mother had died.

"That's better," said Rosemary, giving a last rub to Faris' damp hair.

"Please, Rosemary, I'm not one of the wild creatures you nurse so well." Faris found herself laughing as the owl's head swiveled and one golden eye blinked down at her. She could hear faint snufflings as the rabbits stirred in their wicker cage on the other side of the room.

"You might as well be," said Farin, but he had taken his seat again, and already his dark head was bent over his harp as he tested and tuned its horsehair strings.

"Father said that if the King did not get here before mid-evening, he would go out after him," said Rosemary.

"Then I'm going too", said Farin. "I wouldn't miss the sight of all the fine lords from Laurelynn half drowned in the rain."

"Don't laugh too loud. Eric of Seagate is coming with him, and some of the others who fought with Jehan against

Elaya. And of course he'll have the Seneschal, Caolin. I doubt that *he* would be flustered by a second Cataclysm."

"But the Master of the Junipers is already here," put in Faris, thinking of the little grey-robed man she had seen at supper, sitting like a still rock in the midst of a busy stream.

"Yes, he had to prepare for the Festival."

Faris remembered the wind whipping the starry branches of the almond trees. This was the second week of February, but the winter had been a stormy one, and it was hard to realise that it was already time for the Festival, hard to believe in the coming of spring.

In the distance thunder muttered like a bear balked of its prey. Faris shivered, wondering how the King and his men fared now.

Thunder crashed as if someone had clashed two shields together above Jehan's head, and his horse plunged sideways, almost unseating him. The King swore softly as the clamor faded.

"Stormwing, you white donkey – I thought this kind of weather was your element! What are you afraid of, my swan? See now, it's going away . . ." Still talking, he gentled the horse with firm pressure of knee and rein. He saw his squire, Rafael, watching him anxiously and smiled.

Somewhere behind him he heard a squeal, followed by confused shouting. *Another horse down*, he thought. *I should have stopped at Badensbridge. What fool's pride made me believe I could get everyone to the Hold ahead of the storm?* But the place had been too small for all the lords and clerks and officers, the men-at-arms and supply train that the King of Westria must drag about with him in his quest for a Queen. *And I was a fool to agree to that too!* he thought, but he was past thirty now, and the Council had demanded that he choose a Lady for Westria.

Lightning flared, and for a moment he saw the confused mass of men and animals spread along the muddy curves of the road. Beyond them the land rose gently toward the mountains that gave the Province the name of the crown of Westria, dotted with scattered stands of liveoak and stunted pine. At least they were still going in the right direction!

Stormwing shook his head anxiously and the King loosened his rein, letting the stallion take a few steps up the road while he peered through the freezing rain. They must find shelter soon, but where? *When I was taking my training at the College of the Wise, I knew every twist of the road between here and Laurelynn . . . But that was a long time ago.* The border with Normontaine was quiet, and Theodor was an able lord. Without need to call him there, Jehan had not found time to visit the Hold more than twice in the fifteen years he had been King.

The next flash showed him jagged outlines on the horizon and he pulled the stallion to a halt. The ancients had built a great city here, destroyed when the earth moved and the dam below the Father of Mountains gave way, but he remembered some ruins that might give shelter. Had he seen them just now? Caolin, who knew everything about Westria, would surely know. He reined Stormwing around to find the Seneschal.

Caolin pulled his hood forward and hunched a little more in the saddle, his long legs gripping the brown mare's sides, his strong fingers steady on the reins. His body was settled to a patient endurance; his mind, having determined that there was nothing he could do to make sure that dispatch cases were dry, was focused on the next move in a chess game he had been playing with himself since they had left Badensbridge.

Then he heard his name called by the one voice that could always reach him. As he lifted his head to look for the King lightning struck again so close that he could smell it. In the flare of bluish light he saw a horse rearing and Jehan urging Stormwing forward so that he could grasp the bridle and bring the other animal down, his eyes shining and his face intent as he forced the beast to stillness and spoke to the trembling rider.

"You're not hurt, are you?" The lightning bolt had struck a pine tree beside the road, and now it blazed like a torch despite the rain. Caolin saw the boy whose horse the King had caught shake his head as he tried to smile. "Well then, see to your mount," Jehan went on. "He's frightened out of his skin!" The boy laughed then, for even in that dim light he could see the twitching of the horse's lathered sides.

"My Lord!" came a call. "Are we going to Hell or to the Hold?"

"*I* am going to the Hold." Jehan grinned. "But you are welcome to stay here! I'm just as uncomfortable as you are, but we'll get to shelter soon, so don't despair!"

Caolin saw the King's eyes gleam in the flickering light and thought that although he was cold, wet, and concerned for his men, the opportunity for action exhilarated him. The Seneschal sat still on his horse, watching as the King moved among his men.

"*Don't despair*, he says," came an anonymous voice behind him. "Why doesn't he use the Jewels then? He's their master; surely he could handle a little thing like a thunderstorm!"

"The Jewels of Westria?" came a shocked whisper in reply. "He would be breaking the Covenant if he used them to control a natural storm!"

"What's the use of having them then? In the old days men were masters of this world."

"Well, in the end this world mastered them. Leave well enough alone," his companion answered him.

Caolin peered through the darkness, but he could not see who had spoken. He had trained himself to ignore discomfort, but still he could sympathise with the first man's complaint. There had been many times, when villages were flooded or crops destroyed by fire, that he had wished for the power to protect them. The College of the Wise preached a slavish obedience to the Covenant, but Caolin owed no service to the College now. In other lands men lived by different laws – how different? he wondered. How much could men do without endangering Westria?

The wind shifted, flinging rain against his unprotected face, and lightning stalked across the horizon. Caolin huddled back down in the saddle. *Earth and water, wind and fire – there are the real powers. Might a man truly wield the lightnings if he bore the Jewels of Westria? But Jehan never uses them, so I may never know . . .*

"Caolin." The Seneschal started, turned, and saw the King. "We must find a place to stop. The men are tiring, and I'm afraid we'll wander off the road. Aren't there some ruins near that would protect us?"

Caolin closed his eyes, memory lying out before him the map of Westria with its four Provinces and the red lines of the roads. He could see the Free Cities spaced along the Dorada River like beads on a string, and fortresses like the Hold, where Lord Theodor ruled the Corona. His map showed also mines and grain fields and the ruins of dead cities, where they found metal and glass and sometimes books and strange mechanisms whose use no one in these times cared to know.

"Yes," he said finally. "The Red City lies this way, but there's hardly one wall left standing there now." He looked back at the King. Jehan was standing up in his stirrups, straining to see down the road. The Seneschal pushed back his hood, oblivious to the rain, and thought he heard a distant trumpet call.

A smile was growing on Jehan's face. "It doesn't matter now – don't you hear them? When we fought Elaya together three years ago, I got to know the note of Sandremun's horn – he and Theodor have come out to look for us!"

The King slumped in the saddle, allowing himself to feel the weariness of the long ride now that Lord Theodor and his son had taken over the responsibility for seeing them all to shelter. The excitement of battling the storm had worn off, and his shoulders ached as if he had been carrying half

Westria. Now even Stormwing's steps had grown slow.
More storm clouds were moving in from the southwest,
but for the moment they were assailed by nothing worse
than a cold, steady rain.

The lanterns of Theodor's men bobbed to either side of
the line of horses, casting a fitful light on the road and
briefly illuminating their Commander's beaked profile as
he talked to Caolin about the economics of the wool
trade with their northern neighbor, Normontaine. Seen
in silhouette, without the jutting silver beard to betray his
age, Theodor's erect figure could have been the shadow
of his son's. Certainly the elder and younger lords of the
Corona shared the same relentless good cheer. Jehan grimaced. His breeches were chafing him, water had somehow penetrated his boots even though they were laced
halfway up his thighs, and Sandremun had not stopped
talking in the two hours since the escort had found the
King.

> I took the road to see the world
> When spring was fair and green,
> But now the winter winds do blow
> And I'm for home again . . .

Jehan turned to look for the singer and glimpsed the
slight shape of a dark-haired young man who had come
with Theodor. Sandremun broke off in the middle of a
description of the perils of hunting deer on horseback in
the mountains to join in the chorus.

> But I'll not care for wind and rain
> Nor will I fear the storm,
> If food and fire are waiting, and
> My love to keep me warm . . .

Jehan sighed, remembering the soft curves of the woman
he had left in Elder and wondering whether he should
have brought her along. But it had seemed discourteous to

10

bring a mistress when he was supposed to be searching for a bride, and he doubted her temper would have withstood this journey in the rain.

The creaking of saddles and the splashing as the horses plodded through the puddles made a rhythmic accompaniment to the singing. Forcing his attention back to the present, Jehan glanced back along the line, marking his men. Eric of Seagate's broad shoulders were unmistakable even in this gloom, but he did not recognise the smaller man riding beside him. He heard a familiar name and moved his horse closer.

"It is a pity we do not see people from the other Provinces more often," said the strange voice, the accent of Laurelynn overlaying the more relaxed speech of the north. "These visits provide such a useful opportunity to share our problems."

"I wouldn't know," said Eric. "This is my first trip around Westria."

"But you were down in Las Costas with the King, were you not? The Lord Commander Brian is such a fine man – such a valiant fighter, and with so many valuable ideas too. Did you spend much time with him when you were there?"

"We met."

Jehan grinned in the darkness. It was Brian's name that had attracted his attention, and remembering the instant hostility between the Lord Commander of Las Costas and the Lord of Seagate's son, he wondered how long Eric's restraint would last.

The stranger continued, "Yes, Brian is a truly admirable leader. I trade in furs from the Corona and even Normontaine, and I've visited all four Provinces. It is a pity that the King has not had time to know them as well. Some of the rulings imposed by that precious Council of his really display no knowledge of local conditions. In the circumstances it hardly seems right to insist on central control . . . That's why I mentioned Lord Brian. He's a strong man, and with a little support from the younger lords like yourself, he might win more independence for all of the Provinces. Don't you agree?"

"No, I *don't* agree!" Eric exploded. "I would remind you that Brian is a member of that 'precious Council' himself, as is my father. Let Brian take his valuable ideas to the King. He may find he is not as strong as he thinks!"

The other man opened his mouth to reply, looked beyond Eric, and saw the King. Without answering, he bowed and reined his horse away.

Eric looked around in confusion. "My Lord!" He glanced back at the empty space beside him. "Did you hear what he said?"

"Sandy," said Jehan, "who is the little man in the green cloak who just rode down the line?"

Sandremun turned, not needing to rise in his stirrups to see over the heads of most of the men. "Oh, that's only Ronald of Greenfell – Ronald Sandreson – he's a cousin of ours. Was he talking like a fool again?"

"With all respect to your family, he was talking like a traitor, my Lord," said Eric grimly.

"Treason, Eric?" asked the King.

"Well, sedition, at any rate. All about more freedom for the Provinces, and the like!"

"But, Eric, everybody knows how untrustworthy the Lord Commanders can be," Jehan said seriously, then grinned as Eric's face relaxed into a rueful smile. Sandremun was roaring with laughter.

"Only some of them, only some of them, Jehan!" said Theodor's son. "And only the loyal ones come to the Hold." He gestured up the hill, where an irregular outline bulked against the storm. A second cloud front was moving down on them quickly now, and Jehan thought they would be lucky to reach the fortress before the lightnings were playing about them once more.

The clear baritone of the singer soared above the roar of the storm as they began the last pull up the hill.

And wanderers upon the road,
And caravans and Kings,
Are but the vagrant children of
The Maker of All Things . . .

Sandremun put his horn to lips, and Jehan winced as the sound echoed back and forth between the walls that curved down from the protected side gate that was opening for them now. The Hold loomed over them in a confusion of walls and towers, built from every material and in every style known to the past three hundred years, according to no plan the King had ever been able to discern.

He kicked his weary horse after Sandremun's. People were pouring out of the gate now, waving torches, and Stormwing snorted and reared. The air was full of thunder and the rush of rain. As Jehan fought down the prancing horse, the movement of a window opening drew his eyes upward to the chamber above the gate.

Then the lightning came. Walls and towers sprang into being around him, and in the midst of them a girl's white face framed in a cloud of dark hair.

For a long moment her eyes met his, as if time had been halted by that light, then the vision was gone. Dazzled, Jehan let Stormwing carry him under the arch of the gate, hearing the echo of hooves on stone and the cheers of the people of the Corona. When his sight cleared, he saw only torchlight and the welcoming smile of the Master of the Junipers.

The Master of the Junipers paused in the doorway of the paneled chamber they had given the King. Jehan's squire was helping him pull off his wet tunic. Boots, cloak, and sheepskin jacket already steamed before the fire, and the air was pungent with the smell of wet leather and wool. A partly demolished chicken carcass and a loaf of brown bread lay on a platter on the table beside a stoneware pitcher of mulled wine.

"Jehan?" He came into the room and let the door close behind him.

The King emerged from the tunic, still gnawing on a chicken leg, and reached for his blue robe. "My friend! Thank you for coming to me. I suppose you ought to be resting up for the Festival" – he grimaced – "and I should be in bed. But we'll have to time to talk tomorrow, and we – I thought we had better talk before you went up to the College of the Wise."

The Master had already seen Caolin, leaning against the battered blue leather of the King's traveling chest, blazoned with the radiant silver star of House Starbairn. Somehow the Seneschal had already managed to change into a dry tunic and to sleek back his short pale hair. He lifted his mug to the Master in ironic salute, his gray eyes veiled.

Jehan wrapped the robe around him, poured steaming wine into a mug, and eased down into a chair covered with fox pelts gathered over several seasons' rationed hunting. His squire hung the tunic on a hook to dry and took up a position by the door.

"Rafael," said the King without opening his eyes. "You need to get dry too. And when you've got your wet things off, go to bed."

"Yes, my Lord." The young man flushed beneath his brown skin, then bowed and went out.

The Master sighed and sat down in a straight chair across from the King. "I will visit the Mistress of the College as we agreed," he said, "to inform her about the problems in Laurelynn and Rislin and to have her report –"

"To have her reply!" corrected Caolin. In the firelight the straight folds of his robe glowed as crimson as the red stone on his right hand.

"The Mistress has ruled the College for over ten years, Caolin. I do not think she needs to be told her job." The Master kept his voice low, avoiding dangerous ground.

"She is a member of the King's Council, and accountable. This must be settled – my Lord, don't you agree?"

14

"Forgive me." Jehan looked up, but Caolin's glance fell too quickly for his expression to be read as he realized that the King had not been listening.

Jehan is tired, thought the Master, *and I think he did not choose to have this meeting now*.

"Do you agree that we must make a clear distinction between the areas of authority of the College of the Wise and of the Crown?" repeated Caolin.

"I thought we were discussing jurisdiction," the Master of the Junipers said quietly. "The only *authority* involved is that which both Crown and College exist to serve."

Caolin shrugged. "Call it what you will. But when you go to the Mountain tomorrow, tell the Mistress of the College that we will tolerate no more meddling. Take the case of the priestess in Elder who murdered her child – surely you will agree that no matter who commits it, murder is a civil crime?"

The Master shook his head. "You choose your examples poorly. You know my doubts that something so symptomatic of spiritual illness as deliberate murder can ever be merely a 'civil' crime."

The King eased off his golden circlet and ran his fingers through his dark hair, lines of patience hardening his face. The Master paused, knowing that Jehan had heard this argument too many times before, but there was a principle here he could not betray.

"Then what of the case where the Commander of the garrison in Rislin was arrested for having ordered his men to cut wood?" Caolin leaned forward, and the firelight burnished his hair to the same ruddy gold as the King's circlet. "The wood was on Crown land, the man was an officer of the Crown, and his removal jeopardised the defense of a major city of Westria."

"*Crown* Land? A *Crown* officer?" asked the Master wryly.

The King frowned abstractedly and poured another mug of wine.

"The officer was appointed by Jehan," continued the Master, "but the man himself is responsible for his exercise of that trust. Jehan holds the land on behalf of those who live here. *All* of them. You speak of wood, Caolin, but those were living *trees* until that man cut them down!" The Master remembered the fallen branches he had seen in the orchard. Surely the land was hard enough on itself without the intervention of man. His awareness, tuned to the tides of the earth, felt the movement of the clouds overhead, the hidden rising of the moon.

"So much that is wrong in Westria today comes because we forget that," he went on more quietly. "The King's authority, the duty of the College, the very survival of humankind – all depend on our keeping the Covenant our ancestors made with the Guardians of the other kindreds after the Cataclysm that destroyed the civilisation the ancients made.

"We may not take a life – of any animal, of any creature of air or sea, of anything that grows from the earth herself – without apology or need. Not without need!" His voice grated and he tried to soften it for the sake of the King. Jehan was sitting with his head in his hands, and the Master remembered the many times he had counseled and comforted him since the boy of seventeen had become King. But he could not help him now.

"You need not repeat the Oath of the Covenant, *Master!*" snapped Caolin. "I too have studied at the College of the Wise!"

The Master's attention jerked back to the Seneschal, and his lips closed firmly on the words he would not say, knowing that Jehan heard him anyway. But Caolin could not communicate in that way. Caolin had not left the College voluntarily – he had wished to become an adept as the Master had done, but though his work had been brilliant, he had been denied. The Master had been in Laurelynn at the time, serving the old King. He had had no part in the decision, but he represented the College, and it seemed to him that Caolin had always resented him for that.

The King leaned forward as if he could protect Caolin physically from the memory. "We all live by the Covenant." His voice had deepened. "Assure the Mistress of the College that I have not forgotten what I swore when I first put on the Jewels."

The Master and the Seneschal both looked at him, seeking reassurance in his face, seeing the flicker of pain in the King's blue eyes at their disharmony. Jehan cleared his throat and went on.

"Tell her also that confusion results when communications fails. May the Lord of All forbid that I should usurp the responsibilities of the College, but I and my officers must know what the College intends so that we can know how to respond. If we do not, both Crown and College will forfeit the people's trust." Slowly, holding their eyes, he replaced the circlet upon his brow.

"My Lord King . . ." Caolin bent his head.

"I will carry that message gladly, Jehan," said the Master gently. He thought, *He is still Caolin's master – I should not have feared*.

"It grows late," said the King. "You must lead the Festival tomorrow, and Theodor has lined up every horse in his stables and every landholder in his Province to meet me. We both need sleep!"

"Yes." The circled cross of Westria on the Master's breast glittered gold in the firelight as he sketched a blessing. "Rest well, in the name of the Maker of All Things."

Jehan remained stretched out in his chair before the hearth after the Master of the Junipers had gone, staring into the flames. Images swam before his eyes as the glowing oak logs became coals, and coals fell into ash, fulfilling the natural life cycle of fire. Light and darkness patterned his vision. His saw again the bright face and dark hair of the woman who had appeared in the window when the lightning came. With such hair she was no kin of Theodor's. If she was real . . .

"He was right. You look half asleep, my Lord, go to bed," said Caolin.

"No." Jehan sat up and poured himself more wine. He could feel its warmth burning in his belly, but it did not ease him. His fingers twitched with undirected energy. He wanted to escape from the circlet that bound his brow, from the round of ceremony that would close upon him tomorrow, but he did not want to rest.

The sanded boards of the floor creaked as Caolin came toward him. He felt the other man's strong hands close on his shoulders and knead the taut muscles there. After a moment he let his head drop, trying to relax.

"I thought so," said Caolin. "Well, I can help you get rid of the effects of tension at least, even if at the moment I can do no more about its causes." He gave the King's shoulder a light slap. "Well?"

"I suppose so." Jehan got to his feet, pulled off the rest of his clothes, and stretched out face-down on the bed. The laced thongs of the bedstead gave to his weight as he eased down. Appreciatively he breathed in the spicy scent of the fine grass that stuffed the mattress, and the perfume of the rose petals that had been folded with the well-washed cotton sheets.

Caolin rummaged in the traveling chest and took out the flask of oil, tested it on his hand, and set it beside the fire to warm. Then he came back to the bed, lifted the King's dark hair gently to one side, and began to work on his shoulders again.

"I gather that Lord Theodor has planned quite a celebration."

"Yes, it's been a long time since I was here," answered the King. "It shouldn't take an order from the Council to get me to the far corners of the Kingdom." He remembered what Ronald Sandreson had said to Eric on the ride to the Hold. He ought to tell Caolin that Brian was playing politics, but he knew how the Seneschal would reply. Tomorrow would be soon enough to hear it again.

"Sandy wanted me to sit up and drink with him," he said instead, "but I have too clear a memory of the effects of Berisa's mead, or rather too unclear a memory."

Caolin laughed. "Sandremun *is* the sort of man one calls by his milk name for the rest of his life, isn't he?" He went to the fireplace for the oil, returned, and poured it across the King's back. Jehan felt hard fingers dig into the sensitive spot beneath his shoulder blade and winced.

"You're resisting it – remember to breathe."

Jehan grunted, releasing his breath and trying to draw it in again with the steady rhythm he had been taught at the College, letting go of all the worries that nagged him, letting tense muscles ease.

"Theodor will likely try to match you with his daughter. At least she has the family's golden hair," murmured Caolin.

Jehan shook his head a little. He had met Rosemary several times when her family came to Laurelynn for Council meetings and thought her a nice girl, but she was too tall for him.

"Or he'll find someone else for you," the Seneschal's cool voice continued evenly, inconsequentially, blending with the steady rattle of rain against the windowpanes.

Jehan let the steady murmur lull him as Caolin's fingers traced out the long muscles of his arms, worked down each finger until his hands lay nerveless at his sides. *Did I really see a girl at the window?* he wondered drowsily. *Or was it only a trick of the light?*

"Did you take care of that woman in Elder?" he asked suddenly. Thinking of her, he saw the shining waves of her black hair, but her face was already becoming vague in his memory.

"Yes," answered Caolin impersonally. "She had the bracelet and was escorted safely home."

Jehan smiled to himself. He was aware that Caolin often took the King's women to his own bed for a night before he sent them away. Jehan saw no reason to object to that, since none of the ladies had ever complained. They had,

19

he thought cynically, probably been glad to cling a little longer to the source of power, however vicariously. Did Caolin know that he knew? Sometimes Jehan thought that his friend hardly seemed to remember it himself, as if the satisfaction of his body's need was unrelated to the life of his mind and soul.

Caolin's hands moved down the King's legs, loosing the knotted muscles of the calves, compressing the nerve endings in his feet. Jehan felt a sweet singing in his veins as his blood flowed freely once more. His body remembered the many times Caolin had done this before, and yielded gratefully. *Only one of the many things he has done for me,* thought the King, knowing that Caolin's steady support had been perhaps the best things in his life during the past fifteen years.

"You can turn over now."

Jehan roused himself enough to ease on to his back and smiled up at Caolin. "You should get some rest too," he said.

A little unaccustomed color rose in the other man's face as he returned the smile. "This is one of the few useful things I learned at the College of the Wise," he replied. "It rests me too."

Jehan let his eyes close as Caolin's fingers probed gently at the tightness in his forehead and the clenched jaw muscles beneath his short beard, then moved down his neck and began to work carefully around the old sword scars on the King's shoulders and chest.

The darkness behind his eyelids was shot with flashing lights that formed the face of the girl in the window, her hair full of stars. Darkness was her setting, but she was made of light. *My lady of light* . . . Words faltered in his consciousness and fell away.

He scarcely knew when Caolin finished and pulled the heavy quilts over him, carefully tucking them in. The darkness deepened as the other man blew out the lamp. He heard the click of the door latching and Caolin's soft good night.

20

Good night, Jehan. Caolin's own words reverberated in his awareness as if he had spoken them aloud. The palms of his hands tingled with the memory of Jehan's flesh; he brought them up to cover his eyes and breathed in the sharp savor of Jehan's skin. Dizzied, he leaned against the plastered stone of the wall next to the King's door.

The image of that hard, compact body filled his vision; the shape of every bone and muscle was imprinted in the nerves of his hands – he could have modeled the King's body from memory.

"Jehan, Jehan . . . my Lord and my King," he whispered, then pressed his clenched fists hard against his eyelids as if to suppress both touch and sight. *He is dreaming now and does not even know that I have gone,* thought Caolin. A shudder thrust him against the hard stone.

Once, Jehan would not have gone to sleep after Caolin had worked on his body. That contact might have turned to another kind of touching that would have eased them both. But it had been a long time since Jehan had needed that from him.

"It does not matter!" Caolin said aloud. "What he needs now, only I can give to him. It is enough . . . it is enough for me!"

Slowly he lowered his hands to his sides and made his fingers uncurl, mastered his breathing, and waited for the pounding of his heart to still. He looked around to see if there was anyone in the corridor. Somewhere above him someone was playing a harp. Caolin could hear the notes faint but clear in the stillness of the sleeping fortress, like a memory of love.

Music had been one of those first bonds between him and Jehan. As he walked along the passageway to his own door, the Seneschal smiled.

Farin sat in the window above the side gate with his harp cradled in his arms, looking out at the steady rain. Rosemary and Faris had gone to their chamber long before, but

21

though the long cold ride to bring the King to the Hold had tired him, he could not sleep.

"I sang to the King!" he told the harp triumphantly, "though he may never know it was me!" His fingers brushed the horsehair strings, drawing out the melody of the marching song, embellishing it with the little touches of harmony that his voice could not supply.

Then he stopped, plucked one string again, and reached for his tuning key. The harp was an old one that he had found in a storage room at home, and though he had oiled it, filled its cracks with resin, and carved new pegs for the strings, the sounds was still a little dull sometimes and the strings went easily out of tune.

"But I would not dare to sing to him in public. You are not good enough, old friend, and neither am I." Here at the Hold they praised his playing, but Farin was too painfully aware of the times when his fingers stumbled, or his voice was a little less than true. The others heard the music that came from her fingertips but not the resplendent harmonies that soared in his heart. His hands dropped to the strings once more, plucking out the first lively chords of a war song.

"How splendid the King looked, shining like a star with the lightning around him. He would be wonderful in battle – I wish I could go with him to war! That would be something to sing about!" Realising what he had said, Farin laughed. *What a fool I am*, he thought. *I can never make up my mind whether my hands are for the harp or for the sword*.

The lamp was flickering fitfully as the oil burned low, and the fire had sunk to red coals. Farin yawned, pushing his black hair back from his eyes, and gently set the old harp down.

Caolin sat at the table in his chamber and picked up the book of the stars he had brought from Laurelynn. It was very late, but he had less need for rest than most men, and only the use of his mind could ease him when tension kept him wakeful as it did now.

He turned the pages carefully, for the volume had been printed before the days of the Cataclysm and was held together only by its covering. The language had changed since the ancients described the workings of the stars – he was still puzzled by the distinction they made between astrology and astronomy – but he had become adept at translating it and at preserving pages that threatened to fall to dust in his hands.

He drew out his notebook, consulted it, then looked at the book again. It had taken him years of study to correlate the Westrian calendar with that of the old civilisation. He was only beginning to trust his interpretations. Names, customs, even the contours of the land might have been changed by the Cataclysm, but the stars remained.

Caolin sighed, relaxing as he contemplated the mathematical beauty of the heavenly movements. Here was an order far removed from the confusions of men, yet governing them in a pattern that was plain if one had the wit to see.

There – the planet Venus was riding high in Cancer, the King's sign. But other forces were present: across the horoscope stretched the baleful influence of Mars. Caolin frowned, suspecting danger for Jehan. But from what source? In the years since the Cataclysm, Westria had become a Kingdom of four Provinces that honored the Guardians and kept to its Covenant. Normontaine, to the north, was ruled by a Queen and shared many customs with the people of Westria; they had always been allies. To the south lay the Confederation of Elaya, where instead of mixing, the people of different blood had formed five nations uneasily united under an elected Prince, who were always ready to fight Westria when they were not bickering with each other. But that border, like the wasteland of mountains between Westria and the Brown Lands to the east, had been quiet for some years now.

From where then could danger come? Was Lord Brian of Las Costas planning some treachery? For a moment, intent upon the chart before him, the Seneschal smiled like a cat who waits for a mouse to pass his hiding place. Let Brian only try. He and Caolin had an old rivalry, but Caolin's ally was the King.

Then he sighed, checking the chart against the book again. The power of Mars would be brief and then Venus would reign. Was Jehan destined to find a bride here in the Corona after all?

Carefully he closed the book, eased it into its silken case, and pushed back his chair. He brought his thumb and forefinger together around the candle flame. For a moment he held them so, savoring his own awareness of pain and watching the point of fire thin and lengthen as it sought to escape his touch. Then he smiled faintly and pinched the candled out.

Surefooted in the darkness, Caolin moved to the window, pulled aside the wooden shutters, and unlatched the multi-paned window to see into the night. The wind was hurrying the storm northward, and between the dim masses of cloud great patches of night sky showed now, strewn thickly with stars. Venus had set long ago, but for a moment he glimpsed the red wink of Mars. He stood still, dizzied by the glory that was alternately veiled and unveiled before him.

"When the Masters of the College of the Wise taught us to read the heavens, they never told us how to see the future there. Do they know? Is that a part of their secret lore?" Caolin spoke softly to the night.

"I may always lack the power to link mind to mind, and so they had an excuse to send me away, but I have this knowledge now, and I am not afraid to use it to guard the Kingdom and the King." Unvoiced came the memory of the one time that the doors of his spirit had been unlocked by another – by Jehan.

"Knowledge is power," he cried, "and with that power I can lead this land to a glory it has never known." Caolin spread his arms as if he would embrace the sky.

The Master of the Junipers spread his arms to the east, then slowly traced a star before him that his trained awareness perceived as a flowing pentagram of light. "O Thou Guardian of the Powers of Air . . ." he murmured a Name, "guard Thou the words of my lips and of my heart."

He turned then to the south, making the sign of warding again. "O Thou Ruler of the fires of Earth and Heaven, keep life's fire burning within me until I return to this body."

Moving again; the Master faced the west and, signing it, commanded the Lord of the Waters to maintain him in harmony with all cycles and tides. Then he shifted to the north, lifted his arms once more, and drew the line of light down and up to the right, left and down and up to the point again, finishing the star.

"O Thou Protector of Earth, my foundation, maintain the bond between my spirit and my body until I take it up once more."

He bowed, then seated himself in the center of the circle he had made, legs crossed and hands open upon his knees. His thoughts were still busy with tasks of the day, and for the moment he let them run freely while he controlled his breathing and relaxed his muscles one by one.

He had spent the afternoon rehearsing tomorrow's ceremony with the priestess from the town below the fortress. He had learned all of the major ceremonies when he was at the College, of course, but it had been long since he had been a celebrant. They seemed to think that it would be an honor for one of the Masters from the Father of Mountains to officiate. It surprised him, for in the old days even the head of the College had made a point of performing one of the rituals somewhere at least once a year.

He turned his thoughts to the Lady of Flowers whose festival tomorrow would be, trying once more to bring Her into focus as he had not been able to that afternoon. She was not a physical being, even in the sense that the First People who guarded the plant and animal kindreds could be. He had been presented to the Lord of the Trees during his training, and once, on a journey to the sacred valley of Awahna, had glimpsed the Great Bear, and he knew that they could appear in many forms. But the Masters at the College still argued over the origins of the gods.

Some said the great Powers, like the Lady of Flowers or the Lord of the Winds or even the spirit of Westria Herself, had returned to Westria after the Cataclysm. Others believed that they had always been there, and only those of the ancients who knew how to worship them had been able to survive to found the new nation. And there were some who felt that in truth, the gods were images that men used to focus and contact the universal forces by which they lived. The College itself did not require that men believe – only that they keep the Covenant.

But the Master knew that, whatever their nature, the powers he called upon were real. But in order to call upon the Lady of Flowers he must see Her clearly, and so he sought guidance where he had always found help before.

He straightened a leg that had been cramped by stillness, then crossed it over the other again. Smoothing his features into passivity, he deepened his breathing and willed it to resume the careful rhythm to which he had trained body and spirit to respond.

"In Thy Name, O Thou Source of All, and to Thy glory . . ."

Imperceptibly his open hands relaxed upon his knees. Images swirled across his consciousness and were banished. Releasing its grasp on the world of forms, his awareness retreated until all knowledge of his body was gone.

Within the darkness in which he floated now, he perceived a single point of brilliance. As he rushed forward it expanded until it dazzled his inner sight. Then he waited while the other world took shape around him, until at last he saw his Guide approaching, robed in light.

Light danced with darkness, and Faris' dreaming spirit soared on the wings of the storm. All her troubled dreams had resolved to this – the world spread out beneath her, the sleeping valleys of Westria where scattered points of light marked the dwellings of men, the mountains whose silver peaks thrust against the sky, oblivious to the tumults below.

I am free! she shouted. *Nothing can hold me now*. Not the anger of her father, her sister's solicitude, nor her own fragile body could stop her flight. Higher she rose, and yet higher, lifting her arms to the stars.

Then a bolt of lightning arched across the heavens toward her. She swooped and darted like a frightened dove but she could not escape.

But it was not lightning, it was a falling star, and when it struck, her flesh was ignited and she and the star burned with an equal flame.

Faris cried out as the force of its fall bore her downward, and she and the star upon her breast plummeted earthward in a single bolt of fire.

2

The Lady of Flowers

Faris shivered, feeling a draft though all of the windows in Rosemary's chamber were shut tight. She reached for the mug of green-gold yarrow tea that Rosemary had just poured for her, hoping that no one had noticed her chill. Steam rose from the mug in white curls that twined lazily in the thin morning light.

She swallowed gratefully as the warmth of the tea filtered through her, and pushed her breakfast about upon her plate so that it would look as if she had eaten. But she knew better than to try. She was paying now for her exaltation of the night before and for the dreams that had followed. Darkness and splendor warred in her memory, dimming the morning light.

Something grey and furry slipped by her. She stifled an exclamation as Rosemary's raccoon hooked a honeycake from the platter and, unimpeded by the splint on his hind leg, hopped back to the floor.

"*Scatter!*" Rosemary glared at the animal. "What shall I do with you? You need a good smack, but I don't want to spoil my doctoring!"

"If he tries to wash that cake it's going to come apart," said Farin, watching the raccoon warily. "And if he goes after my breakfast *I* will smack him!" He picked another

28

sausage from the platter as deftly as the animal had taken the cake.

The Master of the Junipers laughed. He looked very much at home here, with the sunlight glowing in his face – a face not so much worn as lived-in, as if its owner had come to terms with his own strengths and failings long ago.

I wish that I could. Faris pushed her plate aside and picked up her embroidery again, frowning as she set neat stitches around the neck of the tunic she was making for Farin. *Life would be easier if I could just accept my flaws.* She shook her head to hold back tears.

"Faris, are you all right?" asked Rosemary. "Berisa will send you home if you fall ill."

"Then don't tell her!" Faris answered rebelliously. She admired her older sister's dark beauty and the efficiency with which she had managed their home after their mother died. Now Berisa bore the keys of the fortress, which Sandremun's mother had been only too happy to give up to her, but when she was near, Faris felt what little confidence she had slip away.

"I didn't sleep well," she added shortly.

"Well, that's no wonder, in such a storm – but at least the Lady has given us some sunshine for Her Festival." Rosemary had finished eating and was feeding her animals. The gopher snake coiled in its basket needed no attention, but the cageful of mice were glad of the cake crumbs. Rosemary's maid, Branwen, was feeding two orphaned lambs in a pen near the fire. The old sheepdog, who had been asleep with his head across the feet of the Master of the Junipers, thumped his tail on the floor as she went by.

"And we brought the King here safely, after all!" said Farin proudly. When he had come in last night with the others, he had been shaking with cold, but he seemed to have recovered his spirits now. "What a rider Jehan is! The horses were half crazed with fear of the thunder, but whenever anyone needed help, he was there. Rosemary! Are you listening to that owl or to me?"

Rosemary looked at him over her shoulder while the owl swiveled its head forward to pick at the bits of sausage she was offering it.

"Huw talks very good sense sometimes, and he has excellent manners!"

The King. Faris could avoid thinking about him no longer, and the vision of the rider on the rearing white horse whose eyes had held her own replaced her awareness of the room, as it had blazoned itself across her dreams. Had he seen her as well?

"They say Jehan is a fine fighter. I wonder if he would take me into his service," Farin went on.

"Shall I arrange for you to sing for him?" asked Rosemary.

Farin looked horrified. "No! He heard me last night, of course – but that was only a marching song, and he could not have known it was me. If I could be trained at the College of Bards, I might learn enough to perform for him . . . but Father would never let me go."

Branwen set down the bottle that had been emptied by one of the lambs and reached for another. Faris saw that she could not grasp it without losing her grip on the second lamb and got up to hand it to her.

"Thank you, my Lady," whispered the girl.

"Let me help." Faris sat down on the bench beside Branwen and coaxed the lamb to suck. She ran her hand across the soft wool of its back and felt her tension ease.

"Faris, you don't have to do that!" exclaimed Rosemary. The Master of the Junipers glanced over at her with one of his sweet smiles.

Faris tried to laugh. "Really, I am all right – it's just lack of sleep."

Her brother looked at her sharply. "Are you getting sick again, or did you have a dream?" She could not evade his eyes – he knew her too well. "What was it, Faris?" he said.

Faris stared at him, images and warnings conflicting in her memory. There had been a confused succession of visions of fighting – Farin had been in them, and the King.

But she must not tell that. Once, she had dreamed that her mother was leaving her, and told her dream, and seen her mother die.

"Faris." His voice was soft, his eyes a mirror for her own. She heard his thought – *I will make her dream into a song* – and envied him, for in Farin all the intimations of power that tormented her had been channeled into the one gift of music.

"So that you can have something new to sing about?" she asked bitterly. Now she remembered her final dream, like an extension of the storm. "Very well. I dreamed that I was struck by a falling star – use that if you can!"

"You must not be afraid," the Master of the Junipers said gently, though his eyes had grown intent at her words. "Such abilities can be very valuable if they are trained. Didn't they tell you so at your Initiation? The College of the Wise would be glad to teach you."

Faris shook her head. She had gone through the classes that prepared all Westrian children to assume their adult names, terrified that the teacher would find out. But there was such peace in the Master's face. She gazed mutely at him, wondering how it would feel to enter the world of the spirit as a citizen.

"You don't know our father, or Berisa," put in Farin. "They would never let her go." A horse whinnied outside and hoofbeats echoed on the stones of the passage beneath the chamber. Farin sprang to his feet and went to the window to see.

"The King is riding into the town this morning so that everybody can see him, since there's not room for them all to come to the Festival," explained Rosemary.

The Master nodded. "That reminds me, it is time I went down to the Hall. Mistress Elisa wants to go over the litany again."

"And *we* should be going down to the orchard to see what blossoms the wind has left for us to use in the ceremony," said Rosemary. "If we hurry, perhaps we can see the King ride out." She began a hunt for the pruning

31

knife while Branwen shut the lambs back into their pen and took down cloaks from the hooks on the wall.

Faris got to her feet slowly, finding herself curiously reluctant to go with them. She was still dazzled by the vision of the King's face in stormlight, and she did not want to see him grown ordinary in the plain light of day.

"Eric, will you go over to the stables and see if they have gotten Stormwing saddled yet?" asked the King, squinting into the sunlight. The rear guard of last night's storm clouds still trailed across the sky – towering silver-edged masses like floating fortresses, driven northward by a chill wind. But the sun shone with blinding clarity through air washed clean by the rain. Jehan breathed deeply, watching Eric stride through the puddles.

He turned to Caolin, who stood beside him on the porch that overlooked the courtyard. "Now that Eric's gone, I need to talk to you."

"I wondered when you would tire of his company," replied the Seneschal. He stood straight and still, the early light polishing the smooth planes of his face. "He is good-natured, but limited in his interests. I suppose it is a function of his rather appalling youth."

"I was appallingly young when I met you – don't you remember?" Jehan grinned. He had been thirteen when he had gone to be trained at the College of the Wise, where Caolin was a senior student. He had been only sixteen, back in Laurelynn with his ailing father, when Caolin, having astonishingly failed to complete his pilgrimage to Awahna and become a Master of the College, had appeared in the capital to take a post with the old Seneschal. Accepting no rebuffs, the prince had tried to penetrate the young clerk's loneliness. But it was in the following year, when King Alexander died and left Jehan to bear the crown, that Caolin had realised that Jehan needed *him*, and the bond between them had begun to grow.

"As a matter of fact, I find Eric's innocence refreshing," the King went on resolutely. "I wanted to talk to you

alone just because I don't desire to disturb it. The Great
Rebellion has finally approached him." Two of Theodor's
men bowed as they passed and Jehan saluted them. Caolin
waited until they had gone down the steps to reply.

"Oh? And what did he think of it?"

"Highly indignant, of course. You know how he feels
about Lord Brian."

"I also know how Brian feels about him. They are too
alike in strength and temper, and Brian is older. Was
Roland of Greenfell the one who spoke to him?"

"Yes – how did you know?" Jehan rubbed at his beard,
realising that this was not such news to Caolin as he had
expected.

"I've talked to him enough to find out he is Brian's
man. Anyone who travels around the Kingdom as much
as he does naturally interests the Seneschal's office, so I
cultivated him. Hopefully he will keep me informed of his
progress. He may be Theodor's cousin, but I doubt that
the Lord Commander knows what he's up to."

The King nodded, remembering the light in the old
man's eyes when he had greeted him. "I don't doubt
Theodor's loyalty. Normontaine is too near, and the outlaws in the no-man's land between the Kingdoms nearer
still. He would not be able to stand alone." *How cynical
that sounds*, he thought then. *Am I becoming like Caolin,
to suspect lies whenever men offer loyalty?*

"Jehan, come down." Sandremun's call brought him
back to the present. "The horses are waiting outside."

The King gave Caolin a quick smile, grateful that for
once the Seneschal had forborne to accuse Brian of treachery. Then he ran down the broad stairs, clutching at his
green cloak as the wind filled it to keep from being blown
away.

Faris hurried across the courtyard after Rosemary, head
bent into the wind. She stumbled, then threw herself
backward as hooves clattered like thunder and a dark
bulk reared over her.

33

"You fool! If you don't know any better than to run under a horse's hooves, you should go back to your burrow in the hills!"

Gasping, Faris looked up, saw a large young man reining an equally massive black horse in tight circles, cursing her and the animal equally as it bucked and snorted, fighting his restraint. She knew that her cheeks were flaming, but she could not get breath enough to reply.

"There now, that's a boy – hold still. Maybe she's never seen a real horse like you." The stallion came to a halt at last and the young man's words died away as he focused on Faris standing there.

"My Lady," he said finally, after a moment of stunned silence during which his face became as red as her own. For all his size, Faris realised that he was scarcely older than she.

"I'm Sir Eric of Seagate, at your service. Did Thunderfoot hurt you?"

She shook her head. Why was he staring at her?

Someone called from the gate. Eric looked around distractedly, then back at her. "Are you sure? Will you be at the Festival?"

Faris nodded, smiling, wondering how long he would keep her standing here. Then his name was called again, and she took advantage of his preoccupation to gather her skirts and cross the courtyard before he could call out to her.

She slipped through the orchard gate and latched it firmly behind her, then stood still for a moment, catching her breath. It was very quiet here, out of the wind. Faintly she could hear shouts as the King's party set off toward the town, and more clearly, the voices of Rosemary and Branwen discussing which branches should be cut for the Festival.

She sighed, grateful to be alone. The plum tree before her was just coming into flower. She rested one hand lightly on its trunk, gazing into the lacy branches. She could feel a light throbbing through her fingertips – was it the response of the trunk to the wind, or the life of the tree flowing beneath her hand? Her breathing deepened, and the flush faded from her cheeks.

Looking from one tree to another, she let the memory of her encounter with Sir Eric slip easily from her mind, and with a greater effort banished the vision of the King. Here among the trees she could escape from the complexities of men.

Her ears buzzed with cold. Her eyes began to water, and the blossoms before her blurred. She blinked, looked up, and was suddenly still. For a moment in which she did not breathe she saw before her not a grove of trees, but a circle of maidens veiled and crowned in white, stretching out their arms to her.

Fear and longing warred within her. Her breath rushed back and, dizzied, she fell to her knees with her palms sunk into the soft earth and her forehead against the trunk of the tree. The air warmed around her and she recognised a subtle perfume. There was a moment then when she might have gained her feet and run away. But she did not move.

The Presence she had sensed approaching grew greater and the heat increased. A sweet fire melted all her stiffness. Faris kept her eyes shut tight, afraid of what she might see.

But words welled unbidden from the depths of her spirit. *Lady! Make me whole . . . let me be free!*

There was reassurance in the warmth that enfolded her, like a mother's arms. Faris bowed her head upon her crossed hands in wordless wonder, beyond self-awareness and beyond time. She heard distant laughter like a chime of silver bells, and the strange heat faded gradually away.

"Faris . . . Faris . . ." How far away the voices seemed. She did not want to move, but she made herself sit up and look upon a world whose splendor was once more veiled. And for that moment she *knew* that what she saw was only the appearance, and what she had sensed, the reality.

"Faris what are you doing? We must get these flowers to the Hall, and then it will be time to dress for the Festival."

Faris slowly focused on Rosemary, standing before her with her arms full of starry flowers.

"Faris, you look so strange. What happened to you?"

But Faris could only shake her head and hold her face to the clean wind.

Wind swept the great Hall of the Hold, fluttering women's veils and ribbons, plucking white petals from the branches of almond and plum that garlanded the long room as the big double doors at its end were opened and shut again. People turned to see who had come in, asking each other if the families from the holdings on the northern border had arrived.

Jehan and Rosemary stood at the edge of a swirl of dancers, sipping white wine. "My Lord, I must apologise," said Rosemary, smoothing her azure gown a little nervously. "Things may begin on time in Laurelynn, but we are less precise in the Corona." The Festival had been scheduled for midday, but it was now halfway into the afternoon, and Theodor had told the musicians to start playing while they waited for the latecomers.

The King turned to her, lowering his voice. "Believe me, a more leisurely pace is very welcome. I am glad of the chance to learn more of the Province from you. For instance, you could tell me the names of some of the dancers. Only the heads of households were presented to me, yet I may have to lead their sons in battle, or . . ."

"Or their daughters in the dance?" Rosemary laughed.

For a moment Jehan's answering grin was as open as her own. "Your pardon, Lady Rosemary. I had not meant to be devious. It is a habit one gets into in Laurelynn." He met her steady gaze.

A boy came by with a wicker tray of sweet white cakes molded in the shapes of moons and flowers, blushing as the King took one and nodded his thanks.

"To be frank, the ways of the capital hold little interest for me. We live more simply here in the north. The companionship of the Master of the Junipers is the only thing I envy you."

"Yes, your father told me you study with him when he stops here on his way to the College of the Wise. I wish I could spare him more often, but my chaplain is like a peaceful clearing in the midst of a very tangled wood, to which I have sometimes great need to repair."

The music changed to the dance called the peacock, and the King offered his hand to Rosemary. Together they paced the length of the hall, the swirl of his dark blue mantle echoing the sway of her skirts. Across the room he saw the crimson splash of Caolin's robe and noted that the Seneschal was talking with Ronald of Greenfell. His gaze passed on, seeking among the dancers one white face framed in a cloud of dark hair.

"The couple ahead of us are Andreas Blackbeard, who is squire to Charles of Woodhall, and Woodhall's daughter Holly. Sir Charles is one of the latecomers we are waiting for. I think you know Allen of Badensbridge, and of course my brother and his wife, Berisa. Sir Eric is dancing with my companion, Branwen." Rosemary paused, scanning the crowd. Colors flowed and blended as the dancers moved, parting for a moment to reveal a white figure like a lily in a field of wildflowers.

Jehan's breath caught for a moment, but the rhythm of the dance carried him on. "And the dark-haired girl in ivory, dancing with the young man who so resembles her?" he asked softly.

"Oh, did I leave them out?" Rosemary looked at him speculatively. "They are relatives of Berisa, from Hawkrest Hold. She is Faris, and her brother is called Farin."

"Fair she is indeed, and her brother looks a likely lad," Jehan replied neutrally. "He is not knighted yet? How old is he?"

"He's nineteen, but he says he will not accept knighthood until he has earned it. I'm afraid he's had little chance to be a hero. Here, he's known for his skill as a singer and upon the harp."

"A singer? Of course, now I remember. His singing was the only thing bearable about last night's ride." Did Rosemary suspect that Jehan's real object of interest was Farin's sister? He was almost certain Faris was the girl he had seen.

The music ended with a flourish of flutes, and Rosemary gathered her azure silk skirts in a courtesy. Jehan escorted her back to her father, and for a moment they exchanged civilities. Her mother, Lady Amata, found events of this kind too great a strain, so Rosemary was acting as her father's hostess. As they talked someone came to her asking whether they should put out more cakes and wine now, or wait until after the ceremony, and Jehan took advantage of the distraction to move away.

He looked around him. The Seneschal had disappeared, and perhaps that was as well, for the King found himself unwilling to seek Caolin's help in meeting the girl in the moon-colored gown. A formal introduction would attract unwelcome attention, and he did not wish to embarrass her. But what about a chance meeting in the dance? Jehan cut through the crowd to find the Master of Musicians.

Soon the hands of the dancers were filled with flowers. Men and women danced together until the melody changed, then each must wander alone for a few measures until the music altered once more, and each gentleman offered his spray of flowers to the lady of his choice and took her as a partner . . . until the music changed again and it was time for the ladies to choose anew.

Like wanderers in some enchanted wood, each one sought the face he or she desired.

Sunlight slanted through the long upper windows, shafting through the dust motes in a haze of light. Dazzled, Faris peered at her partner, recognised him as Allen of Badensbridge, then laughed without replying as he asked her whom she had expected to see. Her pale gown swirled about her like a cloud as they moved forward. She moved as lightly as a cloud, as if she were dancing with the wind.

Ever since that moment in the orchard she had been acutely conscious of the insubstantiality of the veil between the worlds. And now the trees had come into the Hall to dance with her. Faris laughed again, forgetting her aching feet, answering the music. Nothing could touch her now. When the music lifted her, there were no more choices to be made, only the instinctive movement toward harmony.

The melody changed. Her partner left her and Faris waited, poised in the music, dizzied by the flowers' faint perfume. Sunlight blinded her. Then someone drew her into the shadow, and when she could see again she met the blue gaze of the King.

She took from him the spray of flowers, trembling suddenly so that only the steady pressure of his hand kept her from faltering in the dance. She fought for self-control, fear shattering her exaltation as she understood who her partner was.

They turned, and her unfastened sleeve fell back, revealing her scar.

The King turned to face her, almost breaking step. "You have been hurt!" His voice beat heavily across the music. Faris nearly fell, waiting for him to show everyone her shame.

"How did it happen?" he asked softly. Still terrified, she looked up at him and could not look away. She found herself telling him the story that she had tried to forget, as she tried to forget her scar.

"It was long ago . . . our housekeeper had a baby whose gown caught fire. When I beat out the flames, I was burned too."

"Were you afraid?" asked the King, guiding her around the circle. "How old were you?"

"I was six," she said simply, held by his still gaze. Suddenly all that had happened to her seemed very small and far away. "I was afraid afterward, but when it happened everything was very clear, and I knew what I had to do."

The King gave a little sigh and nodded, his gaze releasing her to fix inward on some memory. "It is like that in battle sometimes."

He knows! Faris' heart shook in her breast. *He has seen my scar and still he is dancing with me.* She glanced at him beneath her lashes, and her breath caught as she realised that he was not only the King, but beautiful.

The music swept them forward, but breathless, she could not speak now. She let him lead her, attending neither to the figure nor to her own steps, for it seemed natural for his movements to be reflected by her own. The measure was endless, like music in a dream.

And then, like a dream, it stopped and left them standing together while all around them couples drew apart.

The King's hand tightened, as if he would have drawn Faris through the door behind them. But the breaking of the music had frightened her. Startled, she hung back. Immediately the pressure ceased and he raised her hand to his lips instead. Her left hand. Then he released her and was gone into the crowd.

Horns called, their clear summons dissipating into a buzz of comment as word spread that Theodor had tired of waiting and ordered the ceremony to begin.

Rosemary took Faris' arm and pulled her into place in the line of young women, but Faris scarcely noticed what she did, for even as the first notes of the processional began, the print of the King's lips still burned upon her hand.

"In the Name of the Lady of Fire, be this place purified and made sacred to our purpose here . . ."

While Faris stood dazed, the two priests and the other priestess had already sanctified the room with incense and water and salt, and now they formed three points of a square surrounding the altar where they had placed the most perfect of the flowers. The fire priestess finished her circuit, moved to the altar, where she used her taper to touch the tall candles to flame, and then took her place at the southern corner of the square.

"Thou earth, thou sky, thou sun, thou sea – I am the center of thy circled cross, be thou represented equally in me!" the people cried.

Mistress Elisa and the Master of the Junipers faced each other before the altar, mantled alike over their black and white robes in capes of pale green worked with embroideries of butterflies and flowers.

"Who is this that appears with the dawning?" the Master of the Junipers began the chant. "She is clothed in mist, Her hair is pearled with dew."

"She emerges from the sea, She rides upon the wind," the priestess answered him.

"Her strength is the strength of the seedling surging toward the sun; Her beauty blinds the eye." Back and forth ran the litany.

"Her beauty is as clear as water, Her fragrance stirs the heart like a distant song."

Yes . . . Faris breathed in the scent of the flowers. *I have heard Her . . . I have felt Her touch upon my soul.* The words of the celebrants blended with her memory of the orchard. Overlapping visions dazzled her. Was she surrounded by tree trunks or the carved and painted pillars of the Hall?

"When wind whispers in budding branches and the new moon swings through the sky, She is here."

"When blossoms open to the sunlight and earth receives the gentle rain, She is here."

The Master of the Junipers turned to the people, opening his arms. "Oh my brothers and my sisters, we are gathered here to celebrate the coming of spring and to invoke the blessing of the Lady of Flowers. But winter's sleep was peaceful, demanding nothing. Are you willing to wake, to grow, and with the world to face both the joy and the pain life brings? Is it your will to call the Lady here?"

41

"Yes! We will it, let the Lady come!" came the answer from a hundred throats, shaking the air and setting chills through Faris' flesh.

Do they understand that She will come? thought the girl, *that She is already here?* Abruptly she was afraid.

The Master stood before the altar, lifting his arms as a supplicant, and began to call upon the Lady by names that Faris knew and by others that she had never heard before. Tension charged the air like a gathering of lightnings as he focused the energies of all those in the room into one cone of power. The hair lifted on the back of her neck. The Master's voice rang like a bell in the stillness, names became images, and images a single shining form that stood before the altar, arms outstretched, veils floating upon an invisible wind.

Her cloak was a shimmering fabric of leaves like pale wings, like flames, like the petals of flowers, through which Her body shone like the new moon in a dawn sky. Her eyes were fixed on Faris with a terrible clarity, and Faris could not look away. This was the vision she had feared in the orchard, but she could not refuse it now.

Lady . . . The words trembled on her lips, but no sound came. *What do You want of me?*

Did no one else see Her? The Master of the Junipers stood rigid before the altar, arms lifted in adoration. His face was filled with light. Transfixed by his own vision, he had no help for Faris.

The priestess stepped past him to give the blessing, but Faris saw her slight figure cloaked in the Lady's glory. Her words sounded in the stillness of Faris' soul, answering her.

"I am the kernel in the husk and the seed in the ground. I am the shoot piercing the stone and opening its leaves to the sun. Come to Me, and grow . . .

"I am the rain in the cloud and the tides of the sea. I am the wind of heaven that bears seed to the earth and inspiration to men. Come to Me and bring forth beauty . . .

"I am the lightning in the storm and the star in the dark. I am the fire of earth in the coal and the fire of love in the heart. Come to Me and I will light the eternal flame within your soul . . ."

The words thundered and reverberated through the spaces of Faris' spirit, opening before her vistas that she had never dared to look upon.

The herders were coming up to the altar now, bringing the firstborn lambs for the Lady's blessing, white and bleating with wide, curious eyes. The landholders came, bearing the sacks of seed they would soon put into the ground. Men and women came, smiling, with their children in their arms.

"The Lady blesses you. What will you give to Her?" asked the priestess.

In the midst of the people the unmarried men stood with crowns of flowers in their hands. As they came forward Rosemary led the young women before the altar to face them. "As we are all dresses of the Lady, so we accept your offerings in Her name," she said.

With her back to the altar, Faris was able to focus on her surroundings, though still she felt the Lady behind her as though she stood before an open fire. The men were grouped unevenly before them. Andreas Blackbeard came forward and, after a moment's hesitation, set the wreath he carried on Holly of Woodhall's head. Another young man stepped out and, blushing, presented his crown to the girl next to Faris, then another came. She saw Eric of Seagate towering over the others and smiling at her.

Faris found herself trembling. She had not realised before that it would be so public, that each girl would be singled out from the rest. *Lady, help me!* her spirit cried, and the answer came, *I am here*.

The next man in the line was the King.

Sunlight blazed from the gold that banded his forehead. A light was on his face, and his glowing eyes seemed to see through her to the One who waited beyond. With the stately deliberation of a dream figure he came to her, and in that moment she was not surprised when he stopped before her and set the crown of flowers he bore upon her hair.

He took his place again, and she saw beyond him her brother's astonished face, and in the features of Eric of Seagate a mixture of fury and despair. Other men came forward then, and Eric, mastering himself, strode up to give his wreath to Rosemary.

Then it was finished, and the musicians sounded the first measures of the danced hymn that the girls had been practicing.

"O Shining One," the sweet voices soared, "who from afar bears beauty like the morning star; lend us Thy light who linger here, imprisoned by our pain and fear." Then they began the first verse and moved into the dance.

> O ye who wander in a barren land –
> Behold, the Lady stretches out her hand
> –
> All that was comfortless is passed away;
> She leads the world rejoicing into day.

Faris' feet fulfilled the pattern without her will; her lips moved without her knowing if her throat made any sound as they repeated the chorus and began the next verse.

> Behind Her trail the lengthening daylight hours,
> And in Her footsteps spring the rainbowed flowers.
> Wise as the owl and tender as the dove,
> Her handmaidens are light and life and love.

Faris felt the presence of the Lady withdrawing now, like receding music or flower scent borne away by the wind, but the wreath of flowers the King had given her glowed upon her brow like a crown of fire. She wondered then, *Did the King see* me *when he gave me the flowers, or* Her?

Hers is the rain that nourishes the soul;
Her mirror shows us to ourselves, made whole.
Out of death's sleep . . .

The great doors crashed open, sending tremors through the floor. A cold wind swept the Hall, blowing the candles into streamers of flame and swirling a cloud of flower petals over the people like falling snow.

. . . She rises with the morn,
And, waking to Her kiss, we are reborn.

The singers grasped at the melody and finished the verse, their voices rising resolutely over the confused shouting that was spreading from the direction of the door, but to Faris their voices sounded dull as a cracked bell. The Lady had left Her temple now.

The crowd parted like water breasted by a fleeing deer as someone pushed toward Lord Theodor.

"Commander, you must come." The man burst into the space before the altar. Through the mire that covered him blood showed, caked around a ragged tear in the shoulder of his coat, splashed across his legs and thighs. He fought for breath and clung to Lord Theodor's bony hands.

"Stefan, Stefan, be easy, lad, I'm here. What has happened?" the Commander's voice was low and steady. A little color returned to the messenger's face.

"It's raiders, my Lord, woodsrats from the mountains. They've taken Woodhall and set all the holdings along the Highwater in flames. My two brothers fought their way free beside me, but they brought them down with arrows on the road . . ." Sobbing, the young man sank to his knees, his head pressed against Lord Theodor's hands.

Holly of Woodhall whimpered once and then stood mute and shaking while the other girls tried to comfort her. But Andreas had cried out in a great voice and his hand struck at the air as if grasping for a sword.

He looked around distractedly, saw Holly, and came to her.

"Holly – my lady – Sir Charles is a great fighter; he might be holding out still. I swear to you, we'll rescue him . . . or revenge him." He stopped short, swallowing.

After a moment her gaze focused on him and her hand came up to touch his cheek. Then her face crumpled and, giving way to her grief, she let the other women lead her away.

Two of Lord Theodor's guardsmen were helping the messenger to his feet. Rosemary left her place among the singers to take care of him. Some of the girls tried to finish the chorus, but the Lord Commander was shouting orders and they could not be heard. The Master of the Junipers and Mistress Elisa bent before the altar, hurrying through the closing ritual.

And only Faris, standing still amid the storm of activity, seemed to hear as if from afar an echo of silver bells.

The great bell of the Hold tolled from the tower. Caolin could feel its reverberations in the walls of the passageway two stories below. The ceremonies had been very pretty, but Jehan had looked like a sleepwalker at the end of them. Where had he gone?

Distantly he heard the neighing of horses and the shout of orders as supplies were readied for the war party. There was no need for Jehan to ride with them – Theodor and his men should be perfectly capable of handling this without the reinforcement of the King. But Jehan would think it his duty to go, and Caolin supposed that it was politically useful for him to show himself a warrior.

But he remembered the danger he had foreseen in the King's horoscope. *What is the use of all my knowledge if I cannot guard him?* he thought and quickened his pace.

He heard the King's voice ahead of him, the sound of the words oddly distorted as they echoed against the stones of the passage, and then someone else answering him. Caolin stopped, wondering who Jehan was talking to.

"You gave your flowers to the Lady Faris because you thought it might commit you too much if you honored Lady Rosemary, didn't you?"

Caolin recognised the voice of Eric of Seagate now, and as he rounded the corner he saw the young knight facing Jehan, half crouched as if he would spring at his throat. The Seneschal's hand moved to the penknife that was all the weapon he ever bore, but Eric had dropped to one knee before the King, and Caolin realised that he was pleading.

Jehan's reply was inarticulate. He looked dazed, like a man wakened too suddenly from a fair dream.

"I know that you must marry to serve the Kingdom." Eric spoke as if his throat were closing on the words. "But Faris is not like the other women you –" He broke off, blushing furiously. "She is so young! She would not understand!"

"Eric . . . do you truly believe that of me?" For a moment Jehan's voice shook. "I have known many women, but do you think I would play with a young girl's feelings for my amusement?"

Caolin stepped forward, watching Eric warily, but neither man appeared to notice him.

"Oh no, my Lord! Oh, I had not meant to speak at all, only I saw you here, and – why did you give her the flowers?" Eric sat back on his heels, looking up at the King, his eyes like those of a hurt dog.

Jehan sighed. The glory was gone from his face now, and he looked drawn and pale. "I don't know why. Or perhaps" – his grim look softened a little – "I did it because she stood like a white lily in the sunlight, and then for a moment I saw beyond her the Lady Herself, smiling at me . . . I gave her the flowers because she was beautiful."

"And you are the King," Eric replied replied bleakly. "She will see no one else now. I should have told you that

I – well, it does not matter now." He got to his feet, pulling himself erect. "My Lord, will we be going with Theodor's men?"

"Yes, of course," said the King absently, "but Eric, please –"

"Then with your permission, I will prepare the men to ride!" Eric's face had gone rigid, like a statue of heroic despair. Without waiting for an answer, he saluted, strode past Caolin without acknowledging him, and went down the passageway.

It was no more than his usual response to me, thought Caolin wryly, but in this case he doubted that the young knight had seen him at all. He shook his head and went to Jehan, who stood with his hands clenched in the folds of his tunic, staring at the wall.

"My dear Lord," said Caolin softly, "what are you doing, playing at fighting cocks with Eric, of all people? Does he fancy himself in love with that girl?" He put his hand on the King's shoulder.

"A fancy? Oh no, Eric is perfectly sincere. Oh, Eric!" he burst out. "If only I had known!" Then he sighed and rubbed his eyes. Behind them came the clatter of hurrying feet and the jingle of mail. "They'll be needing me." Jehan straightened, then shivered suddenly.

Caolin's grip tightened on his shoulder. "Jehan . . . Jehan . . . it's all right! It's only a girl."

The King looked up at him, and for a moment his face held something Caolin had never seen there before, evanescent as the light reflected on leaves by moving water. Then his features settled into their familiar lines and his eyes focused on Caolin.

"Only a girl . . ." he echoed. Then he smiled. "And now I must go arm or they will leave me behind, and I would never be able to live that down."

The squire Rafael clattered down the passageway and slid to a stop, panting "My Lord, there you are – I've been looking –" He caught his breath. "I've laid your arms ready and packed your gear. Please come now!"

"Thank you, Rafael. Yes, I will come." For a moment Jehan's hand clasped Caolin's. Then he moved from the Seneschal's side and was gone.

"Take care, my Lord," Caolin called after him, wanting to call him back, feeling the chill draft in the passage as the first breath of a wind that would sweep them all away, but he did not know if Jehan heard.

For a moment he stood irresolutely, wondering if there was something he should do. But war was Jehan's business, not his, and even his usual duties of support and supply were being handled by Theodor's people this time. He shrugged and went back toward the gate to watch them go.

A red sun was glowing beneath lowering clouds as the war band of the Corona prepared to set out. It glittered on helms and mail like a dying flame and painted the bright banners and formal battle gear the color of blood. The forces that Theodor had sent to reinforce the eastern strongholds, were dwindling in the distance, and the men assigned to garrison the Hold muttered in disappointment from the walls. The hundred men whom Theodor had picked to accompany him held their mounts before the gates, waiting for the signal to depart. They included Theodor's own guard, men from the Highwater valley whose homes had been attacked, and the knights who had come with the King.

Faris drew her grey cloak more closely around her, but the bitter wind searched out every irregularity in its weave. She could not stop shivering, and her stomach cramped anxiously. Even the Father of Mountains, rising white-cloaked to the north of the fortress, seemed aloof and implacable now. She looked down at Theodor's little army, pitying the horses who stamped eagerly, not knowing the journey that awaited them.

She found it hard to think clearly. Too much had happened today. That morning Sir Eric had spoken to her like an eager boy, yet now he sat his black horse like a statue in armor. Once, he looked up at the wall, but it seemed to Faris that his eyes flinched from meeting hers.

Rosemary moved closer and took her arm. "Are you as cold as I am? What are they waiting for?" she asked angrily. She was watching Sir Eric too.

There was a stir immediately beneath them, and the Lord Commander came through the main gate, his son by his side. With hair and beards hidden by their helms and coifs of mail, they looked uncannily alike – Sandremun was a trifle taller, with more padding on his long bones. Faris glanced at her sister, Berisa, who was standing with her mother-in-law nearby. They leaned over the parapet, waving as if their husbands went off to war every day.

But she must be worried about Sandy, thought Faris wryly, *or she would have seen me shivering and sent me inside!* Berisa had tried to be a mother to her after their own had died, but her well-intentioned tyranny had left Faris feeling more orphaned than before. For a moment the encompassing love she had felt in the orchard stirred in her memory like the scent of blossoms borne by a changing wind, but she stiffened, afraid to accept it, and it was gone.

The babble of conversation below them lessened momentarily and Faris heard the voice of the King. She had been watching Berisa and had not seen him come out, but now he stood just below them, talking to the Seneschal. Would he look up at her? What should she do?

Jehan and the Seneschal moved forward. Caolin bent his fair head over his master's hand. Jehan slapped his shoulder bracingly and he straightened again, shaking his head. The King let him go and swung up on to his waiting mount. He settled into the saddle and, seeing Lord Theodor's lady on the wall above him, waved a hand in salute. His eyes moved past her to the others, but if he hesitated when he saw Faris among them, she could not tell.

And as surely as she had known he cared for her that afternoon, Faris was now certain that he regretted his choice, that he remembered her scar. She schooled her face not to show her shame, staring out over the warriors without seeing them.

A man desires perfection in the woman he loves. Faris could not shut away the echo of her father's voice, the distaste in his eyes as he turned her marred arm and forced her to look at it. *If men say you are fair, knowing of this, they will be lying to you, and if you let them think you fair, unknowing, you will be living a lie.* Nausea rose in her throat at the memory, and she started to turn away.

Berisa hissed gently, and after a moment's disorientation Faris realised that she was pointing not at her arm but at the courtyard below. "Did you know about this?"

Shaking her head to clear her confusion, Faris joined Rosemary as she bent over the edge of the wall and saw Farin, fully armed, grinning up at them. He shifted his round shield to his other arm and waved. Rosemary laughed and waved back.

"He's too young!" exclaimed Berisa. "He has no experience in war, and who in that crowd will take care of him?"

"Really, Berisa," retorted Rosemary, "if it were not for his own foolish notions Farin would be knighted by now! Surely he is old enough to chase outlaws! They are unlikely to catch up with them, and if they do, not only your husband, but men like Sir Eric of Seagate will be at his back. Farin will be safer with them than he would be at home!"

"He wanted to impress the King," murmured Faris. Another vision superimposed itself upon the scene below . . . an image from one of last night's dreams. She saw Farin's face, not laughing now, but pale and intent as he swung at faceless men who came at him through the snow. Swords gleamed in the fading light. Farin was struggling to remain on his feet. She saw the King's squire, Rafael, beside him, and another man at his back. A blade flashed toward Farin's head, the third man turned to parry it, and Faris recognised Jehan.

I dreamed this battle, and now the King is going to war. Faris whimpered and hid her face in her hands.

The air quivered to the sweet summons of a horn. There was a confused murmur as those who were still afoot swung into their saddles. The hoofbeats became a rhythm as horses joined the line. When Faris was able to look again, she saw only their riders' rejecting backs. Involuntarily she stretched out her hand.

They had not all turned away. As she caught her breath Faris saw one figure still standing in the road and met the considering gaze of the Seneschal.

She stared at him, swaying a little in the strengthening wind, while her cheeks grew wet with icy tears.

3

Trust and Treachery

"By the Lord of Battles!" Eric exclaimed. "There is no honor in this kind of war!" He glared at the ruins of the homestead, whose still-smoldering beams were partly powdered with snow.

Jehan shifted in his saddle, trying unsuccessfully to ease muscles wearied by hours of riding, and smiled bleakly. *Oh, Eric*, he thought. *This is not how I taught you to make war when we fought against Elaya in the south.*

They had ridden northward from the Hold until past midnight and stopped for an uneasy rest beside the road until it was light enough to see their way again. Now the Father of Mountains rose to the east of them, and the beginnings of the Highwater's southern fork trickled through the pasture. A pall of smoke stretched southward, dimming the morning light as its acrid reek clogged the air. The red-stained snow of the yard was littered with household goods the reivers had not bothered to carry away. Nearby stood a single piebald cow, her bag heavy with milk, whose plaintive mooing made counterpoint to the cawing of the carrion birds.

"It is the usual practice of these woodsrats," commented Theodor grimly. "They attack at night, slaughter the people, loot the steading, and then burn it to the ground.

They come down from the north in bands of fifty or more and work their way down one valley and up another and thence back into the hills. But we did not expect them at this time of year. I fear that too many of our fighting men came down to the Festival and the borders were left without adequate defense."

Jehan shook his head, anger burning impotently in his belly. He knew that these outlaws raided the Corona every year . . . and yet if he had not come to the north, this steading might have been better defended and the blood of his people would not have stained the snow.

"Where is Woodhall from here?" he asked.

"Perhaps two hours' hard ride up the road, my Lord. It guards the mouth of the valley, but I fear there is little left of it now," answered the Lord Commander.

"Please, my Lord, let me go and see!" exclaimed a stocky man with a bristling black beard who had been in the forefront of the riders. *Andreas Blackbeard.* Jehan's memory supplied the name from the presentations yesterday afternoon.

"My lord Charles is a valiant man, and he might have held them off! Oh, why did I go without him? He told me to bring Holly to the Festival . . . he said he was too old for dancing . . . but my place was by his side!"

"Peace, Andreas, peace!" said Theodor. "You have no reason to reproach yourself. Your duty was to do as your lord bade you. We will take the main force up the road to Spirit Falls – the tracks of the raiders seem to lead that way – but you take all the men from this valley and fifteen from my guard and go on to Woodhall. Guard the road out of the valley for me!"

Andreas bowed low over his saddlebow and turned his horse up the road, followed by the men Theodor had assigned to him. The others watched him go, pity in their eyes.

"To have one's lord die and be able to do nothing in his defense must be the hardest of all fates for a warrior to bear!" said Eric somberly.

Except to see one's people endangered and be unable to go to their aid, thought the King. A horse stamped behind him and he heard whispering.

"Doesn't this destruction bother them at all?"

Jehan half turned and saw young Farin leaning toward the King's squire, Rafael. They did not see him watching them.

"I would expect the King and the Lord Commander to be made of iron, but don't any of the rest worry about what is going to happen when we catch up with these devils? Do you suppose one acquires this calmness along with knighthood?"

Farin's thin face looked weary, but his eyes were bright. *That girl's eyes, in her brother's face* . . . The King faced forward again, shutting the thought away, while the whispering of the two young men went on. He wished he could tell them that the sickness and the fear never went away, or if they did, it was because a man's soul was already dead, though his body might fight on.

"I don't know," Rafael was saying. "Somehow I doubt it. All I know is that I'm afraid too. Ssh! Theodor's speaking."

The cow mooed mournfully again. A crow was cawing in the trees by the remains of the house. *The music of the battlefield*, thought the King.

"Will someone at least do something about that damned cow?" said Theodor.

Caolin the Seneschal rested easily in a low chair before the fire, his fingers plucking a sonata from the strings of a guitar. It was a beautiful instrument, its wood worn honey-smooth, inlaid around the sound-hole with a geometric design in jet and mother-of-pearl.

Faris, lifting her eyes from her embroidery, wondered at his ability to play with such evenness and accuracy when his attention was not on his music but on his audience. It reminded her of the way a deer fed in a meadow, ears constantly swiveling to catch any hint of danger – except that Caolin's alertness held no hint of fear.

When her brother, Farin, played his harp, he was oblivious to all but the music, and his fingers stumbled sometimes, unable to keep up with the passion he was trying to express. He had no harp to comfort him where he was now. Faris bit her lip and turned resolutely back to the faces around the fire, suppressing her momentary vision of mailed forms struggling painfully through the snow.

The late afternoon light was falling through the window behind her, gray and dim, but the firelight coppered Caolin's pale hair and chiseled profile and warmed the faces of his listeners. Lady Amata sat nearest, her gentle face, too plump to show the wrinkles of sixty years, flushed from the fire. Berisa was beside her, black hair drawn back from her face like raven's wings. Her hands were busy with a darning needle and a pile of stockings.

Beyond them, Rosemary was mixing a painkiller for Stefan of the Long Ridge, whose bed had been placed at right angles to the hearth. Two other men who had been left to guard the Hold were nearby. One of them held up his hands for Holly of Woodhall to wind a skein of wool. In the corner Rosemary's maid, Branwen, sat with her spindle forgotten on her knee. Even Rosemary's old dog had managed to evade Berisa's restrictions and now lay sleeping beside his mistress' chair.

Berisa looked up as the music slowed. "You play well, my lord Seneschal. We are grateful for the entertainment – a welcome diversion from wondering how our lords fare tonight."

"Yes, we *were* distracted, until she reminded us again," muttered Rosemary.

Faris jabbed her finger with the embroidery needle and sucked it hastily, looking around to see if anyone had noticed her agitation. This was ridiculous! Farin was only her brother, and the link between them was such that she would surely know if he were hurt. She had known it when he was thrown from his horse and broke his arm, and the time he was caught in a rock slide while out hunting.

And yet I'm as nervous as if it were my lover, not my brother, who rode away. But I'm no one's lady, she thought bitterly as she remembered how Eric's eyes had avoided her, how the King had not seemed to see her at all, *nor am I likely to be!* She picked up her needle defiantly, but her hand was trembling so that she could not set it in the right place.

"It seems unfair that I should dominate the entertainment," said Caolin, holding their attention with his eyes. His clipped hair brushed the upstanding collar of his robe as he turned his head to survey the company. "Will none of you ladies give us a song?"

Faris thrust her needle slantwise through the shirt, folded it swiftly, and dropped it into her basket. She stood up.

"I will sing if you will provide an accompaniment," she said quickly, forcing her voice to calm.

"Indeed, my Lady, I will partner you with great pleasure. What is the song?"

Her eyes met his, flicked away around the room. Rosemary seemed pleased, the others interested, except for Berisa, who frowned as if she were deciding whether or not to approve. For a moment Faris wavered, afraid that her voice would fail her before all these people, and knowing that her sister would act on the merest hint of an appeal.

And tell me forever afterward what a fool I had been to stand up at all! "I will sing 'The Butterfly,'" she said clearly. It was a ballad she had practiced with Farin a hundred times. "Do you know it?"

"No." Caolin smiled. "But if you will sing the first verse I will join in."

"Wait a moment." Rosemary looked up from her patient. "Let us have some more wood on the fire. As the afternoon fades it will be colder, and I don't wish Stefan to take a chill."

Berisa's two daughters jumped up a trifle guiltily and brought wood from the box to build up the fire. Soon its light reached into every corner of the room, flickering on the painted walls and making fantastic shadows on the carven beams.

Faris' voice wavered as she began, then gained strength and filled the room as the firelight had filled it.

Light is my flight as I float on the wind,
Like a flower given wings I will fly.
I sup on sweet nectar, my drink is the dew –
No creature goes freer than I.

And yet I have trailed all the weight of my fate
Over earth, over trunk, over tree,
Until, wracked by winter, I spun out my soul
For a shroud, and I dreamed myself free.

In beauty I rise as a child of the skies,
I feel the wind's chill without fear.
And when these wings, outworn, flutter earthward, reborn
And more gloriously robed I'll appear.

Faris finished the song and sat down abruptly, feeling her heart pound with the realization that she had gotten through it without losing her voice or forgetting the words. She looked around her, focusing now on the faces that had been a blur to her as she sang.

"Your brother is not the only one with talent in your family," said Caolin, studying her. "My Lady, your singing is as fair as your face."

In her relief at having finished the song, replying to the Seneschal seemed easy. "My Lord, I am not used to performing before such a company. Your playing made it easy for me to sing."

The others murmured appreciation. There was a scattering of applause. Stefan tried to lift his head to look, and Rosemary pushed him firmly down again.

"By the Mountain, Rosemary, I only have a sliced shoulder. You don't have to act as if I were dying," said Stefan fretfully.

Rosemary snorted disgustedly. "It's not dying, but living crippled that you're in danger of if you keep bouncing around like that. I've stitched the wound as well as I could, though I wish the Master of the Junipers were here to check it, but no binding will help you if you don't keep still!"

"I am sure that the touch of your fingers is the best medicine of all," remarked Caolin.

"I appreciate your gallantry, sir, but I have a more realistic opinion of my skill."

"Are you depending on the skill of the Master of the Junipers?" Caolin raised an eyebrow. "He did not specialise as a healer, you know. He has only the general training that all of us who studied at the College received."

"I have benefited from his advice in the past," Rosemary said stiffly.

"Oh, as an adviser, I am sure he does very well."

Faris saw that Rosemary was beginning to smolder. Her exhilaration still buoyed her, made it easy to intervene.

"Were you at the College of the Wise?" she asked Caolin swiftly. "Though we live so close, we know little of it – only that very few are accepted for training there." She smiled at him, suppressing her momentary discomfort at the thought of the powers those so trained were said to acquire.

"I was there five years," Caolin replied smoothly, "studying the things you were all told of when you prepared for Initiation – the doctrines of the Tree of Life, the ways of birds and beasts and the stars."

"I have heard you are a wolfmaster," said Holly of Woodhall.

"That came later," said the Seneschal, "when I was alone. You may meet my friend Gerol when he comes up from the south. It should be soon."

Lady Amata made a small, startled sound, and Caolin looked around him as if enjoying the sensation his announcement had made. Traders from Laurelynn had said that the Seneschal had made a great wolf his companion, but Faris had thought it only a tale.

Stefan grasped Rosemary's arm. "He's right – you've made me well. Let me get up and tomorrow I'll ride after the war band."

Rosemary detached his fingers and stood up. "Lie still and be grateful that your fighting is done for a while!" She turned away from him and went to the window, staring out at the falling rain while Stefan turned his head restlessly and sighed.

"Does the King mean to stay long here in the north, and will you remain with him?" Berisa asked the Seneschal.

"I will stay or go as the King's need requires."

Stefan muttered something and tried to push himself up with his good arm. Faris got up quickly and sat down in the chair Rosemary had left. "Lady Rosemary does not mean to be unkind," she said. "She is worried about her father and brother. But by the time you could reach them, they will have finished with the reivers and be on their way home," she said soothingly, readjusting the quilt around him.

His eyes fixed on her face. Faris smiled, and the lines of pain in his face eased. She continued to talk to him, surprised at how easy it was.

Stefan sighed. "I know that my lord and the others will do all that men can, but it is hard to lie here, wondering. You have been very kind to sit by me for so long."

Faris smiled and took his hand.

Caolin's voice rose above the general conversation once more. "The length of our stay will depend on what news the returning warriors bring."

"What do you think of the Seneschal?" asked Stefan as Faris turned her head to look at him. "He seems such a cold man to be the companion of the King."

"It's that look of his, as if he could see through to a man's bones!" said one of the other men, overhearing them. "And yet he has a name for efficiency, and no one has yet discovered any bribe that tempts him at all."

Faris considered Caolin – the stillness of his lean body within the claret-colored robe, his head poised as if his senses were instruments to be focused at will, the fair skin of his face fitted across high cheekbones and arched nose too neatly for any sign of strain to show. This was the man whom the King had chosen for his chief servant, or as some said, for his shadow, his soul.

As if he had felt her gaze, Caolin's eyes met hers, and Faris looked quickly away. "If they do not catch up with the raiders this time, the King will want to try again. He does not like unfinished business," said Caolin.

Faris listened to the rattle of rain against the leaded windowpanes. Higher in the mountains it would be snow. Where was the King now?

"Are you cold?" asked Stefan. "You are so slender, I would be afraid to let you face a winter wind."

Faris shook her head and smiled down at him, realising with some surprise that she was still warmed by the success of her song. "No . . . I am very well. You should rest now, and don't worry about Rosemary."

"No . . ." His answering smile grew vague. Faris smoothed back his hair, and his eyelids closed as Rosemary's medicine took effect at last.

"Night is almost upon us, and I have work to do before we dine," said Caolin, rising and bowing to Berisa and Lady Amata.

"Oh, you must forgive us, my Lord – we have kept you too long!" Lady Amata fluttered. "Rosemary, darling, bring me my shawl – before dinner I must go to my own chamber and rest."

"Yes, Mother." Rosemary said a last word to her patient, then went to get her mother's fleecy shawl.

"Lady Faris, your singing gave great pleasure. I hope that you will join me again?"

Startled, Faris saw Caolin standing before her. She put out her hand; he bent over it, then drew her to her feet. For a moment he stared at her, and she fought the impulse to pull her hand from his grasp.

"He spoke truly," said Caolin softly. "You are indeed the lily of the north."

Faris drew herself up proudly, feeling as if his eyes had clothed her in silks and jewels. *Who* had told him that? Was it Eric, or Jehan? Then he bowed to her again, and she thought, *It means nothing . . . he does not know about my scar*. He let her go and she curtsied as he moved away.

She was still looking after him when Berisa's hand closed on her shoulder.

"In the name of the Lady, what did that performance mean?"

"My singing? I thought it went quite well." Faris faced her sister, holding her head proudly though her stomach was automatically clenching with the guilt her sister always inspired in her.

"Faris, you know very well what I mean. You were not brought up to lead men on." Berisa's heavy brows bent in a frown.

"Was I? Would they follow me?" She stared at her sister, waiting for Berisa to remember why Faris must not dare to love.

"Naturally they would. A pretty young girl . . ."

"Am I a 'pretty young girl'? You never told me that before." Could her father have been wrong?

"Well . . . you take after Mother," Berisa admitted reluctantly. She sighed and folded her arms. "It's for your own sake I'm saying this! If you court men's attention, they will want to make love to you, and then what will you do?"

Let them? wondered Faris bitterly. Might it be worth it to have the illusion of being loved, if only for a little while? And before they found out the truth, she could send them away, and if they suffered, then at least she would not be the only one.

"Oh, Berisa." She shook her head. "They only look at me because the King showed me his favor for a little while. They'll soon tire of the game. What does it matter what I do?"

"Will they?" Berisa looked at her, frowning as if she had never seen her before. She shook her head. "And if they do, won't it hurt you?"

Faris considered her, trying to decide whether she saw real concern or condescension, or perhaps a mixture of the two, in her sister's face. Her right hand had moved to cover the scar hidden beneath her left sleeve, and she made herself grasp a fold of her skirt instead.

"Compared to the risks that Farin is taking right now, what have I to fear?"

Berisa nodded as if Faris had conceded some point. "I told Farin not to go, just as I tell you to take care, because I'm responsible to Father for you both! If you run into trouble, don't blame me!"

Faris suppressed a shiver, remembering her dream. *But Farin is doing the thing he wants most – defending the King. And even if my Lord never looks at me again, he has given me courage too!* And suddenly, though her Father's words were as true as they had ever been, they did not matter anymore.

"Father stays mewed in Hawkrest Hold like a bird afraid to fly." She laughed a little shakily. "Even if it freezes me, I'll trust to the wind."

A sharp wind drove the snow into the faces of the horsemen who were attempting to climb the curving road. Farin, riding with Rafael close behind Sir Eric and the King, squinted and wiped his face with the end of his scarf. Eric was standing in his stirrups, peering through the snow.

"We will have to stumble right over those bastards if we are to find them in this murk!" Eric exclaimed.

"Relax, Eric," said the King, hunched in the saddle beside him. "You will be worn out by the time we do." Stormwing snorted and shook snow from his eyes. Farin urged his horse closer, eager to hear how these legendary warriors were coping with the situation – eager, in fact, for anything that might distract him from the cold.

"I want something to do! My sword and my arm are both twitching, and there's nothing to use them on – nothing but this damned snow!"

"I'm not surprised," said the King dryly. "You must learn to save your strength, Eric," he went on. "One would think you were going into your first battle, and you a veteran of the Elayan wars!"

"If he doesn't watch out I'll try my sword on that viper Ronald." Eric pointed to two dim figures ahead of them. "There he goes again. 'Oh, my Lord, my Lord, please make haste, they may be burning my home even now! Come yourself, my Lord, and let us hurry to reach Greenfell in time!'" he mimicked.

Jehan laughed. "Don't be so hard on the poor man. You saw the raiders' work. Can you blame him for being upset? Besides, as he informed us himself, he is an archer, not a man of the sword. It wouldn't be fair."

"If he can keep his bowstring dry in this, I will begin to respect him," muttered Eric. His horse stumbled and he swore as he pulled the animal up. "Will this hill never stop? the horses are sliding all over the road. At this rate we will never reach Greenfell before dark!"

"My Lord –" Farin's voice was a croak, and he tried again. "My Lord, I've taken this road before . . . I think there's a pass by the little waterfall ahead a bit, and beyond it the valley widens and levels out."

They all peered upward, barely able to make out the steep, tree-clad slopes that loomed over the road and then fell away sharply to the torrent that they could hear rushing over rocks far below.

But by the time another two hours had passed, it became apparent that it would be night before they reached Greenfell after all. Not only was the narrow road slippery with snow and mud from the banks above, but fallen fir trees blocked their passage, their branches interlaced as they lay. They had to lead the horses, picking their way one by one, step by step, through the tangled mass. The snow had stopped, but the light was fading fast by the time they were all assembled on the road that led into the upper valley.

"I wonder where Ronald is," said Sandremun as he and his father prepared to mount again. "He should lead the way from here." He swung himself up and then, suddenly, collapsed backward with a cry as the air hummed and a flight of arrows materialised out of the dusk.

Farin flinched and yanked at his horse's reins.

"Now we know why our scouts didn't come back!" gasped the King as an arrow snicked by his head. A horse screamed, and the King reined Stormwing sharply around after Farin, then slipped from his saddle. "Down!" he cried. "Get off your horses – the light's going too fast for them to shoot for long!"

Apparently the enemy thought so too, for as he spoke dark figures sprouted from the earth before them and the raiders charged. Swords gleamed dimly, and war cries mingled with the moans of those struck by arrows as the enemy closed in.

Theodor, surrounded by those of his guards who had been able to reach him, battled above the body of his son. His great sword scythed through his foes like grain. Eric stood back to back with the King, both of them cutting as the attackers came on and blocking their blows with neat movements of their shields.

Farin kicked his feet from the stirrups and slid off his hysterical horse, struggled to free his sword, and swung it up to block the blade that was slicing down at him. Another came at him; he slid his own blade over it and then onward, its momentum carrying it through flesh and bone. The raider screamed and toppled headlong at his feet.

Shaking, Farin looked down at the body, but before he had time to realise what he had done, the next man was upon him and he was thrusting up his shield, slamming his sword in the direction where he hoped an opening in his opponent's guard might be. He was gasping, but as he struck and parried he began to find the fighting rhythm that countless hours of practice had drilled into him. He glimpsed Rafael a few feet away. The squire had lost his shield and was defending himself with sword alone. Farin began to inch his way to the other boy's side.

Up and down the road, at the edges of the woods, and on the sheer brink of the riverbank, the fighting went on, and always the most furiously around Lord Theodor and the King. For every one they killed, two more came on, and against the shouts of "Death!" clashed the cries "Lord Theodor!" "Westria and the King!" and once, from Eric, "For the lily of the north!"

The leader of the raiders, a huge man with a fur cloak tied around him that made him seem bigger still, reached the space that Eric had cleared and paused.

"Ho! Plainsmaggot! Do you think you can stand against me in a single fight? We know that all this talk of honor is just a blind – there you are, clinging together like cubs whose mother is gone, afraid to come out and face a real man!"

Eric snarled but held his place, shield up and sword poised.

"I knew it!" the raider went on. "Cowards all of you, both you and that sniveling rat you call a King!"

Eric roared and sprang forward. There was a momentary lull as men drew back to watch the two champions, seemingly equal in size and strength. For a few minutes they dueled, trading blow for blow as if they had been alone on the field. Then the raider gave a cry and sprang backward. His men, disengaging themselves from their own battles swarmed in to separate Eric from the King.

Rafael cried out in horror and began hacking his way toward his Lord, who was whirling like a snow devil, seeming to face in all directions at once. Attempting to follow his friend, Farin glimpsed Eric, roaring, light flaring around him as his sword swung. The enemy drew back before him as Eric charged like a grizzly enraged, and a swathe of bodies lay wherever his sword fell.

Like a hero in an old tale, thought Farin even as he parried, *I will know how to describe it now, when I write a battle song!* His thigh stung as someone sliced past his guard. *If I get out of this alive!*

Around the King the fighting boiled like an ant heap overturned. Rafael had reached his Lord at last, and the raiders were attempting to eliminate this slender reinforcement. The squire, helmet gone now as well, and black hair tossing, was fighting with an ecstatic fury that was in its own way as formidable as Eric's rage.

But Rafael had neither Eric's strength nor his skill. Many of the blows aimed at him got through, though his assailants often paid dearly for their success. But there were many of them, and he was only one. Farin, struggling to reach him, saw his parries slowing, his sword faltering as it fell.

Farin set his teeth and brought his blade down with all his strength on a raider's leather helm. It hit with a shock he felt all the way up his arm, but with only a fractional pause the downward force of his blow drew his sword on through the man's head like a knife slicing cheese. Farin stepped back and wrenched his sword from the body as the man began to fall, and leaping over him, he gained Rafael's side at last.

"Farin! Thank the Battlelord! See, they are retreating now that there are two of us to guard the King."

"If I can fight as well as you have, they will!" Farin gasped, but now that he was close, he could see that Rafael was bleeding freely.

"Have I killed many? It is hard to tell . . . I am so tired. But it is dark now," he added, "and the battle must end soon."

Farin glanced westward, where the clouds had broken and the sun, setting behind the mountains, glowed angrily.

There was a pressure against his shoulder, and he turned as Rafael collapsed against him and slid gently to the ground. Farin bent over him, calling his name, and the raiders charged in once more.

Caught off balance, Farin began to fall as the foremost struck his lifted shield and hurtled past it into the King. Jehan toppled, but Farin, recovering with a convulsive leap, was on his feet again and took the man in the neck as he raised his sword to strike at the King.

He swayed beneath a storm of blows, struggling frantically to guard.

"To the King!" he shouted desperately. "Westria, Westria, to the King!" He saw the blunt menace of a mace swinging at him, felt the shock as it struck his helm. As the world dissolved around him he thought he heard faintly the note of a horn, and he saw Eric striding toward them, breaking through the ring of his enemies like a swimmer breasting a wave.

Farin rushed upward through a well of darkness to become aware that somebody was hitting him on the head with dull, regular blows, and someone else was flashing lights in his eyes and calling his name. Why wouldn't they leave him alone and let him return to the peaceful dark? Farin moaned and stirred protestingly.

"I think he's coming back to us, sir," said a deep voice.

"Yes. He at least will live to fight another day."

Surely he should recognise that second voice. Painfully Farin opened his eyes and looked up into the face of the King.

"It is over then," he whispered, remembering. "And . . . you are safe . . ."

The King nodded. "The fighting is done, and I have taken less harm than you, so be easy. Your courage was not wasted. I have much to thank you for." He had said he was unwounded, but he looked weary, his eyes sunken and his face white above his short dark beard.

Farin smiled weakly. The King smiled a little. "You are very like your sister, did you know?" he said absently.

Farin stared at him. Why speak of Faris now? Had the fighting turned his wits? Then he remembered how the King had crowned Faris at the Festival. *Does the King want Faris? What will we do?* Jehan's love affairs were famous all over the Kingdom, but Faris would not know how to play such a game. It was too much to think about now. He closed his eyes.

"You must rest now, and I must see how the others fare," the King said quickly. "Sir Randal will watch over you."

After a few moments Farin opened his eyes and saw that the King had gone. Sitting by the little fire he recognised the owner of the deep voice he had heard – Randal of Registhorpe, who had come with the King from the south.

"We must have won," Farin concluded. "What happened after I went down?"

Randal put another piece of wood on the little fire, the light glinting like copper on his auburn hair and beard as he bent. Behind him other fires winked as men moved back and forth before them. Farin shivered, even though he lay on a bed of saddlecloths stretched over fir boughs, and several cloaks had been laid over him. He wondered whose they were.

"I'm not sure who would have won," said Randal, "if Andreas Blackbeard had not brought his men straight over the mountain between here and Woodhall. The woodsrats made off as soon as they heard his horn. Some of our people caught their horses in time to pursue, but I doubt they will find much in the dark."

"How are the Lord Commander and Sandremun?"

"Sandremun was struck in the chest, but the arrow missed his heart. They think he will live, with good care. The Commander has wounds, of course, but he can ride. He is a mighty warrior for a man of his years."

Farin lay silent for a little, then asked the question that had weighted his heart.

"And what about Rafael? He was beside me, and he fell . . ."

Silently Randal indicated a long shape covered by a cloak just outside the circle of firelight.

"There was nothing to be done. He had lost too much blood and he was dead when we took him up after the fight."

"If there were only something I could do!" Jehan told Eric as they made their way through the camp. "Rafael died for me like a knight before he had lived long enough to become one. And there's that boy –" He motioned back towards the fire where Farin lay. "He's alive now, but can he live through a night in this cold?"

"He's not the only one," said Eric grimly. "I think that for many, shock and exposure will finish what the woodsrats began. Five of the men I brought from Seagate are dead, and there's no shelter for the others in this wilderness. We came prepared for a celebration, not a campaign!"

"We should not have been caught this way!" the King swore again. "I should have taken command, but I did not wish to hurt Theodor's pride." He shook his head. "I should not blame him – his son's life may well pay for any mistakes he made. And I wonder if even I could have avoided this disaster. I would have relied on the Coronans' estimates of the enemy's strength and plans."

"Their tactics and their viciousness were certainly beyond anything I've ever heard of among such folk!" Eric agreed, pulling his cloak closer around him.

When they reached the Lord Commander, Theodor was saying much the same thing. "I tell you, the whole situation has the stink of a billygoat three days dead!" He turned to the King. "My Lord, I have fought these scum since I was old enough to carry a sword, and always they have hot-footed it down the trail at the first hint of resistance. Why stay and fight? They are after loot, not glory!"

"And why are all those who did not escape dead now? *All* of them are dead, Lord Theodor – I found no wounded at all!" said Serge of Greenforest. "Surely our warriors are not so deadly that none can abide their blows and live."

"I should like to examine those bodies by daylight," said Eric slowly, "and see just how they died."

"Have all our men been accounted for?" asked Jehan.

"Almost everyone, sir. Even those who tried to pursue the escaping raiders have returned. Of course, we could not look in the river."

"Was my cousin among those you found?" inquired Theodor, pulling at his short beard. "I have not seen him since before the fight."

"Oh, I am here, Theodor!" They all turned to look as Ronald staggered into the firelight and knelt before his cousin. His cloak was stained with blood.

"Ronald!" exclaimed Theodor. "Are you hurt? We were afraid you were slain. Where have you been?"

"Oh, it's nothing really. Indeed, I have a confession to make. I slipped away while the rest of you were still climbing the hill. I wanted to see if Greenfell was burning yet. Instead I saw the reivers attacking you. I scrambled down as quickly as I could, but by the time I got here the fight was almost done. I've been searching for fugitives on some of the paths I know. I'm sorry you worried about me."

Theodor snorted, but the others looked at Ronald with no expression at all. So he had missed the fighting, had he? And it was Ronald's holding that the rest of them were bleeding to save.

Something clinked faintly. They looked around and saw Andreas Blackbeard picking his way toward them. He was holding out, at arm's length, a leather bag.

"My Lord –" Andreas paused, but he already had their attention. "I was searching for the wounded, and I found the big man who challenged Sir Eric. He is quite dead, but this was on his body." He handed the bag to his lord.

Theodor hefted it, opened it, and with impassive features let a stream of gold flow onto the muddy ground.

"Well, now we know why, don't we?" said Jehan bleakly. "All that remains is to discover who."

71

In the silence that followed, they could all hear clearly the crackling of the fire, the muffled moans of the wounded, and the mournful whistling of the wind.

The north wind blew down from the mountains, gathered strength as it reached the head of the Great Valley, swirled impotently around the outthrust bulk of the Hold. Behind the thick curtains in the Seneschal's chamber, the shutters rattled as the wind tried to pluck them free.

Caolin shivered and looked up from the papers on the table before him – the reports on every aspect of the Kingdom's functioning that followed him wherever he and the King might be. He smiled as his gaze fell on the great wolf dozing fitfully before the fire.

"You and Ordrey arrived just in time, Gerol," he said softly. "This is no night to be on the road."

The wolf's grizzled ears twitched as Caolin spoke, but he did not open his eyes.

"Jehan was less wise than you. Unless they have found some roof unburned to shelter under, tonight the King of Westria lies on the cold ground." Caolin sighed impatiently. *There was no need for him to go himself, but he would not be ruled by me. Ah, Jehan, I cannot keep you from hazarding yourself, but if I ward the Kingdom well, perhaps one day no one will threaten you.*

He returned to the papers in his hand and began to read.

. . . at present the temper of the College is divided, the majority holding with the Mistress. This faction bases their philosophy on the teaching of the Master of the Deer Park, who held that the wise man concentrates on the truth beneath the appearances of things and lets the illusions of the world came and go as they will. Thus it is pointless for one who seeks wisdom to meddle in the affairs of men.

The opposing view is held mostly by priests and priestesses attached to the communities in the Free

Cities or serving holders in the Marches. They wish
to use the teachings of the College to influence the
lives of those with whom they work, but they get little
comfort from the College, since they have never made
the journey to Awahna to become adepts themselves,
and their vows are made only from year to year. Nor
are they themselves united, since many lay priests are
content simply to do their employers' will . . .

Caolin peered at the cipher with which the report was
signed and began to laugh. "The man thinks I do not know
him, but never mind, I will see that he is rewarded well.
This is the kind of information I need. If I am to govern
this land, I *must* know what is going on!" He laughed
again. "The Master of the Junipers may be surprised at
his reception in the College if he tries to find support for
his ideas there!"

The Seneschal slipped the pages back into their oilskin
envelope and reached for the next packet in the box that
Ordrey had brought that evening. It bore the seal of
Manuel of Orvale, Controller of Highways in Laurelynn.

"Why was this sent to the King?" wondered Caolin,
opening it. The Controller's message sprawled across the
page – obviously not a clerk's writing, but his own.

My gracious King – it is with pain that I write ill news
of one whom you recommended to me.

Caolin frowned, then read on.

Three years ago I took one Waldan of Terra Linda,
called Mole, into the service of the roads. He was
assigned to maintain the way between this city and
Rivered in the Ramparts. I have now in my hands,
and I have seen with my eyes, evidence that instead
of levying labor from the landholders along the way
to repair and improve the road, he has accepted gold
from them and spent it to maintain himself in splendor

rather than the road in safety. I have taken Waldan into my custody, not wanting to give him to the judges since I employed him at your request. I will await your instructions on how to deal with him.

Caolin laid the letter carefully on the table, whistling soundlessly. Thinking back, he remembered the man – a little nervous fellow with sleek dark hair and a livid scar down one side of his face. He had gotten the scar in the southern wars when he threw himself between an Elayan lance and the King.

"The man faced death without flinching, but he could not face temptation," Caolin muttered. "Jehan will take this badly, I fear."

It had happened before, when the King's trust was betrayed. For several days he would have to be coaxed to eat or sleep. He would spend long hours shut up alone. And each time a little more of the youth went out of his eyes.

Oh, Jehan, thought Caolin, *fifteen years ago I swore to serve you, and realised that to do so I had to serve Westria. Sometimes I think that in taking on that burden, I have lost you. But if I can spare you this pain, then I will do what is necessary, even if it means deceiving you.* He tore a page from his tablet and quickly began to write.

Deliver the person of Waldan of Terra Linda to the bearer of this order.

Caolin scrawled Jehan's initials across the bottom, folded the page, and held the candle to the lump of wax until enough had dribbled onto the paper to hold the King's seal. When it cooled, he fitted the order into an oiled envelope and wrote the Controller's name neatly across the front.

"Gerol," Caolin whined softly, and the wolf sprang to his feet. "Come." Gerol's nails clicked on the polished floor as he came to the man, and laid his grizzled muzzle on the Seneschal's knee. For a moment Caolin stroked his head, his long fingers rubbing unerringly the sensitive spots behind the wolf's ears.

"Yes . . . I know where it itches . . . indeed I do." Caolin made a sound low in his throat and Gerol's yellow eyes half closed. "You know all my secrets and care about none of them, do you?" said the Seneschal. "Well, I have an errand for you now."

He took his hand away and spoke in the wolf's own tongue again. "Ordrey – get Ordrey and bring him to me here. Go!"

Gerol sighed, lifted his head, and began to pad towards the door. Caolin growled, and with an impatient snort the wolf increased his pace, nosed open the door, and slipped through.

Caolin got up and began to feed the fire.

It was perhaps fifteen minutes before he heard sounds outside in the passageway and Gerol returned, followed by a short, spare man whose ginger hair was already beginning to recede, though his eyes were still as merry as a child's. The Seneschal stood up to greet him.

"Ordrey, I am sorry to call you at this hour. Were you asleep?"

"Well . . . I was in bed." He grinned reminiscently. "People here are not used to seeing our friend Gerol wandering about. I will have some explaining to do when I return."

"It may be just as well. You are going to need your rest. I fear I must send you off again tomorrow as soon as you can ride."

"Well, I'm sorry for it – they were giving me a warm welcome here. The kitchens are buzzing with gossip about Jehan's newest morsel. Is she just another diversion, or is he serious at last?"

There was a chilly silence. Ordrey looked at Caolin and lost a little of the fresh color from his face.

"Neither the King's name nor the lady's reputation belongs on your lips! I cannot stop the mouth of every kitchen trull in the Marches, but my servants should learn discretion if they wish to prosper. The King has made no decision, and I do not think he will seek your advice when he does." Caolin spoke shortly, his hands busy placing the packets he had dealt with already in the dispatch pouch. Ordrey stood uneasily, watching him.

"These messages must go south as soon as possible." Caolin's tone softened. "That candle is guttering so that it is hard to see. Could you trim it for me?"

Ordrey bent over the candle. Caolin brought his hand up beside it so that his ring of office captured the flame with a flare of ruby light. It caught Ordrey's gaze and held it. As he had done so many times before, he stilled. This was something else the College had taught him, thought Caolin, though they might have questioned the way he used it now. "You see only the light, Ordrey; you hear only my voice." Caolin's tone was very even. "What do you hear?"

"I hear your voice."

"You will listen and do what I tell you to do, won't you?"

"I will do what you tell me," said Ordrey tonelessly.

Caolin held up the letter to the Controller of Highways. "Do you see this packet? You are to disguise yourself and deliver it to Manuel of Orvale in Laurelynn. Wait there until he has read it. When he has done so, he will give into your custody a man called Waldan of Terra Linda. Evade his questions if Manuel should ask who you are and who has sent you – on no account tell him that you come from me. The order you bear is your authority. Do you understand?"

Ordrey nodded, looking at him with unfocused eyes.

"When you have this Waldan, take him to the Merchants' Caravansary in Rivered. You will find Gorgo Snaggletooth there – you remember him, we have dealt with him before. Tell him to hold Waldan with his other merchandise, guarding him carefully, and take him over the mountains on his next journey to the Brown Lands. When he has disposed of Waldan in the slave mart at Arena and has proof of the sale, tell him he shall have another forty laurels from you. Wait in Rivered until he returns. Remember, Gorgo must have the proof – on no account must Waldan ever return to Westria! Do you understand? Repeat what I have said."

Ordrey nodded and in an even voice recounted the orders Caolin had given him.

"Very good. In a moment I will show you the red light once more. When you see it, you will forget that it is I who have given you these orders. When you look at this packet, you will know what to do, but you will tell no one what you have done until I show you the light again."

Caolin stretched out his ring to the candle once more. Ordrey's dull gaze slowly focused on its red glow.

"You see the light, don't you?"

"Yes . . ."

"When I take it away again, you will forget that you have seen it, or that we have just spoken, and you will regain you full senses once more."

Caolin covered the ring with his other hand. "Thank you for fixing the candle," he said. "You see it burns very well now."

Ordrey shook his head a little and looked at the Seneschal. "I'm sorry, what did you say? I have a slight headache, I'm afraid."

Caolin smiled. "I was only thanking you for trimming my candle. I should have warned you about Lady Berisa's mead." He slipped the letter for the Controller into the pouch and began to strap it up. He handed it to Ordrey and sat down again."

"Do you mind if I keep Gerol with me here? You will not need him on this trip, and I missed his companionship."

"Oh, of course. The reivers may haunt the mountains, but I doubt I will need protection on the road between here and Laurelynn." Ordrey laughed.

"Very well, then. Go now, and get what sleep you can." Caolin held out his hand and Ordrey bent over it respectfully, then straightened and went out. Gerol began to get to his feet, but at a sound from Caolin stretched out on the floor again.

Caolin eased back into his chair and rested his head in his hands. In the partnership that had evolved between King and Seneschal, Jehan was the war leader and focus of ceremony, the embodiment of the people's vision of Westria. But the King was free to pursue his pleasure when there was no festival or danger. To the Seneschal fell the daily drudgery of monitoring the life of the Kingdom, from the flow of commerce to the rotation of border garrisons. Instructing, evaluating, admonishing, he was responsible for the work of the entire government. He had set himself the task of forestalling or dealing with every problem, lest it trouble the King. And for the nine years he had been in office, he had exulted in his ability to do so.

But suddenly he was tired. *It is late . . . I should go to bed too. Yesterday Jehan joked about my vigilance, but he should have remembered that even I must sleep sometimes.*

He had done all that was necessary for now. In the morning Ordrey would be on his way. Strange that the man's reference to Faris had made him so angry. Caolin's thoughts went back to the girl's singing that afternoon. She had a subtle kind of beauty, like an exotic flower. Suitably dressed, she could be exquisite.

Caolin laughed softly. *If Jehan doesn't want her, perhaps I will take her myself. She would be a worthy ornament.* He looked at the windows and realised from the faint light that edged the shutters that it was almost dawn.

By the time the sun began to warm the northern sky at last, the men of the Corona were beginning the slow journey home. Jehan and Eric and the unwounded men rode in the lead while Lord Theodor held the rear, close to the litter where his son Sandremun lay.

"Andreas says that the arrow that hit Sandremun, and several others found, were black ones, military issue from Normontaine," said Jehan.

"By the Guardians! They wouldn't attack us – it would mean war!" Eric exclaimed.

Jehan nodded. "Yes, and I believe that Queen Mara has more sense than to do that – nor has she any need. Besides, if it means anything, we found no Montaner badges on the dead."

"Do you think someone else used those arrows to mislead us? Why?"

"I only have suspicions" – Jehan smiled – "and even a King should have some real evidence before he spreads accusations around. Whoever is guilty will probably try again though, and this time we will be on our guard."

They rode on in silence. Stormwing tossed his head and protested the slow pace, less wearied than his rider by the events of the previous two days.

"There is another thing about that skirmish that bothers me," said Eric painfully. Jehan waited for him to go on. "You remember when I fought with their leader . . ." He paused, and for a moment the King thought he would not go on.

"It was the kind of struggle the Bards live by writing about, from all accounts. I'm afraid I was too busy to give it the attention it deserved," Jehan said encouragingly.

"Don't make it harder for me!" Eric cried. "It should never have happened! I left you unguarded, and you could have been killed!"

"Has that been troubling you? Really, Eric, I do have some skill with a sword." Now was not the time to mention Rafael, left behind in a lonely grave in the hills, or Farin in his litter at the end of the column.

"I swear to you I didn't realise what I was doing. I mean it wasn't because –" Eric stopped short, fighting for words.

The King shifted in the saddle to face him. "It wasn't because of jealousy over the lady Faris? We may as well face it, Eric. After all, she is bound to love someone eventually – it may not be you, and it may not be me either, you know."

Jehan frowned, remembering how many others had loved him, and how heedlessly he had received their gifts. Perhaps he should marry someone whose experience equaled his, who would not care.

"My Lord, I am unworthy of her! I have not spoken to her, and I never will!"

"But don't you think that would be unfair to *her?*" Jehan asked gently. "You can offer many things I cannot – youth, honor untinged by any compromise, a peaceful life. As knights, we are bound to fight our best no matter what the battlefield. You would insult me if you were to withdraw from the contest now."

Topping the shoulder of the Father of Mountains, they glimpsed in the distance the tower of the Hold, pink-tinged in the morning light. For the column, it was a full day's ride away, but a single rider on a fast horse might reach it by noon.

Eric reined in Thunderfoot and looked at the King with no wavering in his eyes. "Sir, I accept your challenge!" he exclaimed, bowing low over his horse's neck. Then he straightened, lifting the reins and driving home his heels, and sent the black horse galloping madly down the road.

"Eric, you are a true and honorable knight," Jehan said softly as he watched him go. "And by the Guardian of Men, Eric, if you are not I hope that you never let me know!"

4

A Pledge of Faith

Faris shut the oaken door carefully and leaned against the rough stone of the wall, trying to catch her breath. From somewhere above she could hear the ripple of harp music, distant as a dream. She frowned and peered through the narrow window into the courtyard. Sir Lewis was still there, shifting from foot to foot and gazing hopefully at the door. Faris sighed as he shook his head at last and wandered off.

She supposed she was lucky. Some of the others, like Stefan or Sir Eric of Seagate, would not have given up so easily. She shifted the heavy folds of burgundy velvet to her other arm, shrugging the thought away. She had finished Farin's new cloak just in time for his knighting – surely that was enough to worry about today.

Faris started up the winding stair, passing alternately through the shadows and bars of sunlight from the slits in the stone. The warm breeze was scented with April flowers. The music came more clearly now, and her step grew lighter.

Farin had not practiced much during his long recovery from the head wound he had received in February. It was only in the last few weeks that his full strength had returned. He should have been sleeping now.

When she reached the landing, Faris was able to distinguish the melody, but the sound of the harp was purer and deeper than she had ever heard it before. She opened the door.

Farin was sitting by the window. The morning light glowed on his head and shoulders, glistening on the new streak of white in his hair that marked where the raider's blow had struck him . . . and on the harp, which in that moment seemed carved from living gold.

The door clicked shut behind her. A last trill escaped like a flight of butterflies and Farin looked up. On his cheeks she could see the glitter of tears. Silently he held out the harp. It was not the worn instrument he had brought from home.

This harp was a little larger, the soundbox deeper than broad, but it was the interlaced and inlaid golden wire that ornamented it, and the exquisitely gilded swan that crowned it, that sent back the blaze of the sun.

"*Swangold,*" Farin said simply, cradling it against his shoulder again.

"Where did it come from?"

"From the King . . . he sent it to me as a knighting gift!"

"It's magnificent –" Faris began.

"You don't understand!" her brother cried. "Since I went to war I have hardly thought about music. The King said he would make me knight, and I thought my way was chosen at last. I don't know if I have the genius to be a great harper, and what kind of life is that anyway – always eating at someone else's table and sleeping by a stranger's hearth? I want to be a warrior! To be knighted by the King himself is almost more honor than I can bear, and yet . . ." He rested his forehead against the smooth curve of the harp.

"And yet . . ." she echoed, sitting down on the window seat beside him.

"Yet if anyone tried to take Swangold from me now, I would die! What did the King mean by this gift? Is he trying to tell me I should not be a warrior after all?"

Faris looked at him helplessly. "Surely he wouldn't do that now?"

"He has been coming and going so constantly – chasing outlaws in the north, meeting with the Council in Laurelynn – perhaps he has had no time to think about it until now!"

"Farin . . ." She put her arms around his shoulders, pressing her cheek against his hair. It was the only way she could think of to comfort him. After as few moments he sighed and wiped his eyes with the back of his hand.

"At least you don't tell me I am being foolish, or upset from lack of sleep, as Berisa would do."

Faris smiled and kissed his cheek. For a moment the mirror across the room reflected their two faces, his paled by illness until it was almost as white as her own. Two pairs of dark eyes set above high cheekbones looked back at them, shaded by masses of dark hair, their inheritance from their Karok grandfather. But Farin's mouth was tight, his eyes haunted, while her own mouth was full and soft. Faris could not read the expression in her own eyes.

"In any case, it is the King I want to understand!" said Farin at last.

Faris laughed without amusement. "I don't pretend to interpret *him* – ask the Master of the Junipers what Jehan of Westria means."

"Yes," he said slowly. "Perhaps that is what I should do."

"Not now."

"I cannot sleep," Farin continued, "and there are two hours yet before I must dress for the ceremony. I will fret myself like a mewed hawk if I have to stay here." Abruptly he rose from her embrace and slung the harp across his back by a strap of soft leather stamped in gold. Before she could speak again, he had reached the door and was gone.

Faris sat for a moment, laughing helplessly. Then she got up and closed the door. She began to wander about the room, automatically straightening books and papers, picking up strewn garments and hanging them in the alcove. "Farin thinks that I understand him," she murmured. "I am

83

glad, though I'm not sure that I do. He doesn't understand Jehan. Oh, Sweet Lady! I wish *I* understood the King. I wish I understood myself!" Her hand moved automatically to rub at the hidden scar on her arm.

As she bent to pull smooth the rumpled quilts on Farin's bed she saw a piece of paper on the floor. She picked it up, saw her own name, and began to read. She and Farin had shared everything for so long, it did not occur to her that he would mind her reading this now.

My lord and father [he began], I write this letter during my night of vigil, not knowing whether you will arrive in time for my knighting ceremony . . .

Faris shook her head. Poor Farin. Did he delude himself that the old man would leave his eyrie even to see his only son knighted by the King? The lines were crossed and corrected – this must be a draft of a letter Farin had sent out some days before. She wondered why he had not told her he was writing so that she could add some dutiful postscript.

I would be proud if you could be here. The King says that I saved his life, and he would like to honor you . . .

For a moment the letters blurred before her. "I love you, Farin, even if he does not!" she whispered. She looked at the paper again.

. . . and also because someone must speak to Faris before she comes to harm. Berisa has tried, but Faris seems not to hear.

Faris stiffened, but she could not stop reading now.

Faris is flirting with fire. Men praise her, and now she flutters from one to another like a butterfly. People

are gossiping about her behavior all over the Province
. . .

Faris flung the paper to the floor. "Love him! I *hate* him!"
she hissed. "How dare he judge me. He seeks no woman's
favor, though some seek his – what does he know of the
game of love?" Her skirts swished angrily as she stalked
across the floor.

"The King honored me – once – and so I am the fashion
now. But it is all a sport for the men. Not one has seen
beneath this surface mask I wear . . . not one has even
tried to see! What harm can it do for me to enjoy their
company? Of course Farin does not like it – he never had
to share my attention before. But it will not last. I am not
that beautiful!"

She swept to the mirror and stared at her face in the
glass. She was already dressed for the ceremonies. Her
sleeveless over-robe, high collared and loose in the northern style, was made of soft green Elayan brocade edged
with goldwork. But it was open down the front and cut
wide at the armholes to reveal the tight-fitting long-sleeved
under-gown, made of a silk that was so pale a gold it was
almost cream, ornamented at the neck with a design in tiny
golden beads.

It was the finest outfit she had ever owned. But her coils
of dark hair were already escaping from their pearl-headed
pins. Angrily she tucked the strands back in place. And her
face – her nose was too long, and she was even thinner now
than she had been when the year began. In truth, she did
not understand how her popularity had endured even this
long.

"No . . . I am not beautiful enough." She closed her eyes
so that she would not have to look upon the image in the
mirror anymore.

Berisa's oldest daughter had brought the King a vase of
lilies, creamy and golden-veined in their upright sheaths
of green. Jehan looked at them, then forced his gaze back

85

to the leather boxes on his desk. The last of them had just been locked and sealed for its journey back to Laurelynn.

"You said you had something else to show me," he said wearily.

"Yes," answered Caolin. The Seneschal reached into the case where he kept documents he was working on and drew out a little leather bag, curiously stitched around the top.

"Isn't that the bag that was found on the body of the outlaw leader who ambushed us? Why are you showing it to me again?"

"As it happens, it is not the same bag, which is why I thought you would like to see it."

"Then where did it come from?"

"It came," Caolin paused for effect, "with the taxes from Las Costas. I kept thinking that the other bag looked familiar, but I couldn't remember why. It's from the counting house at Sanjos. They have them specially made."

"That proves nothing, you know. Anyone in the Kingdom could have gotten one," said the King after a moment.

Caolin sighed. "I really find it hard to understand your refusal to suspect Lord Brian of treachery."

Jehan stood up and began to pace restlessly about the room. Suddenly he found the Seneschal's perpetual suspicion of Brian irritating. He had sometimes suspected that it was a reaction to Brian's loudly expressed scorn when he had made Caolin Seneschal. At the time Jehan had shared Caolin's feelings, aware of his need for Caolin's cool brilliance and loyalty, and himself fearing Brian's popularity. But surely they were all older and wiser now.

"Brian does not agree with me on how to run the Kingdom, but that is not treason. Our disagreements have always been open. Of course he tries to persuade people to support him, but he has never been secretive."

"*Somebody* paid the outlaws to ambush your war party. You could have been killed, Jehan! Either you were their target, or it was Theodor, and I don't know of anyone who wants *him* out of his way."

"No. Brian may not love me, but he would no more do murder than you would! And certainly not at secondhand." The King went to the window and stood looking out at the Father of Mountains. As always, it was snow-capped, but the hills at its feet were carpeted gold and purple with flowers.

"Very well. I will drop the question of who sent the gold, and why. Let us pursue another line of thought," said Caolin patiently. "How did the gold get from Las Costas to the mountains? There's one likely suspect – one person who travels all over Westria, and who specifically told Eric that he had been in the south."

"Ronald Sandreson –" supplied the King. "He disappeared at a suspicious moment. We thought it was cowardice."

"Exactly. I hope that you will permit me to suspect *him?*"

"But you won't learn anything if he remains quietly at his holding. We should ask Lord Theodor to invite him for a visit here," Jehan said thoughtfully.

Caolin smiled. "I would like to question him."

"No, not yet. I'm sure Theodor will be willing to invite him on suspicion, but we cannot arrest him without some proof."

"Because he is the Lord Commander's cousin?" asked Caolin.

Jehan turned to face him. "No! Because he is Theodor's sworn man. I was thinking that if Ronald is guilty, he is more likely to betray himself here."

"By trying again to assassinate you? That's why I wanted to arrest him!" Caolin's fist struck the table. "Very well then . . . take the chance. But will you let me at least *investigate* Brian?"

"That would be unworthy. I will find the right moment and question Brian myself."

"And believe him if he denies it all, I suppose? In that case, why let him even know he has been suspected?" Caolin's chair rocked as he rose and crossed the room to the King. He grasped his arm. "Jehan! Why do you do this to me?"

Jehan laid his hand over Caolin's. For a long moment he looked into the other man's gray eyes. "Mine is the responsibility . . . the risk must be mine," he said softly at last. "We'll worry about Brian when we return to the south. In the meantime, you have my leave to suspect Ronald all you please!" He grinned suddenly.

Caolin pulled away his hand, controlling his breathing. "You have a ceremony to conduct today and you are still in your chamber robe," he said after a moment. "You cannot mourn Rafael for ever – why haven't you taken a new squire? Never mind. What are you going to wear? I'll help you dress. Why not – I am your servant, my Lord!"

"I want to serve the King, and I don't know what I should do!" Farin looked at the Master of the Junipers in appeal.

The Master ran his fingers through already rumpled hair and looked at the young man quizzically. "Are you asking me to tell you what to do with your life?"

Farin reddened. "I know – no one can choose for another. But if the King doesn't think that I should be a knight . . . I suppose what I really want to know is the King's mind."

"Why not ask him?" said a new voice from the door.

They looked up and saw the King. He was dressed in an arming tunic of finely woven forest-green wool with no ornament, not even the circlet he usually wore. His voice had been soft, but to the Master it seemed as if there was some hidden tension in his stance.

Farin tried to speak, choked, and for the next few moments both King and Master were busy calming him.

"How . . . how much did you hear?" stammered Farin.

"Only that you want to know what I think . . . about something," Jehan said soothingly, drawing up a bench. "Are you still worried about whether you deserve knighthood? Believe me, you do."

"Not exactly. It was the harp . . ." Farin gestured at the golden harp leaning against his knee. The King's eyes brightened with amusement, though his mouth remained grave.

"Do you like it?" he asked.

Farin's face grew radiant. "I don't know the right words. My old harp and the Hall harp at home both gave me great joy. But Swangold – you know, sir, how it is when you find the one sword that feels like an extension of your hand? This harp is like that for me. She *fits* me."

"Or like the woman who is your mate in body and soul," Jehan murmured. "Yes, I know."

"I meant to give up harping when I took up the sword. But if this instrument can stir me so . . . I do not know what to do!"

"Cannot you do both?" Jehan rested his elbows on his knees, his chin in his hands, watching the boy. His hair was backlighted by the tower window, through which the Master could see the Father of Mountains rising serenely above anxieties of men.

"I don't know," said Farin. "Being a Bard is not so high a vocation as that of a Master –" He glanced apologetically at the Master of the Junipers. "But the call can be as strong. I don't know what will happen if I let it take hold of me, and if it does, how can I fulfill my duty to you?"

Jehan took Farin's hands in his own and placed them on the curve of the harp. "Play for me!" he said.

Startled, Farin met his eyes, and his own widened.

"Much as I value your skill at guarding my back," Jehan said earnestly, "there are others who can do that. Swangold was a gift to me when I was a boy, but I could never make her sing. And yet I need music – being King is not all a Festival! Play for me, Farin, at feasts if you desire, but most of all when I am weary and alone."

Farin studied the floor. His hands were trembling beneath of King's. "I am not good enough."

Jehan shook his head. "I have heard you play! Will you do this for me?"

Farin lifted his head to face the King with shining eyes. "My Lord, to wield the harp or the sword, my hands are at your service to my life's end!"

"Or mine!" laughed Jehan. "So be it!"

For a moment they faced each other. Then Farin glanced at the window and straightened in alarm. "It's almost noon! They will be looking for me for the ritual bathing, and I must check my arms."

"Go then, and we will see you soon!" said the Master of the Junipers. They listened to his steps retreating down the passageway. "You handled him well," said the Master at last.

Jehan shook his head. "Maker of Winds! I wish there were anything I cared about as much as that boy does his art!"

"There is nothing? Not even Westria?"

The King buried his face in his hands. "Farin at least is free to choose his way."

"You could have refused election. Your older sister could have borne the crown."

"Jessica was newly married to the Commander of the Ramparts, and pregnant at the time. They told me that if she became Queen, the Ramparts would be too powerful. They said they wanted a war leader against Elaya. You were there! You know the arguments as well as I. Besides, I was a boy with dreams of glory. What did I know about responsibility and power?"

"You were only two years younger than the boy you just advised so wisely, and you had been bred up to rule." The Master smoothed the worn grey wool of his robe. "But whether the choice is forced or free, what does anyone know about the end of the road? Even the road to Awahna may branch many times. We can only do our best, whatever the path . . . and you did not answer my question. Gently he touched the King's bent head.

"Can there be two answers? I have sworn the oath . . . and I have worn the Jewels," the King said simply. "I care for Westria as I care for my own life, but that does not mean I find either of them easy to bear." His voice came muffled through his hands.

"If it were only Westria – only the land itself – that I had to rule! Sometimes I wish the Guardians would bring down a second Cataclysm, and this time destroy mankind. The animal kindreds act according to their natures and obey their own laws. I can deal with *them*. It is men whose deeds weigh on my soul."

Jehan sighed and looked up. "Sometimes it seems to me as if everyone in the Kingdom were engaged in some plot, that the strong are all out for their own advancement, and the weak are honorable only because they lack the power to do otherwise. I find myself plotting stratagems to make them reveal their plans, deceptions to unmask deceit – all the things I swore never to do or to be when I put on the Jewels. Open force would be more honest, and yet violence ignores the distinction between treachery and weakness, between those who are truly guilty and those who are merely misled."

The Master shifted on the hard bed to face the King. "You must act with honor and forbearance to inspire it in others. If you use their methods, you will be no better than they. But, Jehan, do not close your eyes against evil. It does exist . . . and sometimes blind trust can be as dangerous as suspicion. Trust in the Maker of All – there only will your faith be secure!" He focused his voice to reach the King, but Jehan's face was closed.

"There have been too many treacheries," the King said in a dead voice. "I cannot afford to believe that there may be more. If I cannot trust the men I am supposed to lead, I may as well die!" His body was taut, and he stared through the Master into some vista of despair. "Can you understand what a burden the Crown and the staff can come to be?"

"Jehan . . . Jehan . . ." The Master took him by the shoulders and shook him until the King's blue eyes cleared again and met his own. "Surely it is so in every land. In Elaya the Prince fights for election from among the sons of the Royal House. In Aztlan they say that a man never knows if he is a chief until he begins to move and finds that others are following him. In Westria the throne passes usually from parent to child, as do the lordships of the Provinces, and of every holding down to the smallest steading in the hills. Ours is not the only way, but it is a way we chose from among the patterns of the ancients because we thought it would help us to keep our Covenant. If so many others have borne this, surely you can do as well!"

Jehan tried to smile. "Old friend," he said very softly. "I am afraid – not of pain or death – in battle at least I can see my enemy and I know how to defend myself. But when Caolin brings me an order to be signed, I am afraid. What if I have judged wrong? And when men come to me to be made knight, as Andreas and Farin will do this afternoon, I am afraid lest they betray the faith they swear to me, and I fail in my duty to them. Yet if I fail, the whole pyramid that is Westria may fall. I cannot go on like this!"

For several minutes they sat without speaking while the King slowly mastered himself. The Master was still as an image, his lids half closed. He had opened himself to the King's need, and now he felt his pain. What could he do to ease this agony? If only he could talk to the other Masters and Mistresses of the College of the Wise. But he remembered how indifferent they had seemed to his concerns when he visited there three months before. *There is no help in men*, he mocked himself, remembering his advice to the King. *Trust in the Maker of All*. He regulated his breathing, sending his awareness inward. The air was full of the scent of flowers.

He opened his eyes again. "No, I haven't fallen asleep." His gaze held the King's. "You came here to look for a Queen. Why have you left the lady Faris so strictly alone?"

Jehan brought up his left arm as if to ward off a blow. "You should have been a warrior!" he said, shaken by sudden laughter. "I did not expect that from you!"

"You are in love with her, and I think she is ready to love you," the Master continued calmly.

Jehan's hand clenched in the folds of his tunic. "Am I? Is she?" he whispered. "I thought I loved her when I gave Eric a clear field to court her. I owed that to him, and perhaps to her as well. I thought she would take him or reject him. I did not expect her to play him like a hooked fish for three months – him and every other male in the province!"

The Master sat back and let him run on.

"At the Festival of the First Flowers I saw her, not just with my eyes. I was *aware* of her, as if my soul had touched hers. I thought I knew her then. But when we came back from that first war party she seemed changed, encased in an invisible shell. Was it only my need that made me see her as the goal of my search? Or is the person I thought I saw still there, locked inside her?" He had seized the Master's hand. After a moment he released it and straightened, smiling. "You have forsworn wife and child – I should not ask these questions of you."

"I have not given up women entirely – only permanent companionship! That is what I sacrifice for my calling. Yours does not demand the same!" The Master laughed ruefully. "Perhaps a detached viewpoint can be of some value in this case." He grew serious again.

"What if Faris has begun to love you already? She cannot show it, since you have made no sign. All she can do is distract herself with others, try to make you jealous – which I think she has done. You should at least find out how she feels!"

"Maybe I am afraid even to do that, lest I find my worst fears true."

"Tomorrow is May Eve. Perhaps the fires of Beltane will kindle some courage in your heart. The festival is older than Westria, and our ancestors knew their need for it when they chose to celebrate it after the Cataclysm. If you will not trust yourself, trust them!"

Jehan grinned. "I feel easier already. Do you know I have spoken to no one of this – not even to Caolin? I scarcely knew what I was feeling myself."

Not even Caolin? The close relationship between King and Seneschal had served the Kingdom well, but the Master wondered suddenly if Jehan was now finding that there were things he needed that Caolin could not give.

"I am here to listen," the Master said thoughtfully. "But there is one who can advise you better than I. The Beltane fires reflect the fires of heaven as love between men reflects the love of the Most High. Use the Jewel – ask the Lady of Fire."

"Use the Jewel of Fire for my own need?" The King stared at the Master.

"It is not for your need only, Jehan. The King exists for the Kingdom, but you need a mate to share the burden of the Jewels, to balance your energies, to make with you a child to bear the Jewels after you. You are the King – you stand for the people of Westria. But you have had no Lady to stand for the land. When the High Prince is mated to the Maiden, then will the Great Marriage be consummated at last, and both King and Kingdom will be renewed. Westria needs a Lady as much as you do, Jehan."

The King rubbed at his forehead as if he could already feel the Jewel in its coronet burning there. "I have been taught for so long not to touch the Jewels without the greatest need."

"Think about it. You have the time."

"I hope so," said the King. "But I know that it is time to leave you now. My duty today is to Andreas and Farin! Will you bless me, Master, before I go?" He slipped to his knees before the Master of the Junipers, his dark hair hiding his face as he bent his head.

The older man stood and traced in the air an equal-armed cross. "In the names of earth, of air, of water, and of fire" – he drew a circle sunwise around the cross – "and of the Maker of All Things! May your path be blessed: may you find faith, may you find love, may you find peace!" His rough voice deepened, reverberated against the bare stone walls of the little room like a bell.

He brought his hands down and rested them on the King's head, holding them there as if he could transmit through his fingertips all his love.

Faris unclenched tense fingers from the skirts of her gown, armoring herself with all the praises of her beauty she had heard in the last few weeks, then swept into the Hall like the Lady of Love appearing to Her worshippers. Comment echoed her passing as members of the household bent to tell her name to visitors who had come for the knighting. Her self-image wavered as their interest beat against her awareness. She fought the impulse to panic – she had never before found herself the focus of so large a crowd.

But if she ran away, or tried to blend into the background as she had always done before, she would be admitting that Berisa and her brother were right.

Rosemary was already in her place near the dais with the other girls, but the rest of the guests still swirled at random, waiting for the ceremony to begin. As Faris began to move towards her friend she glimpsed a stooped figure with lank, graying hair in her path, a worn cloak the color of dried blood. She stopped short.

It was her father, Gerard of Hawkrest Hold.

Faris did not need to see his face. He carried his own atmosphere about with him, a molting, broody falcon of a man in a roomful of songbirds. He sensed her presence, turned to stare at her, and her cloak of beauty dissolved. Gerard frowned, and her memory mirrored back the day he had beaten her for dressing up in her mother's abandoned clothes.

She flinched, feeling the familiar cramping of her stomach, the ache of her scarred arm. But his lifted hand and his mental summons compelled her. She felt people looking at them and forced herself to straighten as she obeyed.

"So it's true." Gerard's voice creaked harshly, as if he had not used it all the time she and Farin had been away. "I should not have let you come."

Faris shook her head, denying him.

"You are tricked out like a heifer at a fair, for any man to buy. Your mother played that game well – do you think to equal her? But she chose me after all." . . . *and left me*, came the unvoiced refrain.

Faris felt his shadows engulfing her and stifled her pity. "I am not my mother," she said clearly.

"No. *She* could charm the very trees!" Gerard bit off the words, an ancient anguish distorting his carven features. But Faris had overheard all that he refused to say once when her nurse and the housekeeper thought her too young to understand. Her childhood dreams and nightmares were formed from the story of how her mother had gone out one night to dance with the spirits of the apple trees, and thus took the pneumonia of which she died.

Faris tried to distract him with a laugh. "Now that Farin is being knighted, he will surely marry. His bride will not want to share her home with me. I must find a husband now."

Her father shook his head. "I do not think that Farin will marry. You must stay, daughter. *You* must keep faith with me!"

Faris shut her eyes. *I would come gladly if only you had said you loved me*, she thought. *But now I have learned how it feels to have people care about me – I cannot go back to Hawkrest Hold now!*

"Let my mother's ghost keep faith with you," she said aloud.

Drumsticks buzzed and spattered bursts of sound across the Hall. Faris looked quickly to the great doorway, saw the knights of Theodor's household filing in with a musical jingle of mail. The crowd was folding back before them.

"I must join Rosemary," she said distractedly, but already she was leaving Gerard behind. She reached her place, breathless, as the drumbeat deepened and the skirl of bagpipes overwhelmed all other sound.

The people stilled and turned. *The King is coming! The King* . . .

And then he was in the Hall, walking as if he were alone in the room, walking steadily, as if he could have gone on for ever despite the weight of the emerald mantle that dragged from his shoulders and the Crown of Westria binding his helm.

Lord Theodor marched just behind him, his eyes flickering constantly from the people to his guard, to his wife and family, and back to the crowd again, giving each one a genial smile. But Jehan's face was sculptured into stern lines, his eyes fixed on the circled cross that glittered on the royal banner behind the dais.

Awareness of her father's anger and her own fears slipped away from Faris as she saw the weariness in Jehan's face, the dark smudges beneath his eyes. She watched as he and Theodor took their places on the dais and turned, flicking their mantles behind them with a practiced swirl. Sir Eric and Sandremun, following, continued on to stand at guard behind their lords.

The pipes wailed to silence. Now there was only an expectant rustle of drums. Faris felt Eric watching her. He did not move from his post, but somehow he seemed to bow. Faris felt Rosemary stiffen, but when she looked at her friend, the other girl's face was closed and still. Then the crowd stirred with a sound like a distant wind in the trees, and Farin and Andreas Blackbeard came through the door.

Faris forgave her brother the letter, forgave him everything, seeing his face. His mail had been scoured to silver perfection, the helm he carried in the crook of his arm polished like a mirror, but his face was brighter now. He had called *her* beautiful, but now his face was as radiant as a bride's.

He passed without seeing her, and he and Andreas knelt before the dais. Their cloaks settled around them, Andreas' oak tree and the silver hawk alighting on a harp, which she had worked on Farin's red velvet, glittered in the afternoon light.

"Ye folk of the Corona, hear me!" The Herald stepped forward. "It is said that long ago men bore arms by chance and not by choice and were sworn to serve not their own lords but printed laws. But in the time of the Cataclysm all of men's laws were swept away. And in that time there were some who turned to a more ancient way of fighting that did not offend the earth. They were linked to their lords by loyalty and love, and the old way of war became the new. And so united, these warriors preserved a remnant of the people to establish Westria.

"Since then, those who prove themselves worthy of the service of the sword have been named knights in Westria. You see two candidates for knighthood before you. Will any speak for them and attest their right to the honor they seek here?"

There was a roar of acclamation from Lord Theodor's guard. When the cheering had faded, the Lord Commander took a step forward.

"I will speak for them," he said gruffly.

"And I . . ." added Sir Eric.

"And I . . ." said Sandremun. He still moved stiffly, but otherwise he had recovered from his arrow wound well. Berisa, next to the dais, watched him narrowly as if afraid he would relapse before her eyes. Faris wondered if her sister knew that their father had come.

"My Lord."

Faris' attention snapped back as the King turned to Theodor.

"I would have your leave to speak for the youth Farin, and to make him knight with my own hand."

The King's voice was strong and beautiful. Faris looked at her brother with a terrible envy. He was the King's man now . . . he would go with Jehan whatever might

98

befall. *I have lost my father and my brother – what will I do?*

Theodor bowed assent.

"Farin," said the King, "in recognition of the valor and skill at arms you displayed in the fight against the raiders in the Highwater Valley, which contributed not only to the defense of our party but also saved my own life . . ." His voice rose above the murmur of the audience. ". . . and because of your courtesy and the skill in all accomplishments befitting a gentleman which I have observed in you, I am minded to make you knight. Will you accept this from my hand?"

"Aye, my Lord," Farin replied in a low voice.

The King took from Eric his own great sword of war and poised it over Farin's bent head.

"You are honorable, courteous, and brave," said the King, striking him once on each shoulder with the flat of the blade so that he shuddered beneath the blows. "Rise, Sir Farin of the Harp!"

The Hall erupted in cheering as the new knight got to his feet, and Jehan, handing his sword back to Eric, gave Farin an equal's embrace. He took from his own neck a gold chain, which he passed over Farin's head. Berisa stepped forward to tie the white belt of knighthood about his waist, followed by Lord Theodor, who bent to fasten the golden spurs to his feet.

"My Lord Commander," the King said, smiling, "I am minded to take this new knight into my service, for the sake of his skill with the sword and with the harp. Will you release him to me?"

Theodor laughed. "The gift is already given, is it not so?"

Farin had been blushing, but his face stilled as the King told him to kneel once more. *He loves the King*, thought Faris, watching him. Her eyes moved to the faces of Eric and the rest. *They all love him, and I think he loves them all*. Tears made a blurred shimmer of their cloaks and silvered mail. Her mind shied from the thought of this pledging that was so much more real than any vow that had ever been offered to her.

"I, Farin Harper, do swear to you, Jehan Lord of Westria, to be your man in all things: to speak or to be still, to strike or to stay my hand, to be faithful in wealth or in woe. To your service I bind myself until you yourself release me or my own life ends. In the Name of the Guardian of Men!"

He was trembling, but his voice came true and clear. The King bent over him.

"And I, Jehan of Westria, do now accept you as my sworn man, and take oath to you to be a true and loving Lord. I offer you my hearth for your sustenance, my sword for your defense, and for your trust in me, my heart. As you have given your faith to me, I give mine to you – so witness the four Jewels of Westria and the Maker of All Things!"

The King raised Farin to his feet and kissed him on the cheek, then let him go. Faris could see tears on Farin's cheeks, but the King's face was shining, as if in that exchange of faith he had gained not only a new servant, but a new joy.

Farin stepped to one side, moving as if he were afraid he might break. The applause died away.

Lord Theodor cleared his throat. "Andreas," he called the other candidate. "You served my vassal Charles of Woodhall long and well. In the battle on the Highwater your reinforcement enabled us to drive off the enemy. You have all the attributes of a gentleman, therefore I am minded to make you knight. Will you accept this from my hand?"

"Aye, my Lord."

Lord Theodor took his sword from Sandremun and struck Andreas' shoulders. "You are honorable, courteous, and brave! Rise, Sir Andreas of Woodhall!"

Andreas looked up in surprise at the name. The Lord Commander embraced him, but after chain, belt, and spurs had been bestowed, he held him there.

"Sir Andreas, you know, better than any, that the steading of Woodhall overlooks one of the main roads into Westria. It must be held by a strong man. For many years you helped Sir Charles to defend it. Will you bear the responsibility for it now?"

"My Lord, my Lord –" Andreas stammered. "It should belong to the lady Holly, not to me!"

Faris felt Holly trembling beside her and saw her expression as she looked at Andreas. *Holly loves him! I wonder if he knows.*

"I have spoken with the lady," said Theodor, "and she is willing for it to go to you. The Hold will shelter her, and I will act as her guardian as long as she has need."

"My Lord." Andreas' voice could hardly be heard. "I did not defend Woodhall before – I am not worthy to be trusted with it now." He bowed his head.

The King laid a restraining hand on Theodor's arm. "Sir Andreas, look at me!"

Face working, the young man raised his eyes.

"What shall the penance be for a man who has failed to defend his lord? You could not save Sir Charles, but to send you forth to wander would be too light a punishment, and, by the Lord of Battles, of no use to Sir Charles, to you, or to me!" Jehan took a breath, and his voice rang across the Hall.

"If it is by any fault of yours that Woodhall is without a defender, then the task of holding it shall be your punishment. If no fault was yours, then the honor of holding it shall be your reward! Sir Charles is dead, and no grief will bring him back. Take up his work, Andreas, and guard the land he left!"

Sir Eric had gone dead white, staring at the King, but Andreas gazed at him with shining eyes.

And that is why they love him, thought Faris, *because he reaches out to touch the best in them, and gives them hope again.*

The Lord Commander, his own eyes very bright, spoke then. "Sir Andreas, will you hold the steading of Woodhall for me, as I hold the Corona for my Lord the King, and as the King holds Westria for the Lord of All?"

"Aye, Lord Theodor, that I will!"

"Kneel!"

Andreas slipped to his knees and placed his clasped hands between those of his lord.

When the oaths had been completed, Theodor raised Andreas to his feet and presented him for the acclamation of those gathered in the Hall. All ceremony evaporated as the cheering crowd pressed around them.

The exaltation Faris had felt during the ceremony was suddenly gone. She knew she must go to the feast now – Farin had reserved a place for her. But their father would be there, watching her, shattering the illusion of beauty that had allowed her to respond to Sir Eric and Stefan and the rest. And when she gave them nothing, no word or smile or kiss, they would call her cruel.

But it is only a game . . . surely they will understand if I cannot play it now! Yet she could not still the inner doubt that added, *what if it is not a game for them?*

Faris slipped through the garden gate and latched it behind her, heart pounding as if she were being pursued. But no one was there. Even the babble in the Hall was only a whisper from here. Dim tree-shapes rose around her, mysterious in the darkness, and the air was heady with scent as the earth gave back its stored warmth to the cooling sky. She plucked a spray of lilac and, turning it back and forth between her fingers, began to walk.

The breeze cooled her burning cheeks, and the silence eased her soul. During the dinner her father had been seated by Berisa, who had kept his contempt focused on the people around him and left him no time to think of her. He had made his escape immediately afterward, and as soon as she could extricate herself, Faris had done the same.

Her neck and shoulders ached with the strain of resisting him, of the tension she had picked up from Farin, the myriad emotions of the crowd. A mockingbird began his song of courtship somewhere nearby, and more faintly she heard the beginnings of music from the Hall.

But she continued to walk. She could not face all those people again, and dancing would leave her vulnerable . . . memory shied away from the dance she had shared with the King.

The gate squeaked and gravel crunched as someone came towards her along the path. Faris froze, poised for fight, while she tried to tell her body there was no reason to flee. And as she hesitated she saw a tall figure silhouetted against the stars and recognized Eric.

"You startled me!"

"My lady Faris! I did not mean –" Eric broke off, peering at her. "May I walk with you?" he asked formally.

Faris fought the impulse to refuse, but something in his stance made her respond with a murmur he could interpret as assent. For some minutes they continued along the path in silence.

"Well, your brother is a knight now – it was a fine ceremony," he said at last.

"Yes. This meant a great deal to him." Faris began to relax, wondering why she had been so afraid. Already this conversation was moving toward ground they had covered many times before.

"The King needs good men around him, men who believe in honor – not more cynics like the Seneschal!"

"Yet Caolin seems very devoted to his master . . . in his way . . ."

"In his way – no doubt!" Eric spoke scornfully. "That's what is wrong with these clerks. They don't understand loyalty to an ideal if it means sacrificing one's comfort, much less one's life!" He strode forward as if expecting the forces of compromise to confront him on the path.

"I am sure you are right, but you can hardly expect that to be a popular attitude," said Faris breathlessly, hurrying to catch up with him.

"Oh, forgive me! I didn't mean to run on like that!" Two strides brought him back to her side. "In fact . . . well, now that Farin is going to serve the King, what will you do?" he added suddenly.

She stopped, staring at him, and unable to find a light answer, said at last, "I do not know."

"Faris, why don't you marry me?"

He stretched out his arms dramatically, and Faris, remembering her conversation with her father, found herself on the brink of hysterical laughter.

"Eric! I am not one of the causes for which you must be sacrificed!" They had moved closer to the Hall. Candlelight glowing through the windows laid golden bars across the path.

He seized her hand. "I can never say anything right. Now I've offended you."

"I am not offended, Eric. Don't apologise to me." She tried to smile.

"But you would say that – you are always kind, always gentle, and always beautiful – so beautiful, my Lady!"

His grip on her hand was painful. Faris tried to speak, but Eric charged onward.

"'My Lady' I always have called you in my mind, when I imagined myself finally telling you how beautiful you are, and how much I . . . love you, Faris . . ." He dropped to his knees beside her in the path, seized the trailing hem of her gown, and kissed it.

"Eric! Eric – you must not kneel to me!" His weight on her skirts reminded her of Rosemary's sheepdog. Stifling laughter, she went on. "Please get up!"

He gazed up at her, his face shining in the light from the Hall. As swiftly as he had knelt, he was on his feet again, seizing her in his arms. She looked at him in astonishment, and before she could catch her breath he kissed her.

Faris felt as if she were in the grip of some great force of nature – a whirlwind, a tidal wave, the Great Bear. She was too stunned to even try and break free. She felt the power of Eric's battle-trained muscles and was afraid.

After a moment he let go of her and stood away, breathing hard. The spray of lilac she had been holding at her breast fell in fragments to the path.

Eric looked at her, and Faris realised in horror that perhaps it had not been just his height that had kept him from meeting her eyes before. She had no right to see the nakedness of his soul.

"Eric . . . no!" she whispered, raising one hand.

He stepped back as if she had pushed him. His great fists were clenching and unclenching at his sides.

"No. Oh, my Lady, I did not mean . . . I thought . . . Faris, I love you in all honor! Indeed, I love you as my own honor, and to have you for my lady and my wife would be an honor nearly too great for me to bear!"

His eyes were glowing and his curls had blown back from his brow. Faris looked at his broad shoulders and remembered the strength in his arms. Surely with him she could find honor, comfort, a strong rock on which to build her life anew. But he was looking at her as if he saw the Lady of Fire, and she thought, *Does he really know me at all?*

She raised her eyes to seek his face again and saw in the window above him the silhouetted head and shoulders of the King. Her flesh ran suddenly hot, then cold again. *Jehan . . . Jehan . . .* his name rang in her heart like a knell.

She shook her head. "Oh no . . . what have I done?" and watched the anguished understanding of her answer dawn slowly in Eric's eyes.

"I cannot deceive you . . . I cannot deceive myself. If honor made a marriage, I would be yours –" she stumbled, "but I cannot be what you deserve!" She hid her face. "Oh, they were right – I have done evil – but I swear to you, Eric I never meant you harm!" She dashed tears from her eyes and held out her hands.

He took her hand and kissed it as if it had been some rare flower. She felt him trembling like the trunk of a great tree in a strong wind.

"You have done nothing, my Lady," he said very patiently. "You, surely, have no reason to reproach yourself! It was all my own blind desire. Please do not weep for me!" His voice cracked and he dropped her hand. His face was shadowed now. "I have only one thing to ask. Will you let me serve you still? I ask no reward," he said with a terrible control.

"Oh, Eric," Faris said brokenly, "if you wish, of course you may, until you find another more worthy lady who will return your love."

He laughed grimly. "My Lady, have I your leave to depart?" At her nod he bowed very low and turned away into the darkness. It was only when she heard the far gate close that she realised he had gone to the stables instead of the Hall.

"Eric? Eric! Where are you going?" But no answer came from the night. "Sweet Lady, pity him, and pity me!"

She stood trembling where he had left her. She could no longer see Jehan in the window, but the strangely familiar music was clear. "Jehan . . . oh, Jehan . . . I love you," she murmured, shaking her head while the tears ran unheeded down her cheeks. Now she remembered the words to the song – *As I have pledged my life, so now I pledge my love, nor fate nor death shall ever break this binding*.

And she recognised the tune as the one that Farin had been playing that morning on the King's harp.

5

The Beltane Fire

The Master of the Junipers touched his taper to the green candle. *For the Lady of Fire*. He looked back at the King.

"Are you ready? We could do this later, you know – you will have a hard day."

Although the small windows set around the upper wall of the chapel glowed pale rose in the early dawn, the room was still visible only as dim masses of light and shadow. Scenes from the wall paintings glowed and faded as the candles flickered – men bringing blocks from the ruins of the Red City to build the Hold, Queen Auriane using the Jewel of Fire to turn a forest fire away from the Hold, the symbolic marriage of Julian the Great with the transcendent figure of the Guardian of Westria.

For a moment the King's face mirrored the exaltation pictured on that of the King in the painting. "I must know now," he said in a low voice. "Faris was not at the dancing last night. Her face comes between me and sleep." He placed upon the altar the redwood coffer he had been carrying.

"Since it was my suggestion that we seek the Lady's help, I can hardly deny you my help if you still wish me to be your guide," said the Master. He shook his head to clear it.

The King had wakened him from a sleep filled by troubled dreams before the sun was up.

But Jehan did not look as if he had slept at all. His eyes were shadowed and his skin pulled tight above the dark beard. Had Jehan been suffering this torment since he and Faris met? Surely the Master would have known. But if this was new, it must have been the advice he had given the King the day before that, by sanctioning this passion, had unleashed its full force.

The Master's muscles tensed as he remembered a saying they had at the College – *Be careful what you ask of the gods . . . they may give it to you.* What would come of this morning's work? He breathed deeply, forcing himself to relax. Only good – surely only good could come if both of them held to the will of the Maker of gods and men.

The King turned full into the candlelight, and the Master flinched from the trust in his eyes.

He stepped back from the altar and spoke quickly. "In the Name of the Maker of All! The temple is sealed and the altar prepared!" He spread his hands wide. "Behold the Tree of Life, and obey its laws."

The tall candles set on the nearest corners of the altar flared as he moved, illuminating the male and female pillars, white and black, on either side. Behind them flickered the tapestry of the Tree of Life, which showed all elements and archetypes from earth to heaven.

Jehan stepped forward and laid one hand on the coffer. "Hail, Maker of All. May what we do here today find favor in Your sight!" He opened the coffer.

Inside were four compartments, each containing something wrapped in colored silk. The King's hand moved to the green, hovered a moment, and lifted it out. As he loosened his grip the silk fell away and a copper coronet uncoiled in his hands. The King held it up, eyes averted from the stone set at its center. It seemed dark and opaque, but as the King moved it caught the candlelight, and within its depths the Master saw an answering spark of flame.

"What must I do? I have not touched the Jewels more than twice since I became King, and never for something like this. At the College they said that there have been Kings who could use the powers of the Jewels without even touching them, but I am not one of them."

"Wait until we are in rapport," replied the Master. "I will tell you when to put on the Jewel of Fire." He motioned towards the chairs that had been set before the altar. Jehan took his place with the coronet in his lap, and the Master sat down across from him. For several minutes they were still, relaxing taut muscles one by one, easing their breathing into a synchronous rhythm.

The Master kept his eyes on the King, but he did not focus on his face, for it was not the body of the man that he wished to see. The charged stillness deepened around them. Their regular breathing was the only sound in the room. As the Master's awareness of his own body diminished, he began to perceive a glow around the King that changed gradually from dirty red to deep blue, lightening at last to a pale silver light. The Master closed his eyes and projected his consciousness towards Jehan.

Dim walls . . . a flicker of candlelight . . . the head of a warrior from the wall painting behind him . . . the Master moved deeper, saw Caolin and a blurred memory of Brian of Las Costas, then a glimpse of Faris.

Be still, be still! he sent his thought towards Jehan. *Focus on the Light.* The images in his mind fragmented into flickers of color. He visualised Jehan lifting the coronet and settling it on his brow. *Put on the Jewel!*

When the Master opened his eyes, he was dazzled by the blaze of the Jewel of Fire. The fires in its heart were awakened now, its dusky surface scarcely veiling the coruscations of emerald and flame. Even as he saw it with his eyes, he perceived the reflection of his vision in Jehan's mind and felt the echo of its burning on Jehan's brow.

The blaze flared around them until they were poised within the heart of fire, and for a moment the heat seemed too great to bear. *See flowers*, projected the Master, feeling the wavering of Jehan's will, and the flames shimmered and formed themselves into flower petals fluttering in a warm breeze. There was music around them, and the wind bore heady scents of cypress and sandalwood.

The Master saw the King beside him, robed in a garment the vivid gold of a poppy flower. His own garment in this place was paler, like sunlight shining through a cloud.

"Lead on, my Lord," said the Master then. "This quest is yours."

The flowers opened into a glade hedged like a garden, where the grass glowed as earthly grass grows in the light of the setting sun. All their fear was gone. They felt that they were walking only because it was the most familiar way to move – if they had desired, they could have flown. They hurried forward, their spirits swelling within them, and the music surged.

A scatter of white blooms on the ground before them quivered and rose cooing into the air. They watched the doves settle again, finding it suddenly hard to breathe. Someone laughed in a tinkle of silver bells.

They turned. Behind them stood a cluster of women, some barely budding into womanhood, some with the ripe beauty of an autumn tree, who smiled and sang.

> Mistress of Mistresses, bearer of beauty,
> And world's desire . . .
> The eye She blinds, the soul She binds –
> She is Love's Fire.

Laughter rang again and the women drew apart. Then they saw only one woman, veiled in robes that shimmered emerald and flame. Her face was too bright for them to look upon.

"Seeker, why have you come to Me?"

Jehan bowed. "Lady of Fire, I seek You as the Guardian of human love."

"That I know," she said tartly. "If you were concerned with any other of My aspects, you would see Me in another form. What is your need?"

The heat increased and the perfume deepened until the Master felt faint, but Jehan straightened and stepped forward.

"I must have a Lady to balance me as Lord of this land, and to ease the burden on my heart. But my eyes are too weak to pierce the illusions that surround me, and see truly my own need."

"You do not wish to know what you need," she contradicted him. "You desire to know whom you love. What you ask, mortal, is what you shall receive – do you choose the hearthfire that comforts or the heart-fire that consumes the soul?"

The Lady's voice sang like a viol, and the color of her robes deepened to crimson as she leaned towards them.

Jehan's voice rang in answer. "Show me the one whose soul will be mated with my own!"

The Lady seemed to grow. Her robes rippled away from Her body, and Jehan and the Master were dazzled by the brightness of Her limbs. But Jehan looked up. "Faris," he breathed, and seeing with Jehan's eyes, the Master saw –

Faris robed in green and glowing like the goddess of Spring . . .

Faris bearing the Four Jewels on loins and waist and breast and brow . . .

Faris heavy with child . . .

Faris with eyes huge and burning in a ravaged face . . .

Jehan cried out and sprang towards her, and the Master leaped after him. But the Lady was gone. Her attendants swirled around them, drawing them into their dance. He saw their faces, the transfigured faces of every woman he had ever known . . . they were flowers . . . they were flames . . . and then even the flames were gone.

The Master opened his eyes.

For a few moments he could see nothing. When his sight cleared, the chapel was dim but clearly visible in the early morning light. Jehan lay slumped in his chair, and the coronet with the Jewel of Fire gleamed faintly from the floor.

"Jehan!" The Master grasped the King's shoulders and straightened him. As his head fell back the Master saw a red mark like a burn across his brow. "Jehan – come back!" He took the King's head between his hands.

Jehan's blue eyes opened, catching the new daylight as if they still held the Lady's fire. "Faris . . ." he murmured.

"Yes. I saw her too."

Jehan sighed and smiled, his eyes refocusing on his inner vision. The Master let him go and stood up. Faintly, like the beating of his heart, he could hear the pulsing of the Beltane drum.

On the other side of the field they were playing a dance tune – flute and tambour and the swift rat-tat of a hand drum. Faris pushed through crowds of people, come from the town that clustered below the Hold, or from the surrounding countryside, for the Beltane Festival. From time to time she stood on tiptoe and shaded her eyes to see. Bright awnings and pavilions were scattered about the field, making a loose circle around the Maypole and the two piles of wood stacked for the bonfires. But where was Rosemary?

Faris neared the trestle tables where they were distributing bread, cheese, and roasted mutton and saw her friend at last, her sleeves rolled up and a bread knife in her hand. Faris sighed with relief. She had slept badly, haunted by specters of her father accusing her, of Eric striding desperately into the night. But Rosemary would know what she should do.

"I have been looking all over for you," said Faris as Rosemary looked up.

"Where else would I be? Did you expect my mother to expose her delicate nerves to such a crowd? And Berisa is entertaining our noble guests." She glanced up the hill where the Lord Commander's black and white pavilion dominated the scene. "So I end up making sure that there are enough provisions and helping the people who are actually doing the work!" Her knife.sliced through the bread in precise, vicious strokes.

Faris stared at her friend, then stepped quickly out of the way as a stout man with one child clinging to his tunic and another on his shoulder paused before Rosemary, who cut a long loaf into three pieces and sliced each lengthwise so that it could be used as a trencher.

"Here you are, Jack." Rosemary smiled brightly. "May the Lady give you joy. Have you brought animals to be blessed tonight?"

The man grinned. "Two heifers that we want to breed this year! But my wife won't go between the fires again – she is heavy with our fourth child."

"You finally found out what was causing it, then?" They both laughed at the old joke.

"Oh, we knew that well enough already!" Jack's grin grew broader. "And what of you, my Lady? We had hoped to see you dancing between the fires with the mothers this year instead of around the Maypole with the maidens."

"Everything has its proper season. Mine has not yet come," Rosemary said shortly. Jack coughed in embarrassment, handed the bread to his children, and turned away.

"Can I help?" asked Faris hesitantly. She handed Rosemary a loaf of bread.

The other girl glanced up at her. "Why aren't you on the hill with the rest of them? Are you hiding from your admirers? Or did you think that my company would drive them away?"

Faris stood with the loaf held uselessly in her hand, not knowing what to do. Now she observed the angry flush on Rosemary's face, the suspicious brightness of her eyes. *Have I hurt you too? I never meant to do anything wrong!* her heart cried. She started to turn away.

"It's nothing," she said. "I only wanted to talk to you."

"I didn't think you needed any *female* friendship." Rosemary shook her head. "But now you don't know which of your suitors to choose, and you've come to ask Auntie

Rosemary to tell you what to do? Well, I can't help you. My father's after me to pick any one of those men who are running after you, and I'm tired of competing like a heifer at a fair!"

Faris found her fingers digging into the bread in her hand and very carefully set it down. All the voices that had debated within her since that moment when she had seen the King's silhouette the night before had merged into one voice now. With a fearful clarity she realised that though there might be no future for her afterward, she knew what her next step must be.

"This heifer has just dropped out of the competition."

"What?" asked Rosemary blankly.

"You accused me of playing with men's feelings," said Faris. "I didn't mean to, and I didn't see how anyone could misinterpret me –" She faltered, reached for a mug of wine someone had left on the table. The stuff was too warm, but it eased her tight throat going down.

"But Eric did take it seriously, and I refused his proposal, and he ran away –" she blurted. "I came to ask you if you had heard whether he was all right."

Rosemary's knuckles whitened as she gripped the carving knife. "You came to ask that of me?" she repeated. Carefully she set down the knife and turned to stare at Faris. Her face was red from the heat, and though her golden hair had been braided firmly around her head, escaping strands clung damply to her forehead. But her gray eyes held the same dumb pain Faris had seen in her own mirror that morning.

And Faris heard the words that Rosemary could not say. "Sweet Lady!" Faris put her hand to her mouth. "You are in love with *Eric!* And you wouldn't tell him." She laughed a little hysterically. "Well, that makes two of us! Thank goodness I said no!"

Four boys crowded in front of them, clamoring for bread. Faris handed Rosemary two loaves, and for a moment she was kept busy carving. When the boys had gone Rosemary looked up, frowning.

"Two of us? Who are *you* in love with, the King?"

Faris knew that her own face must have betrayed her as Rosemary's frown changed to a kind of desperate mirth.

"And here I've been wishing you would take Eric and get it over with, while all the time –" Rosemary buried her face against Faris' shoulder, giggling.

"It's not funny," said Faris morosely. She indicated the scar hidden by her full sleeve. "I know better than to think that the King might want me. But at least now Eric will be free to look for someone else."

Rosemary straightened and sighed. "Do you think so? He is in love with an image he calls Faris. I'm not sure you can do anything about that. He might even prefer to serve a lost cause."

Faris nodded, remembering what Eric had said the evening before. Was it a mark of love to understand the beloved so well? Would she ever understand Jehan?

"You might try hitting him over the head," said Rosemary.

The wine Faris had drunk bubbled gently through her veins and buzzed in her ears. The sun seemed very bright, and there was something inexpressibly comic about Rosemary's smile.

"But Rose, I can't even *reach* his head," she began very seriously. Then her control slipped and she began to giggle. Rosemary whooped, and the two girls collapsed into each other's arms.

"I can't marry anybody, and I've quarreled with my father," Faris said at last. "Let's get a cottage together. You can keep your animals there, and I'll work in the garden."

"And we can sell advice to young girls suffering from unrequited love!" added Rosemary.

Trying to catch her breath, Faris brushed the loose hair from her eyes. Someone tugged at her sleeve. She looked down and saw Linnet, Berisa's oldest daughter, beside her.

"They want all the girls to come for the Maypole dancing," said Linnet, "and I promised I would find you. Please come, Aunt Faris – please, Aunt Rosemary?"

She looked up at them with Berisa's dark eyes, but the golden curls beneath her wreaths of flowers were her father's. Three wreaths. As Faris noticed that, Linnet took off the topmost, twined of the little golden lilies that star the grass, and offered it to her. The second, made of twisted rosemary strands, she gave to Rosemary.

They looked at each other, the wreaths held carefully in their hands.

"It is midafternoon. I suppose everyone has gotten something to eat by now," Rosemary said uncertainly.

"Did you make the wreaths?" asked Faris.

"Yes, me and my sister. We want to see you dance," said Linnet.

"Oh . . . well then, I see that we must go!" replied Rosemary.

They bent low while Linnet settled the wreaths on their heads and fussed with them until she was satisfied. Then they let her take their hands and lead them across the field.

The air was heady with the smells of crushed grass, roasting meat, and spring flowers. Faris tipped back her head and gazed beyond the crowds to the hills around them, vivid now with the mingled golds of mustard and poppy, slashed by drifts of purple or white lupine bloom. Behind them the mountains hung upon the horizon like silhouettes cut from blue silk. Except for a few clouds clustering around the Father of Mountains, the sky was clear.

The drum was beating already – the deep-throbbing ritual drum, not the little one used for dancing. The beat moved her feet faster, and the laughter she had shared with Rosemary still bubbled in her breast. *I will not ask for more than this hour, this day, this awareness of love*, she thought, and for the moment her fear was gone.

"Faris, I am so glad that you came to me," said Rosemary softly. "I was growing twisted as a crab apple, keeping all that unspoken. But we are two fools, you know. You should have accepted Eric, and I should let my father try to match me with the King!"

"No . . . Eric doesn't really know me. How could I ever trust him? He is too young. But you would make a good Queen, Rosemary – you manage things so well."

"Except my own life!" she laughed, then abruptly sobered. "You are thinking about your scar, but that's a surface thing. Can we ever really know each other's souls?" They walked for a few moments in silence. Then Rosemary added, "Well, we are all in the Lady's hand."

A little breeze coaxed the hair from its loose braid down Faris' back and carried clearly the lowing of the livestock waiting for their part in the ceremonies. But the drum made it hard to think of other things now.

They reached the other dancers and took their places in the procession of young women and wives who had not yet borne a child. Someone gave them a horn of mead and they passed it from hand to hand. The pipers joined them, puffing and punching at the bags of their instruments until they swelled and the sweet skirling lifted above the beat of the drum.

The girls twirled in a flaring of flower-colored skirts, bent and leaped in place, stretching muscles to be ready for the dance. The piper settled into a frolicking march, and the crowd opened into an aisle before them with the flower-crowned Maypole at its end against the backdrop of the Father of Mountains.

At the retreat that preceded Faris' Nametaking and Initiation, the Master who taught them the history of the festivals of Westria had spent a long time on Beltane. Like many of the customs they used now, the Maypole dancing had been a practice of the old ones – the Edge People – in a land far away. Even the name of Beltane came from a land and language that were only legends now. But those who had brought the festivals to Westria before the Cataclysm were leaders among those who survived it. The Guardians protected those who knew enough to celebrate their powers. Faris knew that in five centuries the rituals had changed – they were not even precisely the same in all parts of Westria. But the purpose and the principle remained, and she realised that if she had refused to join the dancing, it would hardly have seemed like May.

Smiling, she moved forward with the rest. The people were throwing garlands to the girls and draping them with chains of flowers, for it was said to bring luck if one's token was borne in the ceremonies. The crowd cheered and made frank comments on the maidens' beauty. Faris tried to hide her embarrassment as she tied a string of dandelions about the waist of her white gown.

"Well, Ida," said one old woman as they passed, her cheeks burned red as ripe apples by the sun, "they look like a strong lot! They'll last till sundown surely, when it's time to light the fires! I remember one year when all the girls collapsed with an hour yet to go, and we had to wait until someone recovered enough to hold the torch. The rains were bad that year too, and my red cow miscarried of twin calves."

"Who's the warrior they've chosen to stand at the pole?" asked her friend, pulling her plaid shawl around her.

"Oh, it will be the King for certain this year. It's always a high man, and he's the highest of all!"

Ida cackled. "He'll have a fine time then, with all the lasses shaking their titties in his face and him bound too tight by the ribbons to move anything at all!"

"It's a small price to pay, don't you think? In the old days they would not have unbound him before they gave the pole to the fire!"

The King! Faris stopped short, fighting to retain her clarity. The girl behind her bumped into her and jolted her forward again. The drumbeat was deeper now. She could feel it shaking the earth, pulsing through her body from the ground to her heart. Another procession was starting down from the Commander's pavilion to meet them . . . all of the young men of the Corona, crowned with flowers. In the midst of them walked the King.

With much laughter and broad joking they thrust him against the Maypole. He stood still, his arms by his sides, while Sandremun loosed the ribbons that had been looped to the pole. They had dressed him in a new tunic of poppy gold, and there were poppies and lupines wreathed on his dark hair.

As the ribbons fluttered down around him he turned his head, and Faris met his eyes.

She wanted to run, to hide, but the music was moving her on. She looked away, followed the girl ahead of her until the circle was complete. For a moment the music stilled. Every second maiden turned until they were all facing each other in pairs. The ribbons were put into their hands.

The drum boomed twice, and twice again. Shivers ran up and down Faris' spine, and she clutched at her ribbon to still her trembling. The tension built, built, until the bagpipes let loose with a single exulting skirl. The girls facing sunward lifted their ribbons while the others bent. The drum began to beat out a swift insistent rhythm, and alternately lifting and bending so that their ribbons wove over and under each other around the pole, the dancers began to move.

They made the first circle, and Faris looked up and saw Jehan smile. She stumbled, caught herself, tried to focus on the music. She glimpsed her brother in the crowd, standing with Caolin and the Master of the Junipers, and was obscurely grateful that her father was not there. Her wreath slipped; she reached to adjust it and felt the tie slide from her braid and her hair begin to fall free.

And still the music drove her forward, and the shortening ribbons drew her inward to the pole. Faris was warming from the dancing. Her limbs moved more freely now, and she no longer tried to keep from looking at Jehan.

He stood still while the weaving of the ribbons crept down the pole, but his eyes followed her. Faris felt them on her even when she was turned away, burning hotter than the westering sun. His forehead was beaded with sweat, his throat like a marble column beneath his beard. Faris could see a muscle in it twitch as she went by.

The ribbons were touching him now, lacing across his face so that she saw only his eyes and the shape of his shoulders and chest. The sun slipped towards the western mountains. Its deepening glow lit pole and dancers, and the form of the man bound to the pole, with the same fire.

They had to move closer and bend lower to weave around him now. The lacing moved downward over shoulders, chest, waist, molding the shapes of his loins and thighs, tightening around knees and ankles. Faris brushed Jehan's bare foot with her hand as she made the final circuit and jerked away as if burnt.

The music stopped. The dancers straightened, backed away from the pole, and let the long ends of the ribbons fall so that they radiated outward from their center like the spokes of a wheel. Now Jehan was only a swelling at the base of the pole. Why could she still feel his eyes?

The rhythm of the drum changed again, becoming uneven, enticing the body to respond to the lilt of the melody the pipes took up now. The people joined in, clapping, shaking deerhoof rattles, jingling tambours.

Now the real dancing began as each girl tried to outdo the rest. Young men called to them, hoping to claim partners for the evening's revelry. Faris began slowly, meaning to keep on for as short a time as custom allowed and then to drop out. Some other girl could carry the torch and bear the May Queen's crown.

The fading of the day should have brought a cool wind, but the air that fanned Faris' cheeks was hot. Again she lifted the hair away from her neck, fanning it out so that it flared around her when she twirled, and loosened the lacings at the neck of her gown. Her eyes were blinded by the blaze of the setting sun. She should stop dancing now . . . she should . . .

High above the other music came the tinkle of silver bells.

Faris did not need to hear the drumming anymore. It was the pulse of her heart. She opened her arms, and flames ran along each nerve and sparked from her fingertips. She arched her back, feeling the delicious tension of breast and stomach muscles at full stretch. Her knees bent; her feet began to tap out the rhythm of the drums. Music rippled along her body, drew her arms, around her and out again as if they fluttered veils, lifted her into the air.

She no longer saw the sun, or the other dancers beginning to fall around her, or even the King. She was the sun; she was the flame of the torches eager for the pyre.

Faris danced.

The crimson sun sank rapidly towards the western mountains, its shape distorting as it neared the horizon, as if it were melting in its own fire. The clouds through which it fell stretched eastward in ragged banners of flame.

The ruddy light glowed on the faces of the people watching the dancing. The Master of the Junipers felt their emotion building as the pulse of the music increased, flowed back into the dancers, was focused by them and projected back again.

Rosemary stumbled towards him, wiping her forehead and fanning her cheeks. "That's enough for me!" she panted. "It's not fair – the pipers are playing in relays, but we have to dance straight through to the end!"

"I understood that one of the purposes of this exercise was to test endurance," said Caolin without taking his eyes from the dancers.

Rosemary looked at him coldly. "Who's left?" she asked the Master, getting her breath under control. "Oh . . ."

Only three dancers remained, and one of them was Faris, stretching and swaying like a living flame. As they watched, one of the other girls sank to the grass and was helped away by her friends.

"I didn't know that your sister could dance like that!" said Sandremun to Farin, who was watching as raptly as any of them. His fingers twitched as if he were accompanying the dancing on an invisible harp.

The Master braced himself against the force of their emotion – not lust, for although Faris' movements displayed all the grace of her slender body, they were sensual rather than erotic; the desire they expressed was for something not quite attainable by mortal flesh.

"How she dances!" murmured Rosemary. "I did not know she had the strength. I told her that we never really know each other . . . now I wonder if she knows herself."

The Master shook his head. "I do not think that it is *her* strength."

The sun had become a flare of brilliance behind the hills, but the clouds were bright, glowing with opalescent flecks of crimson and gold and flame, purple, and a pale translucent emerald. *Like the Jewel of Fire.*

People looked eagerly towards the Father of Mountains, but the only light on its slopes was the rosy reflection from the snowfields at its peak. Up there the Masters and Mistresses of the College of the Wise would be waiting, but they would not light the Beltane beacon until they could no longer see the sun.

The second girl crumpled to the ground. Now Faris danced alone, and the Master felt the prickling at the back of his neck that told him something more than mortal was here. He glanced around him. Did none of the others feel it too?

At the College they taught that since the Cataclysm, the gifts of the spirit had become more common in Westria, perhaps as a compensation for the skill at making tools and engines that men had renounced. Those with great talent usually ended up in the College, but most people could sense emotion, or even link minds in moments of great joy or fear. But just as some people were deaf to music, some people had no psychic sensitivity at all.

"I have heard of this, but I have not seen it before," said Caolin thoughtfully. "The Goddess rides her hard – there are few who can serve so directly as a channel of Power."

The words focused the Master's attention on Caolin. He glanced sidelong at the Seneschal's clear profile, outlined now in flame. Only long practice in balancing amid the torrent of others' emotions enabled him to withstand those around him, but he opened his awareness momentarily to

Caolin, trying to sense what the other man was feeling now.

As always, he met only a hard shell. *It is observation, not perception then that tells him what is happening here*, thought the Master. *What amazing barriers Caolin must have, and how well he compensates.*

A sound rose from the people around him, as wordless as the wind in the grass. Faris was dancing towards the pole and back again. The sky was darkening to crimson, but her pale dress still glowed. She began to circle the pole, and each circuit increased the tension in the watching crowd.

The Master forced an even rhythm on his breathing and fixed his eyes on the Mountain. He had faced the Lady once already today, and that was enough. Was this dancing the first fruits of the King's petition, or had they themselves been the Lady's tools?

The peak of the Father of Mountains blossomed with flame.

The people gasped. Then their tension exploded in a roar of triumph that engulfed the music and broke the rhythm of the drums.

"The fire!" they cried. "The Beltane fire!"

The Master saw Faris sway. He moved quickly towards her and found Caolin at his side. They caught her as she sagged and held her upright, feeling her body quiver to the racing of her heart. Her eyes were fixed, inseeing still.

Sandremun was cutting through the ribbons that bound the King. The Master shook his head. He had found it hard to withstand even the backlash of the power that Faris was channeling – what must it have been like for Jehan, who had been the focus of it all?

Caolin quivered as the ribbons fell away and Sandremun helped Jehan to step free. The King moved stiffly, his muscles cramped from his long stillness, but the exaltation on his face mirrored the look in Faris' eyes.

"Jehan," whispered Caolin, and the Master realised that this was one of the few times he had heard the Seneschal speak the King's name.

Rosemary and the other girls hurried to take Faris from their arms, to crown her with a wreath of early honeysuckle. Farin was bringing one like it for the King.

The Maypole quivered and groaned as the men worked it free and, shouting, bore it to one of the Beltane pyres. They pushed Jehan after it and put a torch into his hands. The women half carried Faris to the other pile of wood. A second torch was given to her, and her hand closed automatically around its stock.

For a moment she and Jehan faced each other crowned like two woods spirits with flowers. The flickering torches revealed the same unearthly beauty on their pale faces and the same glow in their wondering eyes.

Caolin stood like an image, hands clenched at his sides.

"All hail to the Lady!" came the men's deep cry.

"All hail to the Lord!" the women replied.

As if that had been a command, Faris and Jehan swung high their torches and cast them on to the waiting pyres. The flames caught the sweet oils that had been poured over the logs and licked hungrily down to the tinder within the piles. With a roar the flicker exploded into a blaze of light.

A chorus of lowing and bleating, laughter and ribald commentary, mingled with the crackling of the fires. Two by two the couples who desired children passed between them. Women led their milk-cows, children their lambs, boys tugged at the noserings of the young bulls they had kept to raise. Some had brought chickens or goats to receive the blessing. Some of the young people rode their horses between the fires. One of the King's men led the stallion Stormwing through, snorting and rolling his eyes at the flames.

Over the sea of heaving backs and fire-flushed faces the Master could see Faris, leaning now against Rosemary. She blinked and moved her head, and he perceived warring in her face the bewilderment of the human girl and the terrible beauty of the Lady of Fire.

6

Royal Hunt and Storm

Intent on his prey, Jehan slipped an arrow one-handed
from his quiver and nocked it, guiding Stormwing with his
knees as the white horse plunged through the trees. The
pale early morning light shafted between the trunks of the
firs; the King's eyes narrowed against the shift of bright,
dark, bright, as he focused on the fleeting red-dappled
form of the deer.

*Light and darkness – the radiance of Faris' face, the
shadows of her hair.* Jehan's vision focused on the world
around him again. Cold air rasped his throat, but the blood
was singing along his veins. He was strung taut as his own
bent bow, but soon he would flash free to his goal – the
deer that flickered before him, the woman he had faced
last night across the Beltane fire.

Farin and Randal crashed through the brush behind
him. To his right he could hear Sandremun shouting and
the calling of Caolin's horn. To his left . . . he did not
need sound to tell him that Faris was there. He felt her
presence, as if the dancing had forged between them an
invisible chain.

The deer leaped ahead, slipping through the thickets as
a salmon slips upstream. The hunters followed with more
difficulty, forcing their way among the rock falls and the

jagged stumps of branches as they strained to keep the dogs in sight. It was perilous riding, for the deer was avoiding the bald hilltops and meadows where they might have seen their way.

They emerged from the fir-wood and followed the chase down the mountain, through patches of manzanita and madrone. The hunters had laced their boots to the top and turned them up over their thighs, but still their legs were gouged and their faces welted as they crashed through.

Jehan let a madrone branch slide along his bent back, straightened, glimpsed the deer, and lifted his bow. Sensing his danger, the deer swerved, soared over a clump of manzanita, and disappeared. The King eased back in his saddle and Stormwing slowed, blowing noisily. He had outrun the dogs and must wait for them to give him a direction again.

Caolin pounded up and drew rein beside him. He spoke, but Jehan scarcely heard. The bushes across the clearing trembled; the pounding of his heart deafened him; Faris was there. She bent forward, quieting her black mare. Her hair had escaped its braid and blew around her face like a dark cloud, but in the sunlight her riding tunic and breeches glowed a vivid green.

The sun lifted above the trees and suddenly the clearing was adazzle with light. The hounds called like a chime of untuned bells and swept past them. Instantly Stormwing was plunging after them. Jehan gave him his head, letting the excitement carry him onward, knowing that Faris felt it too.

Sharp branches whipped at his legs as they plunged through the manzanita, up a hill, and down another rocky slope. The ground grew rapidly steeper, and Jehan thought the deer must be seeking some nearby stream in order to lose the hounds. He urged Stormwing forward. The music of the pack changed. Jehan swept after them and saw the deer hesitating, red flanks heaving, where the ground fell suddenly away.

The deer's muscles rippled as he gathered himself. Jehan

raised the bow, bent it till its tension rippled along his outstretched arm. The deer lifted; the arrow slipped from Jehan's fingers, whispered across the top of the hand that clenched the bow, arced through the air to intersect the leap of the deer.

He heard the dull thunk as the arrow hit, saw the clean line of the deer's flight distorted. Then it disappeared below the cliff. The dogs milled at the cliff edge, their frustrated yapping drowning the tinkling of the little stream below. Jehan sighed, slipped the bow back over his head, and started looking for a way down.

He found the deer broken on the rocks beside the stream. He bent over it, hearing the others scrambling down to join him, Sandy calling his dogs away. The deer was not quite dead. The arrow had entered a finger's breadth from the joining of shoulder and neck, and its shaft quivered each time the deer took a breath. A little blood was trickling over the gray stones.

Jehan drew his knife. "Brother, forgive my clumsiness. I would have spared you this pain." The deer's dark eyes fixed on him in mute bewilderment. Kneeling, Jehan laid his left hand across them and held the deer's head down, murmuring, "Father, into Your hands I give the spirit of this my brother. His life will not be wasted, as I pray that my ending my own may not have been."

Then he drew his knife across the animal's throat. The body jerked for a few moments. When at last it stilled, the King lifted his hand and saw the deer's eyes already dull. He rose and stepped back, and Sandremun's men came up to begin the work of butchering, setting aside the offal for the dogs and any scavenger who might have need of a meal, and binding the carcass to a pole to be transported back to the Hold.

Jehan shivered. Clouds had come up from the west and were crossing the sun. He wiped his knife carefully and sheathed it.

"We have been lucky so far," said Sandy. "I think it will rain before noon. I'm going back – this morning's ride has tested my strength. I dare not return to my lady soaked to the skin!"

The King scarcely heard. Faris was watering her horse at the stream. The curve of her bent back, the flexed grace of her arm as she scooped water for herself, made a harmony of balanced tensions that drew him into its patterning.

"We have permission to take another deer," said Farin. "I would hate to turn back when we have come so far."

"I will take the King's deer back to the Hold," said Sandremun.

"We'll come with you," echoed Aramond. "Lady Holly is weary."

Jehan was still watching Faris. "I will stay," he said without looking around. But his thoughts were not on deer. Now he had other prey.

The hounds whimpered eagerly as they sought a new scent. Guided by Sandremun's huntsman, Caolin led the King, Randal, the girl Faris, and her brother through the oakwood. The sky had gone gray above them. Caolin felt moisture, looked up impatiently, then back to the hounds.

"What ails them?" he exclaimed. "We have been wandering for a half hour and they've not started a rabbit, let alone a deer! I should have brought Gerol – he would have found us some sport!" Caolin glanced at the King, who smiled faintly without replying. The King's eyes held the same inward focus that had been there since the night before. What ailed the man?

"You would make a free wolf help in your hunting?" asked Farin, astonished.

"Oh, Gerol is the lord Seneschal's willing shadow," said Randal, "but it might not be fair to the deer."

Caolin let the conversation flow by him, his attention on the King. "My Lord!" he began, but the King did not appear to have heard. "Jehan." He reached out to him.

The hounds gave tongue at last and Caolin's horse plunged forward. For a moment he and Jehan rode knee to knee. How could he breach the King's reserve?

"Ride hard, my Lord!" Caolin challenged at last. "Ride, or I'll beat you to this prize!" He drove his heels into the brown mare's sides.

The trail led straight through the oakwood, then up slopes steeper than any they had encountered, slanted and fissured from some ancient torment of the earth. The line of hunters spread and straggled as they tried to follow.

The air rang with the thunder of hoofbeats and the crying of the hounds. Caolin did not know how long they had ridden when he realised there was thunder in the heavens as well. He reined in and looked about him. He could hear the hounds ahead of him, but he had outpaced the hunters. He eased back in the saddle, waiting for them.

For a moment it was very quiet. Then he heard pattering in the leaves and felt the first raindrops strike his head. The clouds were dark with rain, and he knew this would be no mere uncomfortable drizzle, but a torrent that would wash every trace of scent away.

"Halloo!" he called.

In a few minutes Sandremun's huntsman appeared from among the trees ahead, the hounds frothing about his mount's feet.

"They've lost the deer," he said. "There's no good continuing in this, my lord Seneschal. We'll have to go back."

Caolin nodded. "Blow the rally then." Belatedly he pulled his hood over his hair and fastened it. The rain was now falling so furiously that he could hardly hear the huntsman's summoning. Could the others hear?

A half hour's wait brought them Farin, Randal, and the huntsman's boy. There was no sign of Faris or the King.

Caolin urged his horse a little away from the rest, peering through the rain.

"My lord Seneschal, let us go back to the Hold! If the King and the lady are not there already, they must have taken shelter somewhere," said the huntsman.

"I cannot go back and tell them that I have lost the King!" said Caolin without looking around.

"This rain is too fierce to last long. When it lets up, we can return and look for them," said Farin.

"Who knows – maybe they don't want to be found!" Randal laughed.

Caolin turned on him furiously, and Randal's laughter ceased. The Seneschal forced himself to be calm. The huntsman was right. Surely Jehan could take care of himself. And yet, as he turned his horse downhill at last, Caolin's own words echoed mockingly in his mind. *I have lost the King.*

Faris reined in her mare at the top of the slope and knew that she was lost. The trees around her were half hidden by shining veils of rain. She dashed water from her eyes and peered at them. Faintly she heard the notes of a hunting horn, but the water roared so loudly that she could not tell from which direction it came.

Then the world turned to thunder about her, and lightning split the sky as if the sky-bowl were cracking and all the brilliance of deep heaven showing through.

The black mare, Sombra, threw up her head with a whinny of terror and slid backward down the farther side of the hill. Faris fought to control her and still keep her seat. By the time she had the mastery, they had come to rest in the midst of a small clearing. Far away, thunder continued to roll, but whether the hill provided some protection, or the clouds had simply moved on, in the clearing the rain was only a gentle pattering. She was alone.

Faris drew her cloak around her and relaxed, savoring the quiet that was somehow enhanced by the falling rain. She raised her face to the sky and breathed deeply of the rich scent of wet earth and leaves. She supposed that she ought to be trying to find the others or make her own way back to the Hold, but the forest seemed to welcome her into its peace.

It had been so long since she had sat quietly. The preceding days had been filled with frenzied preparations for Farin's knighting. She remembered her quarrel with her father as something that had happened long ago. At least he was gone home now, though he had left orders for her to follow him after the end of the Festival. But that did not seem important now. She remembered only the dancing and Jehan's eyes burning behind the ribbons. Her memories of what had followed were chaotic – fire, and more fire, and animals rushing past.

She supposed they must have carried her off to bed after that. The exaltation of the ceremony had merged into troubled dreams, into an urgency that had driven her unthinking to the hunting, as if she could outrun the memory of what had happened the day before. But now she had escaped the world and need run no more.

Her hood had slipped back and water was running down her neck, but she made no move to replace it. She became, instead, even more still. Her awareness expanded, touching spirits of tree and bush, of small animals burrowed snugly out of the rain. She felt another consciousness beating against her own and turned and saw the King.

He seemed to have materialised against the dark trees, sitting on his white horse as motionless as she.

"Come," he said softly. "I have found a cave."

The restless flicker of the little fire modeled the slabbed stone of the cave into a shifting frieze of light and shadow. It crackled merrily as flames singed wet bark and bit on the dry wood underneath. The cave was small – perhaps ten feet from its narrow opening to the closing of the fissure. A thin breath of cold air from that crack carried the smoke of the fire towards the outside. The floor slanted downward in a series of broken steps. They had built the fire in a crevice of one of them. Faris perched on another, her arms clasped around her knees.

Through the gap by which they had entered, Faris could see treetops bending under the rain. She felt a momentary pity for the horses, tethered to a manzanita bush below the cave. Their saddles were inside, upended on the other side of the fire with cloaks and outer garments stretched across

131

them to dry. The air reeked comfortingly of horse and wet wool.

But Faris noted these things only subconsciously. Stripped to his breeches, Jehan was coaxing more branches into the fire, the smooth muscles of his back and shoulders defined by the light.

"What do you suppose has happened to the others?" asked Faris, stretching her hands towards the fire. She still wore a short sleeveless shift over her breeches, but her feet were bare. She had spread her hair across her shoulders to dry.

"If they are lucky, they have found shelter too – these mountains are riddled with caves. If not, they are probably swimming back to the Hold." He looked up at her, and her breath stuck in her throat. It was not fair for a man to have such thick black lashes and eyes like blue jewels.

"I hope they are not looking for me," he added, "or for you." His eyes went back to his work and she breathed again.

Faris considered him curiously. She was familiar with her brother's lean body, but the King was more compact, his muscular development more apparent. He stretched out his right arm to lay a larger branch across the fire, and she saw a long purple weal across the muscle of the fore-arm.

"You were hurt!" she protested, not quite touching it.

He placed the stick and turned his arm to the light. "That's a souvenir of the fight where your brother got his streak of white hair. It's healing well. Everything considered, I got off easily that time."

His eyes met hers. "Now I have a scar to match yours," he added suddenly. Instinctively Faris pressed the inner side of her bare arm against her body, but he took her hand and drew it towards him, turning it so that their two arms were twinned. "Faris, you must not be afraid. Do you think I would shrink from the mark of a deed that took more courage than any of my own? Don't you understand yet that there is nothing you need to hide from me?"

She stared at him, finding it strangely hard to focus on his face. For a moment awareness of his essence replaced all other sensation, though he had dropped her hand and moved away. She sensed mixed pain and laughter, an identity as vivid as any scent or color, though it was like none of these. For a moment she lost self-awareness, then, frightened, she looked away.

When she regained control, she realised that he was telling her the history of all of his scars, his voice light with the old note of self-mockery. He stretched out his arms and turned before her, *displaying himself*, she thought with sudden amusement, *like the peacocks at the Hold*.

His body had the lopsided development of the warrior – sword arm knotted with muscle leading to a bulging pectoral, while the shield arm, though more even in form, was supported by a wedge of muscle between shoulder and back. In comparison his hips and thighs seemed strangely slim. Looking at him, Faris found her breathing faltering and once more had to look away.

"Now this lump on my ribs" – Jehan pointed to an unevenness in his side where the ribs showed between the modeled muscles of belly and breast – "I got from an Elayan spear butt two years ago that sent me sprawling. If Eric had not straddled me until I got my breath back, I would not be here today." He sat down again, resting his arms on his knees.

"Eric told me," said Faris slowly, "that it was you who saved his life that day. He said he was surrounded, but you and Stormwing made so much noise that the enemy thought it was an army and ran away." She felt him watching her but continued to stare into the fire. "He was trying to explain to me why you are his model for courage."

"Caolin would say I was a model of foolishness – in fact, that is what he said to me at the time!" Jehan grinned. "And he's probably right. Eric may be a one-man army, but I have to use my head if I'm to stay alive on a battlefield!"

Faris shifted uncomfortably on the hard stone. Looking at him sidelong, she could see the faint white lines of other scars marring his bronzed skin and permanent discolorations from old bruises through his mail. She remembered suddenly his strong hands on the deer's throat that morning and the bright blood gushing beneath his knife.

"Eric –" she blurted. "He went away after Farin's knighting, and no one can tell me where he has gone!"

"Does it matter to you so much to know?"

Faris looked up quickly. Did he think that she loved Eric of Seagate? Was that why he had avoided her so long? Jehan's eyes were steady on hers beneath level brows. She felt her heart beating slow and heavy as a drum.

"He was . . . upset . . . when he left me. He had asked me to marry him and I refused. If it is my fault that he has come to harm – yes, it matters to me to know!" She stared defiantly at Jehan and saw the color leave, then rise again in his face, darkening a line like an old scar across his brow.

It had grown darker outside, though it was just noon. The rain roared against the mountainside so that there was no other sound. This was all that remained of the world – herself, and Jehan, and the fire.

"Theodor's Master of Horse says that Eric was asking the state of the roads between here and Seagate. He should have reached Bongarde by now. As for coming to harm . . . if you have rejected him, I pity anyone who gets in his way!" Jehan replied at last.

How heavy the air had become.

"Why are we talking about Eric?" Faris challenged. She was trembling. She folded her arms across her breast but could not still the shudders that shook her body. Where was the friendly flame that had made it so easy for her to approach him the day before?

"We aren't," said Jehan harshly, getting to his feet. He prodded the drying cloaks, glared towards the back of the cave where the cold draft stirred the air. "You're freezing! I have nothing to stop that crack, and our clothing is still wet." With a single fluid motion he stepped across the fire and eased down at her side.

She looked at him beneath her lashes, trying to speak. But the air was too charged . . . she could not breathe. She started as his arm went around her shoulders, then forced herself to lean against it, marveling at the hardness of the muscles.

It took a moment for her to realise that his arm was too taut and that Jehan was also finding it hard to breathe.

She smiled slowly then and turned in his embrace. The air's tension exploded in a flash of lightning that illuminated the cave and Jehan's face, now very near her own. In the darkness that followed he pulled her closer and guided her to meet his kiss.

The lightning had struck her and was tingling through every nerve. Jehan's arms held her in the center of a star and the world reeled away. After a moment that seemed an eternity he released her lips and she relaxed into his arms, her cheek against his chest. She could feel his heart racing. There was a long roll of thunder outside.

"Sweet Lady!" he said softly, his voice shaken between passion and laughter. "Did *we* do that?" he paused thoughtfully. "There's only one way to find out." He tipped up her head and kissed her once more. This time she wound her arms around him and tried inexpertly to return his kiss. After a little he released her and eased himself and her around so that they lay more comfortably against the rock.

Faris felt laughter sparkling within her, dancing more brightly than the fire. "My Lord," she whispered, "I'm not cold anymore."

His hold on her tightened. "Cold? No . . . not either of us . . . not ever again!" His mouth came to hers once more, gently, coaxing it to open, teaching her how to respond. The silence was longer this time.

When he let her go at last, his sigh was like that of someone who has put a heavy burden down. He lay back, and she wriggled closer so that her head rested on his shoulder. His left arm encircled her, holding her there.

"Blessed Lady," he whispered, his beard tickling Faris' forehead, "you have given me so much more than I asked!"

"You asked the Lady of Fire for *me?*" she said in wonder. "*I* only asked her to ease my heart."

He pulled himself up on one elbow and looked down at her anxiously. "You do love me, don't you? You don't feel bound just because we were linked in the ceremony yesterday, or because of what people may say when they know we have been together here . . .?"

She smiled and ran one finger along the line of a little silver scar just above the line of his beard. "My Lord, without knowing it, I have been bound to you since you first claimed me in the dance. But I did not admit it until I sent Eric away. Now that I know you want me, do you think I could say no?"

He turned his head to kiss her fingers. "Faris, I *love* you! I asked the Lady of Fire to give me a Queen – someone to be Lady of this land as I am Lord, so that the Kingdom will rest firmly on both pillars once more."

She pulled at him, and he eased down so that she could snuggle close again, shutting out that reminder of a world outside the cave.

"I have been so lonely," he went on. "I have needed you so much."

She snorted. "Lonely! In the midst of such a crowd? They all love you – Eric and Caolin and the rest. My brother is your newest slave! I felt like a child peering into a Great Hall where the grownups were enjoying a feast that I could never share." Her hand moved across his chest, learning its contours.

Jehan turned to face her and began to kiss her forehead, her eyelids, the tip of her nose, and at last her lips. "This is the appetiser," he whispered. "The main course will be served . . . soon."

She clung to him, a sweet warmth loosening all vestiges of tautness from her limbs. Muscles that had been tensed all her life began to ease. For the moment she was content merely to feel him next to her. The wind still whispered in the trees outside, but the rain had ceased. It was perhaps two hours after noon.

"I know that they love me," said Jehan soberly after a while. "The weight of their love exhausts me. Caolin wants me to be his idea of a King, Eric wants me to be a hero, and now your brother thinks I'm a figure from some old tale!"

Faris pushed herself away so that she could look at him, feeling suddenly cold, as if a flower were turning to dust within her grasp. "Will my love be so good for you? I love you, but how can I be what you need?" So close, she could see the fine lines at the corners of his eyes crease as he began to laugh.

"You don't have to do anything, my love – only be Faris, and be here! When I hold you, I feel that at last I am linked with reality. With you as my Queen I will finally be married to this land!"

Faris shook her head, then nestled it against his shoulder again. She had seen images of the Lady of Westria, and She was tall, deep-breasted, and strong, with hair as golden as the ripening fields and eyes like the sea. If Jehan saw *her* as the Goddess, thought Faris, he must be in love with her indeed! She sighed. "I will try to be whatever you want me to be."

"Don't be afraid, my butterfly," Jehan said softly. "I will be with you, and together we will learn how to use the Jewels to make this land once more worthy of its Covenant. I have wasted so much time, trying to reclaim the youth the Crown robbed from me, and the land has suffered for my sins."

"Jehan! The sun still rises and sets and winter is followed by spring. The sins of men are their own to answer for!"

"Perhaps so – I *hope* so!" he said somberly. "But I have been raised to believe that the health of Westria rests on her King. What any single creature does affects the whole, but my actions more than those of others, for I have been taught the meaning of what I do. For a long time I tried to forget that – I've no right to be surprised if others in the Kingdom follow that example. But I will change – *we* will change things, my love!" He bent to kiss her again.

She shook her head helplessly. She laid a hand on his shoulder, let it slip across the hair on his chest and the smooth skin of his back and sides. His breeches stopped her; her palm came up and paused over the left side of his breast. She could feel his heart beating heavily beneath her hand, and his nipple harden against her palm. The sweet warmth she had felt before was becoming a fire. Her own breasts throbbed in response, and she moved restlessly against him.

"Jehan," she whispered urgently.

"Yes –" His hand traced the outline of her cheek, slipped down her neck, and paused above her breast. "But not quite like this, with stones digging into our backs! The Lady has been gracious to give us this time alone, but this is not my idea of a bower."

Ignoring Faris' protests, Jehan eased her aside, got up, and brought his cloak from the other side of the fire. He folded it and laid it along the stone step. It was nearly dry.

Faris fumbled with the ribbon of her chemise, then dragged it over her head. She felt a brightness in the air as the sun broke through the clouds outside, but she saw only Jehan's eyes.

He reached out and laid his hand upon her breast. "Yes . . ." Sunlight gilded the ragged edges of their door.

She moved towards him, exulting as his arms closed around her. The friction of their bare skins touching was incandescent, but still he was not close enough. She clutched at him as a circle of light began to form around them that would shut her darkness for ever away.

"Caolin, the King is not *lost*, only mislaid for a little while!" said the Master of the Junipers. "It is barely past noon."

Caolin shrugged impatiently and began to towel his wet hair. "'A little while' is too long." His voice came muffled through the cloth. "I will set out again as soon as this damned downpour stops."

"Don't damn the rain – there has been little enough of it this spring. Both farm and forest must be blessing those clouds." The Master smiled gently from an armchair by the fire in Sandremun's little study.

"Damn the farmers then, and the forests too!" Caolin retorted savagely. He threw down the towel and stretched his hands to the fire, shivering. A gust of rain clattered against the windows.

"Put some clothes on, Caolin! I expect that Jehan and Faris are warmer than you are right now." The Master ran his fingers through his cropped hair.

Caolin paused in the act of drawing on a gray wool chamber-robe of Sandy's. "You are so sure that they will be together! You have had a vision, perhaps? One of the Guardians has personally informed you? You pilgrims from Awahna have all kinds of powers, I understand!" He stopped short, slipped his other arm into the robe, and tied it around him.

The old sheepdog lifted his head from the Master's feet and pricked his ears, but the wolf, Gerol, continued to lie unmoving before the fire. Caolin sat down on the raised hearth next to him.

The Master's smile was troubled. "A vision . . . yes . . . though it was not mine. The Lady of Fire will finish what She began." He gazed into the flames as if indeed he saw a vision there.

Caolin glanced at the windows, where rivulets of rain magnified the distortion of the glass. Surely it was lighter than it had been a little while ago. His hand went out to caress the wolf's great head, rubbing the soft fur back and forth absently as he spoke.

"I agree that the ceremony yesterday was impressive. But surely you build too much on the chance pairing of Faris with the King. She is very sensitive, that is all. She should be trained."

The Master's deep eyes suddenly held his. "It was no chance. The Lady of Fire *showed* us –" He broke off abruptly, frowning.

Gerol growled softly as Caolin's fingers gripped. The Seneschal removed his hand, his mind still on what the Master had almost said.

"The Lady showed *us*," he repeated softly. "Showed what? And who else did She show it to?" The Master's face revealed nothing. After a moment Caolin went on. "Yesterday the King had a mark on his forehead like the scar of a burn. *What did you do to him?*" Caolin's fingers twitched.

The other man's clasped hands were growing white. Caolin's will beat against his silence.

"You must have seen how Jehan has been worrying himself over Faris," the Master said at last.

No, thought Caolin, *I saw nothing of the kind! Jehan has hardly spoken to her for weeks*. But he did not dare to interrupt the Master now.

"He came to me . . . I told him that he had the means to an answer already in his hands." The Master's lips tightened, and Caolin knew that he would say no more. But he did not need to, now.

"The Jewel of Fire!" Caolin could not keep the wonder from his voice. "He used the Jewel? But he never touches them – not in all the years I have served him!" He sat back against the hearth, thinking.

In pictures the Jewel of Fire was set in a coronet – yes, that would explain the scar on the King's brow. And Jehan had used it to turn the element of Fire to his will. A log popped, and Caolin's eyes fixed on the flames. They warmed him now, but if he were to thrust his hand among them they would burn.

The Master sighed. "I know well that you love him, Caolin, so you should know that you have guessed right."

The Seneschal looked at him, wondering how much the Master did know of what had been between him and Jehan, then relaxed as the other man went on.

"I love him too . . . it was *his* will to use the Jewel, but I wonder now if I did well to encourage him. At the College these days they teach that it is better not to ask the gods to interfere in the fates of men. I wonder . . . Faris is so vulnerable, Caolin, can she give Jehan what he needs – what Westria needs?"

What Jehan needs is something to warm his bed, thought Caolin. *After two and a half months without a lover, no wonder he was desperate!* But in sudden pity for the new lines he saw in the Master's face, he did not say so.

Lightning blinked in the window, and after a few moments thunder rolled faintly to the east. The storm was moving on.

"You may be worrying over nothing, after all," he began and saw the Master's body tense and his hands clench on the arms of his chair.

"Nothing!" he gasped. "Did you feel nothing, just now?"

"Lightning flashed," Caolin said blankly. "It does, in a storm."

"He has her! I have been wondering why I felt such tension growing, but *that* was unmistakable! He has touched her at last."

"No," Caolin whispered, but his vision was filled by the memory of Jehan and Faris mirroring each other's exaltation across the Beltane fires. He shook his head. "You are feeling nothing but your own displaced desire!" he accused. "I have lived with him for fifteen years – eaten and slept by his side and seen him take a score of women to his bed – and never felt . . ."

"This time it is different."

"How dare you feed your own deprivation by imagining Jehan in the act of –" Caolin could not finish that sentence either, remembering too vividly the light that filled Jehan's eyes when he made love. He leaped up, and Gerol sprang to his feet beside him, bristling.

"I will not stay to listen to your ravings! The storm is almost done – we must go!" He dragged off the robe, strode about the room snatching up half-dry garments, and flung open the door. "Sandy! Sandremun! I am leaving now, rain or no. Will you give me a guide or will it be said that the Corona could spare no one to search for her King?"

At Sandremun's mumble of agreement Caolin turned back to the room. His fingers were trembling so that he could not get the laces through his hunting leathers, and he forced himself to be still. The Master had not moved. Caolin reached for his cloak.

"I will forget what I have heard you say," he said coldly, "and I advise you to do the same!" But he could not forget the grave pity he glimpsed in the Master's eyes as he slammed the door.

Caolin wiped his forehead and strained to pierce the mists. The rain had stopped, but veils of cloud still trailed through the upper hills on the heels of the storm. Ahead, dark tree-shapes appeared and vanished again.

"I suppose that Gerol knows where he's going?" Sandremun said uncertainly, tucking his scarf around his throat.

Caolin made a sound deep in his throat and, almost on the edge of hearing, received the wolf's reply. "You are confused by the mists. Gerol is taking us by the straightest way to where the deer was killed. He says –"

"My Lord!" came the huntsman's cry. "There's a stream ahead!"

Caolin smiled. They had made good time through the forest, and now they had reached the place where they had been when the storm scattered them. It would not be long now. They clattered down the slope and splashed across the stream.

"I have a scarf of my sister's, if the wolf needs a scent," offered Farin, bringing his horse alongside.

"Do you think that Gerol is some foolish dog?" replied Caolin without looking at him. "He knows our scents as we know each other's faces, and those of our mounts as well!"

"The King and the maiden lost in the forest – it is like a legend," murmured Farin.

Caolin's heels dug into the brown mare's sides and, startled, she surged ahead.

"Ho! Look there!" cried Sandremun. Caolin reined aside and saw beyond the young lord's pointing finger a long white horsehair caught in a bramble bush.

"Stormwing, at least, has passed this way," said Farin.

The mare neighed suddenly, and from ahead of them came a deep whicker of greeting. Caolin set her at the slope. When he reached its top, Gerol was waiting for him, sitting on his haunches and grinning with lolling tongue. In the hollow before them he saw Stormwing and Sombra, Faris' black mare, tied to the same manzanita bush.

"They are near," breathed Farin. "I feel Faris' presence . . . but where?" He looked around in bewilderment. Trees grew thickly in the hollow except where a fall of rock had made a stony slope to the cliff. But though the rock face was knobbed and jagged, they could see no opening.

A damp breeze tore at the mist and ruffled their hair. Except for the sound of their own breathing and the creak and clink of harness as their horses moved, it was still.

"Could they have continued on foot?" began Sandremun, but Caolin motioned him to silence.

The air was brightening, and as they watched, a golden blaze of afternoon sunlight slanted through the parting clouds. Very clearly, they saw the slashed shadow of a gap in the face of the cliff.

Sandy whistled. "Well, Farin, I wonder how your sister will like being Queen?"

Caolin set his horn to his lips and split the stillness with a blast of despair.

Jehan let go of Faris, thrust her behind him, and whirled to face the entrance, his hand closing impotently as he groped at his side for a sword. The horn's bitter blare echoed through the cave, shattering their circle of peace. The shocked pounding of his heart began to slow as the sound was repeated, more mournfully, and he realised what it was.

Faris made a small choked sound behind him, and he turned to her. Her thin skin was pebbled with gooseflesh and her dark eyes dilated beneath the straight brows. Quickly he drew her to him again, wondering at the delicacy of her bones beneath his hands.

"Damn!" he said softly, then repeated it with more force. "Lady of Love, why are You mocking me!" he cried. His body ached with pent longing – he had waited so long! In another moment Faris would have been his beyond all questioning!

"Jehan?" she asked softly, clinging to him. He could feel the tension of anxiety tightening her body and that of passion draining from his own.

"That was Caolin's horn. We have been rescued," he said flatly.

"Oh . . ." Her laugh trembled. "Do we have to go? Can't we pretend we're not here?"

He shook his head. "I should have hidden the horses. They know where we are now!" He laughed suddenly and kissed her cheek. "Get some clothes on, woman, unless you want them to see you half naked. I told you that the Lady had a strange sense of humor, but next time I'll make sure we're not interrupted. We'll have time for our loving – and a far more comfortable bed!"

He pulled on his shirt and threw his cloak around him. Faris took longer to put on her chemise and settle her knee-length tunic over it, then delayed a moment, fussing with her hair.

"You look beautiful," he said, grinning. "Come on, I want to show them their Queen." He pulled her towards the entrance to the cave, then dropped her hand as she stepped into the flood of sunlight. Standing there with her hair loose on her shoulders and her green tunic glowing like peridot, she was as he had seen her in his vision, the goddess of spring.

One of Theodor's ancestors had planted a park to the east of the fortress. Its white oak trees had flourished, growing until their branches interlaced many feet above the forest floor and their leaves formed a roof through which the sun filled the air with green-gold light. As Sandremun led the triumphant searchers homeward with the King and Faris in their midst, they saw Theodor coming to meet them with Rosemary, the Master of the Junipers, and everyone else in the Hold who could sit a horse.

"You have found them, I see," called the Lord Commander.

"Indeed yes, Father," Sandremun replied. "Do you think our storehouses can provide a wedding feast?"

"A wedding?" Theodor reined in sharply, then his eyes lit and he urged his gelding forward. Farin pulled out of the way as the Commander reached Jehan, then trotted ahead to join the other young men.

"My dear." Theodor reached across Jehan's saddle to take Faris' hand and gave it a not quite fatherly squeeze. After a moment she freed it and took Jehan's arm. The King grinned. He wanted to whistle as Farin was doing now, but Theodor had seized his hand and was bending over it respectfully.

"She is the fairest thing in your Province, Lord – can you bear to let her go?" The King laughed. Theodor straightened and began to reply.

The air hummed. A black-feathered arrow appeared suddenly in Theodor's shoulder and his words became a cry. Jehan caught him as he slumped sideways.

Sandy twisted around to see what had happened, and a second arrow went under his arm and took the huntsman beside him in the throat. He looked back as the man fell, in his indecision turning his plunging horse in a tight circle and bringing the others to a halt behind him.

"Spread out and take cover!" cried Jehan, keeping his knees steady against Stormwing's sides and trying to hold the fainting Lord Commander on his own mount. "Faris, lie down on your mare's neck and get over to the trees! Caolin – help her!"

He glimpsed Caolin's tossing hair, turned at the sound

of hooves, and saw Farin and the others galloping back to them. Farin drew up beside him, pointing towards the woods on their left.

"They're shooting from over there, Sir!" he cried, his cloak flapping around him as he waved his arm.

Jehan heard the wasp-whine of another arrow, but before he could look, it had pierced Farin's cloak, struck through the top of his own thigh with scarcely diminished force, through the saddle, and buried its tip in Stormwing's back.

Jehan gasped at the shock of the blow and instinctively reined in, soothing the horse who had begun to buck and squeal as he felt the arrow prick.

Sandremun and the others charged towards the woods. Farin slipped from his saddle and caught Theodor as he slid from the King's arms. A wave of agony pulsed dizzyingly from Jehan's thigh and he gasped, groping for the pommel of his saddle.

"Jehan! Jehan! Lord of All, he's been hit too!" That was Caolin's voice. Jehan managed to focus on the Seneschal, who had grabbed Stormwing's rein now that Theodor's horse was out of the way. Beyond him Jehan saw Faris' white face.

"Get . . . her . . . out of the way!" he whispered through set teeth. There was a shout from the woods.

"They've found the bow – there's no danger now! Jehan, what can I do?" cried Faris.

"It's all right. Stormwing, be still – there's a fine horse – yes, it won't prick if you don't plunge about so," murmured the King, regulating his breathing to keep his voice calm. The stallion quieted, though every irritated stamp of his hooves stabbed Jehan anew.

"Rosemary, take the stallion's head. My Lord, where did it strike – oh, I see."

Relief washed through Jehan like a healing flood as he recognised the voice of the Master of the Junipers. He felt Stormwing relax beneath him as Rosemary spoke to him, and shut his eyes.

"I will do well enough as soon as we get this arrow out!" He straightened, trying to smile, and grasped the arrow shaft. But he could not move it.

Sandremun trotted up, brandishing a quiverful of arrows and a broad warrior's bow. "My Lord, these are brothers to the one you cut out of me two months ago! Normontaine arrows, but did a Montaner draw the bow? I have a score to settle with him if it's the same man – he made me miss a good fight!" He saw the arrow protruding from the King's thigh and his next comment trailed off.

"The arrow's lodged too firmly – we'll have to kill the horse!" said Caolin.

"Oh no." Jehan shook his head. He looked over at Faris, who was growing steadily more pale. "Caolin," he begged, "please take her away from here!"

"Faris, tear some strips from your tunic for bandages – we'll be needing them," said Rosemary without looking around. Faris swallowed and began to obey.

"The arrow head is stuck under the saddle," Jehan told the Master. "If you can get it free I'll do until we reach the Hold."

The Master took his hand, looking up at him, then nodded. "You will have to hold your thigh away from the saddle. Sandremun, undo the girth and be ready to lift the saddle flap. Jehan, give me your knife."

Rosemary's murmur to the stallion made a soft background as the Master slid his hands beneath the saddle and began to saw at the arrow shaft. Jehan bit his lip as his thigh muscles screamed at his effort to avoid putting pressure on the horse's back. In a moment the Master brought out the arrow head.

"Now hold to the other end of the shaft so that it pulls no farther." The Master worked the broken end of the arrow shaft back through the saddle leather. "Caolin, Sandremun, help me to get him down!"

In a few moments they had settled Jehan on somebody's folded cloak with his back against a tree. Nearby, Andreas was trying to keep Theodor from sitting up. Jehan saw Faris, with her hands full of torn cloth, and Caolin kneeling beside him.

"Perhaps I should have asked Faris to help *you*, Caolin. I don't know which of you looks worse . . ." he said faintly. "It's all right. I'll be all right now."

Sandremun paused beside them and whistled. "You were lucky, my Lord – a few inches higher and you would have been little use to your lady!" He laughed uncomfortably, then turned to his father.

"Sir, the men who are tracking our attacker sent Barni back to report. He's still ahead of them, but several are sure they recognise him as our dear cousin Ronald." His voice was colorless.

"Invite him back to the castle," muttered Caolin, gripping Jehan's hand. "'If he is guilty he will reveal himself!' Sweet heavens!" he added in disgust.

Jehan's mouth twitched as he recognised his own words of two days before. "If I judged wrongly, I have paid," he whispered back, "and I promise you, if Lord Theodor does not arrest Ronald, you may do it with my good will!" But Theodor, his voice strengthened by outrage, was instructing his son to do just that.

Jehan could feel Faris trembling beside him. "My darling, don't be afraid – I have taken much worse in war," he said softly.

She shook her head. "It's my fault. It happened because you were with me."

There was a sound of voices as men from the fortress arrived with stretchers. Quickly he reached out to take Faris' cold hand. "My only regret is that those things are not wide enough for two!"

She tried to smile, and the color began to return to her face. Nearby Farin had just discovered the arrow hole in his cloak and was examining it in wonder.

"Well, Sir Farin, you tried," said the King, "but I fear you will not always be able to take the blows meant for me!"

He shut his eyes against the pain as hands that tried to be gentle lifted him on to the stretcher, remembering how they had bound up the deer he had killed that morning for transportation back to the Hold. Today all his hunting had proved successful, but now, grimacing, he wondered wryly whether he was the hunter or the prey.

7

Ascending the Mountain

"To our future Queen – may your reign be memorable!"
Caolin's voice was cool and dry, like Segunda wine. As he
lifted his silver cup men cheered his words up and down the
long table; goblets repeated its flash in the candlelight.

Faris detached her fingers from the crumpled moonlight
silk of her gown and clasped them carefully on the table.
Jehan laid his hands over hers and, stiff-lipped, she tried
to return his smile.

"I feel like a moth plucked into the full light of the sun,"
she murmured. The attention of those who had come from
all over Westria to see her pledged to the King beat against
her awareness. Now her oath was given, and she would
never be free of that scrutiny again.

"Are you already regretting your pledge?" teased Jehan.
His fingers tightened on hers, then he pried open her
hand and brought it palm-first to his lips. The contact
shocked through her body as though she held a coal.
Did he think this would answer her fear? She pulled her
hand away.

He released her fingers instantly, but his darkened eyes
held hers. She saw in his face all the lines of pain that the
slow healing of his arrow wound had begun to smooth
away. And yet he had gone through the banquet without

complaining, and when he swore to make her his wife, his voice had rung against the vaulting of the Hall.

Swiftly she raised his hand to her cheek and was rewarded by an easing in his face as though a window had been opened to the sun. She closed her eyes, turning her lips against his hand, knowing that she could bear a lifetime of judgment in strangers' faces more easily than one glimpse of pain in his.

"I pressed you to this hurried wedding – have I been selfish?" he whispered. "I have kept the Kingdom waiting so long for a Lady, and I wanted them to honor you! See, even the Ambassador from Normontaine is here. I cannot even complete our marriage until my wound heals. But tomorrow we will go to the Mountain, and the College of the wise – I promise it will be peaceful there."

She reached out to him. "If you are with me . . ." she began, but the rest of her reply was cut off by the introductory rattle of the musical consort's drums.

The sweet calling of recorders fluttered across the heartbeat of the drum. Caolin watched Farin Harper lead his sister into the dance and thought how haggard she looked. He wondered briefly if the stress of her new position would force her to something like Lady Amata's fragility. Jehan was watching serenely. If he minded having his lady taken from his side at their wedding feast he would never show it, but one might hope that Jehan was finding Faris less fascinating now that she was his. It was a pity that they would be going away together so soon.

"The King does not dance tonight?"

Startled, Caolin met the innocent gaze of the Ambassador from Normontaine. "My lord Rudiard." He bowed. "Had you not heard that King Jehan was wounded less than three weeks past? He is healing well, but his physicians advise against dancing." Caolin watched the other man, noting the shrewdness in his hazel eyes, wishing his mouth was not hidden by his fox-colored beard.

151

Sir Rudiard grinned. "We did hear something. I hoped you could tell me more. Naturally my mistress is concerned. This border has been peaceful for some years and Normontaine would like it to stay that way."

"Then you know it was a Montaner arrow that we pulled from the King's thigh," said Caolin. The music signaled a round dance. A circle formed among the crowd like a ring spreading from a stone thrown into a pond. Caolin eyed the approaching dancers and motioned to Sir Rudiard to follow him.

They moved casually through the crowd and slipped into the gallery that ran alongside the Great Hall. A small group of listeners surrounded a singer at the opposite end.

"The arrow . . ." said Sir Rudiard helpfully, stroking his beard.

"Did your Lady think we would accuse her?" Caolin raised one eyebrow. "My King knows that you need to maintain our alliance, and he respects Queen Mara's intelligence too highly to suppose that if she stooped to such a deed she would advertise her complicity." The Seneschal sighed. "Despite appearances, we suspect that the arrow's source was closer to home." The Ambassador's face showed polite inquiry, and Caolin went on. "In fact, we intended to ask Queen Mara's help in bringing the true criminal to justice."

The singing had been replaced by the ripple of a harp. At the other end of the gallery Caolin glimpsed a glitter of gold and Farin Harper's dark head. *Jehan's harp*, he thought. Its clear tones rang against the pillars of the gallery.

"Normontaine will be happy to assist you!" said Sir Rudiard as Farin began to sing.

The mists are gathering in the hills and blotting out
    the day.
The embers of my father's Hall are smoldering far
    away.

152

Alas for me that I was born to set men's hearts
  afire –
Death like a conflagration grows because of their desire!

"That's your new Queen's brother, isn't it? He sings
well," commented Sir Rudiard.

Caolin coughed impatiently. "Are you familiar with
Ronald of Greenfell, a dealer in furs? He has traveled
much in this Kingdom and in Normontaine."

Sir Rudiard's hazel eyes came suddenly to his. "I've
heard of him."

Farin's voice rang beneath their words.

My father pledged me to his lord, nor would he
  change again,
Although the one King of my heart was also King
  of men,
  Who ruler, was yet ruled by me, to carry me away,
And slowly died beside the road as slowly died the
  day.

The Rock where I am brought to bay stands like a
  castle tower;
Below, that lord and all his men surround me in their
  power.
Alas, my love, thou hast paid dear to claim my heart
  and hand –
What wergild shall I pay to thee and to this lordless
  land?

"I cannot be specific, but you should know that we are
very interested in Ronald just now, and if you have word
of him in the near future, or . . ."

"Or if we find a reason to detain him . . .?" asked Sir
Rudiard softly.

"You understand me well, sir. Of course, we would like
him turned over to us for judgement."

"The request seems reasonable."

"I hope that we shall have occasion to make it soon. Ronald's outlaw friends may be unhappy with him at present." Caolin smiled slightly. "You might pay special attention to disturbances along the border and be prepared to welcome any 'refugees.'"

> My last defender, true to thee, still stands here by
>   my side,
> Lest she who would have been his Queen should be
>   another's bride.
> My foe has scaled the Rock and now his great sword
>   raises high –
> Shall I not weep that two such men should war for
>   such as I?

"I am only a plain messenger," said Sir Rudiard ingenuously. "I'll tell my mistress what you have said." His eyes fixed on the other end of the room. Caolin saw Faris and Jehan in the far doorway, their arms around each other's waists. As he watched, the King turned a little, his other hand lifted to touch her hair.

"I dare say your King would be glad to have this Ronald as a wedding present," said the Ambassador.

Caolin frowned. If Jehan were too involved with his woman to pay attention to the Kingdom, then his Seneschal must step in. "I am sure you will understand that my Lord is a little . . . preoccupied . . . just now," he said drily. "I would prefer that you send news of Ronald directly to me. Be sure that I will inform my King when the time is right."

Sir Rudiard glanced again at the King and Faris, who had rested her head on his shoulder. As they watched, Jehan's fingers tangled in the dark masses of her hair and he drew her face to his.

"I understand," said the Ambassador blandly.

Farin's voice was louder now, with a bitter clarity.

The swords flash in the faltering light – I know that
  there will be,
If my knight's arm should fail at last, a last sword-
  stroke for me!
The mists are covering the hills, spread like a leaden
  pall,
And I will reign in hell tonight, with thee, and him,
  and all.

"A strange song for a wedding feast, but Bards do not
reason like other men," commented Sir Rudiard.

Caolin shrugged. "It's an old tale from Seagate. The
incident described happened before the Crown was settled
on my Master's House." He suppressed a shiver, felt the
Ambassador watching him, and forced his features to an
equally bland smile. But his eyes remained on the King.

Sir Rudiard made a strange, choked sound. Caolin
turned then, followed the Ambassador's fascinated gaze,
and saw Gerol sitting beside them with an air of having
waited patiently for some time.

"Ah, Gerol," said the Seneschal genially, bending to
stroke the wolf's grizzled head. "Do you have a message
for me?" he concluded with an inquiring whine.

Gerol gave a short bark and growl. Sir Rudiard was
edging delicately backward. For the first time during the
conversation, Caolin grinned.

"Did my friend startle you?" he asked. "Remember, this
is Westria – men and beasts deal as equals here!"

The Ambassador managed an answering smile, bowed,
and walked quickly away. Gerol's ears flicked, but he did
not deign to look after the Montaner lord.

Jehan had left the room.

"So Ordrey is come with messages," Caolin said softly,
his pulse quickening. "They must be urgent for him to send
you into the Hall."

He followed the wolf's swift trot down the gallery and
through the passages to his own chamber. Ordrey was

waiting for him, his freckled face thinned by hard traveling and his clothing stiff with dust.

Caolin let the door click shut behind him and held out his hand. Ordrey set down his wine cup and reached in the breast of his jerkin for a packet wrapped in oiled silk.

"It's from Ercul Ashe, my Lord – he told me to lose no time on the road."

Automatically Caolin ascertained that the seal was indeed his Deputy's, and untouched, then reached for his letter knife to slit the flap. Ashe's precise writing minced across the page:

My Lord – our agent Jonas Whitebeard is newly come with a load of goods from the south, and a tale that men from the fortress of Balleor in Santibar have raided over the border into Elaya. They say the Confederation is buzzing like a overturned hive. You must bring the King back to Laurelynn.

Gently Caolin laid the paper down. "Santibar is in Lord Brian's Province," he breathed. "Ronald is an arrow that may find its mark, but Santibar will be a sword to bring Brian down!"

He looked back at the letter. ". . . *bring the King to Laurelynn.*" Ercul Ashe had a touching faith in his ability to influence Jehan's movements! And yet, in all the years of conflict between Westria and Elaya, the city of Santibar by the sea – the farthest (and some said the fairest) possession of Westria – had been the most frequent prize. It was a major gateway for trade between Westria and the south, and the taxes were valuable. But it had always seemed to Caolin that Santibar's allegiance to Westria was primarily an irritation to Elaya's pride.

In the time of Jehan's father, King Alexander, Westria and Elaya had gone to war and forced upon the Confederation what was supposed to be a binding treaty. Yet only three years before, the Conde de las Palisadas had laid siege to Balleor, and Jehan had gone south to fight for it. And even if Jehan had not shed blood for the place already, Brian would never let it go.

No words of mine could shake the King's infatuation, thought Caolin, *but if war is brewing in the south?* He smiled. "Faris may go to the Mountain," he added aloud, "but I think that the King will go to Laurelynn."

"Jehan lied to me! He promised to come with me to the College of the Wise. I have kept my word to come here, but you cannot make me learn!"

The Master of the Junipers heard Faris' voice from within the low stone cottage, and the murmur of Rosemary's reply. He took a deep breath of the crisp air, drawing strength from the clean line of the slope above the College and the clarity of the morning sky. Then he stepped inside.

His soft sandals made no sound on the stone floor, but Faris curled tighter, turning her face to the whitewashed wall. Rosemary shrugged in exasperation and brushed past him to the door.

Faris' dark hair flowed over the huddle of white wool blankets like an extension of the shadows. One thin hand clutched the sheet around her. She had suffered the two-day ride up the mountain to the College in sullen silence – he had hoped that their arrival would reconcile her to necessity.

"Will you spend the next month in this bed?" His voice grated.

"If Jehan wants me to learn about the Jewels, *he* can teach me." Faris' voice was muffled. The Master settled on the edge of the bed.

"Jehan serves Westria, and so must you and I. Would you give an infant his father's sword for a teething bar? You cannot wield the Jewels untrained, and the best of teachers will be hard put to prepare you to become their Mistress before Midsummer." He sighed, feeling her anger and fear, and doubting whether any words of his could reach her now.

She did not realise her vulnerability, and he knew only one way to persuade her. He frowned, but the thought returned. *Must I bend my own oath to serve Westria?* he wondered. *Lord forgive me, what shall I do?*

He closed his eyes and relaxed, breathing carefully. His sharpened hearing picked up Faris' sobs, the nervous shifting of Rosemary's feet, and the wind, sighing around the buildings of the College like the breathing of the Father of Mountains.

The Master let himself sink a little deeper, still aware of his surroundings, but listening for the inner voice that never failed him. His mind was like a still pool.

Jehan! Across the Master's stillness rippled the image of the King. He saw the jut of his dark beard, the quirked eyebrows that gave Jehan's face the illusion of laughter even when it was quiet – but the Master had never seen such a light in those eyes. This was how Faris saw him . . . and it was the Master's answer. He had invoked the Lady of Fire – he must use whatever means were required to make sure no evil came of it.

Carefully he extended his awareness towards Faris. From among the tumbled images emerged that of Jehan's chamber in the Hold. Gold glittered as the King drew from his own neck a circled cross, kissed it, and slipped the chain over Faris' head. The vision dislimned and cleared. Then the Master glimpsed Jehan's carriage beginning the journey to Laurelynn and recoiled from Faris' despair.

He withdrew until her thoughts grew faint as the murmur of conversation from another room, testing the texture of her mind, sweet and shimmering as a butterfly's wing. Then he focused his will.

Faris, listen to me . . .

No. But her refusal to speak made no difference now.

You have no choice – you cannot shut your mind. He formed the picture of the Hall of Vision in the College, where the Tree of Life glowed in colored glass. *You have never seen this – whence comes the image then?*

Her wordless shriek rocked him. His own shields flashed up and he rubbed uselessly at his ears. Rosemary started towards them, unblocking the door. In the flood of light the Master saw Faris' eyes roll like those of a frightened horse. There were beads of perspiration on her brow.

"What's wrong?" asked Rosemary.

Faris sank back into her welter of blankets. "I thought it was against your oath to do that!" she said bitterly.

The Master's hands clenched. *"Nor shall I ever use these skills to dominate another's will . . ."* The words were graven on his soul.

"It was like walking through an open door." He gazed at her helplessly. "At the least you must learn to barrier your mind. How else could I convince you?"

Rosemary looked from one to the other and swallowed as she realised what had happened.

Faris shook her head. "I must not learn your sorcery!"

The Master rested his head in his hands. Justified or not, he was beginning to feel sick from reaction to what he had done, but he must make her understand! "You are wearing a Cross of the Elements."

Faris' hand went to her breast. "You saw it!"

"No. I saw Jehan give it to you, through your eyes. If you have no care for your own peace, still consider his. Will he be able to share with you only what he is willing for the world to know? If I could read you so easily, what might some enemy of his do?"

"I could resist! Read me now!"

Brutally, desperately, he breached the flame of her anger and saw beyond it almond trees that turned to maidens. Silver bells echoed in his soul. He recoiled, dropped his hands from his face, and looked up at Faris, whose eyes were glittering with tears.

"My poor child," he said softly. "So the Lady already had you in Her hand. No wonder She laughed at me." He felt the feather-touch of fear.

Faris whimpered and collapsed into Rosemary's arms.

Unwilling, he sensed her trying to soothe the wounded edges of her integrity. He knew that shrinking. Indelible in his mind was the face of the Mistress of the Madrones, before her beauty had crystallised to power and, becoming Mistress of the College, even that name had been lost. Only he still called her Madrona when they were alone. He had sought her willingly, prepared by training, and still he remembered the shock of that forced intimacy. But for them it had been a prelude to the union of the flesh as well. Would Faris ever trust him again? If only Jehan had been there – she would have surrendered to him with joy.

"Forgive me, Faris, for Jehan's sake," the Master whispered, pushing himself to his feet. "Once, long ago, this happened to me too . . ."

For a moment he sensed her outrage, and behind it the shadow of some deeper fear. Then she shook her head a little.

"I will try to learn to guard myself, but nothing more . . . for Jehan . . ."

The King braced against the jolting of the carriage, biting his lip at the twinge in his thigh and dipping his pen carefully into the inkhorn. Unappreciated, the meadows of the great valley rolled by, their green deepening to gold now, as May moved towards June.

Faris, there are so many things I had no time to tell you. I wanted so much to share the peace of the Mountain with you. But if I can deal with this crisis while it is small, I may prevent a war that would keep me from you longer than the few weeks until you become my Queen.

Jehan frowned and looked up, taking comfort from Caolin's steady presence on the other seat. He picked up his pen once more.

The wheels of the carriage lag as I long to be done with this journey, and yet they are carrying me too quickly away from you! This separation pains me worse that my wound, but I know we must be patient. We will have time . . .

The writing board jumped as the carriage wheels dropped into a pothole and jerked free. The quill bent, splattering ink across the page. Jehan swore and flung the pen through the window.

Caolin coughed. "I'm afraid that my attempts to write while riding in a carriage have always had a similar fate." His gray eyes warmed a little, and Jehan felt an answering smile tug at his own scowl and a rush of gratitude for Caolin's patience and support. They had been together for so long that he could hardly remember how it had begun, but surely whatever impulse had led him to befriend the aloof young clerk that Caolin had been fifteen years ago had been well rewarded.

Jehan sighed and slipped the ruined paper into his leather writing case. "I doubt that your correspondents were so fair as mine!" He grinned.

Caolin rummaged in his traveling case and pulled out a portable chessboard with holes in which one could peg the men. "Will you play?"

Jehan shook his head and laughed. "Distracted as I am, I could not even give you a battle, Caolin!" When he was playing well, he could sometimes force the other man to a draw, and once or twice he had even beaten him, though he always wondered if Caolin had allowed him to win. Caolin had a chessmaster's mind, adept to feints and deep-planned strategies.

"Never mind," the King added. "I'll finish my letter tonight in Elder. Tomorrow we'll be done with this carriage – perhaps we can play on the boat that bears us down-river to Laurelynn." He turned back to the window, where the shadows were already beginning to lengthen across the fields, and let his thoughts return to Faris.

Only a few students remained in the great hall of the College, their pale robes ghostly in the twilight. The remains of a simple dinner had been cleared away. Two young men were playing chess by candlelight while a woman made notes from an illustrated herbal. The Master of the Junipers and Faris stayed by the hearth.

Faris drew up her knees and clasped her arms around them, gazing into the fire.

"Are you tired?" The Master's voice was soft. Faris looked at him quickly to make sure that he had indeed spoken aloud, and saw him wince. She knew that her suspicion hurt him and supposed that awareness indicated that after two weeks her own hurt was beginning to heal. But she still shuddered with a sense of violation when she remembered that joining of minds. She would not give him the comfort of her forgiveness, not yet.

She shrugged and smoothed the folds of her undyed linen gown. "I don't know why my body complains when it's my mind that is getting the exercise. The Mistress of the Golden Leaves fills my head with every deed of every king since the Cataclysm, and then the Master of the Tidepool tells me to empty my mind of everything!"

There were new lines in the Master's face. "I am sorry – I told you that the time was too short. If you like, I will ask that you be spared the history. You can learn that in Laurelynn."

"I'd rather forgo the mental exercises."

He shook his head. "The mind rules all. Some hold that if it were not for our belief, this world of forms would not exist at all."

She looked around her, reassuring herself with the sight of firelight gleaming on the grain of the oak beams, with the hardness of the stone upon which she sat. "I find that hard to believe."

"Believe? You must know it if you are to wield the Jewels!"

"I won't . . . I must not wield them," she whispered, staring into the fire. "Such things should not be meddled with. You cannot understand – I am so afraid – there are dark things in me that would be too powerful."

For a few moments she could hear only the occasional popping of the logs, mostly reduced to charcoal now, and the Master's regular breathing. Then something brushed her arm. Faris gasped as the Master of the Junipers reached past her and picked a coal from the fire.

Faris flinched from the fire in the Master's hand, looked at his face, and flinched again from the brightness of his eyes. He looked through her . . . he was too beautiful to look upon.

"Put it back!" she whispered, hiding her eyes. "Oh, put it back!"

"In the Name of the Lord of All!" he said suddenly, strongly, and dropped the coal back into the fire.

"It is not darkness, but light," he said when she dared to look at him once more. Light gleamed on the silver in his brown hair, warmed the weathered lines of his face. His eyes were quiet, focused on the outsides of things once more. "You can do that, you know."

She shook her head. "No – you have only convinced me that a Master from Awahna can do that."

"Don't you understand? If your road did not lead to Laurelynn, it might lead to Awahna instead! The power that you fear can be turned not only to darkness but to light! If you had the will, you could learn to do anything that is taught here." He laid his hand on her arm, the hand that had held the coal, and she was aware of him suddenly as a human being like herself. His brown hair was beginning to thin.

"Could you force me to it?" she asked quietly. "As you forced me to open my mind?"

His hand tightened. "No! I could not, not for Jehan's sake, or even for yours. And I swear to you by Those who dwell in Awahna that I will never touch your mind against your will again."

Faris looked at him in surprise, feeling his pain. Had their contact hurt him as well? She laid her hand over his, letting his face replace her father's accusing scowl. "Then I will open my mind to you, and you will show me how to pick up coals."

The Master drew a shaky breath and something eased in his face. He settled himself on the footstool. "Give me your cross." He held it before her eyes so that it caught the light. "Look at this, and listen to me . . ."

Faris stilled her mind, for that moment rejecting all fear. She rested in the Master's honey voice. She was still aware of her own identity, of the room around her. She knew that if she willed it at any time, she could rise and go. But she had no desire to will anything but what the Master told her to do. He hid the golden cross within his sleeve. She waited on his will.

"Do you see the fire?"

Faris nodded.

"There is a jewel among those coals – there, at the edge. It is yours. Take it up – it is the Jewel of Fire."

She saw it, glowing with crimson and purple and gold. *Fire burns*, said the distant voice in her mind, but she had seen the Master handle the Jewel and she believed in him. Her fingers closed on the coal. Without prompting she brought it to her forehead and saw herself reflected in his eyes, a Queen crowned in fire.

"Now put it down on the hearth again," the Master said gently.

Faris laid the jewel on the stone, and the swing of the golden cross drew her eye away. A moment later she was staring at the piece of charcoal that glowed beside her on the hearth. She reached for it and recoiled as the heat stung her fingertips.

"I will never force you," the Master said, "but there are other who might try. That is why you must learn."

She looked at the coal and then back at him, seeing now the strained set of his mouth and the shadows around his eyes.

"You have almost reconciled me to becoming Mistress of the Jewels." She smiled hesitantly.

"You must not be afraid of them," he replied. "Remember, there was a Mistress of the Jewels before there was a Master – it was a woman who *made* the Jewels!"

"They said so little of that when I went for my Name-taking." Faris looked at the Master in appeal.

"Very well . . . you, of all people, ought to know the tale." His gaze grew a little abstracted, and his voice fell into the cadence of the storyteller.

"You will remember that it happened in the days of the Troubles, when every great house fought to make its leader King, and in their fury men used whatever weapons came to hand, forgetting the Covenant. The College of the Wise tried to make peace, but the lords disregarded their words and slew their messengers and employed sorcerers to counter all they could do. So they determined to seek help from Those whose power sustains Westria – from Awahna."

A draft set the flames to leaping suddenly, and the Master paused and looked around. Faris followed his gaze to see the door to the Hall open, and a dark figure standing in the shadows there.

The Master frowned and turned back to Faris, his voice growing a little louder as he went on. "And so they sent a priestess, one wise enough to find the way to Awahna and young enough to make the journey quickly, to be their messenger. I think that she must have been beautiful as well," he added, smiling.

"For as she slept upon the road the sky blazed above her, and a being who shone like a star came to her and courted her and lay with her at last."

"But what *was* he?" asked Faris. "I have heard that he was one of the First People, but he gave her a child, didn't he? How could that be if he were not a man?"

"He could have been a mortal possessed by the spirit of star or wind, I suppose," the Master answered her. "But we have so many tales of such matings – I think that in the moment of union the energy of the Spirit transforms the woman's seed, so that the child, though fatherless in the

165

usual sense, is yet not totally of humankind. In any case, the Lady bore a child whom she called Star until he named himself Julian. And her lover also left her a crystal, like the quartz crystals they mine in the Ramparts, but more perfect than any stone men have ever found."

"And that was the Wind Crystal?" Faris shivered a little, fancying that a playful breeze was stirring her hair. What must it be like to be possessed by such power? For a moment she was aware of profound gratitude that she was married to a mortal man.

"It became so," confirmed the Master, "when the Lady learned to use it to focus her mind on the powers of Air – to understand the structure of the universe, and by Naming them, to cause new things to be. In Awahna the Rulers of the Tree of Life showed her how to find stones worthy of the other elements, and to charge them with Power . . ."

"And ever since then, men have sought their answers in magic talismans and avoided the discipline that leads to true power!" The footsteps of the Mistress of the College rang on the flagstones of the Hall as she emerged from the doorway, but to Faris her dark gray robes seemed to surround her with shadow still. The Master bent his head respectfully as she came towards them.

"I cannot help feeling that Westria might be better off if the Jewels had never been made," continued the Mistress tartly. She pushed back her hood, and Faris saw the planes of her face gleam like polished walnut in the firelight beneath her silver crown of hair. "How can we tell people not to trust in charms and amulets when the King himself never stirs without his trinket box?"

The Master's head came up defiantly. "He doesn't use the Jewels . . ."

"His reluctance comes not from wisdom, but from fear! Jehan left this place without completing his training, and this child will have even less time than he did to prepare for her task."

Faris shrank back, sensing some undercurrent of passion in this argument. Could there be dissension even in the

College of the Wise? Since coming here she had scarcely spoken to the Mistress, who reminded her uncomfortably of Berisa.

"She will be Initiated and receive the Powers," responded the Master. "A lifetime is scarcely sufficient to truly understand the Jewels."

"Or anything else of real value!" snapped the Mistress. "Initiation should confirm knowledge, not try to substitute. You may bend a young tree easily, but if it has not been trained it will snap back again when you let go!"

"My Lady," the Master said formally, "you agreed to the King's request. Surely this is not the time or place to question it . . ."

Faris folded her arms around herself, wishing she could become invisible.

"Well, I suppose it does not matter in the end," answered the Mistress of the College finally. "The purpose of the Maker of All Things will not be denied. It is our own fault if we suffer because we struggle against the flow."

Faris stared into the glowing heart of the fire. *Jehan . . . if you were here I would not be so afraid,* her heart cried out to him. But only the flickering among the coals answered her.

Caolin plunged a sliver into the coals that glowed on the hearth of his chamber, waited until it lit, then touched, one by one, the branch of candles on the polished table. Shadows leaped frantically in the corners until all the candles burned with a steady glow. He straightened and stretched, trying to ease muscles still cramped from the long journey, then turned to the other two men in the room.

Ordrey lay back in a padded chair with his feet towards the fire, his face a little flushed from the heat and the Seneschal's wine. Ercul Ashe sat like an image beside him, lank hair smoothed back, his maroon robe falling in carven folds, long eyes fixed on his master.

"You see that I have brought the King," said Caolin gently. "What have you to report to me?"

"I have made contact with two men in Brian's service – his butler and a clerk in the chancery at Sanjos. And the case of the misappropriation of revenues from the Ardello mill is almost complete. As you suggested, it was the clerk who was responsible." Ashe's tone was detached. "But we have found no evidence that Brian had any knowledge of what was going on."

"Hold the man then, but take no more steps against Brian's people – I have another key with which to unlock that door." Caolin sat down at last and picked up his goblet, turning it as he continued to speak so that the polished surface ran with rivers of light.

"Soon – very soon, I hope – we will receive from Normontaine a prisoner, a very special prisoner, Ercul, whom I want you to take in charge." Ashe nodded.

"He is one Ronald Sandreson, a cousin of Lord Theodor, though that will do him no good now. He gave the King the wound that has tied him to his bed this past month, and he has taken Brian's gold!"

Ashe's eyes narrowed, and Ordrey sat up in his chair, whistling. "Does the King know?"

"He knows who shot him, and he has been told about Brian, but he does not believe it – not yet. I want Ronald, and I want proof of Brian's guilt."

"Oh well," said Ordrey comfortably. "When you have the man, the proof will take care of itself."

"The King has given you full powers in this?" asked Ercul Ashe.

"He told me to arrest Ronald." Caolin shrugged. "It will give me the time to make a case."

"If we can spare the time ourselves to talk to him – Jonas Whitebeard has kept silence, but others have tongues, and the city is full of rumors about the fighting in Santibar," Ashe commented.

"Don't tell me," said Ordrey. "I am barely returned from a dash north and you would send me haring south again?"

Caolin looked at him, and Ordrey flushed and slumped back in his chair. "When I hold Brian in my hand, then you may have leave to lay yours on your lady friends!" snapped the Seneschal. "You know we must have more information than Whitebeard's report gives us." He ran his hand through his hair, dulled now with the dust of the road. *What would he need to convince Jehan?*

"You will go to Santibar," he told Ordrey. "Talk to the townsfolk, to the garrison to the woman who washes the Commander's breeches. Hear it if anyone so much as whispers Brian's name. And when you have gleaned all you can –" His tone sharpened, and Ordrey looked up suspiciously. Caolin wondered whether he should bind Ordrey's will as he had in the past, but for this mission the man would need all his wits.

"You will slip over the border – you can pass yourself off as a clansman again," he said quietly.

"Oh, aye." Ordrey grinned. "I'm to survey the raided village?"

"In passing. I want you to go to Palisada, to the Red Crescent Inn. The keeper's called Arquino – tell him you're the Wolfmaster's hound. He'll give you a message for me. You'll need gold," Caolin went on, ignoring Ordrey's astonishment. "See to it, Ercul – fifty laurels for Arquino and another fifty for Ordrey's needs."

"The Wolfmaster's hound!" repeated Ordrey while Ercul Ashe smiled primly.

"Ordrey – look at me!" Caolin held his gaze. *You are mine, Ordrey, your will is my own.* Slowly the resentment faded from the other man's eyes.

"Just by the way," Ordrey said with a last attempt at bravado, "are we working for war or for peace?"

"The answer to that may lie in the information you bring!" Caolin said tartly. "Peace is good for trade, but a short war now might settle the border for a generation, besides bringing glory to our King." *And in the chances of war, who knows what mistakes Brian may make, and what chances I may find to bring him down*, his thought moved on.

When his servants had gone, Caolin went to the window. He could hear the muted noises of the palace, and the incessant gurgle of the river that surrounded the city, noticeable now because he had not heard it for so long. Laurelynn-of-the-Waters, city of the Kings, to which all roads, all news, came at last. It was good to be back.

He looked around the chamber. Volumes from the Royal library crowded the shelves on three walls; a chart of the heavens was tacked above a map of the four Provinces of Westria between the windows; cabinets full of correspondence and reports flanked the great desk. Caolin peered at the chart and then out the window again. A mist from the river veiled the stars.

The Seneschal frowned. There was not enough room here, nor the peace and privacy needed for mental work. He must find another place – out of the city, but not too far – where he could pursue the study of the stars and perhaps return to the study of ceremonial magic that had been denied him when he left the College of the Wise.

He considered the map of Westria with its cities and strongholds, its mountains and rivers. There were the four sacred mountains – the Lady Mountain for Seagate, the Mother of Fire in the Ramparts, the Red Mountain in the center, shadowing Laurelynn, and for the Corona, the Father of Mountains, greatest of them all.

> We are going up the Mountain,
> We are going up the Mountain,
> We are going up the Mountain,
> Seekers of the Way . . .

Faris' feet moved to the rhythm of the song, feeling out footholds in the steep path. Ahead of her, Rosemary stubbed her toe and swore softly, then hauled herself upward once more. One of the Masters started a new verse to

the song. First the women of the company echoed it, then
the men, then everyone joined in the chorus. If a woman
had begun the verse, the men would have echoed her. Off
and on, and singing had continued since they started the
climb at dawn, the verses growing more sacred in character
as they neared the summit of the Father of Mountains.

Faris readjusted her food bag and the piece of wood
slung across her back. They all bore logs – this was only
one of many trips that would be made to prepare the
Midsummer fire. The trail was too steep for any beast
of burden, even if they had considered it proper to use
an animal for this task, and the trail itself had been worn
by the passage of countless feet out of the living stone.

They were well above the snowline now, the scattered
stone buildings of the College three hours behind them.
Faris wondered at her own endurance. As children, she
and Farin had spent most of the daylight roaming the hills
around Hawkrest Hold, preferring the open air and each
other's company to the dark silences of their father's Hall.
Her feet had not forgotten their skill, and three weeks of
simple food, regular hours, and the training exercises of
the College had restored her wind. She laughed as she
climbed, breathing deeply of the pure air, feeling the cool
breeze on her face and the warm sun on her back as her
body moved to the rhythm of the song.

Jehan was right to make me come here! she thought
suddenly, though her arms ached with the longing to hold
him. She wondered if his leg would have borne him on such
a climb – was it healed by now? Had he obeyed instructions
to rest it until it was well? If only she knew.

She had begun at last to accept something of the mind's
abilities, learned to shield herself from all but a determined
assault, or to try and reach another's soul. *Jehan!* She sent
the silent cry winging outward now. For a moment her
awareness embraced the bright world around her, flinging
it outward as a gift to him. Then she laughed at her own
presumption. The Masters, with their years of training,
could sometimes send messages that way. But three weeks

could hardly be expected to teach her to do so, unless the message was indeed borne on the wings of love.

"We are children of one Mother . . ." The Mistress of the College began the verse, pausing for a moment at the bend of the path. Her robe was as gray as the bones of the mountain, but in the sunlight her hair shone silver as the snow on its slopes above her dark face. Masters and students and mountain alike were painted in monochrome, from the sharp blacks and whites of priestesses and priests on leave from their posts for further study, to the dull gray-brown robes of the adepts who had returned from Awahna, and the unbleached gowns of the students, dull as the discolored snow at the edge of the path. The wind brought a whiff of sulfur from the hot springs near the peak, then wafted it away again.

Was that why they had chosen those colors? Faris wondered, for the Mountain was the crown of the Corona, which was the crown of Westria. Her heart stilled and leaped again as the path curved into the sky before her and she knew they were nearing the top.

The Crown. She thought suddenly of the Hall of Vision at the College, where the morning sun shone through the great stained glass window, casting colored spheres of light upon the polished floor. One could walk among them, ascending the Tree of Life through the spheres of Earth, the Moon, then left to Mercury and right to Venus, and so onward, back and forth through every aspect of the Divine, or else straight upward though the sphere of the sun and on to the crown of all – the Light beyond all created things.

"Bless the Light and bless the Darkness," they sang.

Faris stumbled as the slope eased. There was a boulder beside the path. She sank down upon it, dizzied by that last effort in the thin air. After a moment she lifted her head and looked around her.

Here, at the very top of the mountain, the sun had burned away the snow. The peak held a slight depression, as if the mountain's center had sunk from its own weight.

Steam rose gently from hot springs, melting the snow, and green grass grew.

The Mistress of the College stood on the western lip of the hollow, arms uplifted, facing the Master of the Junipers on the other side.

> Now the Crown is our foundation,
> Now the Crown is our foundation,
> Now the Crown is our foundation,
> Seekers of the Way.

Those who had recovered from the climb began to clear away the ashes of the Beltane fire from the stone platform on the southern edge of the peak. After a few minutes Faris started across the hollow towards them. Weaving among the hot springs, she reached the center and paused, quivering as if some deep vibration shook her bones. The air tingled. Her eyes were dazzled by the noon sun. She held her breath, feeling the light grow around her. The air trembled with meaning . . . in a moment she would see . . . in a moment all would be clear.

She cried out and hid her face from the terrible clarity of that light.

When she opened her eyes again, she was lying on the ground at the edge of the hollow with her head in Rosemary's lap. Students crowded around her, but she sought the Master of the Junipers' clear gaze.

"The Light," she whispered desolately. "I have lost the Light . . ."

"I know." The Master nodded, taking her hand. "I should have warned you to stay away from the Mountain's center."

"Is it forbidden?"

"Does it need to be? It is a pole of power." He smiled.

Faris closed her eyes. "If only I could have endured it a little longer – it was so beautiful. I did not want to come back again."

The Master's hand tightened on hers. "We follow the Way to learn to bear that Light. Few reach it, and of those who do, fewer still return to show others the path."

"Some go straight to the Crown," said Rosemary. "But the Mistress says that is the hardest path. The rest of us must go from aspect to aspect, like a squirrel bounding from branch to branch of a tree." She laughed.

Faris struggled to sit up. The noon sky arched over them like a bowl of sapphire glass. Rosemary looked worried, but Faris smiled.

"Yet we all reach the same place in the end," said the Master. "Come." He drew Faris to her feet. "From the platform you can see half Westria."

Rosemary led the way, the sparkling breeze fanning the wisps from her braid into a golden aureole. "Look – there's the Hold!" She pointed to the fortress, set at the Mountain's feet like an amulet of rosy stone.

Faris shaded her eyes, gazing over the western ranges within whose misty tangle lay the Hall where her father brooded over her marriage, which he would not bless though even he could not break it now. The last ridge ran straight as a sword blade for sixty miles. Beyond it she saw for the first time the shimmer of sunlight on the sea.

"There, to the southeast, you can see the Black Glass Mountain, the Mother of Fire," called one of the students. Faris turned to see.

The other Mountain rose above her companions. Like the Father of Mountains, she was still tipped in white. A thin wisp of smoke curling from her summit reminded Faris that the volcano was still very much alive. Range upon range of mountains shaded into the blue vistas beyond it. The Master of the Junipers gazed into that distance with a curious sadness in his face.

"And there lies the Sacred Valley of Awahna," he said softly, "and the Pilgrim's Road that is never twice the same."

Faris averted her eyes from his face, but her shielding was not strong enough to barrier his longing. She forced herself to follow the glitter of the Dorada down from the Ramparts towards the golden haze to the south. There lay Las Costas and Seagate, and in the center of the Kingdom, the Royal Domain. There, her future lay.

The whole of the land before her dropped into focus, as one sees suddenly the picture inherent in jigsaw pieces spread out on a board. But it was a living picture, and the sunlight seemed to glow through it rather than upon it as if the visible Westria were yet only a veil over some fairer reality.

She stretched out her arms to Westria as she had opened them to Jehan. His words re-echoed in her heart – *I love you as my life, but my life is this land*.

"Behold your Kingdom, my Queen! May your reign be fruitful!" the Master of the Junipers said.

8

The River Passage

The river flowed with light. Through leaded windows
Jehan glimpsed the dappled glitter of the sun, which reflected a glimmering net on the whitewashed ceiling of the
room. It was the beginning of June. The river would bear
his bride to him in three weeks' time.

The King's lips quirked as he realised that if Faris were
already here, he would have had even less taste for the
meeting he was waiting for than he did now, and he turned
from the window.

"You told them to be here at ten?" he asked Caolin.

The Seneschal looked up from the papers he was sorting.
"Yes. Lord Brian –"

"Lord Brian is here." The door swung open, and a shape
like a valley oak tree loomed in the hall.

Jehan stiffened. As usual, he had forgotten just how big
a man the Lord Commander of Las Costas was. Swiftly the
King took his place in the tall chair at the head of the table
so that the other man's advantage of height would be less
apparent.

Brian moved into the room and stood, head thrust a little
forward, poised on the edge of a bow. There was another
step in the hall; the door reversed its backward swing and
Eric thrust through.

He stopped short to avoid bumping into Brian, who had not moved. Jehan's lips twitched. A pair of oak trees . . .

Twice as many winters had thickened Brian's hide, and his luxuriant brown hair and beard were threaded with silver now, while Eric stood straighter and the beard he had started in the North was still a fringe. But they were of a height, and Eric's shoulders promised to equal Brian's breadth soon. This was the first time the King had seen Eric since he left the Hold. He was relieved to see him so well.

Brian looked the younger man up and down, nodded shortly to him and scarcely more deeply to the King. Then he took his place, his amber eyes glittering with amusement. Eric reddened, bowed deeply to Jehan, and sat down on the opposite side of the table.

Two other people, unnoticed until then, passed through the door. Jehan held out his hand to the sturdy woman whose silvered braids caught the sunlight.

"Lady Elinor – Lord Theodor sends you his greetings and his thanks for your reports."

The lady, who was Theodor's half-sister and representative in Laurelynn, smiled and bent over the King's hand. Her companion, Lord Diegues dos Altos, moved majestically forward.

"I suppose Eric can represent Seagate for his father, and this matter is unlikely to trouble the north, but what's Robert's excuse?" growled Brian. "I'd at least looked to see him here. With all respect to Lord Diegues, today's business is a heavy one to lay upon a delegate."

Lord Diegues stiffened. "The Lord Commander of the Ramparts instructed me – I have a letter from him here . . ." He fumbled in his pouch.

"Nay, my Lord. We believe you – be seated now." Jehan indicated the chair to his left. He glimpsed a flicker of irony in Caolin's schooled face. Lord Diegues' irate mumbling died away as the King's gaze rested on him, then passed to fix each of the others in turn.

"Indeed the matter is a heavy one, so we had best begin," he said quietly. "Lord Robert had duties to take him from

Laurelynn just now, but we have spoken of this matter, and I know his mind." The King paused. *My brother-in-law will be escorting my affianced wife from Elder to the Sacred Grove, and if you waste my time I may leave you to your own devices and go to meet her myself!* Jehan's closed lips imprisoned the thought, but something in his expression compelled their attention.

"My Lord of the South," he went on, formally. "I believe you have brought us a letter?"

Brian looked at him levelly and proffered a roll of paper that had been lost in his hand. Caolin reached for it. The Lord Commander looked at the Seneschal for the first time since entering the chamber, and his eyes narrowed, but he did not speak.

Caolin inclined his head and smiled gently as he took the scroll, unrolled it, and in a clear, expressionless voice began to read.

My Lord Brian:

It is with sorrow that I report that on the second of May five men from the second patrol of this garrison left a tavern in Santibar and rode South to Elaya, looting and burning a holding a few miles the other side of the border.

I am told that the Elayan had a pretty daughter whom these men had seen when her family came to market in Santibar (as you know, many of the folk trade back and forth across the border, not caring whether Westria or Elaya holds the town).

They say that the girl was visiting kinfolk at the time, and the men burned the place from resentment at not finding her. I have placed them in custody and offered the smallholder compensation. I hope that you will approve this course. Please let me know your will as soon as may be.

I remain, your servant and true man –

Sir Miguel de Santera
Commander of Balleor

There was a silence when Caolin had done. Jehan heard the wind rushing through the poplars beside the river and the laughter of children, and wondered, *How long until a child of mine will play there?*

The paper rustled as Caolin set it down. "That is all he says." His voice inflected upward.

"That is all there was to say," said Brian, twitching the roll from the Seneschal's fingers as Caolin started to slide it into his case. "You have no need of this, Master Seneschal – I'm sure your creatures will provide you with the same information soon." Brian's teeth showed as he grinned.

"My *employees* can only tell me what happened," Caolin corrected, still gently, though his eyes grew hard.

Brian's head lowered and his beard jutted forward. "My men do not lie to me!"

Caolin shrugged. "I'm sure you know. But if that is indeed Sir Miguel's letter, and he is telling all the truth, why is Elaya so angry?"

"That's so," said Lady Elinor. "One does not like to think it of Westrians, but I have heard that soldiers often lose all sense of decency when they are stationed far from home, as if the natives seem less than human to them, somehow."

Brian's glare became a frown as he considered her words. "Perhaps I should recruit locally," he said thoughtfully. "Local control is what I believe in, after all –" His glance flickered towards the King and then away.

"*If* that was what happened," interjected Lord Diegues.

Brian's amber stared fixed Lord Robert's delegate. "I'll tolerate your presence, sir, but not your insults. I choose my men for loyalty, however your lord chooses his! One cannot spy on every breath they take. If Sir Miguel has betrayed me, he will suffer for it, but I'll not judge the man unheard." The Commander's right hand closed over the massive gold ring he wore on the forefinger of his left, and again his eyes sought the King. It was the ring Jehan had given him when Brian had sworn fealty to *him*, fifteen years ago.

"An effective leader controls his subordinates so well that they *cannot* do wrong!" said Caolin dryly.

Eric looked from the Seneschal to Brian, clasping and unclasping his broad hands on the table before him. "If a lord's example inspires his men, he won't have to *control* them."

"Well said, cockerel," growled Brian. "But a Province is not a tourney field. Men will not follow you for glory alone! They must have a stake in their work. You win their loyalty by protecting their homes and families, or even, sometimes, their good opinion of themselves."

Eric grew red again, struggling for an answer. The dappled reflections off the river underlighted his face.

Jehan cleared his throat. "Westria stands by the bonds between man and man, between man and the land, each one bearing responsibility for his own part. But there are some matters that affect the Kingdom as a whole."

"We differ only in deciding which matters they are," said Brian with the glint of a smile.

"If Elaya comes against us in war because of this, they are more likely to strike the Ramparts, as they did two years ago, than to attack Las Costas," put in Lord Diegues.

"*If* Elaya uses this as a pretext for war," said Lady Elinor. "Will they? It seems to me that this is what we must consider, and try to avert."

The voices of the children outside grew louder, then faded. Jehan heard the smack of a ball.

"I would just as soon avoid a major war right now – mail makes an uncomfortable wedding garment," he said, smiling.

"Pay them off then – more gold for the landholder and a hundred laurels to sweeten the Governor at Palisada. Flog the men involved," said Caolin.

"I suppose that would satisfy *you?*" Brian bristled.

"If we do that, they will think we are weak. They'll conclude we are paying because we cannot fight." Eric's fist jarred the table and he looked at it in surprise.

Brian ignored him, his eyes on the King. "I will transfer

Sir Miguel if you insist, Jehan, but let *me* handle this. The responsibility for Las Costas is mine."

They were all looking to the King now. Jehan focused on the play of light on the wall, marshaling his thoughts. He drew breath to reply.

"*Jehan!*" Faris' voice blazed in his mind and her love rushed over him like a bright wind. Impressions of white-glistening slopes and an endless arch of pure sky were netted by the light on the wall. Light and space overwhelmed him; Faris was more real to him than she had ever been when he held her in his arms. Then, as swiftly as it had come to him, the sense of her presence was gone.

He released his breath. His lips began to move in words prepared in some other part of his mind. "No, I will not insist on Sir Miguel's transfer. After this he should be as watchful a Commander as anyone could wish." Jehan's eyes were still dazzled. The room was filled with light that glistened on Brian's curling hair, glowed steadily in his eyes, modeled the enduring strength of his frame.

"Send no more money to Elaya – send the men. When they have rebuilt what they destroyed, we will transfer them. They will find ample outlet for their energies in the Ramparts, guarding the Trader's Road," Jehan went on.

The light was everywhere. The line of Eric's brow was almost too pure to look upon, and his eyes were like clear pools. Jehan forced himself to finish.

". . . and I will write to the lord of Palisada and to his prince, as one lord to another, equals in honor and strength." Loyalty shone in the faces of Lord Diegues and Lady Elinor. *My people*, thought Jehan. *How beautiful they are*.

"Do you wish my office to draft the message, my Lord?" asked Caolin. The planes of the Seneschal's face were polished; his long fingers flickered as he shut papers into their case; the light struck brilliance from his gray eyes.

Jehan stretched joyfully, resting his palms on the table-top. "No. I will want your opinion, but I will write the letter myself. I bear responsibility for Westria." He smiled at

Brian, wishing he could share his joy, and the other man's eyes dropped to his scarred hands and golden ring.

"Are you well, my Lord? You look . . . strange," said Caolin when the others had gone.

"Did it show then? It was so brief, between a breath and a breath." Jehan thrust back his chair and stepped lightly to the window. "I have my Lady's love and I am very well!" he half sang.

"Jehan . . ." Caolin said carefully. "You are not being very clear."

"Faris is learning things, there on the Mountain, and she has forgiven me for leaving her. She called me just now, and I saw the snowfields of the Father of Mountains through her eyes. We were together." Jehan shook his head, unable to explain, though even the memory of what he had felt sang and shimmered along his veins. "Oh, Caolin – you should fall in love!"

Light rippled across the surface of the Seneschal's face. "No . . . that is not my Way. Besides, someone must keep his eyes on the earth while yours are filled with stars."

The sunlight on the river was too bright. Jehan's eyes had been like sapphire stars. Caolin shut his eyes and leaned back against the balustrade, focusing once more on Ercul Ashe.

"And so, my Lord, Hakim MacMorann has invited me to supper Wednesday eve at the Three Laurels Inn, and I am to give him his answer then. I thought I should appear open to his offers, in case you wanted to know more."

I would like to know if those drunken troopers were inspired by any encouragement of Brian's, or even by any negligence. Balleor is Brian's responsibility – there must be some way to hold him culpable for what has happened there! thought Caolin.

"Yes – you've done well, Ercul," he said at last, looking at the other man through lids slitted against the sun. "And so Hakim MacMorann thinks we do not know that the simple Elayan trader he pretends to be has been sending regular reports to Prince Palomon in Alcastello along with the goods he buys here!"

"It appears that he does not, sir. Naturally he would not be very explicit talking in the street, but I suspect that in the current crisis he feels a need for more detailed information than he can find in the marketplace." The cool wind rushing up the river from the distant Bay tugged at the stiff folds of the man's robe but did not sway him.

Caolin nodded. "The King intends to write to the Prince of Elaya, but if they want war, I doubt –" He broke off – that had come perilously close to criticising the King.

Caolin had never seen Jehan look so beautiful, not even when he had first seen him as a boy more than fifteen years ago, shining with love for the world. Now the King added to that radiance a man's settled power.

"Go to the meeting, Ercul," said Caolin quickly. "Tell Hakim that your worth is unappreciated by me, and if I do not reward you then you will find a master who will. I will be happy to give you information for them . . . and some of it may even be true!"

"Very well, my Lord." Ashe permitted himself a small smile. "There is one other thing. The Master of Signals reports that the Beacon-Keeper on the Red Mountain has died and wishes your recommendation for a replacement."

"The Red Mountain," murmured the Seneschal, gazing beyond the city walls, across the tangle of hill and meadow to the west of Laurelynn. The Mountain rose behind them, its red earth slopes darkened by distance, a looming presence so familiar that it was sensed rather than seen. Caolin had been to its top years ago. He remembered the stillness, the sense of being poised above the turning world.

"Yes, I know someone – a poor creature who hears badly and whose tongue has been twisted since birth. But she will not need to hear or speak to watch the beacon, only to see. Margit can hold the post for the time. I will supervise her while we seek a more permanent keeper. Send workmen to make sure the living quarters in the old fort are in repair."

Caolin's gaze came back from the mountain to the river beside him. Several boats were docked below the balustrade, being repainted to celebrate the arrival of the new Queen.

"Very well, my Lord." Ashe turned to go, paused when Caolin did not follow.

The Seneschal shook his head. "I'll join you soon in the Offices. Just now I have some thinking to do."

The Queen . . . Caolin forced his mind from the way Jehan had looked, to what he had said. To touch the King's mind from so far away, Faris must have in one month gained powers it took most adepts years to master. Could she read the thoughts of others as well? When Jehan held her in his arms, did she touch his soul?

"King's choice or no, Faris is not ready to become Mistress of the Jewels!" The Mistress of the College of the Wise spoke crisply. As she turned, the Master of the Junipers saw her clear profile drawn like a sword against the silver pre-dawn sky.

"Madrona, we cannot stop it now," he replied in a low voice. "The people await her at every holding between here and Laurelynn. From all over Westria they are already traveling towards the Sacred Grove. And any further delay would break Jehan's heart."

"Is it his heart that's so impatient, or another part of him?" she asked dryly. A horse whinnied outside, and another answered it.

"You had Jehan under your eye here for three years and yet you think that of him?" the Master asked bitterly.

After a moment she sighed and laid her hand on his shoulder. "Very well, that was unworthy . . . but you know that I am right about Faris. She should stay here the full year at least. A regular priestess would stay here for four and receive her initiation then!"

Through the window behind her, the Master saw riders in Theodor's black and white forming up in the courtyard, and after a moment Sandremun, reining in his restless mount. Two of the men led riderless horses, and the Master recognised Faris' black mare.

"Faris has learned the basics, and she knows how to shield her mind now. Initiation will give her the spirit of the Jewels. Their history she can learn in Laurelynn," he said evenly.

"Spirit! History! And what of the discipline and detachment she will need to master them? Do you think she will learn those at Court?"

"Why not?" he flashed. "She is not called to renounce the world but to serve it. Her goal *is* Laurelynn!"

"Do not preach the Way of Affirmation at me! Do you regret your own choice now?" The Mistress turned her head without moving her body, and his memory mirrored the movement back across the years, to the days when he had been only a student, and she already a Mistress of Power, and later when he returned from Awahna with a new name and the mystery of the Valley still in his eyes, and she had met him as an equal and given him her love. But that had been long ago, before she had become Mistress of the College of the Wise and he had gone to serve the King in Laurelynn. The light behind her made a nimbus of her hair but left the polished mahogany of her face in shadow. Almost he could see there the flicker of lost laughter, and his throat ached with the weight of words unsaid.

He shook his head, whispering, "All roads lead to Awahna in the end."

A bell rang from the tower. Through the window he saw Faris come out of the dormitory, swathed in a green riding cloak, with Rosemary behind her. The morning light glowed on her face.

The Mistress of the College followed his gaze, and the bolder light picked out all the weariness in her face, all the scars of her struggle to acquire that serenity. For a moment the old face of renunciation, the young one of affirmation, the aspiration that had once shone in the Mistress' eyes, and the tragic vision of Faris that the Master had seen through the Lady of Fire flashed alternately before his eyes. Then they mingled fractionally in one face and were gone. He thrust out a hand, whether in protest or petition he did not know, and when his eyes focused once more, he found that the Mistress had taken it in her own.

"You must go now," she said gently.

"You will not come with us?"

"Between the escort and the baggage, you will be two weeks on the road. I will continue my work here a few days more, then ride across-country to the Grove."

There was a soft knock at the door, but he did not let go of her hand. "It is a punishing journey."

"Has lying in palaces softened you?" She laughed. "I am not so frail – I will be at the Grove before you, never fear!" Lightly she touched his cheek, and he turned to go.

Faris came down the stairs to the commonroom of the Stonecross Inn carefully, clutching at the skirts of her new green gown. It was one of several Berisa had made for her while she was on the Mountain, cut close at the waist in the fashion of Laurelynn, with sleeves tight to the wrist as she had asked, its trailing skirts supported by petticoats. After the simple tunics she had worn at the College of the Wise, its constriction was almost unbearable.

But as least she was clean; the lingering soreness of muscles bruised by six days' riding had been eased by the hot bath that had awaited her here at Tamiston. The worn stairs creaked beneath her feet – Sandremun had said the inn was one of the oldest in Westria – and every few steps a slitted window opened onto the innyard and the circle of the common beyond, now bathed in a rosy sunset glow. Shadows from the houses on the western side of the common pointed across the grass to an upright half-arch of that composite stuff the ancients had used instead of stone. Local tradition held that it had once supported a road that arched through the sky, though no one could say why.

"Faris, wait for me."

She heard Holly clattering down the stairs behind her and paused, gathering the folds of her skirt. The muted roar of conversation from the commonroom rolled and ebbed in the stairwell, but the minds of the people down there were louder than their voices. Faris felt their curiosity, excitement, or boredom, and above all their anticipation, and knew that they were waiting for her.

She closed her eyes, visualising a golden curtain that would veil her from them without cutting off perception entirely. Carefully she drew it around her and for a moment stood still, fixing the physical image so that it would continue to function mentally without her attention.

"Lady of Earth – something smells good down there," said Holly, stopping behind her.

Faris smiled, glad, even with her barriers up, not to have to face the crowd alone. Together they made their way to the foot of the stairs.

At the table nearest the door a big gaunt man with a wolf's grizzled hair paused with a beef bone in his hand. His stillness spread to the four younger variations of himself who flanked him. Beyond them several men in the leathern jerkins of drovers saw Faris and pulled off their knitted caps.

Faris looked around the room as the silence spread, finding at last the long table where they had seated Sandremun and Rosemary, Farin and Andreas, and the others who had come with them from the north, with some of the notables of Tamiston. Empty places waited there for Holly and herself.

Jehan would have had a smile and a greeting for them all, she thought. But Jehan was not here. Faris lifted her chin, gripped her skirts, and started across the room.

"There is rich land along Bear Cub Creek – I could get a good crop of corn from it without stinting the forge, my Lord, if you would let me try." The man's fringe of black beard wagged as he talked. Faris recalled him from the introductions – Jonas Ferrero, the smith.

She turned back to the task of eating enough of her meal to satisfy her host, though her stomach was uncertain. Dietrick of Wolfhill, the holding within which Tamiston lay, was replying.

"I might allow it, but Mistress Esther at Elder would not. She has already warned us about exceeding our bounds."

"Let her! She may be priestess at Elder, but I don't notice the College of the Wise backing her. What's the objection anyhow? The earth was meant to be tilled, and I could trade the corn for more iron. Men from all over Westria have praised my swords – I could make Tamiston famous if I had the metal to work." The smith drained his beer mug and sighed. Faris remembered arguments she had heard at the college and echoed the sigh, grateful that the Master of the Junipers had gone ahead to Elder and could not hear this one.

"Master Smith, that is not quite so!" Rosemary frowned, her spoon stopped halfway to her lips. "The earth sustains all things in her own way. We should be thankful that sometimes she suffers men to impose their ways as well."

Dietrick's eyes glowed as he looked over at her. Down the table his movement was echoed by his sons. "I was bred by this land, and I think I understand it."

"Your pardon, my Lady," Jonas Ferrero broke in, "but we have been frightened by legends too long. The world is wide and men are few – we could accomplish so much more!"

"Have you forgotten the Cataclysm?" Rosemary's voice was very low.

"If indeed the powers of earth ever came near to destroying man, it was a long time ago. I have never seen one of the Guardians, nor has anyone I know."

The murmur of conversation in the rest of the room had stilled. Faris saw an old man watching them, his dark eyes cold in his brown face. Beside him a woman with hair like the fall of night fed her small daughter. Edge People, thought Faris – Old Ones like her own mother's kin. She wondered of what tribe and village they came.

The smith went on. "Even the King has no need to use those magic Jewels of his –" He stopped suddenly, remembering who Faris was.

Her hands clenched in her lap and she turned to the innkeeper. "I saw a pillar of concrete in the middle of your marketplace. What is it for?"

"Well, my Lady," said the woman eagerly, "that's what gave this place its name – Tam's Stone, not Tam's Town as most people think. As to what it's for – it survived the Cataclysm, and who can say for sure how the ancients used the things they made? The booths are set in rings around it when we have our August market fair. Caravaners are always coming through, but there are hundreds of them here then." She waved a hand at the group sitting at the long table nearest the fire. "I wish you could be with us for the Fair." Her gray eyes creased to slits above her red cheeks.

Faris sipped a little wine and smiled. "I would like that." She recognised the men and women she had seen unloading packmules when she arrived. They were carrying cloth of cotton and silk from the Free Cities, salt-fish from Seagate, worked tools and jewelry from Laurelynn, and iron ingots all the way from Elaya. Their destination was the Hold, where their goods would be exchanged for furs, raw wool and leather, and cured meat and cheese.

Two boys in sacking aprons began to clear away the meal.

"We keep no minstrels, my Lady, but we enjoy what cheer our guests can share. Would it please you if I asked whether someone would like to entertain the company?" the innkeeper asked.

Rosemary cocked her head at them. "You could start with Sir Farin over there. His harp was given to him by the King." She grinned.

After Farin had played, the caravaners sang for them, their voices linking in close harmony they had beat out to a mule's pace over scores of weary miles. Imperceptibly Faris began to relax. Some of the candles had burned out, and the dimmer light from the rest flickered on the faces of the company, touching them with mystery. At the College, Faris had learned something of the other kindreds that dwelt in Westria. Now she thought suddenly how little she knew of its men.

The caravaners finished. There was a little silence as people looked for the next volunteer, then the black-haired woman Faris had noticed before rose from her seat, giving her little daughter to the old man to hold. There was a pattering of applause from the local people as she came forward.

"That's Tania Ravenhair, our healer. She's a rare herb-mistress, though she was never at the College of the Wise," whispered the innkeeper.

"Then where did she learn?"

"From her own people, from her uncle – the old man there. He is Longfoot, leader of the Miwok village at the head of Bear Cub Creek."

Tania stood in the center of the room, shaking back her long hair. She wore an ankle-length shift dyed saffron and held to her narrow waist by a woven sash, but her arms and feet were bare. One of the serving lads produced a little wooden flute from his belt while the other lifted a drum from the wall.

Tentative at first, the drumbeats settled to a rhythm. For a while the dancer scarcely seemed to move. She swayed, her feet brushing a pattern on the floor. Then the flute eased into the rhythm of the drum, lilting around its steady beat like a butterfly fluttering across a meadow, and Tania opened her arms as if to draw the company into her embrace.

Faris did not know how long the Miwok woman danced or when it was that Farin's harp entered the music, support-ing and enriching it with a delicate courtesy like a lord at a village feast.

Faris felt her feet twitch. Her heart went out to the dancer, and the golden shell she had locked around her misted away. She felt the stretch of Tania's muscles, the spring of the worn oak floor. She glowed with the dancer's joy as she gave herself to the music, making sound visible, shaping the space around her and drawing her audience into the pattern she made.

Faris was aware of their presence, but it did not frighten her now. Each man or woman brought to the pattern something of his or her own. The dancer, the pattern, the world, were refracted through a score of visions, framed by a score of memories. And Faris knew them all, and through them, Westria. *Jehan's people*, she thought, and then with surprise, *my people too*.

When the dancing was over, Faris stumbled up the stairs and fell into a dreamless slumber. But later she wakened, needing to relieve herself, and paused at the window, looking out at the waxing moon. In its little light the heap of unburied refuse behind the inn seemed inoffensive as a nameless burial mound. Beyond it the common stretched dimly, deserted except for the ambiguous shadow that was Tam's Stone.

Two days later they crossed from the Corona into the Ramparts and transferred to the boats waiting on the Snowflood at Elder. They were met by Robert, Lord Commander of the Ramparts, a sturdy, square man with the weathered strength of his own mountains in his face and their stillness in his eyes. With many good wishes for Faris in the future, Sandremun's escort of Coronans left them, to be replaced by the axemen of Lord Robert's guard. However, Sandremun continued with them, along with Farin, Rosemary, and the Master of the Junipers. They were now two days from Laurelynn and a day farther from the Lady Mountain that watched over the great Bay.

The barge bore them with dreamlike smoothness between banks where ripening grain fields rippled towards the horizon as if the river had overflowed its bounds in waves of gold. People lined the landings as they passed, but the royal barges floated onward without pausing, letting the gentle current bear them down the Snowflood to the Dorada, then on to the Dorada's confluence with the Darkwater.

The misty shapes of the Ramparts disappeared as the river curved. Lower hills darkened to the west and south, and one peak slowly reared itself above the rest – the Red Mountain, Lord Robert told her. Soon they would be there.

They came to Laurelynn-of-the-Waters when dawn was painting the city's brick walls an even deeper rose and were immediately surrounded by a flock of boats as bright as butterflies. Bunting and banners whipped in the river breeze, and flowers were blown from garlands to turn the river to a meadow through which the barges cut their stately way.

Faris gazed wistfully at the city as it brightened in the growing light. Was Jehan still there, where the banner of Westria marked the residence of the King, or had he gone to the Sacred Grove to wait for her? She wished they could stop here. The serenity in which she had left the College of the Wise was ebbing now. She had scorned her father's disapproval of this marriage, but what if he were right? How would she live among strangers? Instead of the Father of Mountains' familiar clarity, there was only the dark mountain that rose above the river's southern bank, its slopes glowing garnet in this dawn.

"I am sorry that my lady Jessica could not be with you now," said a quiet voice. Faris turned and saw Lord Robert, cloaked as she was against the early chill, the wind ruffling his silver-veined brown hair.

"You need not worry, my Lord," said Faris. "She will meet me soon enough, and there is no reason why she should suffer now."

Robert frowned. "It is not so for all women, I know, but Jessica is always so ill the first three months she carries a child. She wished to come with you – she grew up in Laurelynn and could no doubt tell you many things you wish to know."

Could she tell me what Jehan wants me to be? Could she tell me how to be a Queen? Everyone had been very kind, but she found it hard to believe they really approved of the King's choice. She turned away, not knowing how to respond to Lord Robert's scrupulous courtesy.

The deck vibrated to the pull of the river as the polemen thrust them away from Laurelynn and into the main channel, where the force of the Darkwater's contribution to the river could now be felt. To either side water eased through myriad arms and channels around the ephemeral islands of the delta. Only brick-armored Laurelynn resisted the river's power, and that only by dint of ceaseless vigilance.

The channel was too deep for poling now. The barge jerked as four tugs eased ahead of them and the lines drew taut. Oars flashed in the sun. From the corner of her eye Faris saw something – perhaps a river otter – slip silently into the stream. Red-winged blackbirds dipped around the barge as it passed; the graceful neck of a white heron glimmered among the reeds. This was their land – whatever floods passed over them, they would remain. Faris shivered, thinking with what ease even a minor cataclysm might sweep the works of men away. Robert looked concerned and added the weight of his gray wool cloak to her own.

A little past noon they slid by the narrow strip of Spear Island and drew in to change rowers at Julian's Isle, which was high enough to bear a small village on its back. Faris and the others left the barge for a last chance to stretch their legs before they entered the Bay.

"Was the island named after Julian Starbairn?" asked Farin, slinging his harp across his back and hurrying after them.

"In Seagate they say that King Julian created it," said Lord Robert, pausing to wait for them. "According to the legend, he was caught by his enemies on the riverbank and the Dorada was too swift for him to swim. So he used the Earthstone and the Sea Star to raise up an island from the riverbed."

They began to stroll forward along the path at the edge of the island, turning their faces to the stiff wind and holding on to their cloaks. Wind rustled in the reeds, sighed across the rushing waters, whispered of the not-so-distant sea.

"Is all that Seagate land?" asked Rosemary.

"Everything to the north of us, from the west bank of the Dorada to the sea."

Faris followed Lord Robert's gesture from the bare hills they had just passed, smooth as eggs in a basket with their spring green crisping to summer's gold, to the more rugged hills in the west whose brushy slopes hinted at damp breezes from the Bay. Between them a rolling valley opened to the river's edge.

"Rich land," said Sandremun, peering under his palm at a distant cluster of buildings and a herd of fat cows.

"The field would be a good place to hold Games." Farin eased his harp forward and began to pick out a martial tune.

"It would be a good place for a battle," said Robert. "This is the last crossing calm enough for barges before you reach the Bay, and there's no fortress here to guard it."

Faris turned her gaze back towards the western hills. *Seagate* . . . She wondered how Eric was, and Rosemary's closed face told her that her friend wondered too. The Sacred Grove was in Seagate, and all of the Marches were bound to send representatives to see their new Queen invested with the Jewels. Rosemary would surely see Eric there.

And I will see Jehan.

Tonight she was to keep vigil on the Lady Mountain. Tomorrow she would be initiated and invested with the Jewels, and become Westria's legal Queen. Suddenly the day she had awaited with such longing seemed too soon.

She took a quick step towards the river's southern bank and stopped short, facing the mountain that from this vantage point alone reared free of its surrounding welter of hills. As a dark cone on the horizon it had haunted her journey southward. Here its presence overwhelmed her. She cowered back as if even across the waters its shadow could reach for her.

"You are right – the Red Mountain is a place of power." The Master of the Junipers spoke softly at her side.

Faris swallowed. "Is it evil?"

"Few things are evil in themselves – but many can be used for ill. The power of the Red Mountain is only alien to the needs of men. But we have built a beacon there, for it is the center of Westria." He smiled a little. "Do not be afraid. You will find the Lady Mountain very different."

Faris gazed hopefully downriver, where the hills framed the shimmer of sunlight dancing on the Bay. Yet even when they moved out onto the river once more, she felt the shadow of the Red Mountain following her.

Caolin leaned on the parapet of the beacon tower, watching toy boats creep along the river far below. He recognised the green and gold paint of the barge, but even without that he would have known whom it bore – Faris of Hawkrest Hold, on her way to be made Queen. Soon now Jehan would ride down the road from Misthall, the hunting lodge his father had built on the hills overlooking the Bay, and set sail across it to join her. Caolin envisioned them converging, imagined their meeting tomorrow morning at the Sacred Grove.

No horn call of his could stop their union now.

He felt a pang in his fingers. Curious, he looked down and found them pressed white against the guard rail. He detached them one by one and saw etched into his hands the pattern of the stone.

Caolin stepped back, his gaze passing over the swept platform piled with logs for the Midsummer fire, over the lower slopes of the Red Mountain, moving to the folds of the coastal hills and across the stretch of the Great Valley and the veiled ranges of the Ramparts to the east.

Returning, his eyes found the city of Laurelynn glowing in the afternoon sun. Each toy house was picked out clearly by that golden light. Upriver lay toy villages, to the south a fortress the size of the castle in his chess set. How easy it would be to move them on the board of Westria if only he had the reach.

One could see so clearly from this place! The whole world lay at Caolin's feet. The mazes of politics, the morass of human hopes and fears in which men floundered, unable to see the Kingdom's good and their own, all seemed so insignificant from here. Why did he allow himself to be troubled by a toy woman and a toy man?

Caolin's fingers throbbed and he turned abruptly to the stairs that led down from the beacon to the buildings atop the lower peak. The pale wood of new shingles patterned the weathered roofs, but the red stone walls had needed no repair. He hoped that the workmen had followed his directions about the interior.

He passed the door to the main building and turned a corner to a smaller house where a woman was hanging wet sheets on a clothesline. He pursed his lips and whistled a high, shrill note, then waited as she turned and came towards him, wiping her hands on her apron. The sun was warm here, and her full breasts were half revealed by the loosened lacings at the neck of her gown.

"Hello, Margit," he said pleasantly. "Are you comfortable here? Do you have everything you need?"

Her eyes fixed on his face, brightening as she read his expression. Her mouth twitched and she nodded jerkily, trying to force out the sounds that struggled like trapped birds in her throat. On the right side of her face the pure line of cheek and jaw seemed to have slipped, pulling down her right eyelid as if her features were melting.

Caolin sighed impatiently and with a flicker of his fingers caught her gaze. She was still trying to speak, but he bored into her consciousness with images – of himself entering the Beacon-Keeper's dwelling, of faceless others being turned away, of Margit going into the first room to clean and turning away from its inner door.

"Except for you, no one shall enter that place, and

except for me, no one shall enter the inner room at all!" he whispered. "See, here is the key." He drew from his pouch a key of wrought brass, waved it before her, and drew it softly down the marred side of her face, watching shame flare in her eyes. Then, as casually as he had reached into his pouch for the key, he slipped it into the cleft between her breasts.

"Guard it well, Margit, for if ever you fail me, fair one, it will become a serpent to pierce your heart!" Caolin's mind sent image with word, and as she tried to jerk away his other arm held her against him. The warmth of her breast soothed his bruised fingers, and her heart beat heavily under his hand.

"But you won't do that, Margit – because who would take care of you if it were not for me?" He released her and stood smiling while the fear left her eyes.

He went back to the main dwelling and used his own key to enter the outer room. The walls were lined with bookshelves as he had ordered; a long table stood to one side of the stove and a narrow bed at the other. The mattress was a thin pallet stuffed with straw, and there was no rug on the floor.

He hung his cloak on a hook on the door and, scarcely glancing at the room, pulled out a second, smaller key on a chain at his neck and opened the door to the inner room. Then he stopped, smiled, and turned back to light a candle before going in.

The room was windowless, from floor to ceiling painted a featureless black. At present its only furnishing was a square, blood-colored block of native stone. But Caolin, looking around him, envisioned the altars of the elements that he would fit up in each corner and the glowing lines of the pentangle he would inscribe on the floor.

Now it was only an empty room, echoing his footsteps and smelling faintly of paint. When he had consecrated it, tomorrow, it would become a fortress within which he could build his power. Midsummer was a good time for beginnings.

That was why Jehan had chosen it to make his lady Mistress of the Jewels.

Caolin picked up the candle abruptly and went out again, locking the room carefully behind him.

The porch at the back of the house was braced out over the cliff. Although it was lower than the beacon platform, one could see almost as far. Caolin leaned against the wall, breathing deeply in the still air. The afternoon was softening to a golden dusk. There was a bright haze on the valley, and the river glittered like a stream of gold. His eyes followed it through the straits and were drawn onward where the Lady Mountain watched over the bay with her back to the sea.

The west blazed as if the sun had expanded to fill the sky. Caolin shut his eyes tightly against the glare, but the after-image of the Mountain remained imprinted there.

Jehan stood in the bow of the *Sea Brother*, his eyes fixed on the Lady Mountain. His arm was around the dolphin figurehead and he balanced easily as the ship leaned into the wind, her zigzag course bringing him ever nearer to his goal.

Faris should have reached Seahold, he thought – they should be half way up the Mountain by now.

The sky-glow had deepened to a lucent orange like one of those great opals that were sometimes traded up from Aztlan, and the slopes of the Mountain were draped in a purple veil. Radiance flooded across them in a tidal wave of light, spilling down to edge the forested curves of the islands at the Mountain's feet with ruddy gold.

Jehan heard the sailors laughing together, Sir Randal telling his friend Austin, Lord of Seahold, about the girl he had met in Las Costas. But his heart beat in his chest like a ceremonial drum and he could not move.

Often as a child Jehan had had moments like this, when the world held still and the Source of all Beauty was only a breath away. Only now did he realise how long it had been since he had felt this surge of Joy.

"Lady of Fire," he breathed, "You are beyond all praise – only be as gracious to Faris as You have been to me!"

The ship heeled on to a new tack and Jehan blinked at the light, hearing the sounds of the world around him once more. He straightened a little and shaded his eyes with his hand.

They were sailing through a sea of fire.

9

Mistress of the Jewels

Faris trembled as chill water trickled over her bare breasts, across her belly, and between her thighs. She saw her reflection drawn in pale strokes on the dark surface of the pool and erased again as the water moved, like a vision of something not quite in this world. And in this moment that seemed as likely as the idea that she was really here, being readied for her union with the King.

Smiling, the young priestess from Bongarde rubbed rose soap on a sponge and began to scrub Faris' back. The long day was fading at last, and sunset jeweled her pale skin with drops of crystal fire. Another priestess dipped water in a shell and tipped it over Faris' shoulders, while a third combed out the long, shining strands of her hair. The dark robes of the older women made deeper shadows among the laurel trees that edged the pool; their chanting focused the hush of the mountainside.

Faris stood rigid, though each soft touch seared her skin. She ought to welcome this cleansing after her long journey. Why did she feel as if they were stripping away layers of her soul? She had undergone such ritual baths before – at her puberty ceremony, and before that first Initiation that all Westrians shared, when she had chosen her name. Was it because these strangers could see all her imperfections, her scar? But here were none of those shocked glances too quickly turned aside that she had learned to dread. She was being judged by other standards now.

Goosebumps pebbled her skin as the water touched her again.

"Are you cold, my Lady? Tomorrow you will be warm."

The sponge caressed Faris' side. She felt the other woman's memories of hard flesh pressing her own – a man's flesh, like that alien body that would soon possess hers.

Am I afraid of that? she wondered. *I wanted Jehan to take me when we were in the cave, but then it was something between him and me, not this ceremonial offering to the service of Westria!*

"Surely the Lady has favored you," said one of the priestesses, her eyes dwelling on Faris' delicately modeled breasts.

Faris' memory shied from the chime of silver bells. The barrier she had tried to draw around herself shimmered and misted away. Her flesh felt scarcely more substantial, as though her essence were diffusing through it into the soft summer air.

Across the water she met the cold gaze of the Mistress of the College of the Wise, the dark planes of her face as unyielding as the slopes of the Father of Mountains. Faris straightened, wondering if the old woman sensed her fear.

I am Faris! She clung to her identity. *I am thin and scarred and pale. There are things inside me that must not get free, and I know nothing of men and the world. What am I doing here?* Her father's accusations haunted her.

I am going to be Mistress of the Jewels, came the answer, and she did not know if the words were hers or those of another will.

Faris stepped forward in involuntary protest, but the priestesses surrounded her and drew her down to the cold embrace of the mountain pool. For a moment she lay still, her rosy nipples peeping above the surface of the water and her black hair swirling about her like waterweed, then she struggled to her feet. The laughter of the other women echoed against the trees.

I am Faris and I will not let you steal my soul! Warm tears slid down her cheeks to mingle with the cold waters below.

Still laughing, the girls helped her out of the pool, rubbed her dry, and clad her in an undyed linen gown. The sky had deepened to a translucent blue edged by a black fretwork of trees. Through their branches Faris glimpsed the mocking twinkle of the Lady's star.

By the time they had brought Faris to the meadow where she would keep vigil that night, day was only a memory in the west and scattered stars were blooming in the sky like the first daisies in a field that will soon be white with flowers.

The faces of the priestesses glimmered pale within their hoods as they embraced her. Then they turned away and their black robes merged with the shadows, but Faris heard their singing long after they had disappeared.

> Queen among mountains with head star-crowned
> Above the sea,
> Blue-cloaked, your vigil guards the land –
> Watch over me!
> As a mother lays her child to sleep
> Upon her breast,
> Oh, let me seek your shelter now
> And give me rest. . . .

Faris cast herself down among the blankets they had left for her, buried her face in the rough wool, and cried.

A cricket sang nearby, then another. Tree frogs chirred in deeper harmony from the woods on the other side of the meadow. Faris sat up, sniffling, but the concert went on, oblivious to her pain. A last shudder shook her, then she set herself to fold her blankets into a bed.

When she lay down again, she found that the earth still held the warmth of the day, though the hay-scented breeze that played with her drying hair was cool. The steady pressure of the ground was obscurely comforting. This at least was dependable and real. Through the trees she glimpsed the rising moon. Her eyes closed.

When Faris became aware once more, the world was filled with light.

Halfway across the heavens the white moon rode like a queen, paled the stars, and awed the earth to still humility. Her cold light glittered on the tops of leaves. It iced the edges of the bending grass, yet lit the world to deeper mystery.

Something dappled shadows through the trees. Faris thought of maidens crowned with bloom she had seen dancing at the Hold. She heard a singing like the top note of a viol, played at the edge of sound. She shivered then – shapes wavered at the limits of her sight, more luminous than moonlight. Sweet they sang, and drifted towards her through the crystal grass, and beckoned to her with hands that brimmed with light.

Faris' memory strained for the sound of human song, the taste of fresh-baked bread, Jehan's hard strength to hold her. But the moon's strange music drew her to her feet. She freed the gown that weighed so heavily and loosed the shadowed masses of her hair and danced.

Faris woke to a world of shadows, struggled free of her blankets, and looked around her, yawning and rubbing her eyes. She had dreamed – what had she dreamed? Through a gap in the trees she glimpsed mist-shrouded slopes falling sheer to the Bay. The water had the soft sheen of the inside of a shell, an iridescent lavender that shimmered into rose as the light increased. Then the sun lifted above the eastern hills and the transparent world grew solid once again.

Still bemused by the memory of music, Faris began the salutation to the dawn. Then she stopped. Before her she saw the dewy glitter of the meadow scrolled by the printing of a single pair of feet. She *had* danced then – it had not been only a dream. She shivered, wondering, if such things could come to her in her dreams, what the focused evocations of this Initiation would do.

The sudden pounding of her heart was echoed by the inexorable beat of a ceremonial drum. Faris stood still, waiting for them to come for her.

Coalin saluted the dawn from the top of the Red Mountain. Then, ignoring the golden-misted valley stretched below, he went back into the house. To finish the task for which he had stayed on the Mountain, he must not waste a single moment of the day.

He had bathed the night before. Now he carefully combed his fair hair and put on a new robe of undyed linen that he had sewn himself. His tools were laid out neatly on the table. It was time to begin furnishing and consecrating the temple in which he could become a Master – of his own powers.

Taking a deep breath, Caolin picked up his sword. He smiled a little as light quavered its length and picked out his own name etched into the blade. He had filed it from a blank of Elayan steel himself and bound it on a hilt of bone. He doubted that it would stand up to use in battle, but it was not intended to defend him from tangible foes.

The floor creaked beneath his bare feet as he moved to the open door of the inner room. His heart was beating a little faster than usual, but his movements remained graceful and deliberate. He was depending on careful study for his results today, not on intuition or the chance assistance of friendly powers.

Carefully he set the point of his blade to the jamb of the door.

"In the names of the four elements and of that Power that rules them all, I enclose this temple for my own uses by means of this barrier."

Drawing the blade deosil along the base of the wall from right to left as he faced it – the way of the sun – he visualised a mist rising from the scratch it left along the floor, which shone faintly and hardened as it grew. When he reached the corner, he poked the blade through the open window, went out to the porch where he picked it up again, and continued around the outside, reentering the same way and finishing at the other side of the door.

Caolin's mind firmed and strengthened the barrier, bringing it over the building until the inner room was enclosed by a gleaming shell. He could not see it with his physical eyes – it was a mental construct, the foundation of a series of images that would establish his temple at once on the physical and psychic planes. According to his studies, the temple was now sealed everywhere but at the door to entry by any elemental, thought-form, human suggestion, or spell.

He leaned the blade against the wall and rested for a moment, shrugging his shoulders to release their tension. Then his mouth firmed and he cleared his mind of all but his task. He prepared to go in.

"You are to go in." The priestess of the Grove slipped her hands into the green sleeves of her robe and nodded to Faris.

Sunlight, filtered and refracted by countless leaves, bathed their faces in greenish light. The clearing before her was bare except for a veiling of emerald moss. She looked up at a single redwood, huge-girthed and scarred by many winters, yet green as a sapling that has just unfurled its leaves to the sun.

Faris took a few uncertain steps forward, then stopped short.

Like a reflection broken by a falling leaf, the great redwood dislimned. Like an image forming as the water stills, it took shape once more. But now it was a man – crowned with green locks, clothed and skinned roughly in reddish-brown, but human in form. His eyes were as deep as the well of time.

Faris clasped her hands to still their trembling, knowing that she stood before the Lord of the Trees.

"Fair as the lily flower, daughter of the north, I welcome you." His voice whispered through her understanding like the rushing of wind through many leaves.

"My Lord, I thank you."

He sighed. "I was first among the First People to sign the Covenant your mothers made, and it is my right to question all who come here to be sealed to the Jewels of Power. Here they begin their task, and here they are laid to rest when their work is done."

The rich smell of damp earth dizzied her. What did he want her to say?

"You will have honor when you rule this land – will you honor us? You will keep men from sinning against each other – will you punish them when they sin against the other kindreds? Will you be willing to lose all that all may be saved?"

Yes . . . no! What do you mean? Faris struggled with questions, but a great wind roared about her, and when she could see again, both the Lord of the Trees and the clearing were gone.

A pit gaped before her feet. Beside it sat an armed man whose sword gleamed upon his knees. He rose and extended the sword till its point hovered above her heart.

"What is your name?"

"My name is Faris," she whispered, peering at him to see if it was Jehan.

"Not here," he said in a voice like iron, a stranger's voice. "Here your name is Seeker After Truth, until you shall earn a greater one." He lowered the sword and grasped her hand.

"Wait –" She was not yet sure what she had promised to the Lord of the Trees. She needed time.

"Enter in the name of the Maker of All Things!" The warrior stepped into the pit. She tried to hang back, but he drew her after him down the steps and into the darkness.

Caolin paced sunwise around the dark room, scattering pinches of salt from the earthenware bowl in his hand.

"Be this temple cleansed of all spirits of whatever kind! By all the powers of earth I bid ye begone!"

When he had finished his circuit, he replaced the bowl in the other room, returned with the aspergillum filled with consecrated water, and repeated the procedure. The cleansing was performed a third time with a censer smoking with myrrh, and lastly with a candle that searched every corner of the room. Then swiftly he drew the sword across the entryway.

Caolin stood still in the midst of the room, hearing no sounds but his own breathing and the sigh of wind on the mountaintop. It had been long since he had allowed himself to regret the lack of extra sensitivity that would have given him firsthand knowledge that the room was cleansed. But he had based his life on the ability to do without it. He was depending now on both his learning and his will, using the knowledge of the College of the Wise while rejecting both their support and their authority.

"It will succeed," he murmured. "It must!" He turned to each corner of the room and lifted his arms in invocation.

"I, Caolin, do dedicate this temple to the search for knowledge and mastery – of the powers that lie in the world around me, and of those that lie hidden within me! In the names of the four elements I dedicate it, and through that Power by which the elements were made, and on the foundation of this Mountain upon which I stand. If I betray my own truth, may it betray me!"

The floor quivered. Caolin stepped to keep his balance, wondering if the excitement had dizzied him. The blood was singing along his veins.

The temple was ready now, and it was time to furnish it.

Four steps down, then Faris stumbled across an open space heavy with the smell of damp earth. She bumped into a wall of dirt that crumbled at her touch and struck out in panic as her hood was pulled over her eyes.

Metal knocked hollowly against wood nearby. From some unimaginable distance came a reply – "Who comes to the sacred circle?"

"The Guardian of the Gate brings a candidate to the Mysteries." The sentinel's voice was very close. Faris groped, touched cold armor, and clung to the arm it covered.

"Has she been purified according to the Law?"

"All things have been done as the Law prescribes."

"Then enter."

Wood scraped on stone. Gasping, Faris stumbled upward and realised that she had come within the sanctuary.

"Seeker, what are you looking for?" The voice vibrated around her. How must she reply? Jehan would be ashamed if she could not remember, and whatever must happen could not be as terrible as her imaginings.

"I walk in darkness and I seek a door . . . the elements within me are at war." She took a breath and added uncertainly, "The Jewels of Westria have summoned me, and now I seek the wisdom to obey."

There was a short silence. "Who speaks for her?"

"I speak for the College." Faris recognised the harsh sweetness of the voice of the Master of the Junipers.

"I speak for the Jewels!" The second voice was young, and she vibrated to it like a harpstring whose mate is plucked.

A gentle hand put back her hood and she blinked in the sudden light.

All was well. This was still grass beneath her feet, and a circle of redwoods around it, the same sun and sky. She was still in the world she knew. Gradually her eyes adjusted and she saw the Mistress of the College watching her across an altar of granite. She glimpsed other figures positioned around the circle but could not look at them. To either side of the altar two pillars, black and white, pointed to the sky. Beyond them – was that Jehan? Her eyes dazzled again.

"Come."

The Master of the Junipers gave her a welcoming smile and led her to kneel at the central altar with her fingertips touching the stone. Atop it sunfire danced in a golden bowl.

The Mistress of the College began to administer the oath, and the clarity of her voice calmed Faris; the words echoed in her soul to affirm an orderly reality.

"I, kneeling in the presence of these mysteries . . . knowing nothing and having now no will, promise thus – not to speak foolishly of what I may learn or to cease my striving towards the eternal goal, and never to debase what powers I gain, however tempted, to any creature's harm or to the weakening of the Covenant.

"And if I break this oath, then strike me down ye, who journeying upon the winds, can strike where no man can and slay where no man may!"

There was a pause, and Faris saw the shadow of the sentinel's sword poised across the stone. Her throat dried with the knowledge that her own lips were sentencing her, but she went on.

"And as I bow me now beneath this sword, I bind me to their justice with my word. This by my name and by my soul I swear and by that which is All and Everywhere."

Faris clung to the stone altar for her life. Gently the Master of the Junipers helped her to rise. Through her weakened barriers she felt the gentle glow of his concern for her.

"Having been so spoken for, and having so answered, and having so sworn, you may now see the hidden things," said the Mistress in a voice like sunlight. "Let the Mystery of Earth begin!"

Caolin knelt before the northern corner of his temple and lit the yellow candles in front of the tiered altar there. At its top lay a chunk of rock from the Red Mountain's peak. Lower steps bore an earthenware dish of salt and a wicker platter holding a clod of earth with a rooted stalk of grain.

All of these represented aspects of the strength he wanted to claim – the vigor of the soil, the ordered structure of salt crystals, and above all the enduring and eternal resistance of stone.

Slowly he spoke the words of consecration.

"I am Earth, the foundation, the sphere in which all the elements are conjoined."

The words came from the figure before Faris, but the sound vibrated from the ground on which She stood. Her gown folded green-flecked russet highlights and umber shadows around the curves and hollows of a body as rich as the land in flower, below a face like weather-sculptured hills, stripped of all but beauty.

"Hail, Lady of Earth, in whom all things take form!" The litany echoed from the lips of the Mistress of the College, of the Master, of all those within the circle, and as it seemed to Faris, even from the leaves and blades of grass.

"I am Earth. My body is the living soil, the rocks are my bones, the metals flow in my veins. The waves may beat against me, the winds buffet, me, the fire sweep over me, but I abide."

Faris slumped beneath the weight of earth. Into the darkness of the Lady's shadowed eyes she fell; rock formed around her bones. By countless colored strata she was pressed; she felt the interplay of stress and shift and cherished the integrity of jewels that would never see the light. She sensed the elementals' inner forms, which told stone how to grow. She slept a million years.

"I am Earth. I am the Bride and the Mother. Sun and rain quicken me; life springs from my womb to ascend into the heavens once more. From me come all green and growing things."

Faris felt life tingle through her veins, thrust with fierce persistence towards the light, knew warmth, and swayed to a pine-scented breeze. Once more she bowed before the Lord of Trees and danced with spirits sprung from leaf or flower. In joy she rose to life, in joy returned herself to pregnant darkness once again.

"Child of Earth, from Me all your substance comes. Until the end of time when I am united with the Lord of Heaven once more, Earth I am and will remain."

Faris' eyes dazzled. She looked away and remembered who she was and where.

"As you have seen and understood, so shall you be consecrated." The Priestess of Earth sprinkled her with salt, and the Master of the Junipers draped a robe of brown linen over her and turned her towards the altar again.

Someone was coming to her through the light. Faris bit back a cry of greeting as she saw Jehan, holding a girdle whose clasp bore a jewel that shone like sunset shining through leaves. His lips shaped her name, shaped a smile for her. Then she felt the cool touch of the Earthstone on her forehead, her breast, her loins.

Light and shadow swirled around her. For a moment she felt all the growing things in Westria rejoicing in the sunlight, reached with their roots into the earth, knew the structure of the rock beneath that soil as she had never known her own bones. Understanding Earth, she knew suddenly how one might work with it – not forcing it to her will but willing in harmony with its nature and her own.

"Initiate of the Mystery of Earth, I invest you with its power."

Carefully Caolin poured the consecrated water from its crystal vial into the chalice of silver set with moonstones. He raised it reverently and set it on the altar he had placed in the western corner of the room. Water, he thought, so soft, so necessary, which could yet strip branches from great trees in its fury, and in its patience wear away stone. He needed water's strength.

He lit the silver candles and set them down. From the depths of the chalice glimmered a star of light. Like the Sea Star . . .

Caolin thrust the thought from his mind. Let Jehan and Faris play with their toys – he would make his own magic!

The cool touch of water on her face brought Faris back to the clearing once more. She shook her head impatiently, looking for Jehan.

I am Faris, and this is the Sacred Grove of Westria. This is solid earth that I am standing on.

But she felt the strength of that earth flowing up from her bare feet through her bones and knew with a tremor of panic that she was not entirely Faris . . . not anymore.

Water touched her again and she focused on the figure before her.

His pale face filled her vision as the moon had filled the sky. His gray robe shimmered with half-seen rainbow tones – purple, blue, and green – and he bore a silver chalice in his hand.

"I am Water – water of the sky, water of the sea, water of life in man's blood, of death in his tears."

"Hail, Lord of the Waters, nourisher of all things!"

"I am the mist on the mountains, the rain that soaks the earth, and the storm that washes all away. Drop by drop I conquer the hardest rocks; my floods overwhelm the nations; I sink forests and fill plains; from the shores I carve new dominions for the sea."

The grass before her swayed in waves of gray. She sank; bright-armored fish escorted her beyond great forms that stirred dimly in the deeps. She floated, wondering. Then dolphins came and whistled challenge till she joined their game. From sapphire depths in dazzling bursts of spray, she fountained skyward, shimmered as a cloud, rejoined the earth as rainfall, trickled through its hidden places, and became the steady flow of a dark stream that sought the sea.

The cycle was repeated until Faris realised that it was water from the chalice that was drenching her, and that her brown robe had been replaced by one of silky sea green. Light blazed from a stone all the colors of the sea. She tried to see Jehan beyond it, but its touch plunged her into the depths once more.

She felt at once the waters flowing through her own body and through the sea and answered with the waters to the call of the moon. She knew how to flow with them now, to share their power.

"Initiate of the Mystery of Water, I invest you."

Caolin coughed as the sweet smoke caught at his lungs, swirled away from the incense in the brass bowl, and billowed around the room. He went on with the ritual, intoning both dedications and responses as he set in place the wand, the feather, and the bell. The Lord of the Winds was also Lord of Magic, ruler of airborne words that shaped being out of will.

His hand trembled a little as he lit the blue candles, and he forced himself not to hurry, not to give way to the strain of so long a focusing of his will. At the Sacred Grove the joined power of half the College of the Wise was bent on the Initiation of one weak girl. Caolin felt a bitter pride that he must do all alone.

For a moment he wished he had brought someone to assist him. But whom could he have asked? It was no crime for a man to make a temple for the perfecting of his own soul, but building it on the Red Mountain might be considered a presumption by some. Whom could he have trusted not to tell a busybody such as the Master of the Junipers what he had done?

Caolin's mouth quirked as he thought of Ordrey stumbling in this darkness, pictured the responses coming from Ercul Ashe's prim mouth. No – better to be alone than to work with such faulty tools, even though his back ached with weariness and the smoke stung his eyes.

Faris turned her face to the wind and breathed deeply, slowly, trying to reorient herself. The spicy scent of the redwoods drifted through the air; the warm breeze was drying the water from her face and hair. The Master of the Junipers had brought her to the eastern side of the circle, she did not remember how.

But she no longer wondered whether Jehan was there – she felt at once the yielding femininity of earth in her own body and its unyielding strength in his; the gentle tides of the sea and the fury of the storm. She looked back over her

213

shoulder at the two pillars – feminine and masculine, dark and light – and understood why they were there.

The breeze chilled, nipped her cheeks as if it had swept down from snowfields or through the starry reaches of the sky. The air she breathed in tingled through her body, sharpening hearing and sight.

"I am Air – the wind of heaven and the breath of life."

The priest before her had the smooth features of a boy and ageless, merry eyes. The wind whipped his orange robes around him and ruffled his pale hair.

"I draw both heat and cold across the world, carrying the clouds from the sea to give their blessing to the land, to bear seed to the earth and pollen to the flower. Terrible as thunder I can be, or softer than a feather on a breeze." His words were lost in a roaring of wind.

Faris felt the world whirl away, tossed upward with a speed that took her breath, then sank in lazy spirals; felt the wind ruffle feathers, stretched, and spread her wings. She eyed the scrambled patterns of the land with an eagle's vision. Disdaining gravity, she sported with the wind, found in the sky a kingdom freer than mere men could ever know.

"And yet I also bear the sounds that stir your soul – the words by which you understand the world."

A bell's sweet chime divided sight from sound, and sudden harmony of harp and horn laid note by note a pattern on the air that drew her trembling earthward once again.

"What is your name?"
• "Seeker After Truth."
"Who were you?"
"Faris."
"What are you?"
"A woman."

Question and answer followed without cease. Word by word he drew from her the names from which she had built her identity – asking, comparing, and denying them till she no longer knew which ones were true.

Nameless, she stared at him while the soft clouds of incense swirled around her and they laid the orange robe

214

across her shoulders. Jehan held out to her a crystal filled with light, and as it touched her she knew her name, and his, and the names of every thing and creature in the land.

"Initiate of the Mystery of Air . . ."

The light of three pairs of candles danced among the shadows. It gleamed fitfully on silver and brass, glowed on cloth and earthenware, alternately revealing and disguising the trappings of the altars of earth and water and air. Caolin breathed carefully, steadying himself for the final consecration.

Gently he set the large candle on the highest tier of the altar above the sword. The candles were red; the candlesticks of polished copper, the Lady's own metal.

The Lady – whose blessing was being invoked on the union of Jehan and Faris even now. Caolin's head ached with the effort to keep from crying out, to retain control. He brought the taper to the candles on the altar of Fire and touched them to life.

"What can warm can also burn," he breathed. "The spirit of fire is no one's possession, and it too will serve me."

He stared into the candlelight, but all he could see in its steady flame was the light of Jehan's eyes when Faris' message came to him. Caolin remembered a time, long ago, when Jehan's eyes had held such a glow when they looked on him.

Had that also been the work of the Lady of Fire?

Jehan . . .

"Now begins the Mystery of Fire!"

Her heart still ringing with his name, Faris looked from Jehan to the Mistress of the College, and beyond her to the figure towards whom the Master was now leading her. She felt his tension as they approached, glanced at his face and wondered what he feared to see. Then she met the eyes of the Priestess of Fire and sensed Jehan's joy as he sensed hers.

"I am the fire of light and life, and love."

The priestess' robes were made of some shiny stuff shot interchangeably with emerald and flame. They fluttered around her in a blast of heat that seemed to come from the copper lamp she held. Its flame caught Faris' eye and drew her into the heart of fire.

"I am the fire at earth's core, the fire of life in man or animal, the fire of passion and redeeming love."

Shadows circled Faris. Breaching them, she flared against the heavens in a burst of flame. She soared among the stars, became the sun, became the light that fell to earth once more. Burning in each leaf, from light new substance formed; consumed by living things, their bodies made; burned in their blood, gave them the heat to move and join in union with their kind.

And still the fire burned before her eyes, the heat surrounded her, consuming her until she felt herself only a shell through which the light could glow. The brilliance focused to a point, it neared till she could scarcely see. Then she felt fire sear her brow and saw herself reflected in Jehan's eyes.

"Initiate of the Mystery . . ."

Faris scarcely heard. Nor did it matter when Jehan removed the Jewel of Fire from her brow. She walked with his feet, felt him walk within her as she was led around the circle once more. She radiated the steady warmth of every hearthfire in the land; she burned in the veins of every moving creature, transforming matter into energy; she felt the gentle glow of affection between long-wedded pairs, the trust of comrades, the ecstasy of lovers who were each other's fuel. For a moment she sensed the passion of Caolin's mind, bent on his task.

She stood and burned with unconsuming Light.

Caolin had put on a white robe. He stood before the naked stone in the center of his temple and bowed before it. The golden vessel upon it was empty still, as the altar beneath it was still merely stone. He had consecrated the four corners to the four elements upon whose interaction all earthly life depended, but the parts were still less than the whole.

His business was with the center now – the balance, the integration, the focusing of power.

bzl   Caolin turned to his left, continued the circle to the altar of Earth, and laid his hands on the heap of coal piled there.

"Creature of Earth, into you I summon all Earth's power." He visualised all the strengths with which he had hallowed the altar flowing through the hard, powdery surfaces of the lumps of coal. Then he turned again and bore them to the golden basin on the altar.

He moved to the altar of Water then, felt for the brittle heap of dried seaweed he had placed there, and willed into it all the slow strength of the sea. Then he added this fuel to the coals. From the altar of Air he brought incense, placing special intensity in his invocation of the element whose presence was as vital to the life of the fire as it was to his own.

Then he turned to the altar of Fire, whose flame, like all fire, had come originally from the incandescence of the sun. He took a white taper and touched it to the candle, holding his breath as the spark ran down the wax-coated fibers, strengthened, and became a flame.

"Creature of Fire, you are the seed of Light, the catalyst in which all elements will join."

He stood and, holding the taper carefully, began to pace around the room. Softly at first, he intoned names of the elements, the attributes with which he had invested them. As he moved his voice strengthened until it rang against the confines of his skull as it echoed from the walls of the room.

Dizzy, his pulse still pounding with the rhythm of his march, Caolin turned to the central altar at last and thrust the taper into the fuel laid in the golden bowl. It flared in blue sparks and fizzled, flared once more. Caolin's breath caught as he willed it to live. His nostrils prickled with mixed scents of sandalwood and sea wrack as light flickered across the surface of the bowl and the fuel crackled, hissed, and then settled to a steadier glow.

Caolin let the taper rest on the edge of the bowl, forced everything from his mind except the powers on which he was drawing now, and set his hands flat upon the naked stone to either side of the bowl.

"In the name of Earth!

"In the name of Water!

"In the name of Air!

"In the name of Fire!"

His shout became a scream as he willed the forces of all the elements into the altar stone.

Breathless, his sight darkened, his balance gave way. Then he realised that it was not his own weakness but the stone itself that trembled beneath his hands. The floor quivered; there was a deep rumbling, like some great animal stirring in its sleep. Caolin's body convulsed as he received back through his hands all the focused power he had sent through the altar stone into the Mountain's heart.

Caolin cried out again, unable to take his hands from the stone. For a moment he knew the interplay of the elements not with his conscious mind alone, but with every cell of his body, and the passive power of the Mountain balanced the positive energy of his will.

For an instant the sealed rooms in his soul were thrown open, and for the second time in his life he was not alone.

Mistress of the Jewels!

Faris stood before the central altar in the Sacred Grove, eyes dazzled by its pure flame. Her pulse jumped to the steady beating of her heart; her ears throbbed; the ground trembled beneath her feet.

"Mistress of the Jewels!"

Her sight cleared and Faris knew that it was the beating of a drum she heard and that the ground was being shaken by dancing feet. They had clad her anew in a priestess' black robe.

She stood still, trying to master her body – her sight, her breathing, her balance on the earth. But too much had been added to her awareness. She felt within her the interplay of the elements; her consciousness slipped back and forth between Faris the human woman and the Lady of Westria, whose body was the land, whose blood was its rivers and streams, whose breath was the wind, whose life was the light in which it grew.

The priests and priestesses of the four elements had disappeared. Faris saw instead two circles – men robed in white, women robed in black – moving around the pillars and the altar stone. She and the pillars formed two sides of a square at right angles to the square that the elements had made. The opposite angle – Faris glimpsed something white beyond the dazzle of the altar fire . . . was it Jehan?

Blinking, she tried to find among the dancers' faces some she knew, but all were strangers, closed upon a knowledge she did not share. The black circle drew inward; she saw the Mistress of the College reaching for her, pulling her into the dance. She followed unresisting, her bare feet carrying her sideways to the steady beat of the drum. The circle bore her to the other side of the altar, but now there was no one there.

And yet she felt the presence of an Opposite that orbited the center just as she did, balancing her. And in response her awareness of the elements within her changed. She felt the sweetness of the Lady of Flowers and the riches of the Harvest Queen, and across from Her, the hard strength of the Lord of Stone. The chaste simplicity of the Moon drew through her body the tides of the sea, and then she bowed to the driving power of the Lord of Wave and Storm. She was the breath of Spring upon the air, and she fled before the force of the Wind; she was the gentle hearthfire, reflecting the wildfire's flame.

Though her skin burned, she was shivering. She felt a Presence in the air around her, and in some still untouched corner of her mind remembered the Beltane ceremony and how she had been possessed, and was afraid. What waited to use her body now, and for what ends? Where was Jehan?

The other dancers were leaving, black and white robes pairing and disappearing through the trees. But Faris could not follow them. The drum held her in the circle and the Presences around her became greater – the Lady of Wisdom, the Lady of Stars, and She who is the Darkness from which all is born and to which it must return.

Then Faris was alone, and the drum stilled at last. She swayed, trembling. The energy that had sustained her ebbed. She slipped to her knees.

Have mercy upon me, have mercy upon me, O Thou Who Art . . . But she knew not to whom nor for what she prayed. All the goddesses who overshadowed her were merging into one Goddess in response to that other Presence that approached her now. Westria waited for the coming of the King.

Be not afraid.

Faris turned slowly to face it, saw a figure edged in light. It moved into the shadow of the pillar and she recognised Jehan. Light and shadow transformed him as he came towards her. He had shed his robe, and his broad shoulders and narrow hips, his triumphant masculinity, belonged equally to man and to god.

The air burned.

He came to her. His hands loosed the clasps of her gown and it pooled about her knees. His lips saluted her brow, her breast; he bent to her thighs. She reached out to him and tried to shape his name.

But as He rose again to press her down upon the earth, His features were lost in a blaze of light.

Jehan . . .

Her flesh glowed with an answering radiance into which her consciousness pursued his name and was consumed.

The Goddess opened Her thighs to receive the God.

10

The Evening Star

They say a star has come to rest
In peace at last upon your breast –
Oh, sister, will you be the same . . .

Farin muttered the lines, broke off, and shook his head.
Faris' dream of the star, dimly remembered from what
seemed a lifetime ago, had haunted him since dawn. He
recalled promising to make a song about her dream if she
would tell it to them, and suddenly the need to write it
was troubling him, not for her sake, but for his own. He
stood alone in the midst of the throng that milled before the
garlanded platform where the King would shortly show the
new lady of Westria to her people, struggling for the words
that would tell him what he wanted to say.

Like an accompaniment beneath the melody of his
thoughts, he felt the patient benevolence of the Sacred
Wood, charged now with something more – a tension as
if the world were about to explode in terror or in joy. A
chill brushed Farin's skin.

Oh, sister, are you now the same
In any aspect but your name,
As she . . .

"Surely the ceremony should be finished by now. Do you think something has gone wrong?" Rosemary paused beside him.

Farin lost his thought and peered impatiently at the slant of the sunlight through the redwoods. The trees shone in that golden light as if they had acquired an extra measure of reality.

"Is it so late?" he muttered. "How long should it take? Why don't you ask Eric – he came here with his father to see Jehan invested with the Jewels fifteen years ago."

As she . . . As she who was my other self . . . He tried to concentrate, but the tension around him was making it hard to breathe.

Rosemary looked uncertainly at Eric, who stood before the platform like a sentinel. The vulnerability in her face struck Farin with sudden misgiving. It was too like the way Eric and Stefan and the others had gazed at Faris not so long ago. Did Rosemary love Eric? If so, he pitied her and felt an obscure gratitude that he had escaped being kindled by the passion that spread like wildfire around him.

Beyond Eric, Sandremun was talking with Lord Brian of Las Costas. As Farin watched, Brian turned to Eric, grinned, and started to take his arm. Eric stiffened and jerked away with an oath. Brian's face reddened and his hand drifted towards his sword, but Sandremun moved between them saying something that made Brian laugh, and led him away.

"Never mind," Farin said quickly. "I'm sure things are going well. Faris and I have always been so close – remember, she knew I was going to be wounded. I would feel it if she came to any harm!"

The sun backlighted Rosemary's hair to a halo of gold but her eyes were shadowed. "I know that you and she *were* close . . ." She gestured helplessly.

Farin stared at her. *As she who springing from one birth, was twin in soul as twin on earth . . .* No, that was not quite what he wanted to say.

The tension broke.

Farin gasped and staggered like someone turning a corner out of a strong wind. He felt Rosemary's grip bruise his arm, but his eyes were dazzled, his spirit a fountain of joy. The crowd stilled, then broke into excited chatter once more.

"Did you feel that?" he whispered when he could speak again.

"Yes. They must have felt that all the way to the College of the Wise. The Goddess has merged with the God and made a channel for the One. Such a joining renews the world!"

The crowd around them shouted in a babel of accents from every Province in Westria. Farin relaxed and found himself able to focus on the world around him once more.

"Praise to the Maker of all Things that the King has given us a Lady!" came a woman's voice with the lilt of Las Costas. "They say she's from the Corona – one of the Lord Commander's daughters."

"No, Dorian, it was her sister that married the Lord Commander's son – you can see him over there talking to Lord Brian."

Farin sighed and looked after the two women as they passed. *As twin on earth . . .* That was not quite it. He tried to find another line, but his mind homed on what he had just felt. Had Faris caused that? What then had she become?

"Rodrigo said that Lady Faris is as beautiful as the Lady of Light. She must be, considering the women who have been in and out of Jehan's bed!"

Two men laughed, and Farin stifled an impulse to wipe the names of his sister and the King off their lips with his fists. How could they understand?

He sighed instead. Already the legends were beginning – soon reports would name Faris as beautiful as Auriane the Golden Queen or Fiona Firehair. He knew that she could be pretty, but he remembered too vividly other times – Faris smudged and sweaty from working in the garden, or with her face blotched from fever. He remembered how she had looked last night when they took her up the Lady Mountain, pale as paper and bowed beneath the weight of her own hair.

And yet Jehan had chosen her for his mate from among the beauties of a kingdom. That was the mystery. What had the King seen in Faris that her brother, after twenty years of living as close to her as one breath to another, could not see?

> As she who was a twin to me
> In birth, in face, in memory?

Rosemary made a stifled sound beside him. Farin groped for the next verse, swore, and then stopped, hearing what she had heard. Silence was spreading through the crowd as spilled oil calms a troubled pool. And deeply, as if all the people of Westria shared a single heart, came the steady pulse of the ceremonial drum.

Step by step the people moved towards the platform from the groups in which they had been talking. Farin grasped Rosemary's hand and drew her towards Eric, around whose tall figure people eddied like water around a rock. The three of them stood together as the crowd packed itself around them and the last whispers died away.

The drumbeat grew louder. Farin felt a collective sigh as the lines of priests and priestesses in their white and black robes appeared through the trees.

"The Mistress of the College." Rosemary nodded towards the woman who led them, her hair like a silver crown above her black robe. Her dark face held a remote gentleness now.

Farin glanced towards the priest who walked beside her and his eyes narrowed. Surely that was the Master of the Junipers, but how strange he looked. Was it the white robe that made him seem so tall, that gave him the air of a prince as he came towards them?

Praise the Lord and Lady, praise the One
Who Self-divided, is at once Self-known,
And from that knowledge manifests the world!

Farin's song disappeared like a raindrop into the sea.
"Praise the Lord and Lady, Praise the One!" The earth
trembled as the people responded to the litany.

"They're coming." The whisper stirred the crowd. Faris
swallowed, straining to recognise the black-and-white-
robed figures as they mounted the platform and spread
out to either side of the thrones.

They're coming.

Farin saw the King first, looking tired but triumphant,
with the four Jewels of Westria glittering from his loins
and waist and breast and brow. His face held the joy
of a man who has achieved his desire. He disappeared
momentarily behind the platform, then Farin saw him
climbing the stairs.

"Sweet flowers of spring, will marriage do that to me?"
Rosemary's shaken whisper drew Farin's attention from
Jehan to his Queen.

It was not Faris.

Certainly this woman wore his sister's slim body and
shadowy hair and eyes, but the expression in those eyes
was none that he had ever seen Faris wear – none that any
human woman could wear, at once sensual and innocent,
infinitely compassionate and proud. Farin remembered
the Beltane Festival and understood that it was the Goddess looking out of Faris' eyes.

Oh, sister . . . are you now the same?

"All hail Jehan, Lord of Westria and Master of the Jewels!" the people cried until he smiled and held up his hand
to still them.

"As I am King of Westria, I have chosen my Queen; as I
am Lord, I have given you a Lady for this land – does any
here deny my choice?"

"All hail the Queen!"

The sunlight glistened on Faris' hair as she stepped

forward and smiled at the people whose cheering shook the trees.

"As Master of the Jewels, I declare to you that she has been initiated into the Mysteries and may now bear the Jewels of Power," Jehan added when at last they were quiet again.

There was no response to this but a hastily stifled whisper as someone hoped that the Initiation had been a thorough one, since it was said that the Jewels would blast any who bore them otherwise. Tension grew.

Jehan unclasped his girdle of embroidered linen and bound it above the swell of Faris' thighs. The Earthstone flickered suddenly like a forest in the sunlight as she turned to face the people again.

In Her footsteps spring the rainbowed flowers . . . . Words trembled on Farin's lips, but whether they were his own or some hymn he did not know.

The silver mail of the belt that bore the Sea Star flashed in the sunlight as the King fastened it around Faris' waist, and the great stone flared with sapphire light. He drew the Wind Crystal in its eagle-winged sitting from around his neck and passed the chain over her head.

Farin's breath caught, seeing it flame like a star upon her breast. He had heard once that the Wind Crystal was the first of the four to be made and that its power gave the others their potency. But he cared only for the fact that the Lord of the Winds ruled not only magic, but song.

The Jewels glowed against the dark stuff of the Queen's gown. Jehan, gazing upon her face, hesitated a moment as he lifted the coronet with the Jewel of Fire from his head. Then, very carefully, he settled the circlet upon her brow, stepped back, and sank to his knees.

She stood still for a few moments while the breeze sported with the skirts of her gown and blew out her hair. Then she paced forward, gently blessed Jehan's bent head, and lifted her white arms to the crowd.

"People of Westria!" she cried in a voice like a golden

226

clarion. "I stand here before you – will you receive me as your Queen?"

Eric groaned and hid his face in his hands. Rosemary's head was moving in denial even as her lips opened in the cry of assent that seemed to surge from the earth on which they stood.

But Farin could neither cry out nor look away. As he gazed at the Lady of Westria he felt her image replacing that of the sister he had loved, and his eyes stung with tears.

Jehan rubbed at the fatigue that filmed his eyes and took another swallow of mead. Before him the Midsummer Fire roared like a furnace, as if the sun had indeed come to spend the night on earth's breast. The last light of that longest of days had faded from the sky, and the stars danced along their white road as the people of Westria danced below. The air throbbed with the beating of drums and quivered to the high note of the flute as they circled sunways around the fire. The dancing had been going on since sunset, and it would continue until dawn.

He felt sweat trickling down his neck and turned to look up at his Queen, enthroned beneath a canopy of green boughs. Although the heat of the fire was scarcely less where she sat, she showed no signs of feeling it.

Jehan gazed at her and sighed. Her skin glowed and her eyes gave back the light of the fire as if she burned within. She smiled on all, she spoke, she sipped a little water, but she did not eat, and men left space around her as if by coming too close they would be consumed.

"Her beauty is beyond the beauty of women, and she is now in all ways both Mistress and Queen, but you miss the maiden you found in the north," said a harsh voice.

Jehan looked around to meet the unexpected warmth of understanding in the Master of the Junipers' eyes. Seeing himself and the Master robed alike in white, he felt a sudden kinship with the older man, as if the different mystiques of King and Master could for a time be set aside. Both men looked up at Faris.

"I have made her Lady of Westria as I promised," said Jehan thoughtfully, "but though I know that I possessed her in the ritual only a few hours ago, I am as awed in her presence as any man in Westria. We are all her subjects tonight."

"You don't remember lying with her this afternoon?"

Jehan shook his head and the Master smiled. "I have no certain memory of what I did either," the Master said, "though I can guess. It is always so in the rite, when we become the channels for something greater than ourselves. But afterward we are merely human again."

"Not Faris—not yet," sighed Jehan, considering the terrible radiance of her face. "I am married to a Goddess, and all I want is the girl I held in my arms in that cave!" He tried to laugh. For a few moments the two men kept silence in the midst of the revelry.

Then the Master spoke again. "I remember a boy who sat where Faris sits now, with the Jewels of Westria on his body and the god-light in his eyes."

Jehan flinched a little from the Master's keen glance. "I remember a boy who woke the next day," he replied, "weary as if he had borne the whole weight of Westria, not only the Jewels, and knowing only that the glory with which he had been united was gone. And there was nothing between me and despair in that hour, no one who understood where I had been, but one little gray-robed man." He groped for the arm of the Master, who covered the King's hand with his own.

"But at *her* waking she will have you," the Master said.

Jehan felt his heart ease. "Yes. She will always have me." A girl offered them a platter with steaming chunks of roast venison, and Jehan smiled at her and took a piece. He and the Master leaned back against the platform to watch the Festival.

"I had expected Caolin to be here," said the Master after a little while.

"No – he has allowed me a holiday, but he says that the business of the Kingdom must go on, although I think myself that the most important business of Westria is being accomplished here." The King laughed.

"Jehan . . ." The Master shook his head. "You need not always laugh with me. Is Caolin upset by your marriage?"

"Caolin?" For a moment the flames of the bonfires seemed to form the face of the King's friend, bidding him farewell from behind the smiling mask he wore for the world. Strangely, at this moment Jehan could not help remembering times when that face had been opened to him – in the cold loneliness of a mountain cabin, in Laurelynn after the old King had died, and other times. But not recently, not since he had lain with Ronald's arrow sticking out of his thigh.

"I don't think so," he answered reluctantly. "He has given no sign. It's true we are not so close as we once were, but that is natural enough – both of us are older now. He knows that when I have loved someone, I don't change."

"Did you ask him to come?"

"I asked – but I did not want to make him see Faris wear the Jewels." Jehan's voice sank. "That was the first thing I could not share with him, you see, when I became King . . . the thing that he could never understand."

"Be gentle with him now, Jehan. I would be his friend, but I represent the College that rejected him." The Master passed his hand through his thinning hair.

Jehan smiled. "I will. For too long I have left him to hold the helm while I played. Now that I have my foundation, I can begin to pull my weight in the government. Caolin will have the time to play or study, or maybe even find himself a bride."

"That is not entirely what I meant . . ." the Master began, but one of the younger priests came up to them, bowing respectfully.

"Is it midnight already?" asked Jehan. "Well, I know you will be needed to lead the singing, my friend. You must go now." He clasped hands with the Master and watched him

follow the other priest through the crowd before mounting
the platform and taking his place beside his Queen.

The people drew into a great circle as the white-robed
priests came forward, marching together sunwise around
the fire. Gradually the great meadow grew still, and when
all was quiet but for the crackling of the fire, they began
to sing. The music was majestic, and the singers matched
its beat as they sang.

> We hail thee, brother sun, whose conquering light
> Hath captured for the day so many hours,
> And dance our triumph over dwindling night,
> Surrounded and constrained by daylight's powers.

The melody rose triumphant towards the velvet sky as
the marchers completed one circle of the fire and the first
verse of their song. But as they started around again, a
line of black-clad priestesses approached them, moving
in the other direction around the fire and singing in their
turn.

> Think not, oh, man, because the sun is now
> Triumphant, that his power must still increase;
> For it is not in nature to allow
> Growth unchecked, or motion without cease.

The voices of the men confidently replied:

> And yet it is the sun whose burning kiss,
> Touching earth, makes fruitful wood and field;
> Lord of life, by whose bright power it is
> That this world in its beauty is revealed.

The melody with which the women replied was like that
of the men, but moderated with a certain bitter harmony.

> But that same sun whose splendor fills the sky
> At noon, must sink upon the evening's breast

230

When the force that lifted him so high
Has drawn him once more downward to his rest.

From male and female, from white robes to black, the
chorus passed back and forth.

Though he may rest, his warmth enfolds the land
In witness to his power. The barren cold,
Night's offspring, is o'ercome. On every hand
The orchards redden, and the corn turns gold.

The women replied –

Maturity is followed by decline,
And in the eternal cycle of the years,
Earth will sleep in darkness yet again
As the sun's power grows less and winter nears.

The music ceased for a little then, although both groups
continued to circle the fire. Then the women paused in
place as the men sang once more.

If this must truly be, then on this fire –
Sun's image – herbs of fortune let us lay,
And as we make it greater, may this pyre
Retain some power to guard each lessening day.

One by one each man took off his wreath of twined rosemary and vervain, mint and thyme, and threw it into the
flames. As they did so, the women turned to follow them.

Oh, worshippers, fear not, for one thing dies
In order that another may be born.
The sun from his defeat at last will rise
And make the darkest night give way to morn.

The women sang, tossing their own wreaths into the
fire.

A little wind fanned the newly fed bonfire and the flames surged towards the stars. Jehan led Faris down from the platform, and as soon as the priestesses had finished singing, the King and Queen came forward, followed by the rest of the people, to add their own leafy crowns to the blaze. Faris, laughing joyfully, threw her wreath in a high arc above the bonfire, where it was caught by an escaping spark so that it plummeted back into the flames like a crown of fire.

Jehan grinned and sent his wreath to follow hers, then turned away to lead her into the dance. Caught in the updraft, his wreath was blown sideways and fell on the edge of the flames, where its greenery slowly shriveled until it flaked into nothingness without having been consumed.

Caolin yawned, winced, and forced himself to sit up. The damp dawn wind brushed goosebumps across his skin and swirled ashes from the remains of the Midsummer beacon by which he had watched since sunset the night before. He took a deep breath and winced again at the complaints of muscles cramped by sleeping on the stone platform and strained by yesterday's ceremony.

Automatically he began the salutation to the sun, then stopped and stretched out his hands to the Mountain.

"Mountain of Power, I salute you, and I claim your strength this day!"

Caolin smiled then, fancying he felt an answering quiver beneath him, and got to his feet. The mist-wrapped lands of Westria stretched north and south, east and west below him, sleeping at the feet of this mountain whose strength was now linked to his. Jehan's mating with Faris was intended to symbolically marry him to the land. *But I have touched the land directly*, he thought in wonder. *What will that mean to me?*

The roofs and towers of Laurelynn glittered in the early light. If he started now, he could be there before last night's revelers had started their day.

He had what he had come here for and more. He knew his power; it was time to use it. He had been too long away.

"By the time you reach the other shore it will be day," said the Master of the Junipers, looking across the Bay. Jehan followed his gaze to the blue folds of the eastern hills and the dawn-colored cone of the Red Mountain just visible behind them.

"It will be good to be home," he sighed, feeling the accumulated weariness of the past two days weighting his limbs. Faris stirred against him and smiled without opening her eyes as his arm tightened around her. The *Sea Brother* butted hollowly against the jetty as the sailors moved about, readying her to sail.

The Master grunted, rose from his place in the bow beside Jehan, and grasped the rail to step back to the dock again.

"You are sure that Faris will be all right?" said Jehan. The unnatural vitality had left her with the coming of day, and she had ridden from the Grove to the shore like one in a trance, doing as she was bid but making no reply.

"Let her sleep – that's what I will be doing." The Master's worn face creased as he smiled down at the King. He looked familiar and friendly in his old gray robe, and Jehan reached out to him.

"You would be welcome at Misthall."

"I know, and perhaps in a few days I will come to you. But for now" – the Master turned to gaze at the Mountain from which they had come – "I need to spend a few days at Juniper Cottage." He gestured towards the brightening slopes where lay the only bit of land that Jehan had ever heard his friend call home.

"I have never been there," said the King. He wondered suddenly what the Master of the Junipers did when he was not helping other people deal with their lives. Were there those who gave him comfort? Were there things he desired? Jehan glimpsed the dark figure of the Mistress of the College waiting among the trees and thought that perhaps she knew the answers to those questions.

"Perhaps the next time you cross these waters, it will be to visit me," said the Master. Jehan smiled, then shivered in the freshening wind.

"My Lord, we are ready now." Austin of Seahold bowed before them.

The Master jumped back to the dock and waved as a ribbon of water widened silently between them. Jehan waved back, then his arms tightened once more around Faris and he turned to face the sun.

Sunlight barred the worn tiles of the floor in Caolin's office and gilded the edges of the papers stacked on his desk. He had washed away the dust of his journey and changed to fresh robes, but some lingering tension kept him from sitting down to the work that awaited him there. He paced nervously to the window, glanced at the courtyard below, and stiffened as something that looked like a large dark dog trotted through the gate.

Gerol! Caolin peered through the wavy glass, then smiled just a little as he saw Ordrey riding in with someone whose head was hooded and whose hands were bound. He moved slowly back to his desk and sat down, feeling the tension leave him to be replaced by a great certainty that he had indeed tapped into the force that powered the universe. For he knew who that prisoner had to be.

He was sitting at his desk, seemingly absorbed in the work before him, when a timid knock disturbed the door and a clerk answered his summons.

"Tell Ordrey that I will meet him in the lower chamber of the Keep in fifteen minutes' time," he said as the woman was still opening her mouth. The mouth slowly closed; the faded eyes above it rounded with wonder. The clerk hesitated, then nodded and slipped from the room.

Now she will tell her friends that I am a sorcerer, thought Caolin wryly, then sobered, realising that it was true.

"Well, my Lord, it took a long time, but I have had good hunting at last."

Caolin folded his arms and frowned at the man who slumped in the chair before him. His hair was matted and his clothing torn and splattered with mud. The bound hands seemed thin beneath their grime. All in all, this Ronald was a very different creature from the man who had accosted Eric on the road to Lord Theodor's Hall.

"A sorry prey to have given you such a chase," he said to Ordrey. "Where did you find him?"

"In a midden – no, truly!" Ordrey added as Caolin laughed. Ordrey was thinner too, but his pale eyes sparkled. "He had been hiding in a borderer's barn, and when he heard us breaking down the door, he leaped through the nearest window, which happened to be above a dung heap. It had been raining, and the pile was deep, and besides, Gerol was waiting beyond it. We had to sluice the poor man thoroughly before we could stand his company – it did not improve his beauty, I fear."

"It seems an appropriate way for him to end," said Caolin. "You say you found him on the border of the Ramparts? Then he did not go to Normontaine."

"If he did, he didn't stay there long." Ordrey shrugged. "He hasn't told me much, though I suggested that it might be easier to talk to me than to you."

"He should have believed you," said Caolin softly. He placed a finger beneath Ronald's chin and lifted it until the man must meet his eyes. The prisoner's face was pale and as thin as the rest of him now. He was sweating already and began to tremble as Caolin held him, but he could not move his head or withdraw from the Seneschal's gaze.

"I have done nothing," he whispered at last. "What are you going to do to me?"

"If you have done nothing, you have nothing to fear," said Caolin pleasantly. "I would like to help you."

"I'm the Lord Commander's cousin, and I have my rights!"

Caolin straightened and turned away. Rights! This

wretch prated of his rights as loudly as Brian himself
. . . as if the world owed him something for having been
born. He heard Ronald's breathing grow a little ragged and
came back to him.

"I know who you are," he said soothingly, "and it's my
duty to see that you get what you deserve. But you must
be frank with me. There are several points about the past
few months that I find hard to understand." He smiled.

Ronald swallowed and attempted to smile in return.

"We know already that you shot the arrows that wounded
Lord Theodor and the King," Caolin went on without a
tremor, though he was seeing again Jehan's blood bright
upon the grass. A pulse began to pound in his throat.
"That's a terrible crime, you know – to harm the King.
If you want mercy, you will have to be very cooperative
from now on."

Ronald stared back at him like a trapped bird.

"Did you bribe the outlaws to attack Lord Theodor's
war party on the way to Greenfell? Why?" Caolin asked
suddenly.

Ronald muttered unintelligibly. Caolin gestured to Gerol, who padded forward with his muzzle wrinkling in a
silent snarl.

"Yes – yes, I did!"

"But why? What could you hope to gain?" repeated
Caolin.

"Theodor is a hard man, and Sandy a young fool. I was
their own cousin and next heir, but they never gave me my
rights. I lived like Theodor's poorest liegeman. Theodor
does not deserve the Province – if he and his son were
gone it would be mine! But I swear I never meant to hurt
the King!" moaned Ronald.

"It is a pity you cannot prove that, friend." Caolin paced
towards the door, then turned suddenly. "And what about
the gold? You say yourself that you are not a rich man –
where did you get the money to bribe those vermin?"

Ronald started violently and stared at the Seneschal.

"You just admitted that you bribed them. Where did

you get the gold? From someone in the south, perhaps? From someone who would just naturally put his money in a Sanjos bag?" Caolin drew a suede pouch from the breast of his robe and dangled it before Ronald.

Brian . . . the name pounded in his head until he thought that Ronald must hear it. He must speak! As long as Jehan refused to blame Brian for the incident at Santibar, Ronald was Caolin's only weapon against him. The man's life was forfeit in any case – why could he not make himself useful and give Caolin the proof he needed to break Brian's pride?

But Ronald was shaking his head. "It was my own money," he repeated. "I did not mean to hurt the King!" His lips closed like a miser's strongbox and he hunched back in his chair.

The Seneschal regarded him silently, but Ordrey, who had been lounging against the wall, stood up and began to grin as Gerol did when the table scraps were being cleared. Ronald looked from one to the other and grew pale.

"I've told him already, my Lord, that if he didn't talk to me on the journey, and he wouldn't talk to you when we arrived, you might let me try to persuade him."

Ronald's eyes closed and his color became something nearer gray.

"You see, he remembers," Ordrey added happily. "Is it time?"

Caolin looked at him with distaste. Not for the first time, he wished he had the ability to force rapport – but it was not information but a confession that he wanted now. He could rule minds like Ordrey's or Margit's, but they were willing tools. Breaking Ronald's resistance mentally might break his mind.

Unless his life had been made such a burden to him that he would consider Caolin a deliverer.

Images chased one another through Caolin's memory – Jehan's face as the Master dragged the arrow from his thigh . . . the face of another prisoner after Ordrey had "persuaded" him . . . Brian's scornful smile.

His fingers twitched and he clasped his hands, remembering how power had flowed through them on the Mountain. But power was useless if not used.

"You must not be rough with him, Ordrey. I have business elsewhere now. Perhaps you could help him consider the matter until I return." Impassive, he met Ronald's relieved smile and Ordrey's understanding grin.

The door behind him closed on Ronald's first astonished gasp of pain, and Caolin found the Red Mountain, seen through the long windows of the staircase, obscurely comforting as he returned to his Offices to wait.

Jehan raised himself on one elbow to contemplate Faris once more. In the dim light of his bedchamber her face glimmered with an elusive beauty, the clear modeling of her brow and chin belied by the vulnerability of her lips, and her eyes, which might have resolved the contradiction, veiled by the thick lashes that shadowed her cheeks. When they opened at last, what would those eyes say?

Crossing the Bay, Jehan had managed to doze while Faris slept in his arms. But now that she lay in his bed at last, he found himself unable to sleep and unwilling to leave her lest she should wake and find him gone. And yet he felt no impatience. He was content to wait, if need be for ever, till she should come to him.

He heard Farin playing Swangold, the notes as faint and clear as if the wind were singing to itself, and wondered if the boy had found the bench at the end of the balcony, which was his own favorite place here at Misthall. Like the shuttered windows in his chamber, it looked out on fields sloping down to the Bay and across the sweep of the water to the gracious silhouette of the Lady Mountain.

The harping stopped for a moment. Jehan heard voices, then light footsteps passing his own door and going on. He smiled. A small staff kept Misthall for him, and beside Farin and the girl that Rosemary had brought to be Faris' maid, only Rosemary and Sandy were staying here now, waiting for the upcoming Council in Laurelynn. But after

the threats with which he had closed his door, he doubted
that any of them would dare to disturb him. This time was
for him and Faris alone – the time he had been longing for
since their aborted tryst in the cave.

Comparing that setting to this one, Jehan's eyes followed the complexities of the embroidered flowers that
twined across the green linen curtains of the great bed,
then returned to Faris. This was a sanctuary, and she the
goddess worshipped here. It only needed candles to reveal
her beauty.

Then for a moment he saw her lying still upon a bed
of flowers with candles at her head and feet. He held his
breath in contemplation, then grew cold as he realised that
silver threaded her midnight hair, saw her face pared to an
unearthly beauty by pain, and paler than the lilies upon
which she lay. He shut his eyes against the vision and
groped frantically for the living reality.

His fingers closed on Faris' warm shoulder and he collapsed upon the bed beside her, burying his face in the dark
masses of her flower-scented hair. Faris muttered sleepily,
turning and folding in upon herself like a flower closing
its petals against the dark. Jehan released her then, but
it was several minutes before he could lift his face from
her hair.

"Oh, my love," he whispered shakily. "With such fancies
I will end by waking you myself."

He rolled to the edge of the bed and slipped his feet into
the welcome of the sheepskin rug beside it, then padded
across the room. His clothes lay tumbled across the chair,
but he felt in the darkness of the wardrobe for the familiar
folds of a long loose robe that, after having been discarded
by his father, had been worn by him till its weave was bare,
its blue uncertain, and its shape a mold for his own. He
drew it around him, thrust the clothes from the chair, and
sat down.

He could just see Faris from here, her long hair spread
on the pillow beneath the dim shapes of battling warriors
that he had painted on the wall long ago. The picture

showed the battle in which Julian the Great had slain the last of the warlords and checked the fires they had loosed upon the world. The figure of Julian, with the Jewel of Fire upon his brow, was fully colored, and the blood of his enemy spilled crimson on the ground, but the rest of the figures were incomplete, some of them mere outlines on the wall.

Jehan remembered that he had been working on the mural just before his father took him on his first campaign, against the barbarians from the Brown Lands to the east. After he returned he had not cared to paint pictures of battles anymore.

He looked across the room, smiling at all the clutter he had never allowed anyone to disturb – musical instruments he couldn't play, sketches of animals tacked to the walls below dusty trophies of weapons. He had been very proud of the graduated set of throwing knives from the Ramparts, and the Elayan group, complete with tasseled assegai. He even owned, in a special case above the fireplace, the barrel and mechanism of a weapon from before the Cataclysm, which was supposed to have projected pellets of metal as one would shoot a bow.

The shelves to either side of the bed held more collections – shells, feathers, rocks from different parts of Westria, and complete or half-made models of boats and buildings and weapons for besieging them – his own work and gifts from people all over the Kingdom. Looking at them, he tried to remember the boy who had retreated to this room to enjoy the luxury of loneliness, dreaming of a distant future in which he would be the greatest of Westria's Kings.

But the Kingship had been closer than he dreamed, and as for the greatness . . . He looked back at Faris, remembering all his wasted hours. *You are my greatness*, he thought. *For you I will be a true Lord of Westria.* His throat ached with words unsaid, knowing that he must not disturb her with them now.

He rose suddenly and went to the work table below

the western window, next to the doors opening onto the balcony, and began to search through the books and papers piled there.

Below a sheaf of reports on trade between Seagate and the Corona, which should have been filed in Laurelynn, he found a treatise on the art of the longsword and the blade of a dagger with a broken tang. He came to a book of love poems by Hilary Goldenthroat, smiled, and placed it on top of the pile. But that was not what he was looking for.

On the other side of the desk he found a notebook into which he had carefully bound all the letters Caolin had sent him the first time he went on progress alone, leaving his newly appointed Seneschal in charge in Laurelynn. He ruffled the pages, seeing in the exquisitely formed letters the man who had written them. Even when Caolin was writing about his struggle to get Lord Brian to acknowledge his authority, the handwriting remained as legible as a printed book from ancient times. Jehan thought how fortunate it was that Caolin's detachment had been able to foil his own impulsiveness, especially in the first years after he had become King.

Jehan's hands, sifting through the pile, encountered something hard and drew it out. He adjusted the shutters to give him a little more light. The smoothness of the rosewood case he was holding tugged at his memory. Almost reluctantly he opened it.

The lilac scent that clung to the silk scarf and the letters inside had even now the power to bring back memories. Jehan closed the case without needing to reread the letters, testing, as one feels the gap where a tooth has been drawn, the edges of his old pain.

He remembered Mariana of Claralac as vividly as the lilac scent she had always worn and the words in which she had suggested that if her old husband were given a post on the borders, she would be the sooner freed to become Jehan's Queen.

Is that why I delayed marrying for so long? wondered Jehan, considering how desperately he had loved Mariana

and how desperately he had suffered when he understood
that she loved nothing of him but his crown.

He put down the case and rested his fingers on a leather-
covered notebook beside it, smoothing the nap of the
suede back and forth. The only clear memory he retained
of the period just after Mariana's betrayal was of the time
he caught Caolin trying to smuggle two giggling girls into
his bedchamber. As he recalled, he had not taken either
of the girls, but he had laughed at Caolin's attempts to
conceal them, and the two of them had gone out together
and gotten drunk.

*And Mariana had black hair too – Sweet Lady, help
me!*

Jehan shook his head as if he could shake the memory
away, picked up the book, and opened it. Except for a
few notes on the countryside of Las Costas, it held only
blank pages. Swiftly Jehan tore them out, then picked up
his writing case and went back to his chair. For a moment
he sat, staring at the empty page, then he dipped the pen
into the inkwell and began to write.

My beloved, I dare not wake you, and yet there is
so much I need to say. Will I ever show you these
scribblings? Will I find them useful notes, when,
beholding your beauty, I can find no words? Or
will I find that after all, none of this even needed
to be said?

If I had your brother's gift I would make my longing
into music and sing it away. But I can only fumble for
ways to explain how you are the light that shows me
that there is a future – and that the fear that I may
fail you is the shadow that darkens it. Your beauty of
body and soul stands surety for the world.

I have shared my body with many – too many,
perhaps, if I cannot even remember them all – but
how few are those with whom I have dared to share
my soul.

There had been Caolin, he thought, and the Master of the Junipers, but since his mother died there had been no woman to whom he could reveal himself as they surrendered to him. Until Faris. But she was so fragile, so vulnerable – he must go carefully.

The fading light made it hard to see the page. Jehan went to the shutters and half opened them. Bars of rosy sunset light added new color to the worn Elayan rug on the floor, slipped between the bed curtains, and glowed on Faris' outstretched hand.

Jehan stared at it, knowing that all reality lay focused there. Blindly he replaced the book and writing case on the table. Then he moved to the bed and with pounding heart bent to kiss Faris' open palm.

The harpstrings flashed and flickered as Farin's fingers moved over them, as though he were drawing from the air not only music but fire. For a long time he had played without words, evoking the silken stillness of the Bay and the perfect line of the Mountain, whose blue slopes shaded imperceptibly to mauve and purple as the sky burst into flame.

Images moved in his mind like great sea creatures beneath the surface of the Bay, sometimes almost breaking into consciousness, then sinking unrecognised into the depths once more.

Farin played without trying to think while the harp sang of a beauty beyond tears.

"My Lord."

Farin's fingers trailed a descending shimmer of strings and stopped. With an effort he turned from the sunset to the girl beside him.

"My Lord, we have laid out a supper in the hall if you wish to come." She looked at him shyly, her straight brown hair coppered by the sunset, her features in shadow.

Farin remembered vaguely seeing her with Rosemary. She was called Branwen and had been brought south to be Faris' maid.

243

Supper . . . he focused on her words and realised that his stomach had already responded to them.

"Thank you. Just . . . give me a little longer. I will come."

She looked at him uncertainly, then curtsied and made her way back along the porch to the stairs.

Farin sighed. He had been so close to . . . something. His fingers settled on the strings, kissed from them a minor chord, then a matching harmony. Above the hills he saw suddenly the steady glitter of the evening star.

Melody distilled from his random music, words from his tumbled thoughts, like some spell that only the starlight reveals.

> Oh, Beauty like the evening star –
> Oh, sister soul – however far
> You rise above your earthly twin
> (Bright star without, dark star within)
> Still will I follow you, until
> You blaze upon my breast as well.

11

The State of Westria

A wind off the river dappled the poplars and rattled the opened shutters of the breakfast room. The Master of the Junipers took a deep breath, savoring the coolness retained from the night just past; the aromatic response of curing grass in the fields around Laurelynn to the first rays of the sun; the heady sweetness of roses climbing the palace walls. The wind drew his awareness outward till the distinction between self and surroundings blurred.

He felt the presences of the others in the room – the clarity of the Mistress of the College; Robert of the Ramparts' solid strength and the wry cheerfulness of his wife, Jessica; Farin Harper's single note in the midst of the others' harmony; Jehan, burning like a torch; and Faris herself, like all the roses in Westria in full bloom.

Her red robe folded like petals around the whiteness of her breast. She was talking to Farin, but she turned to Jehan as a flower to the sun, and the Master was dizzied by the pliant sweetness of her passing glance.

He savored the moment as he had savored the wind, able for now to forget that it was the nature of both to pass.

"Will you have some honey muffins, or some tea?" Jessica's words and the scent of the food brought the Master gently to the present again. Her blue eyes – less brilliant than Jehan's but with the same sweetness – met his with a friendly smile. He wondered if she had noticed his abstraction – it was always hard to tell how much Jessica knew. He reached out for the muffins, took one, and passed the basket to Farin.

"I was just remembering the first time I met Faris – at breakfast in Rosemary's chambers at the Hold," he said.

"Yes," added Farin, "and Rosemary's raccoon made off with the cakes. Did you know she brought that damned owl of hers south?"

"Huw?" asked the Master.

"Who?" said Jessica.

"Exactly!" answered Farin, laughing. "She's collected another menagerie here in Laurelynn. Don't expect her to show up for breakfast until she's fed them all!"

"What's the joke?" asked Jehan from the head of the table. As Farin began to explain, the Master looked past him to Faris again and was stopped by the considering brilliance in the eyes of the Mistress of the College, as if she had laid a sword between them.

"I don't mean to interfere," Lord Robert continued to speak to her, oblivious of the pause, "but naturally Mistress Esther and I work together, and I share her concerns. Perhaps other Commanders would resent the involvement of the College in the affairs of their Marches, but I welcome you."

"If I were to answer you now, we would be talking until the Council begins. I prefer to reserve my explanation until then," said the Mistress.

The Master of the Junipers looked at her with sudden misgiving. In the weeks they had spent on the Lady Mountain, she had said nothing of politics. He remembered with abrupt clarity waking in the still mornings, content to know she was there; the sweet blending of their two voices making a litany of the daily rituals. And he remembered with a deeper wonder the times when they had shared the gifts of the body as well as of the soul – equals bringing to the act of love the stored richness of their lives.

They had talked as he had never been able to talk to her in the days when she was the teacher and he the pupil seeking his way, a dream of youth flowering in maturity. But the conversation had been all of the hidden ways of the soul. She had not spoken of the affairs of the College, and he had been relieved to forget them for a while.

I did not want to ask her, he reflected bitterly. *I was afraid of the answers*. Her dark face was closed to him, her mind impenetrable now.

"Robert, the Council will be on everyone's mind at the feast tonight, and tomorrow will be given over to it entirely – let us at least leave it out of the conversation now! Faris," Jessica went on, "you aren't eating. Believe me. You will need your strength today."

Faris shook her head. "No, I couldn't now. But don't worry about me – I've gained weight since coming here."

Jessica smiled commiseratingly, but the Master sensed her interest focusing on Faris. "Where have you put it? Shall I help you alter your clothes?" She laughed, setting her hands on her own belly, rounding now as her child grew.

Faris shrugged, embarrassed. "Across the bust, mostly, but Jehan says he likes it that way."

Jessica's glance crossed that of the Mistress, then returned to Faris with a speculative gleam that reminded the Master of a herdsman surveying his ewes. Suddenly he realised what she suspected. It was possible, he thought. The King and Faris had first come together just a month ago, but the Midsummer ritual was known to enhance fertility or hasten it if a woman was near the time.

"I also have finished my meal," said the Mistress of the College. "Let us go to your chambers and you may show me your gown for the feast."

Faris stared at her. Her small acquaintance with the Mistress must still be enough for her to know how uncharacteristic this suggestion was. She looked at the older woman uncertainly.

Awkwardly Jessica pushed back her chair. "I'll come with you." She smiled at Faris and led her out of the room.

Robert had begun talking to Jehan about the Elayan situation. Farin was gazing into space, his fingers tapping out some music only he could hear. The Master sat frowning for a moment, then softly rose and followed the women.

Jessica stopped her questioning and Faris looked up accusingly, face flushed, as the Master came into the room. The Mistress of the College was sitting at the window, disapproval marring the remoteness of her face.

"Is it not enough that I was made wife before the whole College?" asked Faris bitterly. "Cannot Jehan and I wait together to learn what came of it?"

"My poor sister!" Jessica shook her head. "Don't you understand what it will mean to Jehan tomorrow if he can announce the coming of an heir to Westria?"

Faris still looked mutinous. The Master moved forward and took her hand. "If you do not wish anyone to know, I am sure Jehan will abide by your decision – but this would give him such joy."

"But it's too soon. I was sure it was only my stupid stomach again." Faris sighed. "Very well – what must you do to me to find out for sure?"

The Mistress rose. "Lie down and be still. There is nothing to fear." She gestured to the Master. "You may as well assist – you have little practice in this, but you will most likely attend her." Her unspoken thought reached him – *She resists me, but she already knows the touch of your mind.*

Faris looked up at them, lips tightening as fear grew in her dark eyes.

"Lie still," the Master repeated gently, projecting wordless reassurance until Faris closed her eyes. He stood and let his eyes unfocus, breathing deeply until he saw Faris' body veiled in a glow whose muddy red deepened into purple, then cleared to blue as she relaxed.

The hands of the Mistress poised a few inches above Faris' head in a blur of golden light. The Master extended his awareness until he felt her presence. *Madrona*, he named her, *Faris*. . . . Mentally he drew the two together until they touched through him.

The Mistress passed her hands from Faris' crown to her neck, her breast, her stomach, loins, knees, and feet, and the Master's perception deepened until he saw the golden glow of each power point and the energy flowing between them in rivers of light. He had done this himself, to diagnose illness, but not since his student days had he traced the energy flows in someone so healthy.

See, came the thought of the Mistress, *power pulses already around her womb.*

He focused his awareness on the flare of light and stretched out his hands. Radiance pulsed around them, spiraling the womb, brightening as his perception sharpened. He probed deeper, until he came at last to the tiny core of brightness beyond all color, like the light that crowns the Tree of Life, and knew that the seed of life was indeed planted there.

The spark glowed, as yet unaware of anything save that it lived and grew. The Master gazed, aware of nothing but the miracle.

Sunlight flamed in the glass flagon as Caolin lifted it to pour the second goblet of chilled wine. He had seen Jehan crossing the courtyard. Now he recognised the King's step in the hall and heard the door open, but he continued to pour steadily until, the twin goblets filled to precisely the same level, he turned with them in his hands.

Jehan stood by the window, light blazing from the gold tracery at the neck of his tunic and the brooch that closed it, gleaming on the smooth planes of profiled nose and brow, aureoling hair and beard. For a moment Caolin was dazzled. Then the King moved out of the sunlight to the table and sat down. Shards of light danced in the goblets, and after a confused moment the Seneschal realised that the movement came from the barely perceptible trembling of his hands. Quickly he set the goblets on the table, where the surfaces stilled to pools of shadow once more.

"You are early," Caolin told the King, taking his own seat and reaching for his wine.

"Am I?" Jehan's eyes glowed, though he was no longer in the sun. He indicated the goblets. "I thought you were waiting for me."

"I wait for you always, my Lord," Caolin said quietly.

Jehan shook his head a little, drank deeply, and set the goblet down. "We must plan well for this Council – there have been few so important since I was crowned. At least it will be well attended. They tell me Lord Hakon has dragged himself from his sickbed to come; Lord Theodor will be here by tonight; the other Commanders and the lords of the cities have already arrived." He continued to list those he knew would attend while Caolin reached for the agenda his office had already compiled and laid it before him. Jehan glanced down the list.

"Presentation of the Queen . . . yes, that must certainly be first." The King smiled.

"They will approve her," said Caolin.

Jehan had risen and was moving about the room, still reading the agenda. "Yes, there can be no doubt about that now." He smiled again.

"After that, the reports from the Estates of Westria," said Caolin from memory. "I'll have copies ready for you." He waited for Jehan's customary sigh of resignation, but the King had wandered to the stacked coffers at the far end of the room.

"You keep the cities' records here, don't you? They must fill whole libraries! How many years' worth of accounts can you store in this room?"

"Five years," Caolin began, but Jehan had come back to the table.

"Can you tell whether my traveling this past year has had any effects? Are there any changes in the reports, increases in trade?"

"The places you visited certainly reported it, if that's what you mean," said Caolin slowly, watching the King move about. "Trade figures . . ." Automatically his memory transferred the information to his lips while his mind searched the past days for some clue to the King's unusual diligence. Jehan had crossed the room and pulled a map from its pigeonhole, unrolling and rolling it again as Caolin continued. It was a forest map of the Corona. Had the King found out about Ronald?

"You'll have summaries of all this for the Council," repeated Caolin. 'Next comes new business, petitions, and the like," he went on before Jehan could ask any more questions.

The King looked at him intently, then began to laugh. "My poor friend. You must think I've gone mad. The fact is, I think I'm just becoming sane. I ought to know these things as well as you do, but I've had all the pleasure of being Lord of Westria, while the labor has been yours. That isn't right, and I mean to make it up to you, Caolin." He laid his hand for a moment on the Seneschal's shoulder, then turned away again.

Jehan is going to be his own Seneschal? For a moment all other thoughts were blanked out by sheer astonishment. Then Caolin recalled other fits of Kingly efficiency and relaxed. This energy was unlikely to last long, but in the meantime . . . Caolin frowned, wishing that the one man whose questions he had to answer had not chosen just this moment to remember his responsibilities.

"I am told that Lord Brian intends to present a petition tomorrow," Caolin said neutrally.

Jehan put down the folder he had been leafing through. "You are 'told'? Is your evidence sure?"

"I am sure he has completed it, at least," Caolin replied. "The assistant to his Seneschal copied it out for me." He pulled a paper from the pile before him.

"You have a *spy* in Lord Brian's house?"

"I have a subordinate," said Caolin stiffly. "As all the lords of this Kingdom are your men, all the Seneschals and their deputies are mine. It was his duty to inform me of this, as it is mine to inform you." He held out the paper again. "What action will you take?"

"I will hear the petition." Jehan took the paper and set it face down, unread.

"My Lord! Why will you not be warned? Is it dishonorable to feather your arrows until the enemy comes down the road, or to wait for snowfall before you get the harvest in?"

"No . . ." Jehan answered slowly. "But Caolin, it is foolishness to waste those arrows on what may be only the wind in the trees, or to gather the harvest unripe for fear of early storms. Let Brian speak before all the people, and we will know how many follow him. If we strike in secret, secret whispers will call us tyrants – and judged and judges alike will be unheard."

Caolin's eyes fell before the appeal in Jehan's and silently he replaced the copy of the petition in its file. *No*, he thought, *now is not the time to tell the King about Ronald, but it is time to draw from that man a confession that will force Jehan to believe.*

For a moment he longed for the stillness of his temple on the Red Mountain. Since Midsummer he had not found the time to return to it. Coordinating, negotiating, manipulating, he stayed in Laurelynn like a spider caught in its own web and longed for the pure stroke of power that would set him free. Had he imagined that pulse of power? Could he draw it forth once more? Perhaps when next he questioned Ronald, they would see.

Jehan was still waiting for him to reply. "What about the Elayans?" the Seneschal asked softly. "Will they underestimate our strength, seeing us so mild?"

Jehan straightened, head lifting so that he seemed suddenly taller, and his features sharpened. "They will not underestimate *me!*"

The King was not standing in sunlight now, but to Caolin he seemed to glow. *I have been too concerned with my own secrets*, he thought. *What is he hiding from me?* He waited,

staring up at Jehan until the grim look was transmuted into
a joy so transcendent that the Seneschal must look away.

"I would have waited to surprise you with the others,"
Jehan said quietly, "but we have shared so many sorrows,
more-than-brother, let us rejoice together now. Westria
will have an heir, Caolin – I have just learned that already
Faris carries my child!"

He knows about the child, thought Faris, seeing Caolin's
eyes turn from Jehan to linger on her breasts, so clearly
outlined by the clinging green gown. She tightened her grip
on Jehan's arm and returned the Seneschal's smile.

Jehan turned immediately. "Are you tired? Do you want
to sit down?" Colored lanterns reflected rosy light off the
awning that had been set up on the palace lawn on to
Jehan's face; brightened the robes of councilors and their
families and followers who were the King's guests tonight.

"No." Faris shook her head, torn between apprehension
of his solicitude and a need for the reassurance of his touch.
The crowds had given them a respectful space, but Faris
felt their curiosity like the touch of moth wings upon her
skin. Tomorrow they would be curious about the coming
child as well. Why had this had to happen so soon, when
she was just becoming used to the idea that she was Jehan's
Queen? She shut her eyes, reaffirming the golden barrier
that kept her safe from the pressure of so many minds.

Jehan looked at her doubtfully. "Perhaps Caolin will get
us some wine." They turned, but the Seneschal had gone.

Caolin slipped through the crowd, looking back only once
at the two green-clad figures who stood so close together,
like an island around which the people of Westria flowed.
Still dazzled by the King's radiance, he had seen Faris
abruptly as Jehan saw her, as if he *were* Jehan.

But he told himself that to stay talking to them would
waste time. He was not at this feast for his own pleasure,
but to see and hear – to flatter thbzis one, to draw information from that, to plant a suggestion in the mind of a third,

and to test the temper of the crowd before tomorrow's council began.

Expectation strings them like a bow. Even I can feel it, tonight. He breathed deeply, automatically easing his own unrecognised tension as he had learned at the College of the Wise, and veered towards a shimmer of brocade at the edge of the crowd.

The Elayan envoys stood a little apart, Emir Akhbar's dark, deeply lined face impassive, Rodrigo Maclain's fair skin flushed above his red beard, but garbed alike in jeweled caps and flowing robes and guarded by four dark warriors whose plumes towered even above the Seneschal.

"Westria is honoured by your presence at the proclamation of our new Queen." Caolin paused before them, searching their faces for the flicker of speculation or contempt that would tell him that Ercul Ashe's careful confidences had reached their target, and they now underestimated the strength of Westria and her King.

"Indeed, there comes a time when every warrior must turn his mind to more pleasant things," the Emir rumbled in reply, but Caolin was watching Lord Rodrigo's eyes.

"My Lord looks forward to receiving the message of your Prince," the Seneschal replied, continuing to smile even when Lord Rodrigo's face told him for certain that the message would be a challenge Westria could not ignore.

Quickly Caolin disengaged from the Elayans and moved onward. It would not do to be seen too much in conversation with the enemy, nor did he want Maclain to realise how he had revealed himself. Caolin caught sight of Sir Eric's brown curls and turned towards them, schooling his features to concern.

"My Lord." Eric looked around and Caolin went on, "I am told that your father is not well. I hope that the effort he has made to come to this Council has done him no harm."

Eric's surprise faded and he shrugged helplessly. "He is very tired, but he would come. He tells us he will be in his seat tomorrow if we have to carry him there."

Caolin shook his head. "I had hoped that the session would be uneventful, if only for your father's sake. But I am told that Lord Brian intends to present a petition. Of course I don't know what it says," he went on as Eric's face grew red.

"I can guess." The young man shook his head. "It will enrage my father, but he will never listen to me if I ask him to stay away."

A clarion announced that supper was to be served, but Eric was still in the same place, scowling darkly, as Caolin slipped away.

"Will you come to my father?" Eric asked anxiously. "He wants to attend the Council tomorrow, and he is very ill!"

The Master of the Junipers looked up from his dinner, feeling the young man's concern but finding it difficult to reassure him. He had seen the old lord of Seagate when he arrived in Laurelynn and had recognised mortal illness in his face.

"Indeed I will visit him. It's been long since we talked, and I can easily forego the rest of this feast. I promise nothing, Eric, but I will do what I can." Beyond Eric, he saw Farin with Sir Andreas and Holly of Woodhall. Randal of Registhorpe and his new lady were close behind. "Go with your friends now, Eric. Your father would not wish you to miss the feast."

Eric tried to smile. "Indeed, in these past weeks he has often told me I am like a dog with one sheep to guard and has sent me from his room."

The Master saw Eric join the others and then started towards the wing of the palace where the Seagate party had been lodged. He skirted the crowd, climbed the grassy slope beyond the long table, stopped as a shadow stepped from among the fir trees that edged the lawn.

For a moment the Master's neck hairs prickled – knowing more than most men about what things might come in shadow form, he had both more and less to fear. Then he recognised low laughter and the glint of silvered hair as the Mistress of the College put back her grey hood.

"Madrona, must you hover like a spirit of the night? I would have thought to find you at the High Table."

"Night is my Kingdom. Some things are clearer in darkness than by day."

His skin chilled. Not so long ago she had joined with him in service to the Lady of Fire, but she was totally a priestess to the Wisewoman now. He repressed a shiver. A man might court the Maiden and mate with the Mother, but the Crone knew all the secrets of death and darkness, and only the Sage could deal with Her on equal terms.

The Master looked away. With an effort he forced calm into his reply. "Sir Eric of Seagate asked me to visit his father. I think that he is right to fear for the old lord if tomorrow's Council goes ill."

"Lord Hakon will live yet awhile. It is the woman you diagnosed this morning who should be your concern."

"Faris?" He looked at the Mistress in astonishment, then down to the table behind which Faris and Jehan were enthroned like a tapestried King and Queen. "You yourself said that she was in perfect health."

"While you were contemplating the mystery of life, I was examining the vessel that bears it," she said tartly. "Faris may be with child, but her responses are those of a half-awakened maid."

"But that will come. Many young wives –"

"Look at her," the Mistress interrupted, "leaning on her husband's shoulder, hanging on his every word. Today they hail her as Queen of Love, they will hail her as Mother tomorrow, but when will they hail her as Lady of Westria?"

The Master shook his head. "What do you want of her? What do you want of me? Faris is harnessed already to Westria; do not make her draw that load before it is necessary. She will have little enough time to play."

"Go back and learn your catechism." She leaned forward and whispered the name he had borne when he first entered the College, the name that perhaps only she remembered now. "If Faris were 'any young wife' her maturity would be no concern of yours or mine. I said that she was not ready, but not one of you would listen to me." The Master saw the gleam of her eyes as she stared at him.

"The King of Westria stands for all the people of this land, but his Queen must be able to act for the land itself! She receives his service, but she must be his steady reservoir of power, otherwise the Great Marriage is a sham, no matter how impressive the ritual has been. You are her teacher – you must make her understand!"

"No!" He shook his head in revulsion, remembering how he had stripped Faris' soul in order to teach her the need to guard it. His own oath barred him from attempting such a violation again. "I awakened her soul," he said hoarsely. "Her body is Jehan's."

"Do you wish it was yours?" The voice came softly as if the darkness whispered those words. The Mistress of the College withdrew into the shadows once more.

The Master stood, fighting outrage, fear, and then a hysterical impulse to laugh. "Madrona?" he whispered finally in a strangled voice. "Old woman! Are you envious of what you threw away?" he cried out suddenly. But there was no reply.

"My Lord . . . Jehan . . ." Faris pressed her face against his shoulder and felt his lips brush the top of her head.

"Are you sleepy, my love? Soon they will let us go." He tipped up her face, kissed her forehead, her cheek, and then, very slowly, her lips. Around them other couples sat close, listening to singers from the Ramparts twine a love song in close harmony.

"I will be ready," she whispered, "whenever it is right to go." She felt the familiar sweeet lassitude relaxing her as his arm went around her again. Her mind shied from memory of the ceremony in which Jehan had made her Lady of Westria. She knew that he was disappointed because, afterward, her passion did not match his. But she did not want that ecstasy that stole the soul away, only the safety of his arms around her and the awareness of his joy.

"Tonight," she whispered, kissing the palm of his hand. "Tonight."

A hunting owl called once, then slipped by the tower on silent wings. In the basement chamber, covered lamps glowed dimly in niches in the walls, casting shadows that seemed darker than if there had been no light.

"I have been patient with you, Ronald," Caolin said softly. The prisoner's hand moved wonderingly across the velvet of the cushioned chair. Caolin peered into his eyes, saw them beginning to dilate, and held the goblet to his lips again. Ronald drank greedily. The Seneschal had chosen a wine heavy and sweet enough to cover the taste of the drug he had mixed into it and to dull the prisoner's pain.

"My Lord," croaked Ronald. "I have told you what I could. Don't let him hurt me again."

"He will not touch you." Caolin had sent Ordrey away and Gerol as well when he saw how the captive's eyes followed every move the wolf made. He set the goblet back on the table.

Ronald grinned foolishly, triumphantly, but the oblivion he expected did not come. Caolin hoped he had mixed the right dose. When the man was so weak, it was hard to tell what would be enough to loose tongue from will without loosing spirit from body as well.

"We will talk instead," he said pleasantly. "I need clever people to help me, people who have been passed over while foolish men sleep in silk. I know how that feels, Ronald. When I came here, I was only a clerk, and people who could scarcely write their names jeered at me because I would not swing a sword."

"Clever . . . I'm clever," mumbled Ronald. He looked up at Caolin. "I should be Lord Commander of the Corona, you know."

The Seneschal nodded. "Of course. All you needed was some money, and when Lord Brian gave you that gold . . ."

Ronald shook his head, and Caolin let out his breath again as the man went on. "The gold was to get the Coronans to talk about independence from the Crown. The outlaws were my idea, I thought –" Ronald choked and stopped.

Caolin had moved away and was pouring himself a cup of wine. "It's all right, Ronald," he said gently. "I already knew where the money came from. If the outlaws killed Theodor, that would help you, and it would help Brian if they killed the King." With an effort he kept his voice steady, his body still. There was a long silence.

"No . . . it was not that way . . ." The words dragged from Ronald's lips. Caolin stole a glance and saw that the prisoner's eyes had closed. "I could not control the woods rats once they had taken my gold, and I thought that perhaps it would be better that way. The King did not like me. He would never have made me Lord Commander. Brian would have supported my claim as I supported his cause. But Brian was too soft to do what had to be done. I did it for Brian, but Brian did not know!"

Caolin's fingers clenched on the silver goblet until the slender stem bent. He recognised the ring of the truth. He too knew someone who was too soft to do what had to be done.

Brian had begun by teasing a nameless clerk, had protested Caolin's low birth when the new King proposed to make him Seneschal, had sneered at him or ignored him at every turn. He would end by challenging Jehan's own right to the throne. Whether he had conspired to kill the King or not, Brian must be implicated now.

Caolin sighed and touched a taper to one of the wall lamps, then to the unlit candle that stood on the table. Then he slid off his Seneschal's ring.

"Ronald," he called softly, turned the man's face to the flame. The prisoner's eyelids quivered, and he moaned.

"Ronald, here's something pretty – open your eyes to see."
The ring focused the flame to a ruby glow. Ronald's dull
eyes moved towards it, remained there as Caolin kept up
a stream of commands. "You see nothing but the light,
Ronald. You hear nothing but what I say. You will speak
the words I tell you now . . .

"My name is Ronald Sandreson. Say it." Caolin waited
tensely as the man whispered his own name.

"Lord Brian gave me gold to kill the King." Caolin visualised his will as a glowing rod extending to pierce the other
man's soul. *Say the words!*

"Lord Brian . . . gave me . . . gold . . ." The voice faltered. Ronald's breathing rasped the still air. Caolin left
his ring on the table and gripped the man's face between
his hands.

"Say the words!" Will and voice thrust through the link
between their minds. "– gold to kill the King!"

He felt Ronald's head twitch between his hands, and
the eyes that had been fixed on the ruby lifted to his own.
Speak! Caolin stared as if he could see through Ronald's
eyes into his very soul.

"Lord Brian . . . Brian . . . my Lord!" The anguished
whisper grew suddenly clear.

Caolin trembled with frustrated fury, holding Ronald
as he had held to his altar on the Red Mountain. And
as if that thought had released a force greater than his
own, he felt rage flare from his feet to his fingertips.
Ronald's body jerked, convulsed again and again, and
Caolin felt in his own flesh the echo of his victim's pain
and the final moment of release in which the pain became
an ecstasy.

After long, silent moments Caolin realised that Ronald
was dead and very gently laid him down. He looked at the
slack face wonderingly. Had his ritual on the Mountain
done all this? After so many years in which he had felt
nothing, the spirit of the Red Mountain had touched him,
and now the death struggle of this fool – this fool who yet
had died without betraying his master.

Did you love him? he asked silently. *I could forge a confession in your name, but I will let your fate remain a mystery. You were at least a loyal fool. And what am I?* he wondered suddenly. *What am I?*

He sat down by the table and picked up his goblet, but he found that he could not drink. Instead he rested his head in his hands, and so Ordrey found him when he came, some hours later, to tell the Seneschal that it was dawn.

The early morning light had a unique purity, unfiltered by the dust of the day, and soft enough so that one could see things in their true colors without squinting against the sun. But it could be a pitiless purity, thought Jehan, peering into the glass to see if last night's celebration had indeed left a puffiness around his eyes. He picked up a towel and began to rub at his hair, still wet from his swim in the lake that was the heart of Laurelynn.

A ghost of a headache reminded him that he had done due homage to Lord Hakon's gift of Seagate wine. But a sense of ease in his body brought back even more pleasant memories of the night that had followed the feast. His body was content, if not his soul.

Jehan threw down the towel and looked for his robe, then laughed as he realised that even the memory of Faris' sweet yielding was enough to stir new desire, intensified by the yet unfulfilled need for her ecstasy to match his own. He told himself to be grateful for what he already had.

He had asked his sister Jessica whether Faris' pregnancy might account for her passivity and winced, remembering her comments on the way he had hastened Faris into marriage, loosing the wonder of her initiation into womanhood by submerging it in her initiation as Lady of Westria.

"Perhaps after the child has been born," Jessica had ended her lecture. "Give her time, and you will both have youro'z desire."

Mik Whitestreak, who took care of the King's wardrobe in Laurelynn, came into the room with the garments Jehan would wear for the Council today. The King drew on the fine cotton loinguard, raised his arms so that Mik could slip over his head the sleeveless undertunic of white silk ornamented with drawnwork at neck and hem.

It was followed by a full-length tunic of gold silk woven with a pattern of green laurel sprigs, cut fuller than the style was now. Jehan glanced at the emerald velvet Cloak of State draped across a chair, his skin prickling already at the thought of its weight in the summer sun. Fortunately he would do no riding today, and so needed neither boots nor breeches. He slipped his feet gratefully into the sandals of gilded leather Mik held out to him.

"Thank you, old friend, the rest can wait until I've breakfasted. Will you find out if the Queen is ready? That is, if she wants to eat at all!"

Mik's grin answered his own and the old man went out.

Jehan picked up the great jade brooch incised with the circled cross of Westria, which matched the ring that for fifteen years had never left his hand, and pinned the neck of his tunic. The door opened again.

"What does she –" Jehan turned and fell silent as Caolin came into the light, that unpitying light that showed the color drained from his fair skin and marks like old bruises beneath his eyes.

"Well! I thought I had done some carousing, but you look as if you had been through all the taverns in Arena," said the King. The Seneschal's eyes evaded his too swiftly for Jehan to read them, but he realised that they were clear. He caught Caolin's shoulder, pulled him forward, and grasped his other arm. "What is wrong?"

"I . . . was up all night questioning a man who had been badly used . . . and he died."

"Here in Laurelynn? I'll have something to say to the City Guard. But you must not dwell on it," Jehan went on, "the memory will pass. The first battle I was in, I felt everything, but I learned."

Caolin raised his head, and something in Jehan grew very still at the look in his eyes. "You don't understand," said the Seneschal. "It was I –"

"Jehan, I'm ready for breakfast, I'm even *hungry!* And isn't this gown beautiful? Your sister helped me fix it—" Faris drew breath. "I'm sorry, Jehan, I didn't mean to interrupt. Let me wait for you in the breakfast room."

"No," said Caolin. "Interruption is the privilege of beauty."

Somehow he had slipped from Jehan's grasp. He turned and bowed to Faris, and for a moment both men stood still in acknowledgment of the truth of his words. The Queen's tight-sleeved crimson gown was woven with golden roses, cut low across her breasts to display a royal necklace of garnet and gold. But her dramatic coloring and the brilliance of her eyes enabled her to dominate the gown.

"Oh, damn," Jehan said softly. Had he for a moment seen vulnerability in the Seneschal's still face? "Caolin, we must talk about this – maybe after the Council?"

"If, after the Council, we have voices left to talk of anything at all." Caolin smiled. "You remind me – the Council begins in an hour and I still have things to do." His hand brushed the King's sleeve, then he was moving toward the door. "Be easy, my Lord. I am supposed to do the worrying for you!"

"Health and long life to Jehan, King of Westria!"

"Health and long life to Faris, our Queen!"

"Lord and Lady of Westria, all hail!"

Jehan groped for the armrest of the throne behind him, momentarily dizzied by the waves of energy flowing from the people to him. *This is for me*, he thought wonderingly, *not for a poor stand-in for a great King lost too soon, but for the man who has given them a Queen to adore and begotten a child to follow him.*

For once the weight of the Crown, hammered from Ramparts gold and ornamented with medallions enameled with the emblems of the Estates of Westria, did not oppress him, nor did the shepherd's staff he held seem heavier than a sword. He was the guardian of the fairest of all lands, King of a great people, and their belief in

263

him renewed an old ambition to become for them a great King.

At length the cheering died away. Jehan assisted Faris to her throne and was reminded of her radiance when she had first put on the Jewels. He gave silent thanks to the Guardian of Men who had thus rewarded Faris for having consented to become his Queen.

"In the name of the Maker of All Things, and in the presence of the King and Queen of Westria, I command order in this court. Let the business of the day begin!" The Herald's staff rang on the marble pavement.

With a rustle of robes and a last murmur of comment, the seven councilors and the several hundred others – relatives, followers, great landholders from the four Provinces, and Guildmasters from the Free Cities – took their places. For each Estate there was a wedge-shaped section that rose in the fashion of an amphitheater from the circular floor, where smoke curled gently from a perpetual hearth, to the eight-sided walls of the Council Hall.

Behind him Jehan heard the whisperings of his household and holders from his own lands, the Royal Domain, cease as the Herald called the gathering to order once again. The King glanced across the hearth to where Caolin sat at his desk, crimson robe glowing in the brightness from the skylight, fair hair glistening. The Seneschal looked up, and Jehan was relieved to see that though he was pale, he seemed quite self-possessed. Caolin smiled faintly and handed a sheaf of papers to a page to carry over to the King.

Reports – Jehan remembered the agenda and settled back to hear the yearly tally of gains and losses among the population of humans, their animals, and the other kindreds with whom they shared the land.

Lord Hakon of Seagate, as senior Commander of the Provinces, usually reported first. But Jehan saw that Eric's concern was justified. The old warrior lay back in his chair with nothing moving about him but his eyes, while Eric read his report in a voice that gathered certainty as he went on. When the west had reported, came the turns of the south, the east, and the north. Caolin had marked points in the reports where Jehan or one of his officers might want to comment, but there was little that called for questioning.

The King having already given his principal news when he presented his Queen, the floor then passed to the Free Cities, whose place was on the building's southwestern side, for whom Frederic Sachs made a report that the Herald finally had to curtail. Next came Caolin, speaking for the government of Westria, reporting briefly on the status of roads, bridges, foreign trade, and relationships with foreign powers. Most of those present had already noticed the Elayan envoys sitting impassive in their roped-off section, but Caolin's mention of their visit nonetheless caused a little stir. Last came the turn of the College of the Wise, whose Mistress represented not only the College but all priests and priestesses, all shrines, and a link with the Powers who dwelt in Awahna itself.

She rose in her place, waiting a few moments while the silence deepened. Jehan's gaze sought the Master of the Junipers, sitting with other members of his Order in the ranks behind her.

"Fellow-children of this land of Westria . . ." The voice of the Mistress came softly, yet it filled the Hall. "I will not recite facts or figures that you already know. There is little of importance in the world of the spirit that can be described in that way. But I must speak to all of you – and to my own people as well – regarding the role that this College is called to play in our lives."

Jehan thought he saw apprehension on the Master's face and leaned forward, watching the speaker intently.

"My priests and priestesses in the holdings and cities complain to me that men are returning to superstition or fanaticisms from the past and abandoning the rituals of Westria that keep us in harmony with the other kindreds. Lords and holders complain that the College interferes with their legitimate struggle to win a living from the land.

"But I say to you, the only soul that a man can win or lose is his own. If those who are called to the priesthood illustrate their belief with their lives, the lesson will be clearer than any commandment or coercion. Once a ritual becomes a form to be followed, it loses power, but if even one believer walks the path convinced of its truth, its power will endure.

"Look into your own hearts, you leaders of Westria. I will not pass judgment upon you. You will be judged by your own actions, so consider them well!" She gathered her black and white robes around her and sat down.

I must speak to the Master of this. Jehan bit at his lip. *If each man and woman must save his or her own soul, what of their lords? What of the King who is responsible to the Maker for all?*

It was Caolin who signaled to the Herald to proclaim the Council open for new business at last. Jehan watched Brian rise to his feet, deliberately as if a mountain had decided to move. Still shaken by the words of the Mistress, the King did not know whether to be glad or sorry that he did not know what the Lord Commander of the south was going to say.

Lord Brian did not read very effectively, but he did not have to. Copies of the proposal had been passed to each councilor, with a carefully copied list of those who supported it.

"As I understand it," said Caolin, "this proposal of yours is intended to decentralise the Kingdom – to give the Provinces more independence in certain areas, such as relations with those on their borders, and to extend the jurisdiction of the Commanders' courts to cover all except disputes affecting other Provinces?" The others were still checking back over their copies to be sure they understood. Brian nodded shortly.

"But where do you draw the line as to what affects your neighbor and what does not?" asked Lord Robert.

"My Lord of the south and I do not share a border," said Theodor, "so I have not that concern." Laughter was muffled in several places in the Hall. Theodor went on, "But I do have to deal with a foreign power, and I would rather have the weight of a Kingdom behind me than stand alone."

Lord Brian looked down briefly, then turned, surprisingly, to Faris. "My Lady, since you are a strong man's choice, I will credit you with his strength. This Council has always been a place where we might speak freely, without courtly phrases or poisoned compliments" – his eyes flickered in Caolin's direction – "so you must believe that I mean no discourtesy when I suggest that your relationship to Lord Theodor encourages him to support the Crown."

Jehan stiffened, feeling Faris' confusion and fear. He half rose, and Brian sent him a startled glance, but Theodor was already on his feet, his face purple, crumpling his copy of the petition and flinging it down.

"Lady Faris may be too gracious to call that discourtesy, but I am not! Lord Brian, I had heard about your opinions before the King ever came north, and my reaction to them was the same. The strength of Westria lies in unity under a strong King!"

"It depends on how that strength is used. It is well enough when the King is young and honourable, as I believe our Lord to be –"

"You had better!" Eric's whisper was audible across the floor.

"But even when he is," Brian continued as if he had not heard, "the Kingdom is large, and no one man can know it all well enough to be certain of judging rightly all the time. You will say that the King has Deputies to be his eyes and ears, but how shall he know if their report be true?"

By this time Jehan had gotten his temper under control. He reached for Faris' hand. "Don't be afraid, love – wait, and I will show you how I play the King." She looked at him and smiled, and he wished them back in the cave in the mountains or at Misthall, or even in their bedchamber in the palace.

"I speak for the Free Cities," rumbled Frederic Sachs, smoothing the fur on his robe. "If you ask more freedom for the Provinces, the cities must be protected."

Eric was on his feet now, looking anxiously at Jehan. "My father bids me speak for him." He continued before the King completed his nod, "You say that frankness is a virtue, Lord Brian. Well, I can be frank too. You talk about other people's motives, but what about your own? When your boats came into our fishing grounds, the dispute was settled by the King. If we had been under your new system, what would have judged between us, your sword?" His father was pulling at his arm, but Eric charged on, "Frankness indeed – I could give this kind of talk another name."

"Eric, be still!" Jehan found his voice at last. "Westrians do not challenge each other's loyalty in this Hall." Eric looked at him open-mouthed. Someone tittered and he reddened, but seeing the King's gaze soften, he recovered himself and sat down. Jehan looked over at Brian, holding the man's yellow eyes until some of the fierceness went out of them and he too took his seat.

Then the King rose from his throne and stood before them. "Ladies and Lords – such a question will not be settled by hot words. I hold power by the will of Awahna and of the people of this land and may not lightly renounce it – I am as bound by the law as you. If my people find me blind to their needs, I must strive for amendment. But I will not do so by giving up or delegating my responsibilities. So far I will agree with Lord Brian that power and knowledge should be one, and how shall I judge, or you follow, if I pass all my life in Laurelynn?"

Slowly he paced around the circle, drawing their attention to him, to his words. "Therefore look for me not in my own Hall but in yours. For my Lady and I will come to you, and our children after us, and so we shall rule."

He held them. He knew it by the shining eyes of the people in the ranks above him. He would not relinquish leadership of this Council again. He turned, saw in Caolin's face a mixture of admiration and apprehension, followed his gaze upward to the Elayan envoys.

Jehan's arms twitched as if he could protect his people with his bare hands. *Even from Elaya.* He paused below the strangers' box. Everyone was looking at them now, and he nodded to the Herald to announce them.

Emir Akhbar came slowly down the steps, followed by Maclain.

"I bring you the greetings of my Prince, Palomon Strong-bow, head of the House of Ottavie and lord of the confederated states of Elaya. He felicitates you on your marriage and wishes you many children, for the husband of a beautiful wife will wish to enjoy her, and the father of a family to teach his children, unlike young bachelors, who think only of war." His dark eyes paused on Eric's fascinated face. Jehan shifted uneasily, waiting for the insult all this politeness hid.

"And yet young warriors must be kept under control, if fathers of families are to enjoy their homes in peace," Akhbar went on. "In times past the town of Santibar belonged to Elaya. Twenty years ago there there was a war, and your father, my Lord, put his hand to the treaty of peace, and swore" – the Elayan's eyes grew distant – "*that the town of Santibar and the fortress of Balleor should belong to Westria so long as the border between our lands be well and peacefully kept*," he quoted.

"My Lords of Westria –" The Emir's voice rang now against the painted timbers of the ceiling, and men's fingers twitched for the hilts of swords they had left at home. "That oath has been broken, and Santibar and Balleor are now by right Elaya's! These are the words of my Prince, and we bid you peacefully accept our claim . . . for if you do not," he added softly, "be assured that we will write you a new treaty in your own blood with the points of our spears."

"You call the treaty broken when five drunken soldiers burn a barn, when the walls of Santibar still bear the scars of your catapults not four years old?" Brian's fist crashed

on his table, and Rodrigo Maclain, beard bristling, moved
forward.

"The envoys were addressing me." Jehan focused his
voice to the knife edge they had taught him at the College, which could be heard through battle or storm. He
stared Brian down, compelled even the envoys to wait on
his words. He wished that Faris were not here. He would
have to leave her Regent if he went to war.

"My Lords of Elaya," he said evenly, "remember that
men fight most fiercely when they defend their homes.
Tell your Prince that my marriage but makes me more
dangerous as a foe, and reconsider what you say." He stood
up, the step on which the thrones were set allowing him
to look down on them, and grasped his shepherd's staff.
"While the men and women of Santibar wish to remain
Westrian, I will not betray them."

Jehan looked around him, seeing anger, apprehension,
or excitement in the faces of his people, and knowing to
what he committed them if the Elayan challenge were no
bluff. "I have offered reparation to the man whose barn
was burned, but I have had no answer," he added slowly.
"Therefore to the south I will send an embassy, to see this
man and have his story from his own lips, to question the
accused soldiers and send them to me for judgment, and
to hear from the people of Santibar their will." He avoided
Caolin's eye, but he could see the forced stillness of the
Seneschal's hands.

He turned to his right. "My lord Brian. You desire
to take care of your own. You, therefore, shall head
this embassy and face yourself whatever your deeds have
wrought." Something broke like a snapped twig in the silence that followed. Jehan watched Brian pale and redden,
then go pale again as he bowed his assent. "Lady Elinor
of Fairhaven shall go with you." He named three others, all well known and respected in peace as well as
war.

"Tell your Prince what has passed today, and if you will,
send wise ones of your own to join my embassy. The

people of Santibar shall decide, and their decision will be backed by all the swords in Westria!"

As the echoes of his words died the King grew still; a vigilant stillness, which held the Elayans silent as they bowed and withdrew, held even the Westrians, until the Herald had declared the Council closed.

Jehan drew a deep breath, trembling now that it was over, and reached out to Faris. She came into his arms and he held her as if he could draw strength from the thing that his strength was meant to guard.

Beyond Faris he saw Caolin stacking the papers on his table and packing them into a portfolio with swift, precise motions as if he were imprisoning enemies. A pen lay broken beside the portfolio, and Jehan remembered the snapping sound he had heard.

"Caolin, I would rather have consulted with you about the choice of delegates for the embassy, but there are times when one must seize the moment for action."

The Seneschal looked up, his eyes rounding in surprise. "My Lord, it is your decision – you are the King." His voice was colorless.

"Jehan . . . can we leave?" Faris murmured against his shoulder.

The King looked around him. The council floor was clear, but crowds still milled at the upper doors. *My people*, he thought, *my people who would follow Brian or any loud fool who promises something new* . . . He sighed.

"Soon, my love – this herd would trample you now."

"Young cockerels must crow, but not in royal council halls! I have a mind to whip you like a half-grown boy!"

The Master of the Junipers paused in the corridor, recognizing Brian's angry tones. He had hoped for a word with the Mistress of the College, but she was past him now. He turned towards the voice, wondering who Brian was talking to. The long windows he passed were open to let in the cooling air, and the evening wind was beginning to rustle in the willows outside.

"I am old enough to teach you the meaning of loyalty!"

The Master rounded a corner, saw Eric facing Lord Brian. Both men stood with feet apart, hands open and ready to strike.

"You named me traitor before half Westria – do you think to go unpunished?"

"On the field or off it, you are not the one who will lesson me!"

Brian tipped back his head and gave a bark of laughter. "I may lessen you, however, for all they call you the new champion. Men are wagering on the outcome if we fight. You hope for glory, but you will find humiliation."

Eric quivered like a leashed hound and took a step forward. Brian laughed again.

"Brian! Is this how you repay the King's trust? Eric, do you think the King will thank you for brawling in his name?" The Master stepped between the two men, stretching to meet their eyes.

"Prayersmith, keep your sermons for your own flock." Brian did not take his eyes from Eric's.

"I am the King's chaplain, and you are both the King's men. Victory for either would bring honor to neither of you, nor would you get any sympathy in defeat."

The silence seemed long before Brian snorted in disgust and stepped away. "Very well, grayrobe, but one day I will face this cockerel on the field with a good blade in my hand!" His head swung back and forth as he glared from the Master to Eric, then stalked away.

"I will be ready, Brian, only name the day!" Eric cried after him. He turned to the Master, the sparkle dying from his eyes. "And he will be the one left lying on the field."

"Save your strength for the Elayans," the Master said tiredly. "They are even more eager to fight than Brian is. Go away, Eric," he added, seeing interest return to the young man's eyes.

Eric flushed a little, bowed, and turned away. The Master listened to his receding steps, wondering if he should go to the rooms where the Mistress of the College had stayed.

There were words between them that needed to be unsaid. He went to the window, looking across the gardens to the Guesthall, but the Mistress' window was dark.

He rubbed at his eyes and sat down on the window ledge, hearing now no voice but the lonely sighing of the wind.

12

The Lord and the Lady

Faris lay against the low rail of the barge and trailed her
fingers in the dark water, shattering the reflections of the
lanterns into a swirl of multicolored flowers. Petals dropped to add to them from the garlands of red roses on her
hair and at her breast. She raised herself, turned back to
the boat, and Jehan's arm went around her. She grinned
then and flicked her wet fingers so that droplets caught
like crystal in his hair and beard.

"For that, a kiss," he murmured, drawing her to him.
After a moment he let her go, and she settled into the
crook of his arm with a contented sigh, smoothing the gold
silk of her loose gown to admire its embroidery of fruit and
flowers. For a moment she hardly dared to breathe, poised
upon the balance-point of content. *Be still*, she thought,
lest the moment pass.

"Is everyone comfortable? Do you all have your desire?" the Mayor of Laurelynn asked earnestly, by echoing
her thought, destroying it. His dark hair, showing just
enough silver for respectability, lay sleeked against his
head.

"Indeed, Master Joaquin, Laurelynn has outdone itself.
I cannot remember when I passed the Feast of the First
People so pleasantly," replied Jehan drily.

The Mayor's wife stifled laughter as her husband frowned, and pulled nervously at her stiff skirts. She looked older than her husband, perhaps because of her rouged cheeks and the henna with which she tried to cover the gray in her hair. But her gown had the tight sleeves that were now all the fashion in Laurelynn. Faris had not meant to encourage anything so hot and uncomfortable, but she wondered how many would still praise her beauty if they knew of the disfigurement her own sleeve hid.

But surely that did not matter now – she must not allow herself to think of it on such a night as this. She smiled encouragingly at the Mayor's wife, aware of Lady Gwenna's anxiety at playing hostess to the royal party, but it seemed strange to be offering comfort instead of needing it. She heard Frederic Sachs' bray of laughter from one of the other barges across the water – obviously the other guests were enjoying themselves too.

Caolin poured yellow wine into the King's cup and handed it to him as Jehan reached out. Faris looked at the Seneschal under her lashes, wondering how long it would take for her to know what Jehan needed so instinctively. She eased herself closer to Jehan and was rewarded as his arm tightened around her.

"Oh, look – it's a deer!" Rosemary's exclamation focused all attention on the lake, where rafts bearing large lanterns in the forms of plants or animals were being poled across the glittering waters. They floated among the barges and then along the shore, where the people of Laurelynn were gathered. Beyond the lawns that sloped down to the lake the windows of the city glowed.

"Indeed, my Lady, like everyone else in Westria, we open the gates of the city on this night, but it is so rare for any of the other kindreds to accept the invitation that we make these toys to show the children what the Festival means," Master Joaquin explained.

"You should let Rosemary invite them for you," said Farin. "She keeps the Festival all year round. You've collected a family of quail and a lame coyote cub since you came to Laurelynn, and of course you have that damned owl!"

"Should I refuse my help because I am no longer at home? All my doors are open tonight, and if the animals stay with me, it will be because they so choose!" Rosemary turned to Master Joaquin again as Farin picked up his harp and plucked a trill like the call of a bird.

"I expect that Laurelynn has too many people for the other kindreds to feel at home here," she told the Mayor. "The Hold is a way above the town, and so we never know who our visitors will be. One year a great boar came down to our pig barns and sired a new breed on our sows."

"Has Gerol gone to keep the Festival?" Jehan said to Caolin.

The Seneschal smiled. "When the moon rises, listen and you will hear music from the hills. Gerol goes to sing with his pack each year, but he has never told me the meaning of the song."

Farin plucked a series of chords. "In the north we have legends about humans who have gone to the hills on Festival night. When someone is missing from his or her bed the next morning, we never ask where they have been, but the old women are careful to examine the children born at Beltane."

"But why?" asked the Mayor's wife, wide-eyed.

"To see if any of them have pointed ears, or a skin that glows green in the sun!"

Even as she laughed Faris found her arms moving to shield her belly.

"Don't worry," said Rosemary, "your baby will be born in March!"

Faris smiled and shook her head. If the child had been conceived at Midsummer, more than the kiss of a wood sprite had gone into its making. But she remembered only the dreadful sense of loss with which she had awakened, merely human once more, to realise that she remembered only fragments of the ceremony that had mated her to

Jehan. Was the child indeed hers, or was she only a vessel to bring it into the world?

All you Powers of light and darkness, be far from me! she prayed. *Give me no dreams, no ecstasies that set adrift the soul. Let me only be human, and in love, and Faris.*

Jehan's face shone like one of the torches; his eyes gleamed like the stars sewn on to his blue robe. He set his hand gently over Faris' belly, then looked back at the others.

"I only wish I could have offered more today," he said softly. "I have been given so much. I have a wife and Lady for my heart." He turned then and gasped Caolin's hand. "And I have my mind's twin – so much more than friend, and the child who will be my first-fruits, born to the service of Westria."

Lady Gwenna's fingers flickered in the sign to avert ill luck, and Rosemary stretched out her arm and tipped wine from her goblet over the side.

"May the Powers accept our offerings," Rosemary said softly, "and not grudge us the achievement of our desires." Her eyes moved involuntarily towards one of the other barges.

Faris knew she was thinking of Eric and wondered what could change the reproachful devotion with which he served his Queen to love for the girl who loved him. If only everyone could be happy tonight!

Her gaze moved on to Caolin, who sat looking into his wine cup, his face unreadable, his hand passive beneath that of the King. In the north he had seemed as finely tuned as the instrument he played for them. Now, though his dress was still meticulous, he had a faintly ragged quality, as if his flesh were no longer so neatly fitted to the spirit it housed. She let her awareness expand to include him, drew back in surprise as she felt the blank surface of his shield.

Did he accept what Jehan had said? What did he think of her? Once it had seemed that Caolin was going to court her like the rest, then he had seemed almost hostile. But tonight he had left off his brittle mask, and she began to understand why Jehan cared for him. *Let nothing change that. I would not have Jehan lose anything because of me.*

"Caolin –" Impulsively Faris drew the wreath from her head, plucked two white roses from Jehan's wreath, and worked them in among the rest and held it out to him. "We all have flowers tonight except you. Wear this wreath – see, I will take the flowers from around my neck and wear them so we shall be all alike."

Caolin looked up at her then, his gray eyes darkening, holding hers. Then he straightened. "My thanks, Lady. Few can boast of having received such a crown from such a Queen." He took her hand as she reached across Jehan, and she felt the cool touch of his lips on her palm before he settled the bright roses on the gold of his hair.

"You are fortunate indeed, my Lord," said Master Joaquin. "My lord Caolin will keep good watch while you and your Lady travel in the Provinces." He bowed towards the Seneschal, whose eyes gleamed sardonically for a moment as he nodded in return. Loud laughter and a splash told them that someone had missed his step in getting from one of the other barges to the dock. Now other barges were turning towards shore.

Jehan nodded. "The time for celebration has been well spent, but it is the season for work now. The harvest will be starting, and I must keep the promise I made in the Council Hall."

"Then let these last moments of pleasure be spent well," said Caolin softly. "I remember the first time I heard my Lady Faris sing . . . if she is willing, let her sing again."

Startled, Faris looked from Caolin to the others. Farin grinned. "I have done my part of the entertaining this evening, now it is your turn. Sing, Faris, and I will play for you."

"Please," said Jehan. His eyes burned like blue stars.

"Very well," she answered slowly, trying to recapture the words she remembered her mother singing long ago. She cleared her throat and began, so suddenly that she had finished the first verse before Farin caught the tune and began to accompany her.

> Where shall the flower turn, if not to the sun?
> Where shall the river run, if not into the sea?
> Where shall the leaf fall when summer is done,
> If not to earth's bosom? And so it is with me –
>
> For if I sing sweetly, it is because you hear;
> If I have beauty, your seeing makes me fair;
> If I know laughter, then you have banished fear,
> And if I am fruitful, it is your seed I bear.
>
> As you have chosen, so will I decide;
> The same path that you tread, my feet will follow still.
> Where you are dwelling, there will I abide –
> Oh, my beloved, I wait upon your will!

She finished and sat with bent head while Farin rounded out the ending with a series of descending harmonies and a final chord. She could feel approval from the others, and from Jehan, passion that built like a climbing wave.

The music ended. Faris looked up at Jehan and shut her eyes against what she saw in his face. His hands closed on her shoulders; he pulled her to him and her lips opened beneath his as he bore her back amid the cushions.

Her body yielded to his as if in illustration of her song, and yet some separate compartment of her mind was noting the changed motion of the barge as it followed the others towards the shore, the gentle bump as it reached the dock. There was a short silence, then a rustle as the others rose and made their way to the side.

"We thank you, Master Mayor, for a most memorable evening. Since this is the King's barge, I think it will be no discourtesy if we leave before he does," Caolin

said blandly. Feet echoed on the dock, and Faris heard
a shocked giggle from the Mayor's wife.

Jehan's lips released Faris at last and he began to trace
the line of her throat. She turned a little to accommodate
him and saw Caolin, silhouetted against the stars.

"Good night, my Lord . . . my Lady," he said softly.
Faris fought an impulse to laugh – had Jehan even heard?
There was a faint sigh, then a light step on the dock, and
Caolin, too, was gone.

Jehan had pulled down the loose neck of her gown,
imprisoning her arms and baring her breasts to the warm
night air. As his hands moved over her body Faris breathed
deeply of the scent of crushed roses and felt the familiar
sweet lassitude unstring her limbs.

Her heart pounded as the ceremonial drum had pounded
in the Sacred Wood. She flinched from the heat of the sacred fire. She felt a pressure against her mind as Jehan's
body possessed hers, and grew still in his arms, knowing
the Power that waited to overwhelm her if she opened her
last defense.

Oh, my beloved! Her body waited on his will, but her
spirit remained barriered. She felt his longing as he held
back, seeking to kindle her with his own flame, but in such
a blaze they could both be consumed. In that mating of god
and goddess Faris and Jehan would be whirled away like
sparks upon the wind, and she refused to be used in that
way again.

She moved in Jehan's arms, and he cried out, holding
her fast within the tempest of his love. When he grew still
at last, she worked her arms free of her gown and held him,
murmuring his name.

"Jehan!" Caolin turned abruptly, brushing the Queen's
wilted wreath from the table to the floor. "Is something
wrong?"

The King shook his head as he came forward, running
his finger along the backs of the leather-bound volumes in
the bookcase, touching the velvet of the drapes Caolin had

just opened, as if he expected them to have changed since the last time he had visited Caolin's chambers more than a year ago.

"I didn't know if I would find you still here," Jehan said at last.

"There's little point in going to my offices until my staff has had time to recover from the Festival," Caolin replied drily. That was not really true – he rather preferred working alone, but he did not wish Jehan to know that he had slept badly, haunted by the scent of roses.

Jehan looked around him, noted Gerol stretched snoring on the hearthrug with a streak of mud along his side and burrs in his plumed tail.

"He appears to have celebrated rather thoroughly too," the King said ruefully, then met Caolin's eyes. "I'm sorry! I didn't mean for you to have to end the party for me last night. It was the wine, perhaps, or the Festival –" He shrugged helplessly. "I have no reason to hide my feelings, but my control is usually better than that!"

Caolin looked at him curiously. Jehan had never concealed his passions before – why was he worrying now? "It's all right. They all understood."

"I wish *I* understood!" Jehan tried to smile, the beautiful bone structure of his face highlighted by the clear morning light. "What Faris and I have now is all that any man should desire, but if we ever join completely, all Westria will shake!"

"My dear Lord, you should be saying this to your wife, not to me!" said Caolin uncomfortably, picking up his belt and drawing in the full folds of his mulberry-colored robe, but his heart kept saying, *Whenever I turn to you, she is there between us now. What is it you want from her that I could not give you, my Lord?*

The King laughed, and Caolin realised that the moment when he might have asked him such a question had gone.

"Actually," said Jehan, "I wanted to talk to you before I leave Laurelynn this afternoon. Brian has not returned from Sanjos, and people are preparing for our visits throughout the Ramparts. I cannot wait for him. I fear you will have to instruct the Embassy we are sending to Elaya."

"Appoint someone else to lead it and your problem will be solved."

"I was afraid you would not like my choice." Jehan sighed. "But I would rather occupy Brian with a real problem than leave him to invent one while I am elsewhere. If I give him what he thinks he wants, he may change his mind."

Caolin made a sound that was not quite a laugh. "If the Red Mountain fell on his head he might notice. Otherwise . . ." He shook his head. "Well, I will do my best."

"You are the diplomat – I would depend on your advice in this in any case."

"Perhaps, but do you think Brian will be willing to do so?" Caolin asked.

"He will have to." Jehan grinned suddenly. "Caolin, you must be mellowing – we have been discussing Brian for five minutes without an accusation of treachery. Are you waiting to catch Ronald before you go after Brian again?"

Caolin's fingers tightened on the buckle of his belt. *Does Jehan know?*

"Nothing has been heard of Ronald for some time. I doubt we will get any evidence from him now," he said carefully. "I know that you will not suspect Brian until he implicates himself. Maybe he will do so on this trip to Santibar – I only hope the price of the evidence is not too high."

Another half-truth. Caolin moved to the bureau, picked up the Seneschal's chain of office with its golden key.

"Caolin . . ." Jehan spoke with difficulty. Caolin stilled, waiting for the words that would accuse him. "Caolin, the morning of the Council you came to me with some trouble – we had no time to talk. I did not want to go away without giving you a chance . . ." His voice died away.

Does he know? Caolin asked himself once more. *Does his heart feel what he will not let his mind understand?* Slowly he turned.

"So much was hanging on the Council – I was too easily upset. It does not matter now. You must not worry about me."

Jehan took his arm, a smile lighting his blue eyes. "You worry enough for two, my friend. Do not work too hard while I am gone, and if you have difficulties, follow me."

Caolin's arm still tingled with the pressure of the King's hand when Jehan had gone. He stood unmoving, staring at the door. *I did not lie . . . I said nothing untrue,* he told himself. *Oh, my Lord, I do not find it easy to conceal my soul from you.*

The bell in the palace tower tolled ten o'clock. Caolin stirred at last and bent to pick the Queen's wreath from the floor. Something glistened, and he saw tangled among the red and white roses a strand of his own golden hair.

Brian of Las Costas returned to Laurelynn six days after the Royal party had left for Rivered, guarded and provisioned as if he were setting out on campaign. Caolin leaned from the window of his Offices to watch the escort clatter by, wondering which of the Lord Commander's people would have the thankless task of informing Brian that even when the King honored him with a commission, its terms were to be mediated by Caolin.

The next morning, when Brian met with Caolin and the other members of the embassy to Elaya in the small council chamber overlooking the river, the Commander appeared to have recovered from the shock. Despite the open windows and the early hour the day was already hot. Caolin found his fingers sticking to the paper he held and laid it down, considering the other man.

The Lord Commander's face seemed unusually red, and his hair bristled rebelliously from whatever order he had tried to impose on it. Brian looked up, and Caolin let his gaze shift away from the amber glow in the other man's eyes. The fire was only banked, then, not out.

"The King has laid out the purposes of this investigation and asked me to discuss its points with you before you go," he said.

Brian reached for the paper and the Seneschal twitched it back, holding it up. "Copies have been prepared for each of you, my Lords, my Ladies." He gestured to Ercul Ashe, who moved quietly along the table, passing them out.

Lady Elinor slipped a small glass on a chain from around her neck and peered through it at the paper. Ras of Santierra, one of the senior Masters of the College of Bards, leaned back in his chair, moving a dark finger from point to point on the page. Alessandro Cooper, a Guild-master of Laurelynn whose family had traded with Santibar for generations, pursed his lips as he read. Caolin waited as the others looked through their copies, suppressing a smile as he saw Brian's lips silently forming the words.

"As you see, our Lord wishes you to accomplish two things – to find out what really occurred in the so-called 'raid' on Elaya, and to learn whether the people of Santibar wish to remain with Westria. In addition –"

"Whose addition? I'll grant the first two, for the King has put his name to them, but I take no orders from you," said Brian.

"I am sure that our Lord has discussed this matter with Master Caolin, and I for one would be glad of further counsel now," Lady Elinor said quickly.

"Let us discuss it then, but I warn you I will not be bound by what he may say."

"I would never expect that, my Lord," Caolin murmured, slipping his ring of office from his finger and turning it back and forth so that it captured the sunlight in ruby flares.

"I will only offer suggestions for you to listen to . . . only listen to what I have to say," he soothed. Brian's glance fixed on the ring. "There's no need to be upset . . . listen."

"Stop that!" Brian's roar jerked everyone alert. He glared around him like a hunted bear when the arrows begin to sting. Caolin kept his face expressionless. Apparently Brian was sensitive enough to feel that something was being tried, but too strong to be affected. Unobtrusively Caolin slipped the ring back on to his hand.

"My Lord of the South," said Kimi of Longbay, lady of a fishing village in Seagate, "we have no time for this – let the Seneschal have his say. I want to know how we are to be certain of what the people of Santibar desire." Her almond eyes flashed.

"Your people are fishers too; you should be able to win their confidence," said Lady Elinor.

"After I finished at the College, I polished my craft upon the roads," said Master Ras. "I could arrive separately from the rest of you and listen to people's comments as I play for them." They looked at Caolin.

"You speak as my Lord hoped you would," said the Seneschal. "And you, Master Cooper, could find time to talk to the merchants with whom you trade."

"That's all very well, but all this skulking won't convince the Elayans. Let the people of Santibar tell me to my face whether I have been a good lord to them, and then let us look to our arms!" Brian's tone was surly.

Caolin frowned. Could the man be driven, then, since he could not be led? "Seek a fight and Elaya will be happy to oblige – but if the King wished to declare war he could have done so himself three weeks ago!"

"Let them –" Brian began, but Master Ras cut in.

"Our instructions say that we are to report only, to take no action that will commit Westria to any course."

Be quiet, man. Let Brian go on like this and he will condemn himself! thought Caolin, then said, "You are to take your time – gather information, inspect the entire border, delay if you can until the autumn rains begin to fall."

"You would like that, wouldn't you, to keep me away from Jehan while you poison his ears against me. How many other lies have you told in the King's name?" Brian seemed to expand as he leaned across the table.

"In the King's name?" Caolin was startled into response. "I will deal with you in my own name some day!" He gripped the arms of his chair to keep from flinching as Brian rose.

"Don't try me! I could break you, clerk!"

"Lord help your embassy," said Caolin very softly, "if you think you can search out every truth with the point of a sword!"

Caolin heard the scrape of a chair as Master Ras tried to grasp Brian's arm and was shaken off as easily as a bear beats off hounds. He waited, almost eagerly, for his enemy to strike.

But Brian stilled. "No! No – I will not soil my blade." He took a deep breath and sat down again. "I will use your weapons, snake. One day I will find the King alone and tell him what you are."

Caolin looked around the table. The others were beginning to relax, sensing that the quarrel was over for now. He shook his head. *When I have gone to my temple a few more times, I will know how to master you. One day you will learn what I am, Brian, to your cost!*

The remainder of the discussion was subdued and quickly over. Caolin sat still in his place after the Commissioners had gone. *At least Brian no longer discounts me.* He stretched out his arms and flexed his fingers to relieve their tension. *I suppose that is an achievement.*

Ercul Ashe came into the room and set down his papers. "Well, they are on their way."

"I must be on my way as well," said Caolin with a little laugh. "Tell someone to prepare my mare for travel and pack some food. I think I had best ride myself to report on this meeting to the King!"

Rosemary shifted uncomfortably in her saddle. "Oof! I feel as if I'd been riding for a week."

Faris laughed. "No, dear, we spent the week at Rivered, being pampered by Jessica. We left there only three days ago, and we have been riding for only two hours today. If I can bear it, surely you can survive." Her morning sickness had ceased before they left Laurelynn, or Jehan would never have let her ride, and in some ways her health was better than it had ever been. And yet there was something oppressive in the morning despite its brightness, and she understood Rosemary's complaint.

She patted Sombra's dark neck and glanced behind her. Dust rose in a steady haze behind the baggage carts, drifted across the dun-colored fields that stretched to the eastern mountains, shimmering in the heat. To her right the shrunken trickle of the Darkwater coiled through the reeds. She closed her eyes against the glare and shook her head a little, trying to clear it.

Hooves clattered behind them. It was Philip, the oldest child of Robert and Jessica, who was Jehan's new squire. He handled his responsibilities remarkably well, Faris thought, although his behavior alternated disconcertingly between that of boy and man.

The black mare tossed her head as Philip reined up beside them. Faris gave her a warning tap and smiled at the boy.

"Do you see that bird?" He pointed. "That's a red-tailed hawk. I have one at home, and a peregrine. Did you see them when you visited us?"

Faris shook her head. Philip looked momentarily disappointed, then continued, "Perhaps next time you visit us we can go hawking – after you have the baby, that is. I'm glad you are going to have a child," he added in the same tone. "I got awfully tired of being told to be careful because I was Uncle Jehan's heir."

Faris stared at him. "You didn't want to be a King?"

"It's bad enough to be Lord Commander of a Province! I want to enjoy life! Being King – well, now that he's married Jehan's mood doesn't change so much, but still . . ." Philip shook his head.

Faris rubbed at the small of her back, which was beginning to ache despite Sombra's smooth pace. They had told her that easy riding would not harm the baby, and she refused to be cooped up in a cart, but she found it hard to be concerned. Yet lately the idea of the child was taking on more reality. She looked doubtfully at Philip and wondered what kind of life her child would have.

For a moment the boy was silent, and Faris realised that his chatter had distracted her from a growing sense of oppression, as if a headache were coming on. Almost, she recognised the feeling. *No!* She barriered the awareness away. *I escaped such visions when I married Jehan! I don't want to know!*

"Do you see that peak – the one that looks almost transparent in the haze?" asked Philip. Faris shaded her eyes to search among the shapes that wavered in the heavy air, then nodded.

"At Initiation they told us it guards the road to Awahna, but they could not tell us how one gets there. Do you know?" he went on.

"Ask the Master of the Junipers," said Rosemary, pointing towards the Master, who turned his mount towards them when he heard his name.

Faris felt her oppression lighten as she focused on that distant silhouette. "Is that the road to Awahna?"

The Master's gaze followed hers, and the lines in his face eased as if a younger man looked out through his eyes. "It lies close by there, but no one can say for sure where it is."

"But you have been there," said Rosemary.

"I have made my way to the Secret Valley, as all who enter the Second Order must do, but I know only the signposts on that path. The road itself is never the same to any two who travel it . . . and unless the Lords of that Valley please, the path will not appear at all."

"At the College they spoke of it as a valley of wonders – a place not entirely in this world," said Rosemary.

Faris watched the Master, remembering how he had looked when he held out the coal to her and seeing a reflection of that brightness in his eyes now. Involuntarily her awareness sought his, and for a moment she glimpsed granite ramparts laced by silver waterfalls, the reflection of trees and sky in a still pool, faces like those of the priests of the elements who had sealed her to the Jewels. She closed her eyes against the memory, but the echo of the Master's longing had shaken her.

His thought came to her through the link she had made. *Each of us is Called to a different road, nor do we know our true direction until we reach its end.*

The link shattered as a rush of alien impressions broke through. *Run! Death is coming – get away!* Faris clung to the mare, cowering back from the tide of fear, and cried out.

Jehan reined Stormwing back on his haunches, whirled, and set the big horse speeding back, followed by Farin and their escort. He reached for Faris, who was trying to still her horse and herself. She grasped at his hand, a steady point in a spinning world.

"What is it? Are you ill?" They milled around her, overwhelming her with irrelevant concern.

"It's not me!" she cried. "Jehan – Master – reach out! Can't you *feel* that something is wrong?"

They stilled then, staring around them. For a moment the creaking of the approaching baggage carts was the only sound.

"It's very hazy," said Rosemary at last.

"But we often have dust storms here in the Valley," offered Philip.

"Not at this time of year," replied the Commander of the escort, "and not above the hills."

Faris felt the Master's touch on her mind, picking up her memory of fear.

Farin lifted his head, sniffing the air. "Fire –" He voiced the knowledge that had been growing in them all. "It must be fire."

The Master sighed. "The land's self-cleansing is not always gentle, I fear."

They loosened their reins, let the horses move forward again.

"We are expected for the noonmeal at a holding called Ravenhill," said Jehan. "We'll be there soon, and you can rest."

Faris nodded but kept hold of his hand. Twice during her childhood lightning had sparked forest fires that swept the mountains of her home, consuming deadwood and underbrush and clearing the ground for new growth. Men and animals alike fled before the flames and afterward returned to rebuild their lives. Faris had been able to bear the pain of it then – was it because of the Jewels that she felt it so sorely now? Her scarred arm throbbed with the memory of fire.

As they turned up the road towards the holding they saw a rider.

"I hope that's someone from Ravenhill – I could use a welcome!" said Farin. The rider had seen them and was galloping now.

"A very eager welcome." Rosemary tipped back her broad sunhat so that she could see. "It is a priestess."

The woman pulled up before them, wiping sweat from her soot-streaked face. Her dark robe was brown with dust, and strands of her graying hair hung around her face. She nodded to the Master of the Junipers, but her attention was on the King.

"I am Mistress Ramona from the Community at Rivered, sent south by Mistress Esther to serve the people here," she said, catching her breath. "My lord King, I summon you in the name of the Covenant!"

Faris felt Jehan's hand tighten on hers while his face grew paler beneath its tan. "In the name of the Covenant I hear you," he said steadily. "Is it the fire?"

Mistress Ramona nodded. "Lord William's younger son decided to carve out a new holding and set fires to clear the land. In high summer!" She controlled her anger and continued, "And with no knowledge of the winds or the lie of the land."

"And no authorization?" asked the Master of the Junipers.

The priestess shook her head wearily. "I have tried to call the clouds, but they are too far away." The woman looked up. "Two hours ago word came that you were traveling this road. I came as fast as I could – the fire is likely closer by now."

"'The evil that men do men must repair,'" the Master quoted softly from the Covenant, looking at Jehan. "The Jewels are with us."

"I will gladly help fight the fire," said the King, "but the Jewels? I have never used them so – I do not know what must be done here." Faris trembled in the backwash of his uncertainty.

"Let us go and see," said the Master of the Junipers.

Sunlight refracting through the evil gray of the sky bathed their faces in a coppery glow. Before them plumes of black smoke signaled the advance of the fire, and the nearer ridges were edged with flickers of light like the vanguard of an army of flame.

Faris coughed and lowered her head, but she still heard the futile scrape of shovels as men and women tried to clear a firebreak that would stop the flames. Lord William had set up a movable camp on the hill, with food and water on wagons, and pallets where the firefighters could rest.

An old man with hair singed off one side of his head and his arm in a sling was ladling stew. He looked up, saw the King, and started a cheer. The Master of the Junipers smiled a little. He had spent the hour's ride to the fire-camp reviewing with Jehan the means by which the Jewels might be used to control the fire.

"Your presence will give them new strength, but it will not still the flames," he said.

Someone called. A man and a woman ran down the hill and returned in a few moments, helping to bear a rude

291

stretcher. Rosemary stifled an exclamation and Faris swallowed, realising that the blackened thing on the stretcher had been a man. The scar on her arm began to hurt once more.

"He's still alive!" called Rosemary. "Have you salves and bandages?"

"My work is here," the Master told Jehan. "Only you can decide how to do yours." He hurried towards the burned man, rolling up his sleeves.

"Jehan . . ." Faris followed the King to the madrona tree where he was standing with his hand lightly resting on its trunk.

"I know that I must use the Jewels, but I would rather lead a charge against half Elaya!" he said ruefully. "That's my kind of fighting!"

She relaxed her shielding a little to sense his mood and shuddered as she felt the terror of fleeing animals, the pain of dying trees. Jehan touched her arm.

"Go help Rosemary and the Master, and keep anyone from disturbing me here." He glanced down, and Faris saw on the ground beside him the redwood case that held the Jewels. For a moment she hesitated, torn between fear for him and a shamed relief that he had not asked her to stay.

As she moved away Jehan knelt and opened the chest, oblivious to her anxious gaze or the hushed murmurs of the others. Slowly he traced the sign of the pentangle upon his breast and began to bind on the Jewels – the dimly glowing Earthstone, the moonlight glimmer of the Sea Star, the white blaze of the Wind Crystal, and the ember that was the Jewel of Fire. Then he paced forward to face the line of flame. Tremors shook his body as he strove to focus the powers he bore.

After a few moments Faris could no longer bear to watch him and turned to the Master of the Junipers.

The man on the stretcher lay very still. The flames that had engulfed him had somehow missed his face, but his skin was gray, and the eyes he fixed on the Master were dilated with pain.

Faris stopped next to Rosemary, who gripped her hand. "He is dying – too much of his skin has been lost." But Faris had already known that, feeling the man's agony as she felt the martyrdom of the land, which buffeted her shielding until it was gone. She whimpered as if she were still the six-year-old feeling the fire bite her own flesh as she tried to beat the flames from the gown of the housekeeper's child.

"Be still . . . be at peace. I will come with you. There will be no pain," the Master said softly. Wood clattered as Lord William started to pack up the wagons, preparing to retreat from the fire.

Faris began to shiver as the eyes of the burned man dulled. The Master eased back on his heels, his hands resting open on his knees, and his eyes took on the fixed, inseeing expression she had seen at the College when he had picked up the coal.

She felt in her own flesh the dying man's agony fade, to be replaced by an expectance, as if a sweet melody had just ceased to play and might at any moment return. She stilled; for a moment there was something, as if she heard brightness. Then she fell back to consciousness and saw from the slack features that the man had gone.

"Hurry!" cried someone. "The fire is getting too close!"

But the Master did not move. Several minutes passed before his eyes refocused on the outside world, and Faris read in them a last longing for the place to whose gates he had accompanied the spirit of the dying man.

She looked around her, painfully aware of the Master's weariness, the despair of the people around them, the energy of the fire and the torment of the land it devoured. But above all she felt the surges of unfocused power that racked Jehan, the desperation of his battle to control the Jewels. Silence throbbed around her. She knew that Rosemary spoke to her, but she heard no words. Hoofbeats vibrated in the earth, but she did not look to see who had come. Jehan was afraid. The Jewels were mastering him. Faris began to run.

As she reached him the King moaned and dashed the circlet from his head, tore the Wind Crystal's chain from his neck, and fumbled to loose the Sea Star and the Earthstone from his waist and loins. He sank to his knees, clutching the earth, while the Jewels blazed malevolently beside him. Taking care not to touch them, Faris knelt and held Jehan until his shudders ceased.

"I'm all right," he muttered. "Give me a moment and I'll attack again." He looked up, his eyes registering awareness of her presence and the realisation that he was not on a battlefield. "Faris, you and the others must go!"

Faris shook her head, though her cheeks were already smarting with the heat of the nearing fire. "Not unless you come too!" She gripped his hands to keep him from reaching for the Earthstone.

"Faris!" Anguish darkened his eyes. "I do not know if I can win this battle, but I cannot run away! Let me go – how can I fight if I must fear for you?"

She felt his torment, and beneath it, as she had known the Master's longing for the Gates of Light, a yearning for the agony that would justify all pain and end all questioning.

Desire and denial flowed back and forth through their linked hands. To those who watched they did not seem to move, but Faris countered power with power as though she and Jehan were swinging each other in a dance, and imperceptibly their conflict became a balancing of forces. Her expanding awareness began to recall how the Lord and Lady of Westria had come together in the Sacred Grove.

For a moment she faltered, fearing to lose herself again if she accepted this power. Some inner voice whispered, *He cannot do it alone.*

Faris tightened her grasp. "Then I will help you."

With a little sigh she laid down the burden of her fears and stepped into stillness, as she had done so long ago when she saved the child from the fire. Around her the hills blazed like a vision of doom. The sounds of that burning reached her as if from another world. But where she was now all was simple, and she reached for the Earthstone and in one smooth movement bound it on.

"Faris!" cried Jehan, but already she was rooted to the earth and could not be moved.

"You must take the Sea Star and the Wind Crystal and bring wind and water to our aid" – she held them out to him – "and I will bear the Jewel of Fire. Do not fear for the child." She answered his thought, "He was conceived in the presence of the Jewels. He will take no harm."

Still staring at her, Jehan began to put on the Jewels. Faris picked up the coronet and for a moment hesitated as the red glow of the Jewel stirred the embers of an old fear, then she settled it on her brow.

This time there was no warning, no gradual building of power. At once she *was* the earth, screaming within her garment of fire. She felt the agony of every small creature caught by the flames, the extinction of each blade of grass, the heat that seared even the life within the soil. Stones cracked; clods were fired to rock; earth powdered to mix with the ashes of those it had fed.

This was what had defeated Jehan. She heard him calling but could not get free, for the flames were calling to her too, promising freedom in a frenzy that would not fade until all was consumed. And still she struggled, her fear of the pain lost in her fear of the dark fires in her own soul.

Faris . . . Faris . . . turn and come to Me.

And with a last effort she turned and saw a form whose garments pulsed with green and scarlet fires, whose skin glowed like a lantern, whose eyes were flame. The Lady of Fire . . . Faris shrank from the welcome of her outstretched arms.

To save the man, to save the land, to save yourself . . . you must come through the fire. The soft voice seared her soul.

And for that moment Faris knew the answer to her fears. She moved into the Lady's terrible embrace, but her eyes were on Jehan. For a moment there was terror and a pain beyond words, then all the agony of her flesh was transmuted to music, and all the passion of the flames to love.

"My Lady!" said the King. His eyes widened as he recognised her transformation. Still looking at her, his hands closed on the Jewels he bore. He took a deep breath, seeming to grow taller as he drew in their power.

"I am Earth and I am burning – cool me with thy kiss," said Faris, holding out her hands.

"As the wind I will caress thee," he replied.

"I am Earth and I am burning – fill me with thy sweet waters."

"As the rain I will bless thee." His hands clasped hers. Opposing forces arced between them and vibrated to equilibrium.

"In the name of the Maker of all Things!" they cried as one.

Faris set her feet in the earth and held fast as Jehan's awareness whirled outward, coaxing heated air away, drawing cooler air down to replace it and create a wind that would drive the flames back upon themselves. Her head throbbed with the anger of the fire. Like a mother seeking wayward children, she reached out to the fire elementals, set them to herd the flames inward until they exploded in fantastic filigree against the sky.

Jehan's spirit sped westward to bring damp air from the sea, to draw moisture from the waters into the clouds, to raise a wind to bear them back across the land. Cool air soothed Faris' burning cheeks and replaced the acrid breath of the fire with a sweet sea breeze.

Now, my children, be still, for it is time to rest, she whispered to the flames, and over four thousand acres the fires sagged, flickered tiredly, and winked out. Faris staggered, feeling the agony of the earth anew, now that the fire was gone. She looked at Jehan in appeal.

Already the dark smoke that had billowed around them was being invaded by pale swirls of gray as low clouds rolled across the land. Faris turned her face to the sky as the clouds folded the tortured earth in their cool embrace. Very gently it began to rain. Faris drew deep, sobbing breaths, feeling the earth's pain ease as moisture soothed its surface, feeling its grateful expansion as rain penetrated soil seared by the fire.

As the elements mingled Jehan reached for her, and Faris came into his arms. The mists veiled them from the ravaged land and the camp where the others waited. Now all four Jewels were pressed between their bodies. Faris trembled with the powers of the Wind Crystal and the Sea Star as well as those of the Jewels she already bore. Her spirit yearned towards his, striving to pierce the flesh that separated them. Now they were linked not by their own strength but by the flow of power, and the mists around them sparkled with a light more radiant than that of the fire.

Then the clouds thinned and were gone. Voiced and unvoiced, the calling of those they had left behind in the camp reached them, and the Lord and Lady of Westria turned.

Oh, fairer than the evening star! As from a great distance, Faris perceived her brother, Farin, helping support a wounded man.

Lord and Lady, bless me and bring me to the one I love. Rosemary stood with a bowl of soup forgotten in her hand.

Oh, my King! Why did you never tell me what it meant to be Master of the Jewels? That was Caolin – she had not known he was here. His hair clung damply to his skull as if he had been caught in the rain. His eyes were dark hollows in a face that seemed pared to the bone. *Oh, my Queen! You are filled with light – love me also, and set me free! My Lord and my Lady . . .*

Lord and Lady, now I bow before You, the Master's voice echoed, affirming, and the others joined him in the hymn.

> Your radiance burns the darkness from my soul;
> I stand upright between You and am balanced,

When I embrace You, then I am made whole.
Lord and Lady . . .

But Faris did not hear the rest, for the Light was becoming a blaze in which she could no longer see the humans below. The air stirred with music. In a moment she and Jehan would be free.

"Faris! Jehan!" The shout of the Master of the Junipers shattered the radiance into shards that fell about her like rain. Faris staggered as the Jewel of Fire was lifted from her brow.

"You must take them off or you will be consumed!" The Master reached past her to slip the Wind Crystal over Jehan's head and unclasp the Sea Star, then he turned to Faris to take the Earthstone. "I should have warned you, but the power held me too."

Sick and shaking, Faris clung to Jehan.

"No," Jehan whispered, stopped the Master, and unclasped the belt himself. "There is something left to do." He took Faris' hand and drew her a few steps towards the charred, rain-soaked land. Together they lifted the Jewel.

"Lady of Earth! Be gracious to this land!" said Faris.

"Lady of Earth, forgive us, and do not deny your blessing to men," Jehan echoed her. They held their breath, waiting, and for a moment the reek of smoke gave way to a hint of apple blossom, and they heard a shimmer of silver bells.

Answered, they let their hands drop then, let the Master take the Earthstone and replace it in the casket. In the stillness the only sounds were an occasional pop as moisture penetrated some smoldering log, and the patient patter of the rain.

Wonderingly Jehan lifted a hand to touch Faris' cheek. His lips soothed the burn on her forehead, then his head drooped to her shoulder.

Faris looked around her, but the glory was gone; even the memory of what had come to her was fading, as if she were waking from some bright dream. Every muscle in her body was aching, and she knew that she was only a human woman, who could be afraid.

But Jehan was beside her. Because of him, she had been safe in the storm of glory, and now his arms held her in a circle of peace. Beyond him she saw Caolin and the others, and like a glimmer from the future she sensed how the Lord and Lady of Westria might guard them, as the memory of how they had mastered the fire was now a glimmer from the past.

But not yet. For now, it was enough to sigh and bend to heal her scorched face in the raindrops that jeweled Jehan's hair.

LADY OF
DARKNESS

ACKNOWLEDGMENTS

I would like to thank David Hodghead for information regarding the habits and hunting of wild boars, Ken DeMaiffe for data on the capabilities of both horses and carrier pigeons, Clint Bigglestone for suggesting the strategy used in the battle of the Dragon Waste, and Paul Edwin Zimmer for arguing with me about the right way to do a fighting scene.

Contents